ANOTHER VOICE

A MELANCHOLY GIRL

ANOTHER VOICE
A MELANCHOLY GIRL
K.L BUSICK

Color Edition ISBN 979-8-9896225-3-5

Hardback ISBN 979-8-9896225-6-6

Paperback ISBN 979-8-9896225-4-2

eBook ISBN 979-8-9896225-5-9

Published by KLBusick Co.

Library of Congress Number 2026907335

To my fellow daydreamers.
Worlds are waiting, and I hope that you find them.

ARETE
DOUGAL
SENKA GRAVEYARD
CAULDIRA
EROS

RAFFERTY HILLS
ANCORA
GOHMER
GIANT'S PASS

Table of Contents

Prologue

It was a fun game, pretending to be magical. As a child, Clara would grab heaping fistfuls of dirt from her driveway. Feeling the dusty particles trickling from her tiny fist, she hurled them onto the sidewalk. The puffs of dust billowing from the ground looked like smoke. Then, with a gust of energy, she would bolt behind a parked car as if disappearing magically. Being dirty was the least of her worries. After all, there were worlds to explore, and she couldn't wait to find them.

Back then, she lived freely. Such freedom overshadowed any care for peering bystanders who might criticize her silly games. In particular, she took to jumping into rays of light reflected on the ground, hoping to find herself in a new and exciting place. She liked who she was, believing that even in a mundane world, magic could be found.

CHAPTER 1
A Melancholy Girl
MANY YEARS LATER

CLARA

"No one uses 'once upon a time' anymore," Clara whispered harshly. Her eyes narrowed in concentration on the document. As each letter disappeared from deletion, it left behind the haunting nothingness of a blinking cursor fading in and out. Stretching her fingers out, she started over. *She was the adventurous type, never allowing the complications of adulthood...* Fingertips motionless on the keys, she jumped when her phone's timer startled her. The rude interruption left the sentence abandoned. Sucking air through her teeth, she closed the document, not bothering to save her work. "I'll never be an author," she said morosely. "Adventures, of any sort, are saved for the exciting people; not some boring barista who can't even finish one sentence in her story."

Straightening the table in her kitchen, she collected the scattered fashion catalogs, stacking them in the strategically placed basket. She sighed, ideally thinking about how her best friend, Angel, should've done it. But like always, she was left to clean up. Reality was a cruel reminder that nothing would change. She'll always be this way. Stuck.

Shifting her apron, she untwisted the badge hanging around her neck. Sealed under the lamination, the name of the coffee shop, The Bean Queen, was printed boldly above a low-resolution picture of her. Below her image, printed in large font, was her name, Clara Rivers, Barista, and a scannable barcode for clocking in. Frowning, she studied her grinning picture; she looked way too eager to be working at a coffee shop.

Her usual walk to work consisted of beeping cars and rushing pedestrians. Even on a Saturday, people had things to do, and they always seemed in a hurry to do them. As for her, each day was the same. Her life on repeat. Each thud from her feet fell in rhythm with her wandering thoughts.

Thump. *There has to be something more to life than this.* Thump, thump. *I'll keep looking. A better job will eventually happen. It has to.* Thump, thump, thump. *Chances are, I'll screw up the interview and then... my dreams will be reduced to spilled coffee, endless customers, and monotonous work. I just can't live like this forever, daydreaming my life away... but they take me away to somewhere better. Places I'd rather be and... and to someone... I can be proud of."* Such thoughts clouded her mind until the navy blue door, shadowed by the black awning, appeared. With a dramatic exhale, she left her negativity at the entrance before stepping inside.

The Bean Queen was a local favorite, boasting a cozy atmosphere that invited guests to linger. Overstuffed fur bean bags and wicker peacock chairs beckoned from the corners with tables decorating the space between. Gold centerpieces and matching geometric lights dangled from the ceiling, welcoming book signings, open karaoke, and regular trivia nights. It was a neighborhood favorite and the place to be—if you weren't working there.

"Hey girl," Joyce greeted when Clara entered the breakroom. "I know you just got here and all, but that puppy of mine! He's been getting into everything. I mean everything. Last night, he chewed the windowsill. He even tore up my underwear, of all things. Of course, he had to pick a good pair and not a janky one." The casual conversation ushered Clara from the gloomy depths of her mind into the real world.

"Your underwear? Sounds like little Jack's getting really comfortable in his new home," Clara laughed. "But at least he's cute. You probably know what I'm going to say, but if you picked stuff up, you'd have one more nice pair of undies."

Joyce dropped her belongings into her cubby and tied her apron, shaking her head with exaggeration. The smock was white with black threading. "The Bean Queen" was embroidered on the center of the apron's bodice. Above the shop name was a logo with a crown-wearing coffee mug. Black pants and shirts were code and not one to ignore. A white hat with a matching black logo completed the uniform.

"He's a terror. If you ever want to puppy-sit, I won't object. Even cuteness requires a break." Joyce changed the subject while loosening her apron strings, which she had secured too tightly. "Oh, and how did the interview go?"

The question irked Clara. "Well, I landed the ultimate dream job! Can you believe it? Today, I'm giving Carl my two weeks' notice." Joyce's eyes lit up, about to speak, but Clara continued. "But that didn't happen. It's always the same. I'm not in high demand. No experience means no one wants to give me a chance. Not to mention, my nerves get the best of me every stinking time. So, just like all the others. No callbacks for me."

Joyce hummed happily as the two walked behind the granite counter. "I know it's hard, but don't give up. I believe in you, and since there's nothing you can do about it right now, might as well think on the positive side. Make yourself a latte to sip on. Coffee changes everything. It's liquid magic. Smells good, too."

Clara tugged her apron straight, huffed a breath, and forced a grin. Knowing the day would get busier from here, she hastily poured a popular coffee blend into a tall, cylindrical jar while Joyce opened the door to a line of impatient people. Customers grabbed menus from the wooden pocket by the entrance to browse the list of items as they waited in line. There were a few new options today; at least one would become a new favorite.

It's true that making frappes and serving cozy goodies to a flurry of customers made the hours pass quickly. Yet, for Clara, it was a job with little reward. To cope, she let her mind roam into a favorite daydream.

It was another typical day at the coffee shop as Clara frothed the milk. The calm hum of the machine was interrupted by a frightening sound from outside. A tremendous roar cut through the air, shaking the busy coffee shop and spilling drinks! Dropping the paper cup full of freshly foamed milk, she ran outside, heedless of the splash across the floor.

A ginormous dragon, menacing and angry, loomed above, lumbering clumsily on the streets while crashing into tall buildings. People ran screaming as the pieces rained upon them. Intense flames from the beast seared the cold air, breaking a sweat on Clara's forehead.

Now was the time. Reaching her arms towards the sky, in a swirl of colorful energies, she transformed into a sorceress. Her long hair blew in the wind; her eyes were steely and ready for battle. Her friends watched her transformation with astonishment. She had concealed her true self well, and no one had expected anything different about her. At this moment, they were proud. She was finally important.

To stop the fire from toasting The Bean Queen, she drew the flames into herself, accepting the heated blast by smothering it with her own power. But the battle wasn't over. Just when she thought she had stolen its fire, the beast lurched forward—

"Um, excuse me, ma'am. I think that's my coffee," a customer interrupted. He timidly waited for his steaming drink, which she held forgotten in her hands.

"Oh, I'm sorry. Not sure why I stalled. Be careful! It's as hot as fire. As if a dragon brewed it." She laughed. The customer didn't reciprocate the joke but paid for the drink without comment. Clara watched as he carried his coffee to a table where his friends waited.

"Lost in space again?" Joyce teased as she wiped sticky goo from the counter. She lightly butted Clara with her hip. "I almost timed you."

"Well shoot. I hope I wasn't out long. Why didn't you nudge me? Were you going to let me stand there looking like an idiot?"

Joyce chuckled. "I just did, didn't I? You're safe with me, but you need to stop doing that. Carl will give you the stink eye, just like last time. You know how he loves making that creepy face any chance he gets." Joyce tried to recreate the look, but her attempt only succeeded in making Clara laugh.

"I'll do better… It's just that I get so bored! Sometimes I feel like I'm going crazy." *I don't know how much more I can do this. Daydreaming is the only way to get through the day. It's where I retreat, when life gets too hard. When I'm deep in my daydreams, I can be whoever I want to be. I can be brave, smart, and wise. That version of me… she doesn't let me down.*

"Too late for that," Joyce joked, breaking Clara's thoughts. "You done went crazy years ago. But seriously, your life isn't that bad. Life is so beautiful, and all that clichéd crap. It won't be long before it's gone, and maybe you'll miss these mundane moments. One day, we'll be watching our world fade away as we rot on our deathbeds, so enjoy the time you have."

Clara diverted her attention to a stubborn spot of dried foam. "I love your optimism. I suppose being gloomy doesn't help. So I'll try to think of something else… Oh! Have you talked to Carl yet?"

"Not yet. It gives me the heebie jeebies thinking about it."

"But we know he's looking for a buyer. He's been pretty open about selling it quickly. It's almost like he wanted you to know before officially announcing it."

Joyce filled the depleted stack of cups and their coordinating lids while Clara replenished a rack of muffins. "I'll do it soon. I can't take the chance that another buyer is waiting to scoop it away from me. I'll ask him this week. If I haven't said anything by Friday, remind me how you're my accountability partner," Joyce said with a challenge in her tone.

"By Friday, if you don't talk to Carl, I'm sending a wish to the stars that little Jack eats all your good undies and leaves behind only the nasty ones."

The day continued as usual. Treats ordered, drinks brewed, customers served, and counters wiped. With one employee on vacation, her shift was unusually long. When Clara thanked her last customer, she was more than a little excited as she beelined to her cubby. She was free. Joyce followed shortly after.

"What a day that was. I feel like I just got here, and it's already time to leave. But I need to get home to my little fluffball. I can only imagine what surprises are waiting. Thankful for my mom, though. She's been checking on him while I'm working."

Clara harshly untied her apron, causing a string to break. She groaned. She'd have to bring her spare one from home tomorrow. "It's nice how your mom is helping. Having someone shoulder the load is something to be grateful for. Don't forget to give your little guy a pet for me. Tell him Auntie Clara will bring him some treats next week. I can't wait to squish his little face."

"Oh, I will. Safe travels home. I know you're always in a hurry to get out of here." Joyce waved as Clara rushed from the breakroom.

As soon as Clara's feet hit the sidewalk, she popped in her earbuds. An inspiring song lifted her spirits and encouraged her daydreams. She imagined the woman she kept trapped in her mind.

Higher-caliber Clara sat across from a professional-looking man with dark glasses. He peered at her, notes in hand. "I see you work at The Bean Queen. Nice place they have there. I love the Mocha Mustache." The man searched her resume. "Any work experience beyond the coffee shop?"

Back straight and head high, she didn't break eye contact. "Not yet, but I'm confident I'm capable of bigger things than making coffee. I know I'd be a valuable asset to your company. Looking at your job description, I believe this position will help me achieve my career goals, and, in turn, provide your company with a hard-working and loyal employee."

The man nodded favorably. Skipping ahead in time, she envisioned a different version of herself. Learning at a rapid pace, working diligently, and impressing those around her. Promotion after promotion. She would make an impact and help others do the same. Her life would matter, and she would—

Her daydreams faded under the cold winds of logic upon discovering a crusty piece of brownie on her shoe. This was only a fantasy conjured up in her childlike mind. Her lips tightened as she skipped the next song on her playlist. She thought about her current self and the person she wanted to be. *I'll never meet her.*

The sun was setting, and she hastened her pace to avoid walking alone in the dark. Reaching her aging apartment, she climbed the steps and unlocked the door, careful to step over the pesky loose threshold. With a plop of her purse and a squeak from the barstool, she sat. Clara suppressed an irritated sigh when she spotted Angel's fashion magazines on the table, the very ones she picked up that morning. Gruffly sliding them away, she opened her laptop.

Sitting before the blank document, once again, she began to type. *She was a melancholy sort, engulfed in daydreams and stories…* She whispered to the laptop, "No one wants to read about a mindless dreamer." She backspaced the sentence and resumed typing. *She was a brave one, never worrying about the complications of adulthood…* "No, no, no… I can't write today." Closing the laptop without saving, her eyes cast to the pile of catalogs.

Angel was determined to be a fashion designer and notoriously collected any and all media about it. Nearing graduation, her friend pursued any opportunity to make her dream a reality. Blankly staring down the stack of catalogs, a bent corner of a sketch caught Clara's attention. She pulled it from the pile to reveal a gorgeous dress drawn with delicate details. She recognized the style; it was one of Angel's designs. *Wow. Her drawing skills have improved over the years.*

She had no doubt that her best friend would be successful one day. Clara tried college once, but it only lasted a few semesters before she dropped out. The memory made her laugh until she recalled the thousands of dollars in student loans to repay. She grimaced. *Her hasty decision was also an expensive one.*

Wanting to forget the large and useless mound of debt, she

glanced at emails on her phone, hoping to see a response from one of the many job applications sent out. Then, scanning her inbox, she searched for any promising job ads appropriate for someone with so little clout. Her heart dropped. There were only the same basic entry-level options. With so little experience beyond The Bean Queen, she was drowning in a sea of talent.

Opening her laptop once more, she scoffed at the music blaring from a neighbor's apartment. This wasn't the worst part of town, but not the best part either. A bit rundown with dated appliances, her apartment could use some renovations. Knowing their landlord, that would never happen. Her contemplation produced a frown. *I'll be stuck in this apartment forever, and I'll always have to use that horrid pink bathroom and listen to that equally horrid music next door.*

The song vanished from her mind as the front door flew open with a bang. Angel, arms piled high with fabric, crashed in, seemingly mid-conversation as always. "And then I told him from here on out, I'm ignoring him." Her sass lightened the atmosphere. "I don't have time for his drama. Time and time again, he proves to be a loser. Seriously, I can't take another second of it, so I'm not going to."

Blonde hair tied into a high ponytail and dark glasses slipping down her nose, Angel was beautiful and knew it. Clara smirked at the glasses. Her friend had perfect eyesight. Dropping the piles of fabric onto their futon, Angel approached the table where Clara was seated and sat on the other stool, placing an iced coffee on the table's surface. She wrapped up her conversation.

"How the heck did you carry a coffee with all that fabric in your arms?" Clara questioned as Angel put her phone away.

"I can't disclose my secrets," came the reply with a wave of her hand and shared giggles. "More importantly, how's the job search going? Any interviews?"

"Nope. Not even one. Most of the good jobs I don't qualify for, and what's left are the same old options that don't pay enough to survive. No one wants to hire me, I guess.

Angel nonchalantly sipped her coffee. "With that attitude, they won't. Maybe take a walk into the city and find yourself one. Go job hunting. It wouldn't be the first time someone was hired by actually going into a building. Email is great and all, but if they met you ahead of time, I think you'd have a better chance. If nothing else, maybe you'll make some connections."

"You're kidding, right? You know how this city is. I'm not mindlessly walking around. What if I get lost because my phone is acting up? Remember how my maps would randomly fade? I could get lost." She couldn't imagine herself wandering the streets alone for any reason, but she could imagine all the bad things that might happen if she did.

Clara walked the dark street to find her way home. Her phone's map was fading in and out. Lost and afraid, a scruffy man appeared from a nearby alley.

"Hey lady. Whatcha got in your bag?"

Her heart stopped. The man raised his voice, smiling wickedly while exposing a shining blade from behind his back. "Why don't I have a peek?"

She tried to run, but fear nailed her feet to the ground. The thief snatched her purse before stabbing her over and over. There, she would be lying in the alley to rot, all alone, until a poor, unsuspecting pedestrian would find her.

The story played out twice in her head, with the second edition swapping the knife for a gun, as it made more sense. Angel went on as if Clara were paying attention. "I read yesterday about jobs that don't necessarily advertise, but if you stop in, they're willing to speak with potential hires. Put some feet on those dreams of yours. I get it, you're all introverty and stuff, but your current box is too small for you." She pinched her fingers together to express how small the box really was. "Or, you could finish the book you've been writing forever. How far have you gotten?"

Angel squeaked the barstool away from the table to rummage through the pile of fabric on the futon. Grabbing a pair of trousers triumphantly, she returned to the table. Leaning over Clara's shoulder, she pointed at the screen.

"Ooo, started a new chapter?"

Clara cringed inside. "Not exactly…"

"Don't tell me…"

"Yeah."

"Clara…" A cackle tore its way from Angel's gut. "Take a

breath and write something. Anything. Just write. I don't care if it's about taking the trash out. Type. Something. On. The. Page. Every book starts with one word. I think if you saw something on a page, it would encourage you to continue."

Clara watched as her friend retreated, once more, to the couch to root through the fabric mound. Spreading the pile across the cushions, Angel muttered something about textures. "Oh, by the way," Clara said, "can you please clean up after yourself? This morning it was the magazines. Yesterday, it was the mounds of fabric. I couldn't even sit on the couch without having to move stuff. We have a small place, and we both live here. Let's keep it tidy, please." The words spewed more aggressively than intended. She hadn't meant for her frustration and shame to creep into her conversation so verbally. But Angel ignored the disgruntled words.

Seriously? Walk into some random office and ask for an interview? Who does that? Picking up her phone, she began deleting all her unwanted email messages with renewed vigor. Now, both her hopes and inbox were empty.

CHAPTER 2

A Ray of Light

CLARA

THE FOLLOWING DAY, Clara's apron strings felt like eternal ties binding her to The Bean Queen. Pulling her hair through the hole in her hat, she shouted across the hall from the living room. "Angel, I'm thinking about bringing home some coffee tonight after work. Did you want one?"

"Oh my goodness, yes please. It's going to be a late night for me. Don't wait up. I need to look through some vintage fashion magazines at the library. This stupid inspiration block is killing me. I can't put it off any longer, and I probably should return some of the overdue catalogs I still have… somewhere. If I'm not here when you get back," she entered the living area, "can you put it in the fridge for me?"

"Anything for my Angel," Clara replied with a cheesy grin while heading towards the front door. As she reached for the door handle, she instinctively tried to pull the badge around her neck, only to find it missing. Rushing to her bedroom, she yanked it from the hook fixed to her wall before re-entering the living room. She stopped when noticing Angel gathering the pile of magazines

14

from the table. "Sorry about last night. I didn't mean to get cranky."

Angel waved a hand dismissively. "You've got a lot going on in that mind of yours. I'm here for you if you ever want to talk, and I know you've been through a lot. At this point, we're far past the place of holding a grudge against each other. I didn't take it personally."

"Thank you for… everything you do for me. I don't know why I'm in this funk lately. I'm sure I'll feel like myself again soon. Have fun at school today, and I'll see you tonight." Then, with a wave of her hand and a swish of her ponytail, Clara was out the door.

A new favorite song was playing loudly in her earbuds, encouraging her to create a fresh, courageous version of herself as she walked to work. Trudging into The Bean Queen, she deposited her belongings in her cubby before appearing behind the counter to start her shift.

Fighting boredom was a perpetual challenge. A typical mind game was imagining her shift almost over. Pretending to work her last hour, she'd restart the game once that hour passed. Today, she had a new game for herself: imagining it was her last day. Each hour finished would be her very last one working as a barista. Forever. Noticing a familiar face, she waved to the attractive man who approached the register. "Hey, Levi. Are you getting your regular today?"

"Hello, Clara. You got it. Maybe one day I'll switch it up and surprise you." He fiddled with his bank card as Clara crafted the specialty drink.

Brewing, Clara inhaled the aroma with delight. Tomorrow was her day off, and she planned to set aside time to write her book. Maybe Angel was right, even if it was terrible, having a full page or two might inspire her to continue. Sliding the protective sleeve on the cup, she handed the steaming liquid to the man across the counter.

After paying, Levi laid his bank card on the counter to accept the drink. "I noticed they're having karaoke tomorrow. Are you going?"

"I don't think so. Karaoke isn't my thing. I might scare everyone away if they heard me wailing."

Levi laughed awkwardly, side-eyeing the customers waiting beside him. "I'm sure it's not as bad as you think, but if you change your mind, I'll be there. It would be good to see you when you're not working. You could come listen to others, if you didn't want to sing yourself. I think it would be fun. No pressure, though."

Clara returned Levi's strained laugh. The man quickly grabbed a napkin to wrap around his steaming cup and walked abruptly out the door, forgetting his bank card on the counter. Clara snatched the forgotten card and rushed out the batwing doors. The panels bashed against each other loudly, causing many onlookers to watch.

"Levi, you forgot your card!"

"Oh! Thank you!"

Clara tucked rogue hairs behind her ear while Levi fumbled to get his wallet from his pocket. Taking the card, he slid it into an empty slot and paused. Clara spoke as she tightened her ponytail. "I… I'd better get back to work. It's been a really crazy day and…"

"Oh, yeah… of course. But, um, if you don't want to go to karaoke, maybe we could… I mean, if you want to, go to breakfast one of these days. Not here, but the bistro on Ninth Street. The Scramble House. I've been there before, and it's pretty good. You can make your own omelets, and they have a Bloody Mary bar."

"That sounds amazing, yeah, I'd love to go!" Clara glanced at the increasing line of customers. "Sorry, I can't stay right now but—"

"Wait, before you leave, can I give you my number?"

"Of course." Clara shuffled her feet as Levi ran to his car. Rushing back, he handed her his number, written on The Bean Queen napkin. She stuffed it into her back pocket.

"I'll text you later," Clara said as an untethered smile lifted her lips.

"I'll be waiting." Levi grinned back.

Entering the building, Clara once again plowed through the batwing doors before returning to her position. Customers were plentiful today, and even after countless hours of taking orders, they didn't seem to be letting up. Grinning, she wrote another name on another coffee, hoping her spelling was accurate.

"I talked with Carl," Joyce announced as soon as the line of customers broke.

Clara quickly put the cap on the marker. "And? What did he say?"

"He said he has some other interest, but he's willing to look at my offer."

"Oh my gosh. Joyce! That's amazing… boss lady!"

"Remember, you won't be working here by the time I'm bossin' it up, and don't get too excited, I don't own the place yet."

"Your faith in me is inspiring," Clara replied, trying not to shade her words with sarcasm. *I wish I could believe it.* "I have a good feeling things will work out. Before you know it, you'll be the new owner of The Bean Queen." The conversation died when Clara called a customer's name. Handing over the iced caramel puddle, their new specialty drink, she then grabbed a fresh tray of hot buns to display. As the clock ticked away, she kept busy until the very last tock.

Excusing herself from the floor, she hastily darted to the break room. Sadie was back from vacation, and with her arrival, Clara was free to leave. Purse over her shoulder, she pulled off her hat. Tonight, she'd leave the unsightly cap in her cube. Phone in hand, she quickly scrolled for job ads. None of the options seemed promising. It pained her that today, or any day, probably wouldn't be her last at The Bean Queen.

Standing in line like a customer, she ordered the two coffees she and Angel would enjoy later that night. A cup in each hand, and earbud-free, she strolled the sidewalk undistracted by the beat of music. A wave of sadness overcame her. Her brave plans already seemed to be lacking, but her imagination was unbothered. She imagined what her future might unfold if nothing changed.

"Two cappuccinos, please," came the request from a young woman who had freakishly bouncy hair. She reeked of life and the dreams of youth. Old Clara nodded, gray hair thinning from stress and frown lines accentuating her face.

Despite her advanced age, The Bean Queen looked the same, but no one around her looked familiar. All her friends moved on to something better. She was left behind. The once happy Clara, now devoid of life, had run out of smiles to give. Her grins were now replaced with a tired reproach for allowing herself to stay stagnant…

As the sun set, burnt orange and vibrant pink colors cast a warm glow across what little sky was visible between the tall buildings. Yet, amidst the warming colors was a strange, intense white ray of light. It seemed surreal as it reflected into a nearby alley, lighting up the dark, dirty path between buildings. She walked towards it.

Suddenly, she didn't care about entering a sketchy alley. As melancholy led her feet, she stopped only when she approached the shimmering ray. Bits of color flickered brightly as the specks danced inside the pulsating beam. Mesmerizing. The drinks slid from her hands, splashing into a muddy puddle by her feet. Her purse fell from her shoulder, landing on loose gravel and dingy trash. She stooped to retrieve her purse but rose with a fistful of dirt instead.

The memories rushed in: running wildly into the house once the sun set, scalp crusted with dirt, her knees smeared from her many "disappearing" acts. Her eyes burned with the threat of tears. *Where had that girl gone?* She was nothing like her now.

The colors of the light, showing off a white translucent sparkle, summoned Clara to join them and play. Celestial and enchanting, her eyes drank in their majestic beauty. Dirt clenched in her fist, she felt both foolish and strangely empowered. Closing her eyes, she forcefully tossed the dirt onto the ground while landing in the shimmering ray.

"Dear," a masculine voice rang, "there's no reason to throw dirt."

Cheeks flushed, Clara's eyes whipped open. Someone had been watching! Embarrassment fled when she saw the grimy alleyway had been replaced with a brilliant light. Built upon translucent crystal, the space was clear and devoid of markings, save for some specks of dirt, likely brought by her. Thin air filled her lungs faster than expected, forcing her to cough. There was too much air here— or maybe not enough. Her eyes searched the exposed, endless space as she sat on a cold surface. Yet a peace filled her with no rational reason why. Inhaling deeply, she watched some flecks of light dancing around her like golden confetti, spiraling and floating aimlessly.

"I'm sure you're wondering how you got here," came the voice. She directed her eyes to the figure looking down at her, his large hand extended. Supposing that her gallant entrance must not have landed as gracefully as she imagined, she took the hand. The crystal-like floor beneath her was cold on her palms. Even after rising, she felt its coolness linger.

"Am I dead?" she whispered before her voice escalated. "Did I get stabbed or… or shot?" A frigid stream of fear filled her.

"Calm down, child. You're perfectly fine. My name is Kevin, The Guardian of Time, Watcher of Worlds, Perpetual Being… titles mean nothing to me."

"Kevin?" She was taken aback by his name, expecting something longer or maybe ancient. "Hi… Kevin." Her voice echoed with the realization of her barren surroundings.

Clara studied him closely. He was tall and broad with blonde hair and intense blue eyes that seemed far too deep for a human. They made her tremble. He had a pleasant face, his age unidentifiable. Wrapping her arms across her chest, she shuffled her feet and hugged herself. "I'm sorry, uh, I don't know what to do." Tears brimmed, but her sniffle stopped the wetness from becoming an embarrassing mess. "It's not every day that I fall into a dream world… Well, maybe I do, but I have never gone this far before. This… it feels real."

"You're not dead," Kevin said with compassion, "at least not in a way that you think, and this is very much real."

As her mind processed his words, the tiny hairs on her body raised in alarm. Fighting for a solid breath against unstable air, she tried to pull herself together.

"You're at a crossroads," he said without emotion. "A place to which few ever come, although all are invited."

Glimmers of light coiled like tiny whirlwinds. Fixated on watching one small swirl of light, she immediately felt as if she were nowhere. That is, if nowhere could be a place.

Kevin continued, "My role is one of great power, but the power isn't mine to give. Even I can only do so much."

Clara lifted her chin as Kevin's compassionate hand squeezed her shoulder. The man locked his gaze with hers. Softly, he spoke. "There are times when the stars listen to the wishes of those below them. Sometimes, those wishes are so loud, they can't help but tell me. One heard you."

"A star heard me... but how? I think it was a mistake... aren't stars nothing but a ball of gas? How can they hear anything?" Clara noticed the indifferent look on Kevin's face. "But... if that... if that is the case, does that mean I'll never get back home?"

"That's up to you. However, I'd advise against overthinking it. Your arrival was simply a wish. But it's worth understanding that you aren't the first human I've met, and you won't be the last. Rest with the peace that you aren't the only one."

"Why me, though? There's nothing special about me." The words hurt her to say, though she believed them.

"A popular thought, which, in itself, proves your words true. Even I'm nothing out of the ordinary." Kevin paused at the sight of Clara's bewildered look. "I can see you don't understand that. Think of me as a simple gatekeeper to the next adventure."

Kevin stared at his open hands before holding them out, ignoring Clara's confused expression. A small transparent ball appeared in his palms. Inside the sphere spun a shimmering star, invisibly tethered to the center. He rolled the glimmering sphere around from one palm to the other before tossing it into the air. Glittering with a clear kaleidoscope of color, the light flashed across the space with intense brightness. "One way or another, your life is going to change," Kevin said placidly. Catching the ball one last time, he held it firmly in one hand. "I think Arete would be the perfect place."

Clara didn't get a moment to admire the entrancing beauty of the sphere or overthink what Kevin meant, before, to her surprise, it hit her squarely on the forehead.

CHAPTER 3

A Life Worth it

SAWYER

SAWYER, the Commander Knight of Ancora, rose from his seat as King Henric waved a dismissive hand. Sliding the chair to meet the table, the knight bowed, politely excusing himself from the king's presence before turning to the door. The king's proclamation lingered uneasily in his mind.

Many years ago, the king had lost his son, Cyrus. A man of freedom and virtue, the prince had possessed wisdom well beyond his years. As squire to the prince, Sawyer thrived. Although he learned many creative tricks of swordsmanship under the prince's tutelage, the life skills he'd acquired were treasured far more than the battle tactics. It was a mentorship he would never forget nor take for granted.

After Cyrus's untimely death, the king, unable to cope with his shattered heart, locked himself in his chambers, refusing company. Many weeks later, the king left his room to walk the training grounds, where his son had spent much time. It was there he spotted young Sawyer, practicing swordsmanship. Wielding a sword far too large for the small boy's frame, the child's movements were calculated, despite the heavy weapon. More than that, the prince's diligent training, mimicked by the boy, caught the king's attention. Sawyer remembered the day well and how his childish body grunted under the weight of the broad sword...

With a shout, young Sawyer swung the blade upwards to meet the hay-stuffed head, stopping only inches from piercing the cloth. The raspy tone of the small boy's voice lowered while his eyes squinted. He cradled the cumbersome sword with one hand to protect it from dropping as he moved his body to advance towards his pretend foe. Feigned anger was replaced with a smile.

"I take no joy in the death of another. Actually," he said, lowering the sword with a shaky arm. The heavy blade fell with a clang onto the rocky soil. Sawyer fumbled to locate the sword's grip without breaking eye contact with the sewn-on eyes. Successfully locating the hilt, he pierced the ground with the blade, relieving his small arm from its weight. His stance regained, he repeated the words learned from his mentor.

"I take no joy in killing another," young Sawyer said, starting over. "Actually, I hope to meet you again, my friend, but under different circumstances. Now be free." Reaching to squeeze the dummy's shoulder, the boy yanked the sword from the soil and turned to walk away...

It was a scene Cyrus had coached Sawyer on many times before. Kindness paired with concession was the prince's way. Visually touched by the memory, Sawyer could still see tears forming in the king's eyes as the monarch approached him and said, "Hope has found me this day, as my son is yet living inside his young squire." Many would say that King Henric thought of Sawyer as his own, a replacement for the son he had lost, and those people may have been right.

The servant closed the door of the king's chamber after the knight left the room. The soft click marked the conversation officially over. When the king summoned him, Sawyer thought it was about a pesky beast or keeping the peace in a nearby town, but neither had been the case. The knight would've preferred a good battle or ordinance to what had transpired. Running his hands through his hair, he replayed the last hour in his mind.

"Sawyer, Princess Adeline from the mountainside Kingdom of Cauldira... you've met her many times before, I'm certain, will be arriving at Ancora in three days' time," the king said with a nod, folding his hands upon the table. "Cauldira has heard of your heroics, and if I might say so, experienced your bravery a time or two themselves."

Standing from his oversized chair, the king declared, "Since I have no other heirs, I have commissioned a marriage treaty. As you know, I'm no longer a young man. Ancora's unity with Cauldira would entitle you as the future king." The king paused, anticipating Sawyer's excitement.

But the young man carefully searched his words instead. "Your Highness, although an honor, I ask for some time to consider this."

"Sawyer Lydon, the state of our kingdom depends on strategic advancements," the king said firmly. "I know how much you love the people of Ancora, and this marriage will help us all. We're aware of the strength of Cauldira's military, not to mention the wealth of their harvests and livestock. With this union, we'll all prosper." He pounded his fist on the table to emphasize his seriousness. "I'll not let this offer pass us by!"

Sawyer held back his words, as he knew trying to communicate with someone with so much passion was futile. King Henric, unwilling to hear any possible conflict, waved his hand to dismiss his knight.

The knight sighed. It was, of course, common for nobility to marry for treaties and status. It happened all the time. But having humble beginnings, it wasn't something he thought he'd experience. Marriage wasn't something to take lightly, and he had yet to settle down with any of the ladies in his past. Beyond that, he wasn't fond of the notion of the complexity of being king. It was true that royalty had a great deal of power to improve their kingdom, which he desired, but Sawyer didn't feel worthy of this responsibility. Desiring reprieve, he made an impromptu turn to the stable to grab his trusty palomino, Willow. A day or two away from the castle would be beneficial to decide how to approach the situation. Reaching Willow's stall, he saw his squire, Rory.

"How're your chores coming?" Sawyer smiled as he ruffled the boy's hair.

"Well enough, Sawyer," Rory replied casually. Having a close relationship, the two dropped formalities and picked them up only when circumstances demanded otherwise. "Willow's been extra energetic today. She must be feeling her oats. She didn't want to come to the barn, so I had to coax her with an apple."

"Smart boy. I can foresee you becoming a great horseman one day. Speaking of Willow, can you saddle her for me? It seems adventure is calling, and I've decided to find it."

"Certainly," Rory answered. Grasping the stiff brush with enthusiasm, the squire opened Willow's stall to clip the lead onto the leather halter. Sawyer stroked the bridge of Willow's nose before walking the well-trodden path back to the castle.

Entering the stone archway into the castle, he traveled through many hallways till he reached the kitchen. Following the hearty aroma, he spotted Jasper, the chief cook. Every time he saw the burly man standing over a pot, it made him smile. As hairy as he was thick, Jasper looked more likely to swing an axe than stir soup.

"Hey, Jasper! Whatever you're cooking, it smells wonderful."

"Ho, Sawyer! Making a fine soup for tonight's meal. Got me some rabbit for rabbit pie," he replied, smacking his lips with anticipation. "I'm only waiting for the crust to brown."

"Rabbit pie sounds delightful, but I came for more packable meals. I'm headed to the Village of Gohmer. I'd like to check in with the people and possibly run a hunt or two. I think four days of provisions would be sufficient. Been feeling the itch to battle something and keep my real-world experience sharp," Sawyer stated.

"Well, you'll be missing out on a fine meal," Jasper said ruefully. "But I'll gather you some nourishment for the road, nevertheless." Turning his attention from the soup, Jasper quickly packed a waxed cloth bag full of travel-ready snacks and some dried meats. "This should do it. I even packed a cup of rabbit pie, although your crust might be a bit doughy." Handing over the food, Jasper returned to his masterpiece, which would be fully ready as soon as the crust browned up a bit more.

Not willing to wait to taste the rabbit pie, Sawyer opened the cup and ate the delicious stew immediately as he retraced his steps to the stable. He reasoned it wouldn't travel well anyway.

Willow, tied to the post and tacked, gave a friendly snort at the sight of her master. Her hooves pawed the cobblestones as she shook her head. Giving a gentle stroke on her muzzle, Sawyer stuffed his saddlebags before mounting.

Rory rushed over to bid farewell with large eyes. "You'll be careful, won't you?"

"More than, and when I return, I'll teach you all the new things I've learned."

"That would be great!" Rory shouted as he pumped a fist into the sky, watching with admiration as Sawyer nudged Willow into a trot.

After passing the castle gate, the knight galloped across the plains. Willow's gait was consistent and smooth—a true pleasure to experience. The breeze from her pace quickly dried the stubborn, sweaty hairs from his brow, leaving behind a restless, albeit refreshed, feeling. Ancora's wilderness was no stranger to the adventurous knight. Sometimes, he rode with friends or colleagues, but it was times like these when he was alone that he especially enjoyed.

Looking into the horizon, he slowed Willow to a walk. Shifting in the saddle, he let the reins drop to stretch his arms above his head, pulling the stiffness from his body. Releasing the tension from his lower back, he settled into the saddle for the long ride ahead. It would be some time before he'd reach Gohmer, but he wasn't in a hurry to get there. Leaning back to face the heavens, the sky became his muse. The clouds were fluffy, showcasing the sky's incredible blue. It was going to be a good day.

After a day's ride and a night under the stars, Willow's hooves clopped into Gohmer. Most towns had notice boards pinned with announcements for hired work. A renewed sense of adventure sparked as the hope of finding a well-paying hunt filled his chest. Hopefully, Gohmer would provide some excitement for him.

Dismounting, he fastened his horse to the hitching post outside the inn. With a pat on Willow's hindquarters, he entered the building. Rundown and dusty from the dirt roads and even dirtier travelers, the atmosphere was typical. Living at the castle, he'd gotten used to all the luxuries it provided. The harsh realities of life hit him anew each time he sauntered into a place outside the protective gates.

"Good day, ma'am," he said to the weary woman at the counter. "A room for tonight, if you will."

"Hmm? 'Ello, jest a minute," she greeted tersely.

The young lady grabbed a small key from the wall behind her and handed it over the counter. "It'll be twenty coin, Commanda'," she said, while looking at his badge that displayed his rank and name. "I've saved ya the best room, I 'ave. Tis' the one on the end to the right. Room number six. I even 'ave a bath drawn for ya, if ya like."

"What a nice surprise that is! Thank you, m'lady," he said as he grabbed the key from the counter and headed to the job board. A slew of hastily scrawled notes layered the makeshift panel. Lifting a corner here and there, he searched its surface for something of substance.

Dishwasher for the inn. Must tote the water from the stream yourself. No complainers!

Need a helper at the garden. Weeding and harvesting time! Free strawberries fer pay!

Varmint infestering! Ratz ruining my grain. Will pay coin for each dead one.

Don't trust Henry Forman! He runned off with my mrs...

Sawyer tsked. It seemed there were slim yet interesting pickings. Continuing to sort through the mess of stacked notices, one caught his attention. The paper was thicker than the others and a little crisper.

*Notorious hag scaring the town women and children.
Head must be presented for reward. 200 coin. See Mayor
Hans Gribble - Town Mayor.*

Aha! Sawyer's eyes flashed with excitement. It had been a while since he'd battled a hag. Tearing the paper from the board, he turned to the innkeeper.

"Hello again, maiden," he greeted with a dashing charm. Through his travels, he noticed that simple things, like calling townswomen "maiden" or simply acknowledging their presence respectfully, brought great joy to these downtrodden ladies. It worked. Her countenance transformed as her weary eyes widened, as did her grin.

"I'm looking for your mayor, Hans Gribble. Can you provide some insight into his whereabouts?"

She nodded, smile widening. "He be in the big house yonda, Sir Commanda'. The one that sets upon the 'ill."

"My greatest thanks to you, dear lady," he said with a heart-warming bow that caused her to blush. It was time to find Mayor Gribble.

Sawyer hated seeing people suffer. Formal education became less and less common the farther away from the castle one lived. In some places, it was nonexistent. He wondered if King Henric was aware of the situation. Perhaps he should provide a census for the king upon his return. If he were to marry Princess Adeline, he could use his influence to implement change. Even so, the idea of settling down with the estranged princess wasn't his ideal way to resolve these problems.

The mayor's villa was a short walk, but on a surprisingly steep hill. He shook his head. He was rethinking his idea of leaving Willow tied to the post, as she could have saved his legs from the unwanted burn.

Mayor Hans Gribble - Town Mayor was crudely inscribed on the sign outside the home. Sawyer's eyebrows rose. Given the small size of the town, the idea of a mayor was surprising, but this sign surprised him more. Poorly made sashes and banners hung outside the villa, and an iron bench sat lonely on the porch next to a dead potted plant. The mayor had apparently gone to great lengths decorating his home like the estates in Ancora, although he had not done a great job in doing so. Approaching the door, Sawyer gave it a solid knock.

"Imma commin'! Jest hold onta yer breetches," croaked a voice from inside.

The door swung open. A tidy-looking maid appeared in the doorway, eyes surveying him. Bonnet tied snugly under her chin, she shuffled from one foot to the next, broom in hand. Sawyer bowed. "Ma'am, I'm looking for the mayor," he cleared his throat, "Hans Gribble."

Her eyes settled upon his badge. Her mood brightened. She leaned the broom against the wall. "Come on inside, then! 'Ave a seat right 'ere, sir! Sir Commanda'," she exclaimed as she motioned to a wobbly-looking chair that wasn't as inviting as the maid seemed to believe. Back in its day, the chair must have been beautiful, but now the fabric was faded with dry rot from many years of dampness and sun. He doubted the fragile heirloom could hold a small child, let alone a full-grown man.

Crossing the threshold, the chair waited on unstable legs. Knowing that in the unfortunate event the chair could not withstand his weight, his ego would be bruised far worse than his rear. The maid, who was still motioning toward the chair, swished her arms toward the antique, rushing him to sit. Slowly following orders, he carefully lowered himself onto the seat. The chair groaned. Sawyer shifted his weight to his legs so he wouldn't find himself sitting on the floor.

To avoid this undesirable fate meant squatting over the woven cushion for what seemed like many minutes. Way too many minutes for someone who was most likely not that busy working a position probably created for himself. Legs burning, Sawyer coughed. He needed the mayor to arrive soon, before his legs gave out. The maid finally squeaked open a door. "'Ere comes Mayor Hans Gribble." Her announcement cracked her voice.

"To who do I owe the pleasure of visitchure?" the mayor said with a forced roll of his tongue.

Sawyer lifted himself from his hovering squat. Saying that Mayor Hans Gribble was a strange-looking man would be an understatement. His outdated, yet clean, attire was pressed for the occasion, but judging by the style, he must not have too many of those. Small glasses balanced on his nose, and he sported a hairpiece, though not one made from human locks. The only authentic thing about the peculiar man was a small pinned flower, obviously taken from the bush outside.

"Mayor Gribble, I'm here about the hag. The one scaring the women and children." Mayor Gribble's face illuminated with surprise and relief. Seeing the relaxed expression, Sawyer knew the truth. The hag frightened more than the women and children.

"Yes, yes, yes… the hag," the mayor puffed his chest out, stressing his wooden buttons against the button holes. "I'd do it myself, you know, but this town here, it has me so busy! No time to be getting rid of hags when everyone needs my leadershipness! I'm sure you know how that is."

"No doubt, " Sawyer concurred. The knight pushed back a chuckle. He could imagine the mayor, red-faced and huffing while the hag turned him in circles.

"Sawyer, 'tis it?"

"Yes. Sawyer Lydon, the Commander Knight of Ancora."

Hans pushed his eyeglasses back up from resting on his nostrils. "The hag's been a nuisance around these 'ere parts." The excitement over the hag prompted the mayor to slip into his usual accent. Sawyer kept his face stoic despite his amusement. What a performance. The mayor continued, "She's been scaring the children and lady folk. Ate a few of our 'attle, too," he huffed with his fists clenched.

Strength came to Sawyer in the form of composure. "The notice states you desire the hag's head. Is this negotiable? I find that hags often travel for a reason, and I may be able to convince her to leave." Sawyer always tried to reason with any foe willing to hear him out. Although it wasn't always possible to negotiate before battle, he'd try to make the effort.

"No!" gasped Mayor Hans, fear flashing across his eyes. "The head or nothing!"

Sawyer sighed. "Fair enough, Mayor, and where should I search for the fiend?"

"Near the banks of Giant's Pass."

"It's settled then. I'll retrieve the hag's head." Sawyer turned toward the door in haste as his composure was wavering. Keeping his weight on his heels, he headed down the ridiculous hill to rejoin Willow. What a story he could tell once he returned. Feet in stirrups, he departed for adventure.

Giant's Pass was about an hour's ride from Gohmer. A hag lingering within the swampy mire seemed out of the ordinary. Hags were known to hunt close to a town only if someone had insulted her or stolen something she loved. Partial to collecting things, they typically resided in old barns or abandoned buildings. Giant's Pass didn't have any of those things.

The hour passed swiftly, and soon Sawyer smelled his destination. Giant's Pass was known for its sloppy, muddy swamp that carried an unforgettable smell. Not wanting to slide around and splatter himself or his steed with the stinking muck, he loosened the reins to allow Willow's head more freedom to navigate the foul terrain. Gagging, he held his nose. No matter how many times he visited the swamp, he never adjusted to its unique aroma. Searching for his target, his eyes darted back and forth and down the banks until a swift shadow caught his eye. Off in the distance, circling a mound protruding in the mud was the hag.

He nudged Willow forward, but not too quickly. The hag saw him and let out a scream. It was a good one. Hags were infamous for their screams—high-pitched and shrill. Knotted hair peeling off her scalp and long, unsightly fingernails scraping at the air, her delight to see him was apparent. However, there was never a time he enjoyed seeing a hag, and each time he found himself in their presence, he shuddered.

"Tasty young man! You'll make a fine soup," she said with a grin revealing rotted teeth.

"Miss Hag, I'll not be simmering in your soup tonight. I've heard you've been visiting the town nearby. The town of Gohmer."

"Ahhhh, tender snack for Hag!"

"Please explain yourself. Why have you been terrorizing Gohmer?"

He stood in his stirrups to glimpse at the lump the hag had circled, but he couldn't decipher the source of her obsession. Since his arrival, she no longer seemed concerned with it.

"They've taken my haaaair," she screeched at full volume. Sawyer could tell she was upset about the whole thing, and judging by the few twisted tendrils she had left, each piece of mud-crusted hair must be special. Hags were strange in that nature. Once they had something they wanted or believed was theirs, they would stop at nothing to get it. And if a person tried to take it back, somehow, hags knew where to find them. In his dealings with her kind previously, he had seen some odd things stolen. Cows, chickens, and livestock were typical targets, but some hags had unique taste. Jewelry, outdoor decorations, and trinkets left outside during the night. One even stole a chamber pot, although he couldn't fathom why.

"Hag," Sawyer began, "if I return your hair, will you cease to terrorize the townspeople of Gohmer?"

She seemed to consider his offer in her decaying brain as she rolled her neck with a crack and pop. "Give me my hair, and I'll only take a bite of the tender one," she croaked.

"No, Hag, you shall not harm the tender one in any way." Sawyer pictured the mayor sweating as he screamed and ran from the hag chasing him, mouth open and teeth bared.

"He shall be mine just as you'll be," came her hiss. She rushed towards him with her spindly gray legs, moving much quicker than one might think.

Realizing this hag was not a reasonable negotiator, he avoided the attack and awaited her next move. He supposed trying to talk her out of a fight would prove futile, although he would try one more time. "Hag! If you do not listen to reason, I will collect your head. Do you understand me? You will not leave this battle alive," he warned. He disliked the idea of chopping off her head, especially on such a nice day.

She responded with a hideous cry before circling her target, but he was no fool. Chasing a hag in circles would only make him dizzy and her lunch, so he let her decide the next move. Once the hag was satisfied with her circles, she lunged with fury. Seeing the perfect opportunity, he lashed out, sword swooping across her neck, lopping off her head. As the disgusting thing flew into the sky, he was amazed at the simplicity of the battle. A quiet night alone was coming sooner than expected.

One never knew how a battle would play out. A seemingly timid creature could transform into a difficult enemy, or a large, hideous beast into a food-searching beggar. Each victory wasn't taken for granted, and each loss was a learning experience. It's true that Sawyer felt terrible about hurting any creature, but at times, it was a necessary transaction.

As her decapitated head fell, he caught it neatly by the hair during its trip back down, but the rotted tendrils parted from her scalp from the impact. Consequently, her head landed in the mud with a solid plop, leaving Sawyer with a fistful of stringy, lank hag locks. Staring at the lifeless, cross-eyed face, he thought of her precious hair. It had meant so much to her. So much that she had traveled an entire hour to find it and ultimately risked her life. Picking up his virtually bald, dismembered bounty, he decided to abandon the separated tresses in the mire, as a remembrance.

With the job successful, he searched for the lump that intrigued the hag. Locating the muck-covered protrusion, he was surprised to find a mud-covered maiden, a sight most unlikely for the middle of the swamp. Her attire was curious, unlike anything he had seen before. She wore an embroidered smock. He studied the emblem but didn't recognize the crest or colors. Stooping to investigate closer, he saw that she was very much asleep but very much alive. Breathing a sigh of relief, he brushed some gunk off her face. Searching her clothes, he located an inscription on her apron stating, "The Bean Queen."

The Bean Queen? What kind of silly idea is that? Of all the places, near and far, none had such an absurd name. Despite her unfamiliar origins, he desired to ensure this very alive human stayed that way. Yanking the limp body, he pried her from the smelly muck that suctioned her by a thick cover of mud. She dislodged with a pop. Slogging through the mud, he grabbed Willow's reins between his knuckles.

It then occurred to him that trying to ride with a lady strewn across his saddle would be impractical. He would need some way to transport her. Carrying the maiden while leading Willow back to the grass was only one part of the conundrum. Situating her in front of him, the fresh muck caused her to slide around. More than once, he caught her body from falling off the saddle and hitting the ground. However, before long, the sun and breeze hardened the mud, turning it into a rather reliable glue. Keeping a steady pace, Willow and Sawyer eventually made it to the village, bounty and all.

By the time he returned to the mayor's residence, it was dusk. Dismounting, he gently peeled the lady off Willow, causing a crumble of smelly dirt to scatter across the ground. Without a place to lay her safely, he carried the unconscious woman to the threshold. Shifting her slightly to free his hand, he knocked on the door.

"Jest a minute!" called the maid. It seemed she never left for the day. Opening the door, she was immediately repelled by the scent. "Oh Sir! I jest can't let ya in. The mayor will be vexed with ya tracking in all that mud, ya know. I'm sure ya understand." She was waving her hands again, but this time to blow away the stench that quickly wafted. She eyed the woman in his arms but didn't comment.

"Ma'am, I have your mayor's request. I'll wait for him out here, as you mentioned," he said, relieved to know he wouldn't need to pretend to sit in that rickety chair a second time.

"Stay where you be, sir! I'll git the mayor." She bustled inside.

While waiting, Sawyer contemplated his reward. The job was posted for two hundred coin, although he wasn't sure if the mayor truly had that much. In that case, Sawyer reasoned, he should barter for a small cart. Knowing that a cart costs much less than two hundred coin, he was willing to take the loss for a prompt return home.

Once again, more time than necessary was spent waiting for the mayor. Eventually, the pompous official appeared, dressed in the same outrageous threads as before. Chest puffed out, his buttons still stressing the seams of his outfit, and his glasses still pinching the tip of his nose. It was certain that Hans believed he was dressed in the highest of fashion, but sadly, he didn't travel outside of Gohmer often enough to know the truth.

Sawyer motioned to the saddlebag. "Mayor, I've completed your hunt, as you asked. Here you are. A decapitated hag's head."

Seeing the crazy eyes peering from the bag, the mayor nodded to his maid, who promptly took the prize out of its holding place, with much distaste and exaggeration. Mayor Hans Gribble pointed to the maiden in the knight's arms, but was distracted when his maid handed over the head.

"Now about my payment," Sawyer said before the mayor could question him.

"Yes, yes, yes… " Hans fiddled his fingers and nodded his head, slipping his hair askew on his sweaty brow.

"I would like to propose a small cart, instead of coin. I've found a lost maiden at Giant's Pass, and I'll need to bring her back to Ancora."

Mayor Gribble let out a sigh of relief. "Well, I'm sure you're aware our carts are worth far more than the coin posted fer the hag, but I shall see that ya get one, anyways. I've been known to be a generous leader, ya know."

"Your kindness is noteworthy," Sawyer stated with a polite nod and a hint of sarcasm coloring his tone.

The maid, sensing that it was also her job to retrieve the cart, hurried to the back of the house, where a tired old barn leaned precariously. She returned with a small, used, two-wheeled cart. It looked sturdy enough, and if Sawyer was judging correctly, it should last the trip home.

"Thank you, and good day, Mayor." He nodded quickly, more than ready to leave the Gribble residence.

He laid the maiden in the cart and wrapped her tightly in his camp blankets. Fastening the harness to Willow, he lifted himself into the saddle. It would be a long and sleepless trip back, but a human life was always worth the effort.

CHAPTER 4
A Nameless Phantom

CLARA

CART IN TOW, Willow walked the smooth, well-trod path leading back to Ancora Castle. The pace was slower than Sawyer would have liked, but the cart holding the maiden was more rickety than he thought. Historically, traveling was restricted to those with the luxury of hired protection or battle skills. However, with scheduled knights on the common roads, per his request, bandits and beasts alike would be less of a danger. Each time an Ancorian knight passed by, a positive sentiment filled him that his plan for safer travel would come true. Yet, even with knights patrolling the roads, he dreamed of the day when everyone could travel without the worry of monsters or bandits.

Many of the wealthy were oblivious to the living conditions of the average townspeople. As they lived carefree, their countrymen fought for simple shelter and meager meals. If classes solely mingled among themselves, much potential for opportunity and economic growth would be lost. Even the smallest towns had something to offer, but awareness was key. Compassion could come later. His rally for safe travel would open the possibility for positive change between classes—or so he hoped.

In any case, he was relieved to have an easy ride home given the circumstances. A time or two, he stopped to check on the crusty woman, but she seemed to be sleeping deeply, despite being wrapped in a smelly blanket of swamp. If the mud dried any harder, he'd have to chip her from its cocoon.

Walking slowly, Sawyer diligently allowed Willow an extra break or two from pulling the cart, as they both had lost sleep. Willing himself awake was a well-practiced skill, but it didn't ease the burning in his eyes or the regret felt from not packing an energy tonic. Lamenting the warm bath and night's rest at the inn, he recalled the sweet lady at the counter. Her grateful smile told him that his choice to let her keep his refund was a good one.

In the distance, a faint gray image of a woman snatched his attention. He rubbed his eyes. Had she been there all along, or did she materialize before him? Wisps of shadowy hair tossed around her. Interest piqued, he guided Willow towards the mysterious phantom. A mirage of a form, the gaunt shadow turned. Willow snorted but stayed still. Sawyer stared, unable to divert his attention elsewhere.

Her face was vague, with deep-set eyes peering from hollow sockets. She returned his stare. Amidst the emptiness in her eyes, there seemed to be anger... even sadness. Her gray lips turned downward as she swayed. Blinking, her empty eyes flashed red as she glared at him through the tangled tresses hiding her face. Thin arms swung lifeless from her shoulders as she moved forward. Stopping only after one step, she raised her arms in front of her with a forceful swing.

Never had he seen such a creature before. With no physical body of blood and bone, he was unfamiliar with her species. Even hags, as ghostly as they are, had something to pierce, but this creature faded in and out. Dismounting, his back straightened from the shiver running down his spine. He had a strange feeling that he was inadequate to handle such a foe. Unable to look away, he was transported back to another time and place, where a long-hidden memory came vividly alive.

Prince Cyrus lunged at the enemy soldier. Young Sawyer, scared of the warrior clad in spiked armor, hid behind the fallen cart. The army had advanced quickly, taking the group by surprise. It had been his duty to keep watch while the knights slept.

Out of excitement for his new grown-up role, he stayed awake all day, which later deceived him when he found himself asleep. He would only awaken to the frightening clash of cold metal and loud voices.

The knights fought in earnest, all too engrossed in the rage of battle to notice the quivering boy. Each one was solely consumed with killing their target and saving themselves, but none would experience the latter. The prince, locating the frightened boy, rushed to protect the young lad, fending off the brute force that surely would have killed him in an instant.

The phantom dropped her head from side to side, wispy hairs floating back and forth. There was neither sound from her movement nor blinking from her eyes. Feeling emotionally exposed, he shuddered and brushed his hand through his hair. Sorrow, anger, and shame all pushed to darken his spirit. His reverie turned dark as his breath became shallow. Reality fading, his memories, once vivid and alive, muddled with real-life. Dream faded into reality and reality back to dream. Legs shaking, he fell to his knees.

The forest surrounding the path altered. This new forest was dense, with little color, and smelled of dead leaves and musty dirt. This wasn't the forest leading home. Then he remembered. He remembered who he was and what he needed to do. There was a reason he was here… it wasn't to reminisce, but to help someone else… His eyes opened in shock to see the shadow mere inches from his face, eyes glowing deadly. Her closeness was familiar, as if he had always known her. It invited him to dwell upon memories and slumber in them. Her call was strong, but his conscience pulled stronger. Swallowing the dryness in his mouth, he regained awareness.

He was in the woods, the real woods, and on the road to Ancora Castle. *My name is Sawyer. Commander Knight of Ancora. I found a woman in the swamp. She needs help. She might be sick or hurt. I must help her, and not linger another moment.*

The darkness disbanded, leaving him dizzy. Rising to his feet, he steadied himself by resting his hands upon his thighs. The ghostly woman shook her head and retreated quickly, flying backwards. She stopped far down the dirt path. Arms swinging, she remained.

"Hello there, what should I call you? I don't believe I've come across your kind before. You seem… troubled," he asked, his voice shaky. There was no answer.

A sudden unworthiness filled him. He knew she possessed unknown power. Neither advancing on the other, she broke the stare to sadly cast her eyes downward. Moments later, in jerky motions, she lifted her head with renewed strength. Lifting her chin, her mouth gaped open to suck in a large gulp of air. Exhaling, she left behind nothing but the slight echo of a moan.

Sawyer squeezed his thigh to calm its shaking. Searching his surroundings, he was still on the path to Ancora. He needed to get the maiden help. Drawing in an intentional breath to refocus, he held it firm until his heart quieted. Mounting Willow, he continued home. Then, when a groggy sigh escaped from behind him, the memory of the shadowy figure was forgotten.

CHAPTER 5
The Bean Queen

CLARA

CLARA'S ATTEMPT TO open her eyes failed. Raising her arm to rub her face, a scratching sensation scraped at her skin. She gently rubbed her eyes. Disturbed hardened particles crumbled off, tickling her ears on the way down. Plucking crust from her lashes, she gazed into an open dark sky filtered through watery eyes. Blinking frantically, she cleared her vision.

The stars. So clear and bright. They beamed proudly in the dark. She instantly knew this was not the city. Her lungs filled with cool, crisp air, and the most terrible smell. Albeit, the breath was invigorating, despite her involuntary gag. With renewed energy, she gained the strength to move the rest of her body. Creaking her head side to side, more crusted particles tumbled off in clumps. Worn wooden slats beneath her moaned while she thrashed. Pausing to catch her breath, she peered through the large gap between the spaced boards to see a dirt road passing by. The pace was neither fast nor smooth.

Why can't I move? Tilting her head back, she wiggled to test the tightness of her bondage, only to discover that she wasn't constrained after all. A rough blanket, tightly swaddled, was the culprit of her minor kinetic setback.

Rolling to her stomach, she quickly suppressed a painful groan. Achy and stiff, she pulled herself onto her knees with great difficulty and noise. Globs of brown matter rolled off her like small avalanches as she scrambled to her knees. Free from the blanket, cool air caressed her newly exposed skin. Her heart skipped a beat, maybe two. A pungent odor slapped her senses. She gagged, spitting out lumps of gritty, sour dirt. Grasping for the blanket, she wiped her face and hands while trying to calm her nerves. The cart jostled, sliding her around. She planted her feet to keep her balance. A horse was pulling the cart, with a man riding it. Placing her hands on the tops of the slats, she studied the rider cautiously.

Calm down… I'm being kidnapped… on a… he's on a horse? He didn't seem to notice that she was awake or alive. She pulled her ponytail to tighten it, but it was stiff and uncooperative. Leaving the mess for later, she rubbed her mouth. Slapping her hand to her lips, she muffled another gag. *Kevin… was he real? I jumped into the light… I was bringing coffee home.* The experience organized in a confused cluster in her mind. None of it made sense. *"Stay calm,"* she soothed herself again, although her hands continued to shake. Her mind, in protection mode, took her out of the moment into the perceived safety of her thoughts.

The horse trotted unbothered. The rider never turned but stayed focused on the road ahead. Being on a dark and bumpy road, he didn't notice her moving behind him. Her eyes searched the cart to find a single crowbar, almost hidden under an old dirty blanket. She snatched it from under its cover, tightly gripping the handle. Standing on the bumping surface, weapon in hand, she put one foot on the slat of the cart and used it as momentum to jump behind the rider, landing perfectly on the horse. Smacking him on the head, he fell to the ground with a satisfying thud. Screaming victoriously, she took off on the horse to safety…

Clara blinked her dry eyes. *I don't know how to ride a horse, and even if I did, where would I find help?* A jolting bump from the road pulled her from her story, and the cart slowed. *Shoot, I wasted too much time thinking!*

"You're awake," came a cheerful voice from the rider, who

didn't turn around. Pulling back on the reins, the horse stopped and he dismounted.

More than ever, she wished to be one of the higher versions of herself. Thinking of her brave alter egos, she pretended that she, too, was brave. A cold rush streamed through her body. She frantically looked for the life-saving crowbar, but could only locate blankets, splinters, and stinky crumbled mud. Not knowing how to escape, she scooted to the back of the cart and wrapped her arms around her legs. She had to wait this one out.

The man was much bigger on his feet. It was highly unlikely she could take him down without a weapon. He walked to the back of the cart and placed his hands upon the edge of the bed. Slowly leaning forward, the cart groaned from the pressure. Clara kept her foot pressed firmly to keep herself from sliding towards him. Using her hand as an extra anchor, a splinter pierced her palm, but the persistent stabbing was only an afterthought.

Dangling from a sheath at the man's side was a double-bladed sword. The perfect size to kill her, or worse, cause significant damage. Without a weapon of her own, she pushed hard into the corner. Even now, during this dire situation, her mind didn't let her down. She winced and shut her eyes tightly as the story unfolded…

The man with the sword drew his weapon. The moonlight emitted a beautiful yet manipulative shine on the blade. She was a trespasser fit only for a proper beheading. Jumping off the cart, she ran, but alas, she wasn't fast enough. Catching her, he would cut her up into pieces and feed her to the dogs. Old Fido would get an arm, while Cassie got her foot. Her head, of course, would be hung by the hair as a warning to others who did not belong…

The creaking cart snapped her from her thoughts. There wasn't anything she could do, save for hoping for the best. The man, still leaning, watched her with interest. *I suppose if he makes it quick, I wouldn't feel it for long. I hear that your body can go into shock, to protect itself and—*

"You're frightened," he said gently. He leaned harder on the cart, and Clara pushed harder to stay in her corner. Mouth gaping, she watched as he pulled his sword from the sheath and tossed it to the edge of the grass. Without its master, it appeared innocent and lifeless.

Her mouth snapped shut, leaving behind a lingering sour taste. Tacky and thick, she held the muddy syrup in her mouth not knowing if she should spit it out. She swallowed it. The man laughed softly and lifted himself into the cart, sitting beside her.

Silence between them, she shyly studied him. He, too, had a coating of mud, although not as severe as hers. Sitting a few inches away, he didn't meet her eyes, but stared off into the distance.

"The mud. It always tastes bad. No matter how much you visit the swamp. One can never get accustomed to the smell or taste," he said, amused. The knight shifted and put a hand on his bent knee. "Queen Bean, is that your name? They call me Sawyer Lydon. I'm the Commander Knight of Ancora Castle." Clara didn't move. "Please, there's no cause for concern, I'm nothing to be afraid of."

Queen Bean? Where did he get that idea? Oh. My clothes… How in the world did I get from work to a— "You said swamp?" her voice wavered. "My name is Clara Rivers. I'm not a queen… or anything like that. The Queen Bean is where I work… um, worked. I'm guessing I don't work there now that I'm here. Somehow."

"I see. Lady Clara, it's a pleasure to meet you officially. I hope you haven't found your traveling means too crude. I hadn't come prepared to rescue a maiden, and although I was able to locate this small cart, it's a rather uncomfortable way to travel. You see, I found you at Giant's Pass in a very unfortunate manner. A hag was acutely interested in you. Thanks to the stars that I found you in that moment."

"Hag?" Clara wanted to imagine such a creature, but she willed herself against it. The last thing she needed was another daydream to haunt her for the rest of her life. "Where am I?"

The knight smiled warmly. "Currently, you're about four hours from Ancora Castle." She met his gaze, connecting with a set of kind, green eyes.

"I know it sounds crazy, but I'm not sure how I got here, and… thank you… for saving me from that… hag."

"I'll count it a pleasure, although it's not my regular act of heroics, if I'm being honest, but I did well. However you got here, your timing was impeccable. From what I gather, it sounds like you need a place to stay. Please know that I won't insist that you go to the castle with me if it doesn't suit you. You have a choice, in case you were unaware."

"Thank you for helping me. I have nowhere else to stay, so I guess I'll come along. I mean, as long as I'm not going to end up burned at the stake or cut into pieces."

"What an imagination you have." The knight chuckled. "I don't typically participate in such things, at least not when it comes to maidens. Now, I'll need to retrieve my sword, as it can be a bit dangerous out here, especially at night." The knight rose, rocking the cart. She swayed with the movement as he jumped off the back. Retrieving his weapon, he walked to his horse, stopping abruptly to peer over the side of the cart.

"Forgive my rudeness, but the horse, who is so kind to transport us both, is named Willow." He winked. Clara surprised herself by returning a smile. Gathering the filthy blankets, she settled into the cart and fell asleep surprisingly quickly. As miles passed, the sun woke to the image of Ancora Castle appearing in the distance.

The castle was as sturdy as it was beautiful. Lilacs covered the entrance, filling the air with a heavenly scent. Pink blossoming trees lined the entryway leading up to the oversized wooden drawbridge. A banner hung from a pole, waving proudly, a welcome and reminder of the hope and compassion it symbolized, the knight informed her. With the palette of blue, brown, and gray, the colors portrayed loyalty, endurance, and intelligence.

As Ancora Castle's stone towers loomed above, Clara felt the change of surroundings as the atmosphere shifted from struggling creaking planks to a bustle of activity. Sitting up, she stretched as the sound of voices filled the air. The large, heavy door creaked open, exposing a gray stone entrance. She brushed herself off as the man who found her offered a hand to help her off the cart.

People were hustling, seemingly excited to see them. Clara stood in confused silence. Unfamiliar faces welcomed her, though she couldn't be sure why. They were dressed in lavish medieval-style clothing. She tried to adjust her crooked shirt but it wouldn't budge. She didn't belong here. She wrung her hands together nervously.

"Clara," the knight's voice was soft, "this is Delilah. She'll be your maidservant during your stay. If you don't mind, follow her. She'll guide you to your room. I'm sure you're looking forward to a relaxing and quiet place to rest and refresh." With a groggy smile, Clara thanked him and followed the maidservant. Her legs mindlessly trailed after Delilah while her mind blankly tried to process the recent events. *This can't be real.*

The solid door opened into a massive, lavishly decorated room. Long, heavy curtains hung at the sides of each window with thick braided rope tiebacks. A weighty, ornate dressing table sat against the wall, adorned with many eye-catching bottles and vials. The room contained large pictures, a strange fur rug, and fancy oversized furniture. Each piece appeared expertly crafted and placed with care.

Delilah lightly touched Clara's shoulder. "Welcome to Ancora Castle, Lady Clara. This will be your room. I hope you find it to your liking. I'll send servants to help you... clean up." Delilah gracefully left the room.

Clara was alone. Sitting on a small corner of the bed, she noticed the trail of mud left behind. *I hope the smell comes out of my hair...*

"Hello, Lady Clara," came a perky voice that woke Clara up from her sleep. "My name is Holly, and this here is Annabelle," she said, motioning to a little girl.

Holly's face was pleasant, round, and youthful-looking despite a few wrinkles. Happy and welcoming, she seemed to possess the talent of making others feel comfortable. Annabelle jumped next to Holly. Her mass of unruly blonde-white curls bounced around. She had a big smile on her face, as if something really funny had happened.

"Tis 'a pleasure, Miss Bean," came her sweet voice. "Sawyer told us how he found you near Giant's Pass. He pulled you in his cart all the way here. You were all wet and smelled of swamp. You still smell horrid." Annabelle's words were fast and excitable, as she pinched her nose to demonstrate her thoughts about Clara's scent. "He said the giants weren't around when he found you, but an old hag was." Wide-eyed, she jumped closer to Clara. "I think she was going to eat you."

"Hush now," Holly scolded, pulling the little girl back. Annabelle obeyed but continued to stare rudely.

Clara's mind raced, but she could acknowledge one thing as fact: she did, indeed, stink. More concerning, however, was the idea of the hag. Fear shot through her as she smeared away mud from her pants. The fear encouraged her eyes to burn with threatening tears.

"Oh dear," Holly said, pressing her hands against her full cheeks. She looked akin to a chipmunk that stored way too many acorns in her mouth and now regretted it. "You are fine now, my dear. Sawyer found you just in time. Nothing to fear. Come this way, let's get you out of this attire and into something clean."

Holly grasped Clara's shoulders and faced her towards the tub. While Clara cautiously undressed, Holly stooped to address the child. "Annabelle, go fetch the maids to fill the tub with some warm… err, hot water. We want to scrub this muck away, now don't we?"

"Yes, Momma," Annabelle replied while rushing towards the door. Seemingly unwilling to miss any action, she hastily dashed out of the room to yell down the hall. "Come quick, she's awake! Only hot water to scrub the stench," her voice echoed.

"Holly, I don't want to overshare since we just met and all, but I'm confused, and I don't know how I got here or if… if this is real." Clara's tears were drying up, but her inner self trembled. Despite the fear, the goodness in Holly's eyes eased her emotions.

"Lady Clara, of course you are. You only just arrived and in such an unusual way at that. It's only natural to be a little disoriented."

It wasn't long before a group of maids scurried into the room, hauling buckets of steaming water. Holly helped Clara into the sudsy bath. Across the room, Annabelle was stripping the bedding and complaining loudly. "Good golly, it smells so bad! These sheets will never be the same! 'Tis the worst smell I've smelled in some time, and… and… I have to empty the chamber pots," her high-pitched voice rambled.

"Hush now," said the nearby maid helping with the sheets. She pinched the young girl's arm, and Annabelle squealed.

"You're going to meet the king later this evening," Holly announced. "He took an interest in your appearance and your whereabouts. You don't look like the rest of us, you know. Oh my, the entire castle is fussing over you. We're curious where you came from, and how you ended up in the swamp, of all places." The woman softly chuckled.

"There's a king here?" *Of course there is.* "I'm going to meet him today? I—I haven't met a king before."

"Dear girl, now don't be ashamed. Not many have had the privilege of meeting the king officially, myself included. It'll be fine, now. You will see."

Sitting in the once clear water, Clara frowned at the dirt under her nails. Taking a stiff brush, she roughly scrubbed at the gunk and the mystery behind its origins. It was still possible this was only a dream, but it felt real. Too real. Finishing her scrub, she took the offered arm from a supervising maid and stepped into a robe to dry off.

The next few hours were disorienting as Holly and her maids gushed over dresses and hairstyles. Once the final choices were set, they swiftly pulled Clara's look together with a flurry of mindless chatter. Clara listened as they discussed cute love interests, the unsurpassed quality of the fabric, and what they planned for dinner. Yet, no one asked about how she got here or where she was from.

When the transformation was complete, Holly's smile matched the beaming tone in her voice. "What a lovely sight you are," she exclaimed, folding her hands. Clara grabbed the sides of her billowy velvet dress. The detailed work was stunning. The fabric was rich and heavy, and she loved how the weight of it hung on her body. The navy blue and white velvety material shimmered. She lifted the hem to find ruching on the bottom, exposing dainty eyelet fabric. Swinging her dress side to side, the maids stared at her oddly.

"No time to waste," Holly announced as she took Clara's arm and guided her out the door. "On to see His Highness, King Henric!"

Holly quietly bowed to the usher guarding the grand and extravagant double doors before passing Clara off. The usher offered his arm to Clara, which she felt pressured to take. Creaking from years of service, the doors opened into a lavishly long room with a noble red carpet, trimmed in gold.

CHAPTER 6
Clara of America

SAWYER

SAWYER WISHED for sleep as he tossed and turned in his bed. No matter how he lay, a comfortable position wasn't found. Fresh from a much-needed bath, he stared at the ceiling, arm stretched above his head. The mud-covered woman filled his thoughts, hindering any chance of sleep. *Her accent is unlike any I've heard. The clothes, the mannerisms. I feel there's more to the story. There always is.* Pushing the mystery aside, it had been the most unusual day all around, a strange woman buried in mud while another seemed to be haunting the woods.

The phantom. What a peculiar exchange. It was as if he were pulled vehemently from reality into his most hidden memories. Was it magic or another force the hazy phantom possessed? Of course, the foggy woman might have been a crazy mirage from lack of sleep and long hours on the road. Still, thinking about her was nothing short of chilling, despite his questioning her reality.

Turning to his side, he slid from the bed, abandoning the idea of a quick nap. Instead, he checked his reflection to ensure he was fit to represent in the King's Audience. Combing through his wavy brown hair, the last few days, paired with the harsh scrub, had aggravated his locks. He wasn't one to dress up often, preferring his casual attire of light armor and the king's colors—blue, gray, and brown. He wore them proudly, but sometimes he thought about his life prior to living within the castle gates.

His parents died when he was young. He often wondered if the faces he recalled were truly theirs or devised by his imagination. Holly Puckett, his mother's dearest friend, lived down the road from his family. After being orphaned, Holly immediately took him in. Unlike many children who found themselves without the protection of a family, he had a loving home with the Pucketts.

Being a diligent worker with exceptional multitasking skills, Holly secured a position as a castle maid. Regardless of rank, it was considered an honor to work for King Henric, and it paid well considering the alternative options. Eventually, she was promoted to Head Maid, which rewarded her with a hut secured within the castle gates. The hut wasn't roomy, but no one cared about that. The price of fond memories far outweighed the small size. On warm winter nights they huddled around the fire while telling stories, while Dave, Holly's husband, strummed his mandolin. Some nights, if they were lucky, Holly would bring home sugary leftovers from the castle, which they would enjoy with freshly brewed tea.

Sawyer recalled Holly's pride in her hard work. On one occasion, he had heard her cheerful voice addressing the younger staff, "Work hard, ladies, and it will pay off. Smile and do as I say. You will see." He felt lucky to have his second-chance family and the opportunity to live within the castle walls.

Early on, he was intrigued by the Ancorian knights. Around the age of nine, he pleaded to Holly and Dave to permit him to work at the stable. There, he learned more about the knights and what Ancorian commanders looked for in potential prospects. There was more to being a knight than being trained for swordsmanship, especially if one would be fighting mages. Although each castle was specific about recruits, Ancora preferred those with outstanding natural ability. Eventually, he caught the eye of the prince.

Not giving up on the hair battle, he wet the comb to push his stubborn cowlick into place; it rose from his hairline, protruding prominently from his scalp. Dipping his comb in a gel, he pasted it down. Victory. He happily surrendered the comb back to the table. Grabbing the brown leather boots from his bedside, they shone from the polishing wax that Rory had used. Feeling fresh in his coat of arms, he exited the room and walked towards the King's Audience.

During his stroll, many young maids batted their eyes and smiled coyly. A part of him liked the attention, but he kept that to himself. It never served anyone to be too full of themselves. Yet, at times, he would send them a wink, just to watch them huddle with a cluster of giggles. Today, however, he had no such thoughts. *Who, exactly, is Clara and why was she wandering around Giant's Pass alone? Didn't she understand the dangers of traveling alone, especially near the swamp?* He recalled the flurry of excitement after she was escorted to her chamber.

"Is she a mage?" one maid had asked.

"No, she must be a bard," said another.

"She stinks," Annabelle shouted, causing the maids to stare. She could be both loud and talented at causing one to jump. "Did you save her from the giants? Were they going to eat her?"

The recollection amused Sawyer. He loved the brazen child and enjoyed joking with her. "Well, Annabelle, no giant in their right mind would touch her while she smelled like that, but there was a hag that showed a bit of interest," he said, raising his eyebrows. Annabelle jumped back in a fit of giggles.

Sawyer left the memories behind as the heavy doors to the King's Audience opened. He bowed when he approached the king, who was already seated.

"My boy," King Henric exclaimed, hoisting an arm in exclamation. "I'm sure Princess Adeline's appearance tomorrow has you excited?"

Sawyer took his place at the left side of the king's throne and hid his shudder well. "Of course, Your Highness."

The king nodded enthusiastically. "We'll continue the discussion tomorrow. I'm sure you're ready to get things in order, as we all are. Big advancements will come to fruition with this union."

To the right of the king was the king's advisor and long-time friend, Merrick. Although known to be harsh and sometimes quite direct, his heart was good and his smile authentic. Having fought in many battles together, Merrick and the king were like brothers. Merrick acknowledged Sawyer with a nod, "Commander, I hope to get your thoughts about Clara later this evening."

Sawyer nodded in agreement. "Unfortunately, she slept the entire trip. I have little information to provide, except that she seems frightened and somewhat unaware of her surroundings. A hag was acutely interested, but has anyone else mentioned anything beyond this?"

Merrick replied, "We'll discuss it in detail later, but Zerpith was madly intrigued. He speaks of nothing else."

"Zerpith has? I can't imagine why." Sawyer paused when he noticed a group of court members trying to decipher their conversation. "I'll follow up later."

The King's Audience was a long, dimly lit room full of courtiers, all hoping to discuss and discover the most recent gossip. Dressed in extravagant garb, they clustered against the walls lining the aisle. Having a carefree time eating and drinking, they stopped when the doors opened, and a stranger entered. The usher, leading Clara arm in arm, bowed when they reached the platform before the king. Clara's curtsy was tense and uniquely her own. Yet, she managed to clean up nicely.

"Your highness, King Henric, I introduce Clara Rivers of America!" the usher broadcasted loudly. The room went silent. Clara stood still. So did everyone else. Clara cleared her throat and wiped her hands on her dress.

In a small, shaky voice, she spoke. "I—I guess it's my turn… Your… Your Highness, as you know… um… my name is Clara Rivers. I'm from a place called America. Not that long ago, I was home… um… in America. It was just a silly game, really. I jumped into a ray of light… um… now I'm here. I have no idea how it happened, and no idea how to get back home. It sounds crazy, I know… but…"

Sawyer's face was stoic despite the awkward display. *She's nervous.*

Clara visibly swallowed a hard lump. The court observers remained still. Their merriment would come later, Sawyer was sure. The court loved good gossip, and this strange woman appearing from a glowing light was a delicious tale to tell. Many leaned in, hoping to hear more. Sawyer glanced at Merrick, who glanced back without expression.

The king broke the heavy silence. "Clara of America. I sense our meeting was hurried. You're still not well from your excursions at Giant's Pass." The king turned to Sawyer. "Commander, please escort Clara to the gardens so she can renew her mind."

On command, the knight left his post and gently took Clara's arm. "Ma'am," he bowed, "allow me to show you the gardens."

CHAPTER 7

Dirty Dishes

CLARA

THE KNIGHT LED THE WAY. Clara watched her feet as loneliness overcame her. She was alone in this strange world, and her chance to represent herself became an unfortunate shamble. Each step forward, her shoes peeked from the hemline. When she first wore the dress, her obsession with it was distracting, so much so that her shoes had become an afterthought. But now, she fought anxious tears as she watched each bejeweled velvet shoe emerge from under the dress's hem.

Keeping her gaze low, she firmly squeezed the knight's arm. *If there's magic in this world, I hope I learn to disappear. But then what happens when one disappears?* As her dress rustled, her thoughts did the same in her head. *I just spoke with a king... A real-live king who sat on a real throne. I should've been more collected. I should've explained more about America. I made a fool of myself and ruined my first impression. He dismissed me so quickly, too. Great. Everyone was staring. I bet he thinks I'm an idiot.* Heat rose to her cheeks. *I wonder if I can ask for a second chance so he understands I'm not rude!*

Feeling her hand cramp, she loosened her grip on the man's arm and continued to observe her feet. The jewels still played peekaboo from under her dress, she was still holding the knight's strong arm, and she still didn't wake up from this bizarre dream. Her daydream continued, and her steps slowed to play it out.

Clara stood tall in front of the king's platform. "King Henric, it's a pleasure to find myself here in Ancora. You see, I was walking the streets of my mother-home," she pondered if that was the correct verbiage, *"when an enchanting spot of light appeared out of nowhere. I was curious, so I went to investigate and found myself in a mysterious place. It was then that I realized what an opportunity it is to be here. Surely, there is something that I'm destined to help you with."* Of course, the king would then be delighted to know how much of an asset she'd be, so he would invite her to lunch, train her in their ways… Perhaps things would work out. Perhaps—

Sawyer broke her train of thought. "I think you'll enjoy the gardens very much."

His deep, soft voice pulled her back to reality. Diverting her eyes from her shoes, she looked at him. He was cute. Her cheeks flushed, and she hastened her steps until they were outside. The gentle breeze cooled the warmth seeping across her face. The smell of wet dirt and fresh flowers soothed her senses. For a moment, she forgot she was in a strange realm where she didn't know a single person.

Butterflies flitted about, living their lives as butterflies do. Birds sang songs of contentment and peace in the trees above. Flowers of all colors and shapes danced in the breeze. Releasing Sawyer's arm, she ran ahead and stopped on the cobblestone path. Flowers surrounding her, she gazed into the most incredible blue sky. "Oh my gosh! This is so beautiful!"

Clara rushed to a blooming rose bush that appeared to glow with the sun's light. An untethered laugh escaped the knight standing behind her. Clara bounced from plant to plant, smelling and stroking the velvety petals. She stopped when she saw the knight quietly watching her. *He's judging me… He thinks I'm crazy.*

Calming her excitement, she shyly strolled through the walkways, hands behind her back. She felt at peace, regardless of her embarrassment. The feel of the velvet dress. The smell of the charming flowers. The mystery of the plants. This place felt magical, a world that might have fairies or unicorns. Perhaps both. Flowers of all colors bloomed and offered their unique perfumes to anyone who would stop to smell them. Taking the invitation, she sniffed a few, careful not to pluck them from their stems. Backing up to study a flower she had never seen before, she huffed out a breath when she hit something firm. It was Sawyer.

"Please excuse me, Lady Clara. I can see you are smitten. The Kingdom of Ancora prides itself on its well-planned gardens. Here, you won't only find plants of the decorative sort, but also of a medicinal nature. Tell me, are you familiar with the Lily Weed?"

"Really? That's so cool. I don't think America has anything called Lily Weed, although I'm not sure about that, as I don't know that much about plants."

"No, I wouldn't say it's cool..." repeated Sawyer skeptically. "Lily Weed is neither cool nor warm."

Clara swallowed. "Um... In America, we have a good bit of slang words. 'Cool' is just one of them. For example," she paused for a moment. "For example, cool means..." She stopped again, since she had just realized the difficulty of explaining it. "I guess cool would... mean..." She wanted to say awesome, but that wouldn't work. She couldn't say neat or fun either. "Cool means... great? It can also mean having good style, or even that you agree with something," she said confidently.

"I see..." The knight looked puzzled.

"Well, I'm sure if we're together more, you'll get the hang of it." Clara's heart sank. It was becoming all too real she wasn't home. How was she to process this strange occurrence? Yet, there was nothing she could do about it. She continued the conversation as if discussing slang with a knight was a normal thing to do.

"Sawyer's your name, right?"

"That's my name, Lady Clara."

"Sorry, um... you can just call me Clara. I'm not familiar with your world, as I'm sure you've noticed. I don't mean to come across as weird, but Lily Weed, kings, knights, or even castles are new to me. I know this sounds like I'm crazy, but I highly doubt I'm even from this realm."

The knight lifted an eyebrow while standing eerily still. Clara wrung her hands together. She suddenly felt the need to be alone. "Would it be possible for me to go back to my room? I'm feeling a little tired, that's all."

Her anxiety killed the beauty of the garden. The once lush plants, with their planned topiaries and extravagant flowers, became invisible by her racing mind. Wonder fading, all she wanted was home. She was going to find a new job and get her life together. She had a book to write and a life to plan. For once, she was going to make everyone proud. She was going to make herself proud. Her deep inhale escaped shakily, but she held her emotions in check.

Sawyer replied calmly, "Of course. I understand how overwhelming this is for you. I'll find Holly to see if your room is prepared. Follow me." He offered his arm politely. Clara took it. It seemed to be a normal thing to do around here.

Sawyer addressed the servant cleaning up an iron table placed at the edge of the garden. "Gretta, have you seen Holly?"

"I have, Sir Sawyer," the maid exclaimed, almost too hastily. "Holly's planning for the festival. She told us not to bother 'er unless it was urgent." She continued to stack plates.

"Do you know if Clara's room has been arranged for tonight? Will she be sleeping in the same chamber?" Sawyer questioned.

"I believe they're cleaning her room as we speak. From what I understand, the king would like her to stay, for now. If I find Holly, I'll ask her and let you know for certain."

"Thanks, Gretta." Sawyer turned to Clara. "I know you're not comfortable with me, but Holly has a big role in the festival. Today is the main planning day, and it will prove difficult to pull her from her duties. It's best not to hinder her. Since your room isn't prepared, would you mind keeping me company? I promise I'll try not to bore you or burn you at the stake," he winked.

An unexpected laugh escaped her.

Sawyer's tone of voice brightened as he led Clara back into the thick of the gardens. "Now, let's revisit the Lily Weed. It's one of my favorites."

The Lily Weed was sectioned off from the surrounding plants

and marked appropriately. "Not everything is what it seems." Sawyer began, "The Lily Weed teaches us an important lesson about life."

Clara beheld the patch of leafy stalks sprouting ugly brown bulbs, white closed flower heads, and extravagantly open blossoms. Mixed and tangled together, the lively blooms contrasted with the browned, dead-looking bulbs. Sawyer gently brushed a few of the ugly stalks. Long, flowing petals emerged, revealing a center bulb that shone with a prism of color. Her breath caught in her throat. *They look magical.*

"The Lily Weed appears to be a simple, pesky intruder, but it's only a bit shy. With proper care and a gentle touch, it will bloom into what it's supposed to be. All the Lily Weed parts are important, but it's most potent while blooming."

"No one knows why some Lily Weeds bloom while others stay dormant in their stems. I find them fascinating because of it. But beauty is only superficial. It holds many medicinal properties, which make it useful in this way. Once mixed into a poultice, it can aid with headaches and even help with bruising or burns... like that mark on your forehead."

Clara instinctively reached for her brow. "There's something on my forehead?"

"You aren't aware? A ring is branded upon your brow. Looks rather bothersome." At the mention of the mark, Clara felt a faint pulse. Her hand caressed her forehead but felt no marks. "Are you okay?" the knight asked with genuine concern.

"Yes, thank you. I'm fine. I guess I didn't notice it before. It just took me by surprise." She continued rubbing her brow.

Sawyer bent to one knee to cup the flower's head. He glanced at her, flashing a dashing smile. "Would it interest you to learn how to make Lily Weed into a solution for your burn?" His smile melted her skepticism.

"Sure, I'd like that."

The careful hand that cupped the flower head yanked it with force from the stem. The center prism popped off and plinked across the cobblestone. Clara flung a hand to her mouth to muffle a loud laugh. It was a funny sight and most unexpected. Sawyer swiftly retrieved the rolling bulb. Tossing it into the air, he deftly caught it in one hand. "Now, onto the next ingredient, m'lady."

Trailing behind, she watched him gather tools and a few other plants while he explained the process along the way. Captivated, she wished she had a notebook and pen. *Maybe if I stayed here…*

A flock of blue birds flew overhead, breaking Clara's concentration. She was so engrossed in the moment that time passed unnoticed. His knowledge and skill to transform nature into healing elixirs amazed her. Even if she had her phone, it would've been untouched. With the Lily Weed mixture smeared across her forehead, a slight burn from its contact irritated her skin. The sectioned-off space where they worked opened into the gardens through tall stone archways. The breeze softly blew the ivy growing from the archway tops. Dangling carelessly, they gently rocked against the stone. Clara watched a bug crawl from the ivy and sneak into an adjacent clump of moss. It soon reemerged and spiraled down the stone from a thin thread. The room, although partitioned by the archways, was covered by a thatched roof and filled with shelves of potions, tonics, and other curiosities.

Alchemists quietly minced, stirred, and pounded ingredients on thick wooden tables around them. One alchemist, carrying a tray of potions, opened a heavy stone door that seemed to lead into the castle. The creak from the opening door tore her away from the crawling bug. "Where did you learn all this?" she asked, drawing her attention to the knight.

"I've lived in the castle since I was a child. There's no shortage of healers, mages, knights, you name it. Whatever trade you wish to cultivate can be explored. Now, it doesn't mean everyone is a proper fit for the position or permitted every opportunity, but it's one of the many reasons why working for the king is desirable. Life is good within the safety of the castle. I can't say as much about its surroundings."

"There's villagers?"

"Of course, all castles have them. I was one myself, as was Holly and her family."

Clara pondered this. The knight continued to smash away at the poultice he was mixing. She studied him. As he worked, his expression was concentrated, but he stopped when he noticed her looking. Glancing away swiftly, she stared off into space. *This world is more than the castle. Stupid. Why didn't I think that before? Sawyer seems kind, but I don't know him. What if I'm on the wrong side of a battle? What if the villagers are neglected and want to chop off the king's head?* Her mind wandered.

The villagers surrounded the castle with pitchforks and shovels as weapons. They crashed into the castle door, all intending to chop off the monarch's head. He caused them so much misery. They wanted revenge. She tried hiding as the villagers crowded around the garden, but she was found. One of the dirty peasants lifted an old, rusted axe and lopped off her head. It rolled like a soccer ball into the midst of random rushing townspeople. It then tumbled across the cobblestone until a panicking servant's reflexes kicked it into a bush. She would be forgotten in a land where she didn't belong, missing head and all.

Clara cleared her throat. "Sawyer? Are the people here happy?"

"I'd say so, but I guess it depends on who you ask." He stared at the oily mixture before thoughtfully continuing to smush the concoction. "I can attest that the king loves his people. But, no matter who you are, some won't like you. Such is life, especially as a royal. Decisions are made for the greater good. Unfortunately, not all benefit from that."

"Yeah, that makes sense." Her anxiety lifted. Perhaps a massacre resulting in her beheading wouldn't be an impending threat after all. "Sawyer?" she asked quietly.

"Yes?" He ceased pounding the mixture in the stone bowl to look at her.

"What's going to happen to me? I have nowhere to go besides what's offered. Will I... be okay?" Clara fiddled with a leaf she took from the table.

"Don't wash your dishes before they're dirty. All things work out in due time. For now, enjoy the moment you're in. I believe you have a room here, at the castle. Even if you didn't, I wouldn't abandon you. Especially after digging you out of the swamp. Trust me, it took some great bravery to pry you out of that stinking mire. Way more than battling the hag."

The way he said it, so confidently, made her believe it. She dropped the small leaf she'd been twirling. Curled and torn, it left behind an oily stain on the velvet of her dress. She scratched at it, but it sank into the fabric leaving behind a dark, wet-looking spot. Glancing to where Sawyer had been, he was now missing. Searching her surroundings, she calmed herself. *How did he leave so fast?*

Relief washed over her when she saw his broad form in the near distance. He was talking with Holly, who smoothed down his hair and patted his shoulder. *They must know each other. She can't be his mom. He calls her Holly. Perhaps his nanny or sister?*

"The day is going quickly, isn't it?" Holly exclaimed as they approached. "How ya finding your time here at the castle?" Clara had only known Holly for a short period, but her voice gave her a sense of security.

"I'm finding my way around, thanks to Sawyer." She nodded in his direction. He returned her friendly gesture.

"I was on my way home when Sawyer found me. Would you care to join us? We don't have a big home like the castle, but it's clean and cozy," Holly said.

"I'd love to," Clara answered honestly. Her stomach growled. Assuming the castle would continue feeding her might be presumptuous. She should take each meal offered, just in case. She had to look out for herself, after all.

"Sawyer, would you join us as well?" Holly pleaded. "It's been some time since you've been home."

"Of course, I'd be happy to come. I apologize, it's been such a long time since I've visited. I can't wait to taste your cooking again."

Holly wiped her hands on her apron. "I've missed you. Dave will be so happy, that's for sure!"

Sawyer offered his arms to each of the women. "It would be my pleasure to escort you both."

It was a short walk to the Pucketts', and an absolutely gorgeous evening to be taking one. Not long after they joined arms, a delightful cluster of small, cozy homes appeared. The scattered huts resembled a cozy village painted upon a page of an old storybook. Clouds of smoke rose from chimneys, the result of lovingly crafted dinners and warm homes. Livestock nibbled on grass contentedly in fenced yards, and free-range chickens plucked at the dirt. It reminded Clara of an old fairytale, perhaps a place that Hansel and Gretel would live—minus the eccentric witch and cooked children. Thinking of witches, she shuddered. She wondered if the hag was a witch, and what she wanted with her. It was possible the hag was going to throw her in a pot and eat her with candy. *Candied Clara…*

The Puckett hut didn't disappoint Clara's imagination. The main room was illuminated by the warm glow from a fireplace and scattered candles. To the left was placed a steaming cauldron perched on top of an open hearth. Various kitchen pans and tools hung over the hearth and clinked together as Dave retrieved a small cast-iron skillet. The counter contained a washing sink stacked with dirty dishes. To the right, a worn table was surrounded by eight equally worn wooden chairs. Handmade rugs littered the floor, adding interest and color to the weathered floorboards. Facing the fireplace, a rocking chair creaked from Annabelle's movement. Next to the rocker, two padded chairs were placed side by side, and one held a sleeping calico cat. Thick cushions faced the fireplace while a pile of knitted blankets, tossed carelessly into a large woven basket, decorated the nearby corner.

"Sawyer!" Annabelle screeched when she saw him enter the room. She jumped from the rocker, scaring the cat. "And here comes Bean Queen!" She jumped up and down. "Queen Bean, Queen Bean," she yelled while pulling on Clara's sleeve. "You look pretty! You don't even stink anymore! Are you really a queen? Do you have any family? What's your mother's name? Do you have kids?"

"Hush now," Holly scolded.

After general introductions, Holly made quick work of preparing dinner. Dave had started the meal, and Holly was more than happy to take the task over. Soon, the room overflowed with the scent of a hearty meal and calm, mindless chatter. Clara quietly listened to Dave's mandolin and watched Sawyer play a game of jacks with Annabelle on the floor.

Annabelle was competitive. She attempted to cheat by swiping Sawyer's arm during his turn. Clara laughed lightly and brushed her hair behind her ear. Uncertain how to start a conversation, she folded her hands onto her lap, crushing the velvet under their weight and covering the dark oil stain. Convinced there were no dry cleaners in these parts, she could only imagine how they'd get it out.

Stain or not, what a picture this was. Straight from a fairytale. If only she could text Angel to tell her… but she didn't know if she would ever text again, let alone speak with her best friend. She allowed the sadness to cloak her. It was only yesterday she was making lattes and laughing at evening sitcoms. Now, she found herself in a medieval predicament, and a rather unbelievable one at that.

"Dinner is served," Holly announced cheerfully. She carried a large pot to the table and set it on a chunk of wood. Beef stew and fresh bread greeted their noses, wetting their taste buds.

Pleasant candlelight cast a comforting glow around the room. Perhaps, Clara thought, once she got home—if she got home—she would include candles at her own table. The flicker of light gave the room a sleepy feel, accentuating the magical tone of the cottage. The flames danced across the table, showcasing a face here and there. A time or two, the candles lit Sawyer's face, during which their eyes met. Glancing at her plate to break the exchange, she relaxed. Then, in that moment, she pictured herself living in this world.

"Clara," said Holly as she sopped up the last of her stew with her half-eaten bread, "why don't you stay in Annabelle's room tonight since it's so late?"

"I appreciate the invitation. I really do. I think there was a room for me at the castle, but no one confirmed it and…" A lump formed in Clara's throat. She sniffed and took a drink, "I have nowhere else to go if they change their mind."

Holly placed a hand over her heart. "Now, now, don't you fret, dear. You have a place here for as long as you need," she reassured.

"Sawyer," Holly said, looking in his direction, "You're welcome to the loft, if ya will."

"That brings back many fond memories, and yes, I accept the offer."

Clara placed her hands on her lap and took a deep breath. "I hope I'm not being rude, but how do you know Sawyer?"

"Ahhh," Holly smiled. "Sawyer's mom and pop were killed when he was a youngin'. Evelyn, his mother, was a dear friend of mine since we were spry girls." Holly leaned back in her chair, eyebrows pushed tightly together, as if reliving the memories. "When I heard the commotion next door, I ran over to witness the horrible scene! Evelyn and her husband—murdered." Holly's cheery face dropped, but she turned it around. "Sweet little Sawyer was crying in the corner, trying to hide under a chair. He came a runnin' when he saw me and took a part of my heart that day. I adopted him as my own. Now, every time I see him, I see Evelyn. He has her eyes, ya know. Green as the fields in spring."

"Thanks for sharing. Sawyer… I'm sorry about your parents."

Holly joyfully responded. "Of course! Such a pleasure to have some chit chat and get to know each other better, ain't that so?"

Sawyer nodded towards Clara. "I'm one of the lucky ones. So many orphaned children are left without families after their parents are gone."

Annabelle interjected, "Holly's my momma too! She didn't birthed me, but she's still my momma."

Holly laughed. She set her napkin next to her plate. "I have three children of my own flesh and blood, all grown. But blood relative or not, I think of Sawyer and Annabelle as my own."

Dave stayed quiet during the telling of the story. With both Holly and Annabelle as chatterboxes, he didn't seem rushed to add to the conversation. Clara considered sharing her story, but decided against it. There was no telling how much longer she would be here. Getting close to these inhabitants might not be the best idea.

The meal finished, Clara helped Annabelle clean the dishes. *Don't wash the dishes before they're dirty.* She liked that. She would try to be more relaxed about things. For tonight, she had a place to sleep, and for now, her belly was full.

CHAPTER 8
Spilled Coffee
MEANWHILE IN AMERICA

ANGEL

IN A FLURRY, Angel rushed up the entrance steps to the apartment she shared with Clara. It was her typical way—arms full, fake but fashionable glasses falling. Despite having perfect vision, certain outfits looked better with a smart pair of specs. Pushing the door open with one leg, she squeezed herself through the opening. Forgetting about the pesky loose threshold, her foot caught the lip of the detached seal. Simultaneously, her other foot stepped on the hem of a long dress she had been sewing. With an exaggerated *oomph*, she tumbled the rest of the way in. Fabric piled in front of her, and she banged her head on the scratched wood floor. Thankful for the cushion of fabric, she lifted her head and fixed her glasses. Twisted among the fibers, she thought of better things.

Coffee. Clara was bringing her a King Carmel Latte with an extra shot of espresso and oat milk. Peeling herself off the floor, she gathered her fabrics and studied the dress that caused the fiasco. "Ugh, I ripped it. I needed this for tomorrow's project, and it's already after seven."

It was going to be another sleepless night. The torn dress only added to her list of tasks. At least she had coffee to keep her awake. Moving the pile of fabric from the floor to the futon, she set off on a mission to the fridge. Opening the door in anticipation, she searched for her coffee. But scanning the shelves, she didn't see anything special.

"Clara, did you forget my coffee?" Silence. She searched again, moving a few items out of the way. "Clara, my coffee?"

Still, no answer. Angel clicked her tongue and shut the refrigerator door. Glancing around the apartment, she noted that her friend wasn't in the bathroom. Peeking in Clara's room, she saw nothing of interest there. Spinning on her heels, she returned to the living area. No Clara.

Grabbing the torn dress, she located a needle and thread. Taking them to the small bar-top table, where they both usually ate, she sat while mending.

Pulling the needle through the fabric for the last time to finish the darning, she tied a knot. *Maybe she's still at The Bean Queen. It's possible they were hosting an event tonight.* Tapping her fingers on the table, she grabbed her phone and typed a text.

> Hey girl! Are you at work? Don't forget our coffees!

Back to the fridge, she grabbed the last yogurt and leaned against the wall, mindlessly eating spoonful after spoonful till gone. Checking her messages, she ignored one from Kyle, her most recent ex. Still nothing from Clara. Dialing The Bean Queen, the line rang busy. Intuition pushed her to grab her keys. Pocketing her phone, she ran out the door, locking it behind her.

Her heart raced as her feet hit the sidewalk. Running, she retraced Clara's typical path. Peeking into each dark alley, she shouted her friend's name. *I told her to go to the city and search for jobs… Did she finally take my advice for once and get lost?*

Pushing the door open into The Bean Queen, Sadie, who usually worked the evening shift, was wiping tables. Only a few customers were left, many of whom were gathering their belongings to head out.

"Sadie, is Clara still here?" Angel asked, winded.

"No, she left hours ago. Is everything okay?"

Angel's lip quivered. "I don't know. She's not at home. I'm getting concerned, but I don't want to overreact. What if something happened?"

Sadie dropped her wet rag with a flop. "Call the police, Angel. This isn't like her. She's the biggest homebody I know. She never goes anywhere alone."

"No, it's too early for that. There's so many possibilities of where she could be. Let me look one more time, and if she still isn't home… I'll call the police or something. I'd hate to jump to conclusions. I don't think anything can even be done after a few hours anyway."

Angel left, walking a few strides past the coffee shop. *It's possible she went to the bookstore and got swept away.* Climbing the steps, she tugged the handle that didn't budge the door. She sighed when her eyes focused on the closed sign. Jumping off the landing, she walked home. Searching across the street and behind her, she called for Clara. But Clara didn't answer.

Just when she was about to give up, a light caught her eye. Clara's phone. Face up and lying in a dirty, vacant alley, the displayed home screen caught her attention. Alongside were two spilled coffees and Clara's purse.

"Please no," Angel panted, tears falling down her cheeks. It looked like someone had already found the purse and had a good time rummaging through it. Leaving the coffees behind, she grabbed what was left of her friend's belongings. Reaching for her own phone, she promptly called the police on her way back to the apartment.

The night was endless. Interviews with the officers, calls to what little family Clara had. No evidence was found to guide the officers to where her friend had gone or who might have taken her. Most of her stuff was there, even the drinks. Only Clara was missing. It was possible they may never know what happened. The officers seemed optimistic, but she knew better.

The night was torture. Sobs soaked her pillow as she tossed and turned. Sleep would not visit, but all the horror of the night would. Getting up, she paced the apartment while checking her phone over and over. "Where are you, Clara?" she wept into the darkness. "You realize we were supposed to be in each other's weddings. We were gonna have kids at the same time so they could grow up together." Heavy cries escaped her, "Please… come home."

The darkness never answered. Clara would not answer. A great loss tore through her heart. Wondering if her friend was sleeping somewhere, terrified, she hugged a pillow as memories filled her… Complaining about the gaudy pink bathroom, walking on Sundays to get lunch at the nearby café, laughing at childhood recollections of the crazy cop and robber games. So many wonderful memories. Memories that might cease this very night. These would be taken from her.

Eventually, the sun would rise and life would continue. But, for now, her scheduled classes would have to wait. There was no way she could concentrate or go back to her normal life so quickly. Yet, a small spark of hope poked at her heart. Grasping onto that, she drifted to sleep.

CHAPTER 9
Princess Adeline

SAWYER

THE SUN ROSE over the Puckett house, awakening with shades of red and yellow. Sawyer woke to the sounds of jingling pans and a bossy rooster. Stretching out with a yawn, the loft still felt familiar after all these years. He was also thankful to have a silent night without his sparring partner, Onyx, who was prone to snoring.

"How'd ya find the loft? Been some time since someone slept there," Holly chirped when she saw Sawyer climb down the ladder. The patriarch of the family was already gone. It wasn't uncommon for Dave to be the first out the door, but never without a kiss from Holly first. Many times, Sawyer witnessed the love that Holly and Dave shared. He hoped to find the same.

"Good morning, Sawyer," Annabelle said in a raspy voice.

"Good morning, I hope you slept well."

"I did. Queen Bean doesn't snore."

"Well, it appears your cheating didn't keep you up either. You have a conscience of stone," he snarked.

Holly laughed, enjoying the voices of her loves while the smell from the kitchen filled the entire hut. "I've got some pancakes and eggs for breakfast. Get yourself some before you head out, hear me?"

Sawyer nodded. It'd be a shame to leave the Puckett hut hungry. Not only were the meals good, but refusing one would break the matriarch's heart. He scarfed down the food, which was much better than the mess hall's, and there was less competition for a plate.

"I'll return for Clara later. When she rises, can you tell her to wait here? I'm pretty sure the king will schedule an audience with her today."

"Oh, of course. Don't be a stranger. I enjoyed having you over." Holly's smile pushed her cheeks up, squinting her eyes.

Pushing away from the table, he gathered his things, waved to the ladies, and headed out the door. Jogging to the castle, he fancied a relaxing bath to invigorate and refresh himself. Upon his entrance into the knight's quarters, his buddy, Onyx, was gathering a few vials stopped with corks from the small dressing table.

Onyx, due to his unnatural-looking ink-black hair and eyes, was named after the stone of midnight, despite his sunny personality. As a competent battle partner, Onyx was skilled in weaponry but brilliant in the art of alchemy. "Where've you been?" He questioned with a smirk. "Sleep under the stars?"

"I'm not against that," Sawyer replied. "But no. I was at Holly's last night."

"Didn't that Clara lady, the one you found in the swamp, stay with Holly too?" He squinted his eyes and put his hands on his hips. The nobles seemed to see and tell everything.

"She did, but it wasn't planned. It just happened to work out that way."

"Hmmm." Onyx's smile widened.

Sawyer collected his things as Onyx's dark eyes watched him amusingly. Stashing clothes and personal items, Sawyer rushed out the room. Onyx poked his head out the doorway. "Perhaps love happens the same," he echoed into the empty corridor.

Sawyer ignored the alchemist's words echoing down the hall. It was a preposterous idea to mention love for someone you recently met. Infatuation, yes, but not love. Besides, he was already arranged to be married. He knew his friend was only teasing, but it irritated him. Yet, there was something about Clara that intrigued him, even if it wasn't love. Heading to the bathhouse, he ignored any nagging feelings. It was another passing feeling, just like the others. He hadn't told his friends about the king's order for the marriage treaty. Thinking of it spoiled his day and made him uncomfortable. Reaching the doors to the bathhouse, an usher pulled them open.

The bathhouse had an atmosphere of serenity and was typically reserved for nobility. Although knights were not noblemen, they were still considered high-class, much like celebrities. Many esteemed nobles, mages, and healers soaked in the warm, steamy tubs. Talking business and pleasure, they enjoyed invigorating drinks and light snacks while washing. On rare occasions, a servant who'd performed a great deed or was a residential favorite was gifted a soak or two. Statues and plants lined the walls surrounding the inviting, deep pools of heated water. One particular pool held the esteemed burly cook.

"Ho, Sawyer," Jasper greeted.

"Morning, Jasper."

Sawyer raised his arm to flag a nearby attendant with a tray of cool drinks. Taking a minted refresher, he placed it on the thick ledge of the pool. He quickly slipped into the water and laid his head back on the warm cloth pillow. Jasper downed an orange drink containing crushed cranberries.

"The hunters brought in some clemmies during their forest hunt last night," Jasper announced while Sawyer washed. "Dropped them off early this morning. I have the kitchen tearing off their legs as we speak. I'm thinking a generous portion of butter sprinkled with rosemary, thyme, and just a dash of spice. Of course, I'll add my special ingredients as I go. But not too much of the spice, as we know King Henric isn't a fan of spicy food," Jasper explained while putting his glass down with a clink. A nearby servant quickly retrieved it.

"Clemmies? I haven't eaten one in a long while. I'm guessing they planned something special for the meal with Princess Adeline and King Boren?"

"Ah, so you'll be attending. I figured as much. It's going to be a large group. Petunny is even making her special cake and caramelized pears."

"I'll be attending. The king's excitement is evident. Each time he sees me it's all he mentions... It's the whole marr—" Sawyer stopped himself.

Jasper waited for Sawyer to continue, but instead, the knight dipped his rag into the water to rinse. As his rag submerged, rude bubbles rose to the surface from the direction of Jasper.

Sawyer glared hatefully. "Come on now. I no sooner get here and you're already behaving badly. It's no wonder you're not married. No respective lady around would... would stand... for such disrespect." He grimaced, not only from the waft that was starting to rise, but also from the idea of his future marriage. Both stunk.

Onyx, who had followed Sawyer to the bath house, towel draped over his shoulder, witnessed the unfortunate event. "Perhaps I should bottle that up and use it in a bomb. Might kill a whole army," he joked with a subtle seriousness.

"If you create that bomb, you'll kill both armies," Sawyer snapped while throwing his rag at Jasper. It slapped the cook's face before splashing into the water. With a disgruntled heat, Sawyer exited the pool.

"Ah, you are a weak one, Sawyer," cackled Jasper.

Onyx backed away from the pool. "As I'm undecided what you may have released, I'll be moving on myself." Jasper sat alone until frantic servants ushered him out of the tub.

Sawyer quickly dried off. Dressed and feeling clean, despite the deplorable event, he left the bathhouse in search of the king. The greatest chance of finding the royal at this time of day would be in the King's Audience. King Henric spent most of his time there, watching over nobles who loitered around the borders of the room and listening to the woes of those permitted to express them. Reaching his destination, he walked the gold-trimmed carpet leading to the king's throne.

Seeing the king in his usual spot, Sawyer joined him at the

platform with a noble bow. Judging by the large rolling cart, the king had decided to eat a late breakfast in the King's Audience instead of his bedchamber.

The king downed his morning refresher from a small crystal vial and shook his head with disgust. "Good morning, Commander," he greeted with a cough.

"Good morning. Your Highness, I humbly request a word with you in private, if you don't mind."

"Of course." The king waved his hand to his right. "Merrick! Please see to the people. I'll be speaking with Sawyer in private."

The king led the way out the back door and down the connecting corridors. Passing the portraits of past royalty, they reached a compact room. Sawyer knew the space well. Many strategic battle plans occurred among the hanging maps and tiny carved armies. Knight and king each took a seat around the worn wooden table. A servant quietly approached with a rolling cart containing a charcuterie platter. Depositing it between them, the servant exited the room to grant privacy.

Sawyer, usually at ease around the king, felt his heart pump in his throat. "King Henric, I've recently been in the village of Gohmer. It's a day's travel from the castle. While there, I noticed what seemed to be extreme poverty." Sawyer's fear dissolved while thinking of the impoverished people.

The king settled into his chair. "Gohmer, you say?"

"Yes, your highness. Gohmer had many villagers who looked far too thin, and their homes were in disrepair. They're barely surviving. I believe this is due to the self-proclaimed mayor, Hans Gribble. He seemed much healthier than the rest of the villagers. I presume he is taxing them dry. I believe we should intervene to help them," he recollected, his heart aching for the people.

The king's jovial face clouded over. "What do you suppose we do here concerning Gohmer? We should be concentrating on the treaty and your upcoming marriage. Speaking of the princess, she should arrive any hour." The king munched loudly on the food, as if the thought of the marriage feast was already making him hungry. "As for Gohmer, I'm sure they can secure resources if they're in need. We can't aid all the towns. It's not practical. Now, once your marriage is consummated, you can do as you please. Within reason, of course."

Sawyer watched the food quickly leave the plate. He couldn't help but remember how the king had eaten two breakfasts, while the people in Gohmer might not have had one. It didn't sit well, yet he couldn't question it. Sitting in silence and hearing only the crunching of grapes, he politely shook his head when the king motioned him to take part in the feast.

"Sawyer," the king said, before pausing to chew. "Clara of America… I'd like to speak with her today when the clock strikes two. Bring her to my audience room. I have a suspicion there is more to her than your average maiden." The king cleared his throat and took a noisy drink.

"It would be my pleasure, Your Majesty." Sawyer noticed the abrupt wave of the king's hand. It was time to leave. Getting up, he bowed and departed without another word.

Walking the hall of painted faces, he stopped at the portrait of King Henric. *Forget about Gohmer, his own people? This is not the king I know. King Henric was kind and thoughtful, even to those far from Ancora. Perhaps the contract details for the marriage have him in a peculiar mindset.* This was certainly a difficult situation either way. Challenging the king would not be an option, but something felt off.

Shaking the feeling, he continued walking until he found himself at the stable. Smelling the fresh hay and leather corrected his mood. As usual, it faded some of the ill feelings that had crept in. Looking down the line of clean stalls, he located Willow's and gave her nose a pet.

"Sawyer," came the call from a young lad. Rory was running joyously towards him with a stiff-bristled brush in his hand.

"Hey, Rory," he acknowledged while pretending to throw a punch at the boy.

Rory punched back and laughed at the antics. "Will you teach me how to parry today? Please say you will."

"We'll see. I have a few important matters to attend to, but if the day goes well, then why not?" Sawyer loved Rory like a little brother.

His squire's work ethic, as well as his infectious personality made the boy a pleasure to mentor. Although too young to tell, there seemed to be a good chance of the boy developing special abilities.

"I'll be waiting," the boy informed him with a swipe of the brush.

Sawyer surveyed the stable. Everything appeared to be in order. Squires hustled, mucking and laying fresh hay. Horses nickered, waiting to spend the morning out in the pasture. This year, they had an exceptionally talented group of squires. He nodded proudly at the orderliness of the stalls. Willow banged on her stall door when he stopped to pet a beautiful black gelding. She snorted her disapproval. "Now, Willow," he assured, "I won't be replacing you." He dropped his hand from the gelding's nose to give her forehead a gentle stroke. "I'll be back after I pick up Clara."

Entering the breezeway leading from the stable, a delicate voice called out to him. "Hello, Sawyer." It was Princess Adeline. Stopping abruptly, he felt a sour rush in his stomach. He turned to face her and bowed. "Good morning, Princess Adeline."

Adeline's braided blonde hair was twisted with ribbons, cascading off her shoulder. She was accompanied by two rather intimidating guards and four ladies-in-waiting. The ladies giggled at the sight of him. He was their princess's future husband, and they were smitten.

Sawyer hesitated to gather his composure before rising from the bow. "You look well. How was your trip to Ancora?"

"As smooth as one could ask. Not a beast nor bandit in sight. It seems that your army has been keeping your land safe from danger."

"You've heard of my declaration? I'm glad it aided in your safe arrival. I've been sending my men to survey the lands, as I know how travel can be harsh. Thank you for noticing. How's your father been?"

Adeline's father, King Boren, was a jolly and humble king. He loved a good meal, a hearty drink, and a full belly laugh. Being fond of Cauldira's king himself, Sawyer hoped to speak with him during his visit.

"Father's been well. He hasn't stopped talking about the gardens and your cook's fine cuisine. Apparently, he can still taste the roast he ate on his last visit. He's already been asking about tonight's meal," she laughed.

"That would be Jasper's doing. He's a master at his craft, and we're glad to have him." Sawyer replied proudly.

"Perhaps, one day, Cauldira will borrow his fine talent! Until then, I apologize for my quick departure, as I do need to freshen up. We've recently arrived, and I'm afraid I may look a bit disheveled. In any case, it's a pleasure to see you, Sawyer," Adeline said softly. "I'll be hosting a lunch for us later. I'll send word once everything is settled."

The knight bowed and watched her depart. In the past, when they had interacted, she didn't seem the least bit interested in him. Most times, she was buried in a book or writing in a journal. She was pretty and polite, that was true. But he never felt a spark with her. As for now, he was occupied with picking up the mysterious swamp lady. A welcomed distraction.

When he arrived at the Pucketts' hut, his heart lightened when he opened the door. Clara locked eyes with him. She smiled endearingly, skipping his heart a beat. Perhaps it was he who produced that grin. At least, he would like to think. At that moment, all thoughts of Adeline disappeared as he entered the hut.

CHAPTER 10

Wake Up

CLARA

DESPITE THE PERSISTENCE of the ever-cawing rooster, Clara slept past the normal rising time for the average Ancorian. Deep in slumber, she didn't wake until the sun burned hot in the sky. The sunlit rays filtering through the curtains reminded her that yesterday had, indeed, happened. Reluctant to leave the cozy room, she stepped around the makeshift bed of crinkled blankets bunched on the floor. The lingering smell of pancakes made her stomach growl. She finger-brushed her hair and located Holly scrubbing a cast iron pan in the deep kitchen sink.

Annabelle jumped in circles, hair flying. Anxious to be the first to greet their new guest, her sentences rambled at auctioneer speed. "Queen Bean, you're finally up. We thought you would never stop sleeping. I asked if you were dead. Sawyer's coming to get you soon. I was going to wake you, but momma told me not to."

"Good morning," Clara quietly greeted. The spirited girl's pigtails had fallen from her hyper jumps. Clara thought this made her all the more endearing.

"It's not morn—"

But Holly cut the child off. "I hope you slept fine, dear."

"I did. Thanks so much for letting me stay. Sorry I slept so long. I guess I needed some extra rest." Sawyer opened the door, wearing light armor and looking striking. His eyes flickered shades of green in the bright sun. An odd sense of happiness filled her.

"Well, if it isn't Clara." He winked cheekily.

"The very one. It's good to see you. Sorry… I got up really late," Clara said sheepishly.

"What is happening here, hmm?" Holly mused while pulling Annabelle's hair up for the second time that morning.

Annabelle, seemingly enamored at the thought of a blossoming love, but not so happy about her hair being tied back, yelled out, "What's happening, momma? Ouch! Are they getting married?"

"Sweetie, hush," came the correction, but with tenderness.

Clara dismissed any idea of a relationship. If, perchance, she settled down, she could disrupt time! That is, if she had gone back in time. If time travel were the case, she, herself, might not even be born. She had seen it in the movies, so it made perfect sense. Yet, time travel didn't add up. She knew enough history to know that Ancora wasn't historically accurate. Perhaps she was living in a fantasy realm parallel to her own? *I always wondered if anything or anyone lived in the galaxies. It's far-fetched, but how else can I reason with this?*

"Clara," began Sawyer, "The king requests your presence today. If you don't mind, I'm here to bring you to the castle."

"The king? Yes, I mean, okay." *I'll get another chance.* It amazed her how she went from serving coffee to speaking with a king in just one day. If she ever got home, no one would believe her.

Sawyer waited while she finished breakfast before escorting her to the castle. Stepping foot in the courtyard, a gorgeous young woman dressed in a regal gown approached. A group of equally fancy ladies were with her. They stared skeptically.

"Sawyer, we meet again. I have yet to refresh myself. I've been overcome with the Ancorian welcome bestowed upon me." Adeline laughed softly. "My, who do I have the pleasure?" The woman smiled at Clara with perfect white teeth.

The knight bowed and Clara curtsied, with no signs of

improvement. "Princess Adeline, I'm happy to hear we've made an impression. Please allow me the courtesy to introduce Clara of America. We recently met, but I'm sure you'll find her easy to speak with. She'll be residing at the castle awhile."

"America? I'm not certain I've heard of it."

"Nor I. I discovered her unconscious during a hunt at Giant's Pass only yesterday. I apologize as Lady Clara must freshen up herself. King Henric requested to see her shortly. Would you like a servant to escort her to her chamber?"

"Although your company would be desirable, I'll not keep you as I'm headed to my room. I mustn't tarry any longer. Lady Clara, it's a pleasure to meet you. Perhaps you can tell me all about America one day."

Sawyer spoke, "Princess, given her unknown nature, I'm sure she could use a friend. So far, she has only me to accompany her. I know she could benefit from a woman's companionship."

Reaching for Clara's hands, Adeline nodded. "I've been here for a few hours, and the court has already been speaking of you. Welcome to our land. I'm sure you miss America, but take heart, as you're in good company. Perhaps, during my stay, we can meet again. I'd love to extend my friendship." Adeline released Clara's hands and placed her own properly by her side.

"Thank you, Princess Adeline," Clara said, slightly out of breath. She was speaking with a real princess! Remembering the stain on her dress, she folded her hands over the spot. "I do miss America and I—I appreciate any friendship offered to me here."

"Of course. Sawyer, I shall see you later. Clara, I will schedule a time to meet with you before I depart."

"Princess, if there's anything we can do to make your stay more comfortable, please let us know," Sawyer said. Adeline gracefully excused herself. Clara released the air she hadn't realized was trapped.

When the door to the familiar chamber opened, Sawyer departed without setting foot inside. A flurry of activity was alive in the room. A clothing rack on wheels hung many dresses displayed from silk hangers. Maids bustled about carrying beautifully decorated boxes, white frilly petticoats, and pretty bottles made from stained glass. Another maid, sitting on her knees on the floor, unpacked clothing, which she handed over to another maid standing beside her. They stacked them in a gold-trimmed dresser. It seemed she might be staying after all.

"Come along, Lady Clara," said one of the maids as she gently took her elbow and escorted her to the bathing area. "We can't have you looking a mess for the king, now can we?" Clara stepped into the porcelain tub. Yesterday, it felt odd to have people around while she bathed. Today was no different. Watching a maid take the blue velvet dress, she hoped they didn't notice the stain but didn't mention it. It would only be a matter of time before it was discovered. Rushing to break the news wouldn't benefit her now.

After an invigorating scrub, she waited for the bickering group of maids to choose her dress. Two maids were engaged in a heated debate over the options, while another assisted Clara in putting on her petticoats. Holly suddenly burst through the door, making the room jump, Annabelle in tow.

"Ladies! I have just the dress in mind," Holly announced, pushing through the servants. Shortly behind her, another maid entered the room with the most beautiful gown. It was white with gold trim. Circlets of gold metal crested the bodice. The empire waist proved flattering for her figure. It was the most beautiful dress Clara had ever seen.

The material was soft and thinner than velvet, with a slight sheen that hinted at magic and mystery. This fabric was undoubtedly expensive, possibly ancient. Swallowing to wet her dry mouth, she vowed to keep this one clean. The dress fit her well, and she glanced at her shoes. They were white with hints of gold sparkles. The slightest heel elongated her legs without hurting her feet. Angel would freak out over this getup. She played a conversation with Angel in her head while Holly carefully tugged at the dress to ensure the thin petticoat sat perfectly beneath it.

The maids piled her hair into a sophisticated updo secured with a dainty pearl comb painted with gold accents. She beamed at herself in the mirror. Leaning into her reflection, she checked her forehead. There was nothing there. Whatever had been there before must be gone. She was now ready to meet the king, at least physically. The maids filtered out of the room, each carrying something with them. Clara smoothed her dress and sat on the chaise, waiting. No sooner had she sat, she stood when a soft knock was heard. Holly rushed to the door. It was Princess Adeline, this time without her usual crew. Bowing in surprise, Holly welcomed the princess in. "Princess Adeline, how may I help you? Please, come in."

"Holly." Adeline gently placed a hand on her shoulder, a signal to Holly to rise from her bow. "I'm here to see Clara. May I speak with her in private?" Holly nodded and swiftly left the room, pulling Annabelle, who stared, unblinking, at the Princess.

Princess Adeline addressed Clara, "Lady Clara, Sawyer mentioned you'd be meeting King Henric today. I understand this will be your second time. There's no shame here, but I understand you require instruction."

"He said what?" Embarrassment flushed Clara's face. It's true that she didn't know the ways of this land, but by no means did she feel that she had been that out of place.

"I've asked about your country, but no one seems to know of its location or culture. This is a bit unnerving, as we don't understand your intention. If you're willing, I'd be happy to instruct you quickly so you can make a strong impression this time around. Perhaps blending in would secure you a place at Ancora indefinitely. As a princess, I typically don't perform such teachings, but I've seen you walk—"

"Oh! I'm so sorry, Princess Adeline. I'm so sorry. I hope I don't bumble around like a monster. I could use all the help I can get. I need to be better. I don't mean to offend anyone."

"It's agreed then. First, Lady Clara, you must refrain from interrupting others while they are speaking. Never open your mouth unless you have something of substance to say. A true lady is an exemplary listener and a tactful conversationalist. I know it can be difficult, especially when you're listening to something you don't agree with or find boring, but you must pay attention. A solid word of advice is to count to five after the speaker has ended. This will help you refrain from over-talking and provide a moment to respond gracefully." Clara blushed, staring at her hands.

"Next, proper deportment is vital if you desire to be taken seriously. You must sit up straight. You cannot be slumping. The same goes for your head. Do not cast your eyes to the ground or your lap. Keep your chin level to the ground and push your shoulders back. Yes, just like that. Now, rotate them down. You are proud and elegant, not self-disrespecting. Do not forget this. Ill confidence has done no one any favors. Even servants should hold themselves with pride, in my opinion. Regardless of status, all people should respect themselves enough to stand tall."

Clara straightened her spine as Adeline continued. "To be clear, if you remember nothing else from your lesson today, remember to hold yourself with dignity. A slouching back will convey the message that you permit others to treat you with less respect than you deserve. How you carry yourself is a model for others. You can be in a room full of enemies, but if you hold yourself with pride, they will never truly defeat you."

Clara swallowed as Adeline lifted her chin with a graceful hand while continuing her lesson. "A downcast gaze may portray you're easily manipulated. Lady Clara, you're not easily manipulated. Remember that. Posture with confidence will make all the difference in how you perceive yourself. Trust me on this." The princess smiled, satisfied with what she saw. "There now, don't you look refined. However, you don't need your hands to hold you up. Your posture does perfectly fine without them. Place them in your lap… There you go. Aren't you a lovely sight of dignified grace?"

Clara couldn't hold back her grin. She already felt her confidence shining. Adeline resumed. "Please don't take this personally. I'm here to help you, after all. Your curtsy could use some refinement. Bowing is a form of respect, and one must show such respect by using proper form. I'm sure in America your curtsy is acceptable, but in Ancora or even Cauldira, your bow is akin to mockery."

Rising from the chaise, Princess Adeline showed the correct way to curtsy. After a few tries, Clara learned the skill well. The princess spent a few more moments teaching the basics of manners, resulting in a good-natured laugh or two.

With the hasty lesson complete, Adeline left the room promptly when her entourage knocked. Holly returned shortly after. Tugging the dress here and there, Holly smoothed out some stubborn wrinkles before nodding. Her authentic smile pushed her plump cheeks up and wrinkled her eyes. "Just lovely. The dress fits you perfectly. Now, come along. I'll lead the way to the king."

A knot formed in Clara's stomach. She needed to make a good impression. Walking the hall, passersby admired the shimmering dress. She didn't recognize any of the faces. Realizing no one knew her here, she could be whomever she wanted. It's not like anyone would know any different. She could be confident and brave... She could be any of the versions of herself she had created. Now was her chance to start over. Noticing her shoes, she lifted her head to remind herself to remain straight and tall. She felt dignified with her new corrected posture. Allowing her mind to drift, she imagined being an honored guest escorted to the king. She had done a great deed. The king was proud. Keeping her chin up, her daydreams played out...

King Henric grinned. "Clara of America, we're happy to have you in Ancora. You did an excellent job healing our warriors. The war was challenging, but you proved to be a great asset. You have great power that has surprised us all."

"It's a pleasure to be here, and there's nothing more rewarding than helping those in need. I'm happy to help the kingdom any time."

"In honor of your good deeds, we have decided to let you stay, and we are going to enroll you in our herbal class. You'll work in the infirmary, healing the wounded and caring for the sick."

"Thank you so much, King Henric. I would be honored to serve you and the people..."

Reaching the King's Audience ceased the continuation of her daydream. An usher waited outside the ornate double door. He politely bowed and offered an elbow, which she took. Men liked to do that around here, she came to realize. The doors opened, revealing the three… no, four men who graced the platform at the end of the aisle.

Merrick was once again to the king's right with Sawyer to the left. Clara met the knight's eyes, but he didn't hold her glance or give her any assurance of comfort. Her heart sank. Perhaps she had read him wrong. The king was the only one seated but that did not lessen his authoritative presence.

Unlike her previous visit, there was a fourth man. He was gnarled and hunched. The bald spot atop his head shone as the light from the windows reflected on it. Standing next to Merrick, he shifted side to side and forward to back. Wearing many layers of robes, she could see a visible bony hand holding a curious-looking staff. The usher bowed, and Clara followed suit.

"Your Highness, King Henric, I introduce you to Clara of America." She flinched at the usher's unique ability to project his voice and destroy her ears. The king stood, putting Clara on alert. *Why is he standing?* She licked her suddenly dry lips to keep them from sticking to her teeth.

"Clara," the king said, "we're happy you're here at Ancora Castle. I sense there's a reason you're here. I've invited our Ancient Mage, Zerpith, to accompany us today." Zerpith gazed at Clara, his hazy eyes void of emotion. The shine from his bald spot distracted her. She wondered why, if he was so powerful, he did not grow his hair back.

"Clara of America, eh…" He hobbled off the platform and into her personal space. His firm confidence was apparent up close, despite his hunched stature. She froze as he crept closer. Out of the corner of her eyes, she noticed Sawyer grab the handle of his sword. She tensed up. Even the usher next to her flinched.

The ancient's eyes were cloudy with a crash of lightning darting back and forth, so fast that one would second-guess they had seen anything at all. Clara held her breath and leaned away when he shuffled only inches from her face. Scanning her hands, he bobbed his head. He peered into her eyes and sniffed. Then his murky eyes fixed on her forehead. He paused, untamed eyes rolling around in his sockets. Eyes darting, his countenance changed. Hunching his shoulders even more, he jumped from her, in a fashion far too agile for one his age. Throwing his head back, he screamed into the air. "She has met The Guardian of Time. Cursed she is!" His gray, stormy eyes danced back into his head until only the whites were visible. The room darkened from an overcast sky. Outside, storms brewed in the heavens. A strong wind disrupted the room.

Merrick shielded the king, and Sawyer, sword drawn, stood guard. The wind blew so intensely it turned over the tables lining the room. Drinks and snacks from the court's indulgence littered the air. The court, afraid and cowering, either ran for cover or stayed present. Hiding behind tables, they peered over the edges.

Head lifted, the veins on the whites of Zerpith's eyes grew thicker and thicker until his eyes seared red. He chanted eerily, *"The tale is told when one is young. Fairy tales aren't spoken for fun. Mind behind bars, lost among dreams. Her eyes may be open, yet they don't see."* The wind strength escalated. Clara crossed protective arms across her chest. Her gown blew about her legs. She closed her eyes, bowing her head to shield herself from debris.

Zerpith's voice rose an octave. He cackled recklessly. *"A circle that's branded, she landed in mud, cursed with a power, she knows not what she's done. Wake up, wake up! Lectus is here!"* The ancient mage convulsed as he reached towards the ceiling. Sparks rolled from his palms, crashing on the floor, burning the gold-trimmed aisle rug. *"She listens to one, then retreats to another; her arrival decides our fate or survival."*

His head rolled forward, and his eyes returned to their natural position. The storm outside dissipated as quickly as it had come, leaving behind wet grass and scattered puddles. The usher had abandoned his post next to Clara, and most of the court exited the room, ready to share the gossip. Clara stood alone, legs shaking.

Zerpith returned to his haggard self. "Clara must find the windowless castle where Lectus lies, ehhh. If she doesn't overcome, we perish." The ancient mage nodded to the king as if his job here was done. With a twist of his staff, he was gone. Clara dropped her arms from her chest and broke into a cold sweat. She held back the bile rising in her throat. Her legs shook violently. Sawyer left the platform to help her to the floor.

"I—I don't know what to say," Clara whispered. "I wasn't expecting this. Do you think I'm cursed? Did he say I'm… I'm responsible for stopping whoever Lectus is? I promise I didn't do anything wrong. I—I didn't even try to come here." She searched the knight's eyes, but found no comfort in his concerned gaze.

The king, who had been sitting during Zerpith's chant, rose once again. "Clara, you have an important role to defeat the fabled Lectus, and my premonition was correct. The symbol on your brow holds a cursed power we must leverage." With those words, he walked away from his throne, with Merrick following behind him.

CHAPTER 11
A Cryptic Prophey

THE KING'S Audience was empty, save for two. Clara sat folded on the floor, her once radiant dress bunched up and resembling crumpled tissue. Sawyer gently helped her to her feet. "Mages are a fascinating sight, don't you agree?" He said with a surprising calm.

"I've never seen anything like it. He summoned wind and a storm... He's so powerful, he even... disappeared. People can't do that in America. I was a nobody in America, and I'm even more of a nobody here. I'm not magical. I can't save anyone. I can't even get a decent job. I promise... I'm not cursed..." Clara rambled, then trailed off.

The door creaked. Holly, who usually wasn't permitted within the King's Audience, scurried into the room at a hurried pace uncomfortable to watch. "I just heard the news. Merrick informed me. He told me to take Clara to her room. Promptly." Holly wrapped an arm around Clara. "Now, now, my dear. Don't you worry, we'll figure this out." But the cheery pretense didn't seem to fit.

Clara stumbled when she attempted to step forward. Fear

dilated her pupils as she spoke. "I wish I could go home," she whispered. "At least I know what to do there. I just got up, went to work… then I ate and slept. It wasn't what I wanted then," she said while gingerly shifting her weight from one leg to another. A heartbreaking sob escaped her. "But… I'd take it now."

Holly took Clara's hand and patted it. "No need to worry, dear Clara. I find that we always miss home when we're not there and miss adventure when we are. But, for today, this is your home. We care about you, ya know. No use thinking about the past. You even have your own room. In the castle, too! Isn't that fancy? A nice change of clothes and a hot meal will ease your mind. It always does for me. Ah, that and a warm blanket by the fire. I'll make sure they stock your hearth with extra wood."

Sawyer waited till Holly and Clara were out of sight before finding Merrick, who seemingly recovered quickly from the haunting prophecy. "Princess Adeline will be ready in three hours. The servants are hosting you both in the north parlor for high tea. It should go without saying, but let go of any inclinations you have toward Lady Clara. The officials will take care of her from here. A pleasant break with your bride-to-be would be a welcome distraction. It's imperative to keep your future in mind. Clara isn't part of that."

Sawyer brushed off the unexpected irritation threatening to rise. "Merrick, a word in private, if you don't mind." Merrick nodded. They stepped away from the ever-nosey ears of the court. "It's about Princess Adeline…" His heart hastened. "I'd like to request a leave… er… from my scheduled nuptials with the princess… at least until Clara finishes her task. I'd be a valuable asset to help her reach her destination, wherever that may be. Then, in turn, I'd help ensure the safety of all. I sense she isn't much use in battle. I'm thinking her purpose is something outside melee attacks."

Merrick folded his arms across his chest. A broad smirk emerged, which straightened out quickly. "Sawyer, compose yourself. I saw the gleam in your eyes when Clara entered the room. Think this through. We don't know who she is, how she got here, or if she will stay. Her powers, if they are anything, are undiscovered, at least to us." Merrick put a firm hand on the knight's shoulder to bring his point home. "The sooner you realize what your true duties are, the better. Don't allow your temporary feelings to destroy your future."

Shifting his feet, Sawyer ran his fingers through his hair. "I understand. However, despite this, would you consider speaking to the king to postpone the marriage? At least for now? I believe I'd prove valuable in the effort towards Clara's success. If the prophecy is true, and she doesn't fulfill her mission, we are doomed. In that case, none of this shall matter. But, if she does fulfill her mission, it'd be wise to consider other options, since she would demonstrate great power. This could also be of use to Ancora. Perhaps more so than Cauldira. I don't see an argument, as everyone will get what they desire in the end."

"It's true that if anyone could lead a successful mission, it would be you. However, the heart of a woman is involved. A royal at that. This could cause a lot of angst among kingdoms."

"I understand. Even so, I don't think Princess Adeline will be as heartbroken as you think. She doesn't seem interested—"

"We won't discuss this further. I'll speak with the king, but I make no promises."

"Also," Sawyer called as Merrick turned to leave. "I propose that during my… um… exclusion from duty, I'm granted the freedom to do as I wish. I'd like to ask Clara to the festival." The last part spilled out of his mouth, unfiltered.

Not turning around, Merrick laughed. "Sawyer, your heart deceives your mind. Even courageous knights such as yourself may surrender defeat at the bat of a pretty lady's lashes. Perhaps the toughest opponent a man could face is no beast at all, but womankind. I'll ask, as I said before. With that in mind, I don't believe this will be an issue. It seems our so-called heroine can barely compose herself in the presence of a mage, let alone a fabled threat." Merrick's lighthearted tone became serious. "After seeing her frightful reaction, I highly doubt she'll survive the mission. That is, if there is a mission."

Hours later, Sawyer sat across from Princess Adeline. A lavish display of food spread before them. The private table, secure from the view of onlookers, was decorated with hand-embroidered linens and a lace-trimmed umbrella. "Oh, have you tasted the biscuits Jasper baked? They are divine and incredibly flaky. I don't think I've tasted anything like them. Perhaps he can share the recipe with Cauldira's cook," Adeline exclaimed as she politely spread jam on the other half of her biscuit.

"Hmm… Yes, Jasper. He's an expert in his craft. I think sharing the recipe would be cool." Sawyer dropped another sugar cube into his tea. It plunked into the cup, spilling some brew over the rim. The image of Clara, adorned in the white gown, replayed in his thoughts. The dress cast tiny reflections across the room as she entered. His heart stopped when he saw her, but it was more than a dress. It was how everything else faded when she walked into the room standing tall and proud. Confidence looked good on her.

"Pardon? I don't understand what you mean. Are you saying that sharing the recipe is… cool?" Adeline's brows pushed together. "Are you well? How can one manage to hear temperature?"

"My apologies." Sawyer snapped into the moment. "I mean… um… fool not cool," he hastily replied, now with regret.

Adeline's eyes lit up in the most intimidating way. "Are you saying the idea of sharing the biscuit recipe is foolish?"

"No, that wasn't what I meant. Please forgive me, Princess. I've been less than a gentleman. You're definitely not a fool, rather, I admire your intelligence. I've never seen another woman, princess or not, with the desire to learn as you. 'Cool' is a slang word I heard from Clara. In America, they use it to express style or a way of agreeing. At least I think that's what it means. For example, Clara once said 'that's cool' about something I had said."

Adeline's eyes calmed. "How clever! So, I should say it is cool to share this biscuit with you." She then cut the buttery delight in two and placed half on a plate for Sawyer.

"It appears you catch on faster than I." Taking a bite of the flaky layered crust, he relaxed. "Jasper always outdoes himself."

The conversation lingered until Adeline's ladies came for her. Now Merrick sat in Adeline's abandoned seat. "I spoke with the king. He was engrossed in a plethora of stories about the storybook villain, Lectus. There were papers scattered everywhere. When I entered, he was fixated on an old book with pages falling out."

Sawyer leaned across the table to keep their conversation low. "Has the king uncovered any additional information?"

"From what I gather, yes. Zerpith has been using spheromancy. His crystal ball has unveiled a starting point, but King Henric will debrief in a round table tomorrow."

"Excellent news. What are your thoughts about Lectus?"

"From the stories I heard as a child, Lectus, no matter the tale told, usually ended badly for all. As a child, I dreamt of him once. Unnerving to think he may be real. This is grave news, if true."

Sawyer leaned back into his seat. "I'm unsure what I believe about Lectus, but I'll support Clara either way. I have no doubts about her success, especially if she has a solid team backing her up."

Merrick tapped his fingers on the table. "Speaking of Clara. King Henric is willing to postpone your contract until the mission is over. He's going to meet with King Boren and relay the news on your behalf. With this in mind…" Merrick leaned across the table and squeezed the knight's shoulder. "When you return, the contract will be revisited."

"Revisited?" Sawyer queried, wondering how that ended up in the negotiation.

"Take the win for what it is."

"I agree then."

"It's done," Merrick confirmed. "I suggest waiting to tell Adeline until her father gives her the news. Women-folk tend to be sensitive about these things, as you may already know. We don't want to upset her." Merrick walked away, stopping only after taking a few steps, "One caveat. The king has the idea that Clara is your mistress."

Sawyer watched Merrick leave, unclenching his fist only after he was out of view.

When night cloaked the sky, Sawyer yanked his boots off and jumped onto his bunk. Onyx, sprawled on the bed below, was nose deep in an alchemy text. "Hey there buddy. Are you okay?"

"Why wouldn't I be?"

"King Boren and Princess Adeline are leaving early."

Sawyer ran both hands across his hair. "What a fine mess this is. How do you know about my postponed marriage?"

"It's being discussed all over the court."

"The court never ceases to amaze me at how resourceful they are at spreading rumors. I'm all out of ears for gossip these days." Lying his head on his pillow, Sawyer pushed the nuptial from his mind to reminisce about Clara. She looked enchanting. Her white dress floating around in the wind… and the mark on her forehead glowing. No Lily Weed around would heal the spot that graced her brow. It was more than a burn. He knew that now.

Onyx, who had fallen asleep, snored loudly into the book that now covered his face. Ignoring the disruptive noise, he closed his eyes. Early on he learned to sleep quickly and soundly, despite his environment. It was a vital skill learned by all those training for battle. Sleep was a precious commodity in the open wild. Many times, quality didn't mean more. But tonight, sleep wasn't coming, no matter how hard he tried. Turning on his side, he wished for slumber. He begged for rest. He even considered summoning one of the mages to cast sleep, but he hated the feeling of grogginess it caused the next morning. So he lay there, thinking of the mysterious woman in the blowing white dress.

CHAPTER 12

Hey

CLARA

CLARA STARED AT THE CEILING, contemplating life. The night's sleep was what she needed to reset. Still in her robe without a desire to change, she blew a tangled lock of hair from her eyes. The haggard wizard's chant played repeatedly. Lectus is here. What doesn't she see? Why was she responsible for defeating Lectus, and why did that old kook think she was cursed? The servants had long since taken the beautiful dress away. A new frock hung on the hook near the tub. Sighing, she figured it was time to face reality. She recalled the disapproving look of the maid who confiscated the relic. Once gorgeous and stunning, the prophecy had taken its toll on the dress. Her hair had fallen out into a tangle of tresses. The unfortunate, delicate comb barely hung on to a persistent strand. Now, her hair was washed and dangling lifelessly wet.

That was not how her second meeting with the king was supposed to happen. She expected to meet the monarch and make a great impression. Instead, she became the cursed thing. Nothing made sense. The empty tub reminded her of home. At her apartment, she would give herself spa nights, sitting in the colorful water with a fun bath bomb, reading or watching shows on her phone. She'd smear on a facemask while enjoying some self-care. Then, after her indulgence, she and Angel would paint each other's nails while talking about their latest love interests. Angel usually had a boyfriend or admirer to discuss. She was always more than excited to hear Angel talk about the men in her life. Her friend would jump from one to the next, usually finding something wrong with each one. "He has to be Mr. Right," she would joke.

As for herself, she had a date now and then. Nothing serious. For a moment, she considered Sawyer. But she had no idea what kind of future she would have, if any. She was presumed to be cursed, not exactly a charming quality. Besides, there was definitely something going on between him and Princess Adeline. Angel would be intrigued by the gossip about Sawyer and the mysterious princess. Speculating alone would produce memories full of laughter and presumed stories about the two. *Should I ask him if he's single? Is that considered being too forward? What if they are supposed to be married, then what? I'd be so embarrassed!*

Clara leaned into the vanity mirror to smooth out her eyebrows. There were no marks of any kind on her forehead, despite what she was told. Checking the drawers, she spotted toiletry items, thankful for some options for staying fresh. She spoke to herself in the mirror. "Good thing they have deodorant," she said with amusement coloring her tone. There were bigger things to worry about than body odor. But, might as well laugh about it since she might die soon. She dabbed on the scentless liquid and used the lotion provided in the pink etched glass container. Unfortunately, she didn't see anything to dry her hair with. Sliding the tufted stool from the vanity, she flashed a fake smile when Holly entered the room.

"Clara, today's a big day… Oh dear, you aren't dressed."

"Good morning, Holly," Clara replied, trying to hide her disappointment. Lately, there seemed to be way too many big days. If this were the normal routine for Ancorians, she would like to relocate.

Holly continued, "King Henric ordered a round table later today. You'll be the topic of discussion." If Holly was concerned, she showed none of it. "Isn't that exciting?" Despite the reason for the gathering, the kind woman somehow managed to make it sound like a fun thing to do.

"I feel like I've been the topic of conversation way more than I desire. I really don't like being the center of attention." Clara stopped complaining when she saw the hurt clouding Holly's eyes. "I'm sorry. I guess I'm just nervous. Anyway, thanks for letting me know. I'll make sure to be ready." *It appears there'd be no way out of it.*

Maids once again filtered into the room. Soon, Clara was dressed in a beautiful, but much simpler, linen outfit. Since she had ruined two dresses, one for each day being here, she supposed they decided against destroying another. This time, they had adorned her with leather boots and tight-fitting pants. A white linen blouse, secured with a blue corset-like contraption, pulled in her waist. She felt comfortable enough and could move around well despite her cinched waist. Looking in the mirror, she willed the outfit to be practical for laundering, rather than agility.

Leaving her room, urgent steps brought them to a room with a curiously carved door. Sparsely furnished, a large table was situated in the center, surrounded by numerous chairs. Not much else was showcased in the room, except for the carved wainscoting lining the walls and a few scattered wall hangings with maps and old rusted weapons. Every chair circling the table was filled, save one.

Twenty-nine expectant attendants sat around the table with another twenty noblemen standing around the walls, all hoping to get a glimpse of the mysterious stranger. Clara's insecurity rose as she scanned each face. She straightened her back and lifted her chin. Some of the onlookers had sincere interest on their faces, while others appeared amused. One looked like he had eaten something that didn't settle well.

King Henric motioned for Clara to sit in the vacant seat beside him. As soon as she did, he stood. She waited to see if anyone else stood, but no one did, so she remained in her chair. Surveying the room, he waved his hand, commanding the bystanders loitering along the walls to leave. They filed out slowly, and when the last person exited, the king addressed the room. "We have a very grave matter at hand. Many of you are already aware of Zerpith's prophecy."

Zerpith sat across from Clara. In the King's Audience he seemed so powerful, even frightening, but here, he merely looked like a tired old man nodding his head, attempting to evade sleep.

"Zerpith has analyzed Clara," the king said.

Zerpith's eyes opened, "Ehhh yes. The prophecy spoke through me. Lectus is waiting. He is here. Clara is destined to find him."

Analyzed... the word feels so exposing. Clara stopped her internal dialogue before it got out of control. She couldn't afford to miss out on anything important.

The king commanded the room with his voice. "There have been fables of Lectus. We've heard of them in storybooks and in ancient texts. We all know of the doom he brings, if the tales are true." The room filled with muted conversations. "We have no cause for alarm at the moment, but we must be vigilant." Nervous gasps escaped from the table. Some laughed. "Of all the stories I've heard about Lectus, there's not one that concluded with a positive ending. Yet! Listen up! We won't know for sure until Clara finishes her journey. Nothing is ever set in stone, as we are aware, and circumstances can change without warning. I caution anyone from spreading the news. The court has already been warned. Although we trust and support our Ancient Mage, Zerpith is at the end of his days. He may be incorrect." Zerpith's sleepy eyes opened, showing red veins. He hissed. Clara shuddered. The king moved forward with his speech.

Clara glanced at Sawyer, emotionless except for a slight movement in his throat. *This Lectus guy doesn't sound like a good time. Don't they understand that I'm mediocre at best? There's no way I can help anyone... I can barely help myself. Even if I make it to Lectus, what am I going to do with him? Brew him coffee? Politely ask him to leave? The only magic I have was when I wrote a name on someone's cup correctly. But, like the king said, Zerpith could be wrong. Maybe there's no Lectus, windowless castle, or curse.* Merrick stood from his seat. Great, she had missed a portion of what he said.

"Zerpith's crystal ball displayed an image of Eros, the city of magic. So, she must go to Eros to gather additional information. The Preceptor may be able to provide the insight needed to locate the windowless castle. Then, she must simply defeat Lectus. This morning, and with much deliberation, we have decided upon a party to accompany Clara on her journey."

Clara's throat tensed. She had no idea how "simple" had anything to do with this.

Merrick commanded the room, "To whom I name, stand up!" The table grew silent. "Sawyer Lydon, Commander Knight." Clara's heart lightened. Her new friend would be joining her. At least she'd have good company and someone she could trust.

"Onyx Farfalex, Alchemist."

"Sorceress Mage, Jade Crist!"

"Rory Dextin, Squire and Equipment Manager." Clara noticed Sawyer wince when he heard the boy's name.

"Jasper Birnstock, Chief Cook and Wagoneer!"

"Healer, Eleanor Wingwright!"

Six people were standing around the table. All so different. All knew their place in life. How was she going to compare?

"And lastly! Clara Rivers of America! The one who will slay Lectus and save our kingdom." Noticing the introduction as hers, she stood. Hearing it aloud, it seemed surreal and, if she was honest, a bit dramatic.

Merrick sat when the king stood to speak. "In a few months, we'll have our yearly festival. This event is eagerly anticipated. I won't have anything disrupting the celebration and causing undue panic. Instead, we'll plan for the group to depart shortly after. In the meantime, perfect your craft. Gather supplies and get acquainted with Clara. What happens in the next few months will be crucial to your success, which is the success for our kingdom."

The king dismissed the table. The party remained. Jade, with her dark skin and tall stature, looked as beautiful as she did confident. She took the initiative to be the first to approach. "Clara, I know you heard it from our Highness, but I wanted to introduce myself properly. My name is Jade. I've worked in the magic arts for most of my life, continuing my family's legacy in elemental magic. I understand you possess unknown powers, and I hope to help you discover them." Jade's jewel-toned eyes gleamed stunningly. Her thick lashes would be the envy of anyone. Jade continued, "The king has given me strict orders to work with you. I'd recommend making yourself available as much as possible, so we can test exactly what you possess."

"It's nice to meet you, Jade. I'm looking forward to your training. Of course, I'll make myself available whenever I can. I'm going to need all the help I can get."

Behind Jade was a guy with dirty boots. "Clara. Onyx is my name." He bowed gracefully, his cloak swooping behind him. Circular goggles rested on his head, bringing Angel to mind. She wondered if he wore them for need or show, but looking at his muddy boots, she guessed fashion wasn't his top priority. "I don't suppose we'll be working on a one-on-one basis, but if you care to learn a few things about alchemy or enhancements, let me know. I've been known to mix up a pretty reliable bomb, among other things."

"Thank you, Onyx, I'm delighted to have you a part of the journey. I'm sure there's a lot I can learn from you. I've spent a little time mixing some basic stuff in the alchemist's room. I did enjoy that. I hope we can spend some time together so I can learn more."

After the alchemist was a young boy, Rory. Lanky and thin, he grinned excitedly. "Lady Clara, my name is Rory. I'll make sure everything stays in order. Don't you worry about the horses and equipment. I'm the best squire around. And, I'm being trained by Sawyer," he boasted.

Horses… why didn't I think about that? Obviously, there's no cars. I hope I don't have to ride. Horses are big, and what if I fall off? "Rory, I know I'll be impressed with your work. Perhaps you can pick out the perfect horse for me, unless there are other ways to travel. I've never ridden a horse before."

Rory looked shocked. "Lady Clara, only Onyx doesn't ride a horse, but I'll make sure to pick a steed that you'll be comfortable with."

"Thanks, Rory. I appreciate that."

Up next was a small and delicate woman with lavender eyes who studied her cautiously. She looked young, despite her white locks. Clara realized that not everyone in this world looked like a typical human. Most of the people she had seen, save for Zerpith, had appeared to be fairly ordinary. This woman, however, appeared to be straight out of a fantasy book. A golden band around her head gleamed. It made the whiteness of her hair look even brighter and her eyes more captivating.

"They call me Eleanor." She took Clara's hand delicately. "This journey will be dangerous. I'm here to protect the fighters, heal their wounds and help the fallen."

Clara swallowed. *The fallen. I was so concerned about my own life, I didn't even think that someone, other than me, might get hurt.* "It's a pleasure to meet you, Eleanor, and thank you for coming along. I've never met a healer before, but I'm already relieved to have your support."

"It's my pleasure to serve on this important journey." Eleanor let go of Clara's hand and, with a flick of her hair, walked out.

Seen easily behind the healer was a burly man who strutted on thick legs. With a shaggy beard and more hair than Bigfoot, she was glad to see such a robust warrior on the team.

"Ho, Clara. Jasper is my name. I'll be cookin' and the like. I think you'll enjoy what I bring to the table." He hooted at his joke. "No one goes hungry with me around."

"Thank you, Jasper. Actually, your name does sound familiar. I've heard a lot about your cooking talent. I'm excited to see what you'll have for us. Thank you for coming along." Jasper patted his belly with a stout hand, grinning broadly before leaving the room.

There was one left. Flashing a cheeky wink, he approached. Standing close, she could see his freckles.

"Hey," he said with a grin.

She smiled back, "Hey."

CHAPTER 13

Fear Withers

THE NEXT DAY

SAWYER

CLARA HIT the ground with a force that expelled the air from her lungs. "Couldn't you go a little easier?"

"Easy benefits no one. Instead, get better." A frustrated laugh escaped Sawyer as he offered a hand to pull her from the dust. "Trust me. Out in the wild, you can't plan on easy."

"That really hurt, though. You know, maybe we can start easy and work our way up? I've never done any of this before," Clara pleaded with a frown.

Sawyer didn't pity her. He watched Clara brush herself off. Skills such as these were essential to survival. If they had more time, a slower learning curve would be acceptable, but they had no such luxury. Clara's way of thinking was a curious endeavor to unravel. Just days ago she was crying about her fate, yet today she begged for ease. No one must've told her that success and easy don't marry. "If you desire a version of easy, you're experiencing it. Next time, parry. Like I showed you."

"Well then," she said, rubbing her palms on her pant legs, "now you see what you're working with."

"It's true I had no idea your reaction would be so… delayed. Please accept my apology for hitting you as hard as I did. I did hold back, as I promised. But, as much as I love your creative excuses, I really don't care what we're working with, and neither will Lectus. Now, try again. I know you have it in you." Sawyer retrieved the dropped training sword. Standing close, he once again demonstrated how to hold the weapon correctly before placing it in her waiting hands. He explained his next move and how she could complete the lesson by evading. He walked back to his position, sword in hand. "True swordsmanship can't be learned in months or even years. In your case, a few basic techniques with a concentration on defense will be most useful."

Clara nodded and reached her arms above her head, pulling her left wrist for a deeper stretch. Dirt smudged across the brand on her forehead. Sawyer lightened his tone. "I'll be with you until the end, but adventures are never predictable. So we must plan for the worst-case scenario. Anything less may find you on the wrong end of Lectus's sword. I'm going to charge again. It's up to you to knock me over. Don't hold back, and don't worry about hurting me. Give me your entire self. I can take it."

Taking a stance, he charged. Clara reactively dropped the sword to cover her head. Grasping her arm, he swung her around before carefully dropping her on the ground. He purposely fell with her, pinning her arms back by trapping her wrists.

"Clara, listen," he said sternly. They were nose to nose. "What will you do if an enemy holds you back? Like I am now?" Clara's eyes opened widely. Sawyer stared into them, unblinking. "Your life depends on your ability to protect yourself. Stop thinking and start doing. Thinking is vital and necessary, but overthinking only robs you of implementation. Remember what you've learned. Don't think about what's happening. Simply do it." The corners of his lips raised into a smile as he saw the flush loom across Clara's cheeks.

"Well, hey there, Queen Bean."

"Oh… uh… hey…" Clara laughed awkwardly.

She locked eyes with him. His heart beat faster. He felt hers do the same. "I just want to ensure your safety." Sawyer searched her eyes. Lost in the moment, he jump-started the conversation. "If fear locks you from action, that very fear will wither you into something you don't recognize." Lifting himself from the ground, he helped her up after he stood. "I'm only being hard because I care about what happens to Ancora and that we all come back home alive. Beyond that, your potential is there for the taking. That is, if you stop being afraid to wield it." Clara's mouth opened as if she had something to say, but she quickly closed it.

Sawyer, once again, took his post. For added effect, he snarled as he rushed forward. He had to concentrate. A few good knocks to the ground would teach her to defend herself. Safety was a top priority, especially for someone unfamiliar with the land. He knew how to fell her; others would not be so kind. This time, she almost evaded, but he was quicker. He snatched the sword by the hilt and spun her until she lost her balance. She tumbled to the hard ground with a huff. He could have caught her, but he didn't.

"Come on now," she screamed with frustration. "I told myself not to be afraid this time! And, did you see me? I did evade!"

Sawyer held back a laugh as Clara stood. *Good. She's angry. Perhaps that will motivate her.* "That you did, but you also stalled before doing so. I've decided you're going to fall and continue to fall until you stop me."

"Sounds fun, for you. I'm not made for this. My body hurts, and this training sword feels heavy. I'm sorry, but I don't think it's reasona—"

Sawyer cut her off. "Again. Lectus will not care. The past doesn't matter. What your experience was in America doesn't matter. All that matters is what you're doing, right now, to ensure a future you can be proud of." Clara paused. Looking at her feet, she kicked the dust around. He let out a silent breath of air. "I'm not doing this to frustrate you. There may be a time when you have to protect yourself. Then, what's your plan? Cower while they kill you, or worse? I know I sound like I'm repeating myself, but until you understand how to overcome your fear, you won't advance."

Taking stance, once again, the knight charged before she could prepare. Clara lifted her chin as her eyes narrowed. Brilliant. He wanted her to seek revenge. She rushed towards him while he wildly sprinted towards her. Her sword raised, he grabbed her arm and bumped her firmly. She fought to regain her balance before hitting the ground. In anger, she pounded both fists into the dirt.

"A warrior in berserker mode cannot be stopped. You must parry and evade. Please Clara, evade. I don't remember teaching you to rush an enemy."

Clara rubbed her ambushed shoulder. Her voice was tense and shaky from being out of breath, "I know what I'm supposed to do, but when it comes to me doing it, I freak out. I don't know why I keep doing that; evading is harder than I thought." She rubbed her eyes, smearing more dirt that mixed with spilled tears.

Sawyer wished to console her with his promise of protection, but that was a dangerous venture. *I don't think she means to be this terrible. But I'm not sure how to teach her how to be brave.* "I'm going to charge again. I expect you to parry my attack, unless you want pinned again." He smiled when she laughed and then charged without notice.

Clara's sword brushed against Sawyer's blade. The force didn't stop his running but pushed her off to the side. Seeing an opening, Clara ran behind him to kick the back of his knees. Sawyer plopped to the ground with a huff.

"Good work, Clara! See that? You did it. Even if you hadn't kicked my knees, it gave you a way out."

"Finally," Clara ran to help him off the ground. She held an open hand up in the air. "High five!" She cheered.

Sawyer stared at the hand waiting for him to do... something. "Come again?"

"In America, when someone does something we like or want to celebrate, we slap hands together. We call it a high five."

"I'd say it's high-five worthy." Sawyer agreed as he slapped her hand. He quickly refocused. "Let's keep practicing."

CHAPTER 14
Where Magic Lies

CLARA

CLARA ATE her midday meal next to Sawyer. Placing her fork on the table, she circled her shoulders, easing the stiffness. Her entire body was sore, especially the arm that held the sword. The first half of the day had been spent evading, most of which found her on the ground. Yet, more and more trials left her standing, impressing herself. Perhaps she could learn the art of basic swordsmanship after all. More than ever, she wished for a hot bath with some scented salts, a luxury left only to her previous life, or so she thought.

"I'm proud of you. It's not easy to evade, especially once the anger sets in," Sawyer mentioned, scraping his plate clean.

"Oh… so you noticed."

"Mhmm, it was hard to miss." A wink told her he wasn't offended. "I'll have Onyx bring one of his healing tinctures to help with the soreness."

"Thanks. Maybe I'll have huge muscles once this is all said and done. Ugh, I feel it, though. Feels like I was hit by a bus."

"A bus?" Jade questioned as she and Eleanor set their plates down across from Clara. "Tell me about this bus."

"In America, we travel using cars, buses, trucks... all these things are built for transportation. They have wheels and many people can ride in them at once. Mechanics keep them moving. The buses are especially big. I'm joking, of course, about feeling like I got hit by one because if I really did, I'd probably die."

"So," Jade asked, interest enhanced, "you would ride a bus in case you encountered enemies during your travels? Seems like a tactful way to exterminate an entire group at once."

Clara laughed. "Not exactly. There aren't enemies in America. At least not in the way you have them here. The buses only transport people from one place to another."

"Why is the bus hitting people if it's mainly for travel? I can't imagine Americans are so unaware they would walk in front of one... but maybe they do. The American I know is pretty delayed," Sawyer joked.

"Hey now! I'm getting better, you have to admit that," Clara laughed as she pushed his shoulder. Feeling the ache in her joints, she winced before shrugging it off. "Accidents happen. They might hit another vehicle or forget to stop when they're supposed to. Sometimes people do get hit from not paying attention, but no one does that on purpose."

"Your world is interesting, but I feel it's not all that different from ours," Sawyer said, wiping his mouth on the cloth from under his plate and excusing himself. "I'd love to stay and talk, but Rory is waiting for an overdue training. Clara, I'll find you after I've fulfilled my duties. You'll be with Jade the rest of the day, so I'll collect you after dinner."

Eleanor delicately cut the meat from the chicken leg bone and chewed it lightly. Picking up the goblet to take a small sip, she glanced at Clara, then placed it down. "The mages have been speaking of nothing else aside from you."

Clara diverted her eyes from the healer. "I'm sorry if I caused issues. I promise all I did was jump into light. I had no intention of causing problems, and if I could go back home, I would."

Eleanor's eyes softened as she spoke with an empathic tone so low Clara could barely hear her. "Of course you would…" The healer left her plate and utensils on the table and quickly excused herself.

Clara turned to Jade. "Is everything okay with Eleanor?"

The mage picked up her empty plate and gathered Eleanor's and Clara's as well. "Eleanor hates traveling. She loathes battle, preferring the luxuries of the castle. But there are so few healers capable of providing adequate support during battle. Many times she mentioned how she wished she were an infirmary healer instead."

"There are different types of healers?"

"There are many classes of healers and mages. I'd be happy to talk about them, but daylight is limited, as is our time before leaving to find Lectus. I promise we can revisit this conversation when time allows for it. For now, follow me, we're headed to the Mage Arena."

The Mage Arena, or what was referred to as "the arena," was enclosed in a transparent dome. Stands of weapons, most untouched, lined against the tall wood fence. A few booth-like structures were scattered around the perimeter. The center was empty except for a few mages practicing inside. Magic spewed from their palms and scepters.

"Sawyer mentioned how you've made a little bit of progress, but I expect you'll learn magic faster. All those in battle should have melee experience, but I don't think that's your strength. Even I can wield daggers, if needed, but I'm not all that proficient." Jade opened a metal door etched with a symbol. The door swung open, leading into the dome. "The Ancorian Axiom states how all those in battle must be proficient in more than one discipline. As an elemental mage, I can't heal, but I could learn some alchemy or weaponry. I chose daggers since they came most naturally to me. I don't plan on needing to use them, but I keep the practice sharp, just in case."

The interior of the dome was far more intimidating than the outside. Raging pulses of light skipped across the top and sides of the dome's interior. They quickly fizzled out before hitting their target. Clara halted. Jade pulled her arm. "The barrier you see was conjured by a group of mages. The purpose of the dome is to dull magical powers. This allows us to practice without serious injury. It's nothing to be afraid of, just a bunch of smoke and mirrors."

"So, why wouldn't your enemies use this to stop people from fighting back? Wouldn't it stop mages from attacking?"

"It would also stop theirs. No one is looking for a checkmate when it comes to battle. The barrier is a creation of Master Zerpith. He only instructed a few mages on the chant and only bits and pieces of it. No one but him has the entire spell. There's so few ancient ones left to create such a spell anyway. It's not written in any texts either. It's nothing to fear."

"Zerpith is an ancient one?"

"One of the few. I've yet to meet another, but I've heard of more." Jade sighed. "Clara, now isn't the time for mindless chat. That has nothing to do with what we need to accomplish today. You see, the heart of magic isn't an outward thing." She paced the dirt where she and Clara were standing. A few feet away was a flour sack stabbed on a stake—her target.

Clara pointed to one of the booths next to her. "Real quick, what are these for?"

"Dispel bays are for emergency purposes."

"Emergency purposes? Like, in the case someone gets hurt?"

"It can happen. The barrier keeps others from getting hurt but does nothing to protect the one using it. Magic is stored deep within. It's kept within your being until you need it. When that time comes, it's up to you to guide it up and out." She stopped her pacing. "No barrier of any kind can shield the user from themself."

"Oh… um, can you elaborate on this? Should I be looking out for something to lessen my chance of needing a booth?"

Jade put a hand on Clara's shoulder. "No. Most mages concentrate magic from their palms. Some can even alter the path through the eyes. One moment…" Jade jogged to one of the racks against the wall. She handed Clara a basic-looking wand adorned with a simple shiny ball at its tip. "I think this might help with your projection."

"I hope it's an extra powerful one."

Jade rubbed her hands together as she walked a few feet away from Clara. "Scepters are merely tools, nothing else. They are only powerful if the steward is. Think of it as a way to concentrate."

Clara held the scepter. Swishing it around, she felt like a child pretending to play princess. Until now, she had only heard talk about her powers, like a dream that would never happen, or maybe a character in a poorly written novel. But now, holding the wand, reality hit. She was expected to use it for real. *I wonder what it's going to feel like to use magic?*

"Now, hold the scepter and point at the sack. That bag over there. Think, Clara. This target is going to hurt you and your friends. You need to stop it before it stops you."

With an outstretched arm, Clara pointed the scepter at the sack. She tried to concentrate. She stared at the sack, locking her gaze on the sloppily drawn eyes. Nothing. She pushed her arm forward. Still nothing. She grunted from the soreness in her muscles. The wand did nothing. She did nothing. Over and over, Jade instructed. Clara tried to follow. She was losing energy and hope. She grasped the wand so tightly her hand began to cramp.

"I don't know what's wrong with me," Clara began to cry, but she blinked the wetness back. *I can't look like a crybaby…* Jade's eyes bore into her. Her heart pounded.

Jade relaxed and gently took the scepter. "That's what's wrong. Right there."

"What's wrong?"

The mage interrupted her. "It's been hours. I think it's time we rested. Let's get something to eat. Since we stopped, I'm realizing how hungry I am. Sometimes I get so carried away I forget the hour."

Jade led the way to the hearty expansion of food. Looking over the smorgasbord of choices displayed across the large table, Clara grabbed a tin plate, which she filled with options that reminded her of home. Roasted potatoes, seared meat, and a leafy vegetable that looked similar to collard greens mixed with cooked-down tomatoes. She bypassed the options that stared back at her with charred eyes. Sitting, she ate with Jade until she felt a body plop next to her. A strong smell of rosemary and herbs permeated her nose.

"Good day, Lady Clara," came the cheerful voice of Onyx. "How are your studies going?" He clicked his boots together under the table, scattering grass to the floor beneath him.

"I'd love to say they were going well, but sadly that isn't the case. I'm really bad at all this. Like, abnormally bad."

"Sounds like a case of beginnerism."

"I could only hope," she laughed. "But I doubt it. I'm just not magical or coordinated. Just because I relocated to a magical world doesn't mean my skills changed. I'm still Clara from America."

Onyx shoveled food into his mouth at a speed fit for competition. It was normal for him to pause before responding, as Clara would soon understand. Only when she thought he had nothing else to say, or perhaps chose to ignore her, did he speak.

"Jade is an incredible instructor. Eventually you'll get it, or you won't. Either way, have fun during the process."

"I feel a lot of pressure to be what everyone needs me to be. That's stressful."

Onyx shrugged. "The pressure never leaves. I find that when I feel overwhelmed, I reflect on how time passes either way. Why add in the weight of expectations? You're the only one who knows how hard you're trying." Clara waited while he sat back in his chair, goblet in hand. He finally continued. "As far as I'm concerned, all that matters is if you're happy with yourself. Did you put in everything you had?"

Clara held back her amusement. Somehow, he had managed to eat all his food during their brief conversation. With the last bite, he slammed down his goblet. "I did try," she said. "My reflexes kept working against me, but I eventually figured out how to evade. The magic though... I tried my best. Nothing happened."

"As far as I'm concerned, you've done your best, and that's about all you can do. Excellent meal! Oh, I almost forgot, here's a tonic for you." Onyx left a small vial on the table. "Sawyer asked me to give this to you for your sore muscles." Without another word, the alchemist rose from his seat, leaving a trail of scattered grass behind him. Shaking her head with mirth, Clara finished her own food.

Jade shook her head, entertained. "Onyx is always like that. I think he's got so much information swirling in his head that he takes some extra time to spit it out. It's frustrating sometimes." She finished her meal and took a long drink. "I wish he would just say what he needs to without wasting time."

Clara stared at her folded hands while Jade switched topics. "Your projection isn't revealing itself through focus alone. There's so many classes of mages and everyone is different when it comes to how they learn. For example, although I'm an elemental mage, I can mingle with other magics, but my strength is within the elements. For me, it started very young. When I was little, my temper was always short. One day, I got so mad I felt the fire burning inside me. I'll never forget the feeling. I thought it would consume me. My father found me crying just as I began to catch on fire. He calmed my fire by explaining how I could summon water. The coolness eased the searing pain of the flames. It was the first day I understood. I had everything I needed to be powerful."

"I don't think I'm an elemental mage. What other mages are there? Could I be one of those?"

"It's always possible. Besides elemental mages, there are parlor mages who are simple jesters. Then there are house mages. I doubt that would be you. We have phantom mages. They practice dark magic. I don't believe that's you either. I don't feel that darkness from you. Dynamic mages are rather unpredictable. They are powerful, and although they can wield all kinds of magic, there are times when they get a little… complicated. Personally, they drive me crazy. Sometimes their magic works out, sometimes it doesn't. Hmm… maybe that's your power?"

Clara laughed at Jade's sarcastic eyebrow raise. "Are those all the kinds? Are there more I should be aware of?"

"There's the druids, but I wouldn't classify them as mages. That's beside the point. I don't have the time to explain magic theory, and we don't have time to appoint you with a proper mentorship to explore them all."

"I understand," Clara said. *I guess I have to make the best of it, however it works out.* Clara's serious expression lifted when Sawyer tapped her on her shoulder.

"Hey there. I'm hankering for some dessert. Holly mentioned she's making pie. Care to join me back at the cottage?"

CHAPTER 15
Wild Pain

CLARA

IT WAS dark when Clara and Sawyer reached the Pucketts' hut. "Queen Bean," announced Annabelle as she squeezed a hug. The young girl wore her hair in one large braid with an even bigger smile. "I'm so glad you're here! Did you want some pie? I helped momma make it."

Clara hugged the girl back. "Wow, Annabelle. I'd love some. I bet it tastes incredible."

"It does," Annabelle answered with confidence, despite not tasting it yet. Sawyer sat next to Dave, and they talked quietly.

"Pie's ready, just in time, it seems," Holly announced, wiping her hands on her apron. "Annabelle did a splendid job helping."

The little girl smiled broadly, aware of her fine job. "I know."

"You outdid yourself, ladies," Dave praised as he took a second bite. The pie melted in Clara's mouth in a mixture of sugary cinnamon apples and flaky dough.

"Clara, care to sit with me?" Sawyer asked, patting the empty spot on the blanket in front of the fireplace.

Clara sat with a plate of snacks, including a few chunks of cheese, a roll with butter, berries from the bushes in the yard, dried meat, and the rest of her pie. The fire burned the logs greedily, heating the large room and spitting ashes against the fireplace screen. Clara accepted the hot tea handed to her and took a careful sip. "In America, we have these things called TV dinners," she said, recalling peeling off the hot plastic which always seemed to burn her fingers. She would always scrape the chewy parts off the sides of the segregated compartments before digging into each section. "We'd take one of these prepared meals from the freezer and heat it for a fast dinner."

"What's a TV?" he asked, looking off into the fire.

"Guess. If you guess right, I'll give you this piece of cheese." She held up a chunk and wrinkled her nose.

"With such a grand prize, I can hardly resist. Let me think. Tinctured Victuals?"

She chuckled. "It means television. It's like this box filled with colors and light. Inside are pictures that move. People play out stories. Then, they recorded the plays so we can watch them whenever we like. It's like watching a live play, but from your house."

"And you eat the once frozen dinners while watching TV?"

"You could, but you can eat whatever you want when you watch TV, not just TV dinners. The frozen dinners don't always taste the greatest. I used to have so many favorite shows…" Clara glared into the fire. The dancing flames mesmerized her with their fiery swaying. Lost in thought, she was pulled into a memory…

"You have to get off the couch. You can't keep watching trash TV… and stop eating all the chocolate chips."

Clara, with unwashed hair and still wearing the same sweats after days, lay on the sofa. Wide-eyed and concerned, Angel pulled the blankets off her friend, snatched the chips, and shut off the TV. Tears streamed down Clara's cheeks. She grabbed for the blanket, but Angel was too quick.

"Sit up. I bought you something." Angel held out a perfectly wrapped gift.

Clara slowly took the gift, unwrapping it cautiously to keep the paper intact.

"You got this for me? Thank you. I'm… sorry. I know I haven't been myself lately. I—" The package revealed a journal with a matching pen.

"I thought a journal might help you process things. Maybe write a story. I'd read it, even if it wasn't a best-seller."

"I don't deserve this. You already do so much for me. I'm not the best person to be around right now, and—"

"Stop that. Seriously, get off the couch. Get a shower and put on something cute. I want to go somewhere with you. I'm not going anywhere with you looking like a bum."

"I… I really don't feel like going out or being around people right now."

"Did I ask you what you felt like? You've been inside for weeks. Now, get your butt off the couch and get changed."

"So, in America, they make horrible food that's frozen, just so you can heat it up and hate how it tastes? Then, while eating the nasty meal, you watch stories from boxes? Can you at least use the TV to transport?"

Sawyer's voice seized her from her mind. "Oh, no… the stories? They were recorded on something called film, and you can replay them over and over if you want."

"Ah, so you came back to join me. I thought I lost you… Care to tell me where you've been?"

"Oh… no, I was just thinking about my home. I have a best friend. Her name is Angel. I miss her a lot." The heat from the fire slapped across her face, burning her cheeks. Black spots from the intense light speckled her sight; she blinked to remove them. Shutting her eyes tightly to reduce the blackness, the image of a ghostly woman with hollow eyes flashed.

"Dry eyes?" Sawyer laughed. "Either that or you saw something frightening."

"I guess you could call it that. About the dry eyes, I mean. I find fire entrancing. Its depth seems eternal. Once you stare into it, it's hard to look away."

"I can tell you're troubled far beyond missing your friend. Care to discuss?" he asked gently.

Clara scooted herself farther from the fire's intensity. "I'll tell you mine, if you tell me yours."

"A fine deal you strike, m'lady," Sawyer said, "but I'll pass on disturbing you with my woes. However, I'm a steady ear for listening, and I'm not triggered by much, if anything at all."

Annabelle cried in the background as she lamented her spilled pie, upset that she couldn't lick it from the floor. Dave's mandolin was the accompaniment to Annabelle's desperate pleas. Holly laughed as she wiped up the mess. Clara listened to the exchange to distract herself from her emotions.

"When the sun sets on your adventure, and Lectus is defeated, where do you find yourself?" Sawyer asked.

Clara paused. "When it's all over? I… I'm not sure. I haven't thought about it. I'm not even sure if I'll survive. What happens if I die?"

Sawyer's eyes shrouded with concern. "Why would you say that?"

"If you knew me in America, you'd agree. Everyone here sees a higher version of me than those back home… I'm nothing to believe in. I know I sound…" *I don't feel like explaining.* "I know everyone is tired of hearing about it but the reason I'm repeating myself is to set expectations. You see, I wanted to be successful in America but I—I wasn't."

"I wouldn't think that way. It's only robbing you of this peaceful moment with the most dashing man, not to mention your very future. If I didn't believe you were capable, I never would have joined the companionship. I don't like losing, in case you were unaware." Sawyer smiled, trying to lighten the mood.

"What about my curse? What does that mean?"

Sawyer leaned back on his hands. "That could mean so many things. Curses aren't always bad."

"So, you don't think my cursed power will cause problems?"

Sawyer laughed with a wink, "That's up for interpretation. But, no. You said you encountered a magical being, perhaps it came from him."

It's true, I did meet someone but who? I can't remember anything about him except he was there. "Yeah, maybe… So, do you think I'll win? You know, it was the strangest thing." Clara stared at the glowing embers. "When I was in America, I was walking home from work one day."

"The Bean Queen?" Sawyer asked. At the mention of the coffee shop, Annabelle plopped herself on Sawyer's lap.

"Bean Queen," shouted Annabelle joyously, drawing a laugh from the room.

"Yes, The Bean Queen." Clara punched Sawyer's arm. "On my way home, I saw this light. Now, that doesn't sound all that interesting, but the light looked unearthly and absolutely heavenly. The place I lived had tall buildings. So tall they blocked the open sky. The building lights never went out there. But, this light… There was something different about it." Clara's hands began to animate to the pace of her story. "Something drew me to it. I can't explain it, but I needed to get a closer look. It reminded me of a game I used to play when I was a kid."

"Oh, tell me about the game," Annabelle pleaded.

"It's silly, really. I wanted to be magical when I was your age, Annabelle, but magic isn't real in my world. It never was. We don't have ancient ones, mages, or healers, but we loved wishing for them and pretending to be them."

"A world without magic," Sawyer repeated while shifting Annabelle on his lap and tickling her side. Her infectious giggle filled the room, drawing Dave and Holly to stop and listen. "So, if your world never had magic, how do you know of it?"

"Good question… It's something everyone talked about, like a story. It was made up, but it wasn't real. It's funny because everyone knew what it was, but no one had it."

"Interesting, although hard to fathom." Sawyer grabbed a piece of meat from Clara's plate.

"It would be something, if it were true—having magic. But I highly doubt it. When I was little, I wanted to be magical so bad. I remember it so clearly. I would take handfuls of dirt and throw it on the walkway, you know, so the dirt would create dust. I would pretend that dust was the magic."

"Dust is magical?" Annabelle leaned in, entranced by the story. "Momma, we have lots of magic."

"Hush, now," said Holly from behind them.

"It was only pretend, but to me, I secretly wished it to be true." Annabelle left Sawyer's lap and sat between him and Clara. Holding Clara's hand, she looked up at her in anticipation, begging for more. Clara continued.

"In my game, you had to throw the dust when you saw a ray of light. The light was supposed to be a transport to other worlds, worlds that were far more exciting than mine. I could spend hours pretending with just a handful of dirt and a reflection of light. So, anyways, after an especially stressful day at work——"

Annabelle's shriek made her jump, "The Bean Queen!"

"Yeah, that place. Crazy girl." Clara laughed, then settled back into the story. "Well, I was walking home when I saw the light. Out of nowhere, my childhood game popped into my mind. I hadn't thought of it in years, but I did then. Something urged me to recreate it, one last time. So, I took the dirt and jumped into the light."

"Then what happened?" asked Annabelle, wide-eyed.

"I found myself in this strange place with a strange being. It feels like a dream now that I'm talking about it. But I believe it happened. He said some things to me. I can't remember what. After that, I woke up in the cart."

"All stinky and covered in swamp," Annabelle cackled.

"Yes, that. I can still smell it when I think about it," Clara said with disgust.

"Annabelle," said Sawyer, "I'm going to take Clara outside. You stay inside until we come back in. Agreed?"

"But I want to go, too," she begged.

Seeing the exchange, Holly collected Annabelle for bed. The young girl resisted before pouting her agreement. The back door of the cottage opened and shut with Clara and Sawyer on the other side. Stars speckled the clear sky. *I wonder if Angel sees the same sky,* Clara thought, refreshed by the crisp night air. They strolled through the village past neighbors wrapped in blankets and quietly talking on their porches.

Sawyer broke the silence, "Nothing smells as good as a fire."

"I'd agree to that, but I recently smelled apple pie."

"I wouldn't disagree. Apple pie is a comforting scent, especially as the nights grow colder. Clara, I know you're still figuring out who you are. I can only imagine how you might feel. Being in one world one day to wake up in another… You've been quite vague about your life in America, other than that there's no magic and you felt helpless. If it matters, I think you're supposed to be here, even if you don't see it. People don't appear out of nowhere for no reason."

"It doesn't make sense. I've never been great at anything. Believe me when I say how no one needed me to save them in America." They walked in silence, both ensnared by their own thoughts.

"What happened before you leaped into the light?"

"I… I was struggling. Life hadn't exactly panned out the way I hoped." Clara felt a catch in her throat and a rise in her heartbeat. Side by side, they walked until they sat on a bench overlooking a small lake. "I always wanted to be someone, to make a difference in the lives of others. To just be… somebody people were proud of. Somebody I could be proud of. Instead, I was kind of a nobody." Looking down, she wrung her hands together, cracking her knuckles. Placing them back onto the bench, she felt a warm hand take hers.

"What made you think you were a nobody, and that no one was proud of you?"

Unwilling to meet his eyes, she continued, head bowed. "I know it's hard for you to understand, but I keep telling everyone I'm not special because it's the truth. Even in America, I was nothing to celebrate. I scraped to get by financially and struggled to make something of myself. Please don't be disappointed when I let everyone down. It's only a matter of time before everyone sees that, and if people get hurt… I don't know if I could forgive myself."

Sawyer remained silent. Wiping her eyes, Clara thought about her past, the part of herself she couldn't escape. There are times her pain was so strong it would fill her, drown her. Clara, having cut the wound anew, couldn't stop the tears from coming. The pain escaped as her tears flowed freely. This wound, like her tears, ran wild. The knight squeezed her hand and put a tender arm around her. He lifted her chin. Clara's tear-filled eyes met his.

Above them, an owl hooted in the distance while searching for prey, unbothered by the destructive sobs under the mellow light of the moon. The air's caressing breeze rustled the leaves on the trees, creating a ripple on the lake. And the slight outline of a gaunt, faded figure watched, unnoticed, while the woman cried.

CHAPTER 16

The Open World

CLARA

THE GRAVEL PATH to the training grounds crunched under Clara's feet, so different from the sidewalk she took to The Bean Queen. Horses being led or ridden clopped by with a nod from their master. A group of mages passed by holding books and scepters. A slight breeze carrying the smells of nature surrounded her. This was different, but a difference she welcomed. During these walks, she didn't have her headphones to drift off into a daydream. Instead, she rehashed the night over. *I never should have opened up to Sawyer. Why was I so stupid? He probably thinks I'm crazy. He probably thinks I'm weak. Everyone here is so strong… and then there's me. Even Annabelle would have a better chance at defeating Lectus.*

She'd spilled the contents of her heart. Now, the spattered leftovers left her feeling raw and vulnerable. She wished she'd remained silent. Who knows what would happen once things ended? She wasn't even certain about what would happen after all this was over. Sharing too much had little benefit, yet she had done it.

The training grounds were hard to miss, and Clara spotted

Sawyer conversing with Jade. Jade handed over a glimmering stone. He looked excited to get it. Clara listened while she stood nearby.

"I just infused it. It should have enough power for around five uses. After that, let me know when you need more. Do you still have enough on the fire stone?" Jade moved over to allow Clara to join them.

"Yeah, the fire stone is still good for a use or two. Clara, good to see you. Are you ready to begin?"

Clara blushed, casting her eyes to the ground. Just last night, she shared her most hidden pain. The exposure embarrassed her, and she wondered how he truly felt.

"So, how are your muscles? Day two is always the worst. Especially after the tonic wears off." Sawyer's warm smile told her he held nothing against her.

She perked up, his icebreaker diffusing the awkwardness. "They hurt, but I'll manage. It's not all bad since the pain means I'm getting stronger. But if there's another tonic, I'd take it."

"So you become stronger. If Jade gives you up this week, I'd like to continue our lessons."

"Yes, I'd like that."

"When you're done training, come find me at the stables." Sawyer turned to the mage. "Jade, don't go too hard on her now. Make sure you leave something left for me to break," he said jokingly.

Jade interrupted the conversation with intent, ignoring the knight's comment. "We need to make some progress today. I think we can make that happen."

"I'm trying to look on the bright side. I'm sorry yesterday was less than productive. I really am trying. I promise."

"I know you are, but trying isn't enough. We have to explore deeper. There has to be something more or something you're holding back."

On the horizon, Onyx, knee-deep in mud, dug up roots. When he saw her, he stood and waved eagerly, flinging weeds. She waved back. The things she saw here never ceased to amaze her. A man, knee- and elbow-deep in the mud searching for precious roots, a maid carrying baskets of snacks to court members, a jester dancing around hoping for monetary tips. It was not her world, and she liked it. *If only there wasn't Lectus.* Taking the scepter from Jade, who was impatiently waiting, Clara swished it around in fun.

Unamused, Jade cleared her throat. "We tried this yesterday, but I'm hoping a night's rest helped. Concentration is key, only at first. Once you get comfortable with it, it will come naturally. As soon as you feel something, let me know."

Clara concentrated on the target. Pointing the scepter, nothing came out, then again and again, the same outcome. "I'm frustrated. Are you sure I have any magic at all? Could Zerpith be wrong or do you think it's because I'm cursed with a power I can't use?"

"Both are possible. Zerpith's already passed retirement. Even mages eventually age, although they take centuries to do it. Some may experience their powers lessening as death nears. Still, magic isn't going to stop you from using it until the user grieves it. When that happens, you'll know. Personally, I'm not wasting my time thinking about your curse. I don't feel any ill will from you or evil intent. Magic is still new to you. I'm sure you'll get it eventually, or we'll all be in trouble."

"Sounds like no pressure at all."

After wrapping up another uneventful training, Clara searched for the stables to find Sawyer, per his request. She looked forward to nights at the Pucketts', and he was going to take her again today. Wandering the halls, she walked down a few shallow steps into a narrow hallway that didn't look familiar. Old, ornate shields hung across the dimly lit hallway. Many appeared to have seen a plethora of battles. As she continued, she heard voices from a door to her right. She stopped, compelled to listen.

A smooth, refined male voice was the first to be heard. "I understand you've acquired a new mage, one with extraordinary ability. Perhaps, you'll allow me to transport her. I don't see the need for battle companions or a long journey." Clara pressed her ear harder into the door. Surely, they were speaking about her.

The king's voice rang deeply, much louder than the other voices heard. "Clara has her own path to take. She must travel with her designated coalition."

"I don't recall Zerpith's crystal ball showing anything outside of Eros," the refined voice said flatly.

"It wasn't his ball, but… I saw it in a vision… No… it was… an old book…"

"You'll chance Clara's life prematurely for the sake of some old book when I could quickly transport her within days?"

"Ancora has equipped her with companions to aid her. I believe she'll find the windowless castle, and win the battle, but I doubt her ability to survive after she defeats Lectus. I have no interest in trading her at this time. Perhaps, if she comes back to us, we shall speak then."

Trade? What the heck? And… he doesn't think I'll survive? What the double heck! It appeared the king's faith in her was wavering. She understood his allegiance was to his kingdom, but he didn't have a shred of hope for her well-being. She kept on listening through gritted teeth.

"King Henric," said the refined voice again, this time with an authoritative tone. "Zerpith predicted Lectus. He's well beyond his years, even for an ancient one. Perhaps he's a bit senile. I don't believe Lectus is a valid threat, or real, for that matter. Certainly you aren't caught up in children's tales."

Zerpith wrong? I was just talking about that with Jade. I hope it's true…

After a moment of silence, the king replied, "Although Zerpith is advanced in age, I have no reason to think his predictions aren't true." The king's voice escalated angrily. "I could feel the prophecy in my bones. Lectus is alive and Clara must find him, with her team of companions, and by completing the journey." The king cleared his throat. "Without the help of transcendence. Do not try to convince me otherwise."

"King Henric, I'd advise you to listen to reason," the refined voice said bitterly. "If Clara is surrendered to us, we'll know the proper way to train her. Zerpith mentioned her power came from a curse; we can help her overcome it. We can also help her accomplish her mission. Our training would ensure a successful slaying of Lectus, if that's what you believe. A world beyond our imagination is living right here at your castle." Clara heard other voices murmuring in the room. None were clear enough for her to decipher.

"Although I cannot disagree, that'll have to wait. We cannot keep her from her journey. If she holds enough power to make it out alive, then so be it."

"Your Majesty, if there's no compliance, we'll need to resort to drastic measures. Do you understand? Consider what allies you'll lose and all because of something you believed from a book." Someone banged something down. Hearing footsteps rumble from behind the door, Clara quietly, but quickly, snuck away on her tiptoes, legs shaking and heart racing. She couldn't be caught. *I should probably tell Sawyer...*

Following the detailed instructions given by a passing maid, a building with a dirt path opened to a clean, busy stable. Trees guided the walkway. The other side of the stable was a wide gate beckoning to a wild, open prairie. Entering the barn, Sawyer and Rory waved to her. Rory held the reins of the familiar palomino.

"Clara, you made it," Sawyer teased. "I don't know if you remember, but this fine steed is Willow. She is the valiant one who pulled us from Giant's Pass." He patted the horse on the neck.

"Thanks, Willow." Clara slowly approached the horse to pet her nose. Willow shook her head. Clara stepped back. "Horses are bigger than I thought."

"Depends. Willow is average in size. Riding is a valuable skill and will be sorely needed once we leave Ancora Castle. I know you've been bounced from magic and melee training, but a quick trip to a nearby town will allow you to practice horsemanship. In a few weeks, depending on how your riding is coming along, I'll take you to Rafferty Hills. Of course, Jade will come along, for training purposes, as will Onyx."

Clara frowned. She hadn't even mounted a steed yet, but fear was an anxious visitor. "That would be fun, I think."

"Now, what's that face for? Come now, horses are nothing to be concerned about. What will alarm you, however, is Holly's scolding if we miss dinner."

Taking Sawyer's arm, they strolled back to Holly's. A few minutes into their stroll, Clara spoke. "I got lost in the castle trying to find the stable. While I was trying to find someone to ask for directions, I heard the king talking with someone." Sawyer continued walking, albeit, a bit slower. Clara continued, "The man he was speaking to wanted to transport me to Eros and skip the journey."

Sawyer stopped. "Skip the journey? What an entitled thing to suggest. Did King Henric agree to this? It seems like a dangerous venture, as there's no way to transport the entire coalition and our supplies. You'd be without a trusted team, and much-needed experience. There are no shortcuts to growth. Trust my words when I tell you how much the adventure becomes one's right of passage into a higher version of self."

Clara halted. Sawyer lifted an eyebrow. "Is everything okay?"

Clara pushed herself back into a walk. "Yeah, I'm fine. So, the king. He wasn't on board with it. He said he felt it best I take the journey. But, I am curious about transportation. Is that what Zerpith did when he disappeared?"

"The very same. I suppose it must have been one of the leaders from Eros suggesting such things. Yet, they'll need to wait for you to get there. It seems silly, when you overthink it, but I'm thankful King Henric wasn't persuaded into this risky venture."

Clara smiled when she saw the huts peek into the horizon. "I'm glad to take the adventure with you." *Perhaps the person I need to become is waiting for me on the way. And, I'm happy to have more time before I meet… Lectus.*

Time seemingly passed slower at the hut. Even dinner didn't cook as fast as in America, with open hearths cooking food in cauldrons. Time was enjoyed, not rushed. Clara helped Holly with the feast, all while trying to learn from the matron's masterful skills. In the meantime, there was time to visit. It was moments like these she forgot about her mobile phone, TV, and social media. All faded into the past. Oddly enough, she didn't miss them. In its place were people she was growing to love.

Dave strummed his mandolin. Sawyer gracefully bowed to Clara. "Ma'am, it would be my delight to have this dance with you."

Moved by his request and enamored with his charm, she took his hand. They laughed and occasionally fumbled over each other while Clara learned the dances. Holly smiled with an approving nod. Picking up her yarn, she knitted, smiling warmly while the food simmered.

Clara improved in her dancing skills quickly. Before long, they were waltzing around the room. A time or two, dance partners changed. Sawyer would invite Holly while Clara invited Annabelle. Clara tossed in modern dance moves to shock and awe. Outbursts of laughter would fill the room with the outlandish and silly movements. She laughed through tears as they tried to replicate them.

There was love in this house. Clara began to forget about the life she used to have. She even forgot about Lectus.

THE TRUTH about time is how it always moves forward. One must learn to walk alongside it and accept where it finds them, ready or not. As for Clara, time went fast during the day and slowed during the nights. Most evenings, she spent time with her newfound family, dancing, eating, and conversing by the fireplace. Time, however, did not halt for her to master the art of magic, much to her dismay.

Weeks passed by. Clara awoke in her castle room to the excited chatter of Annabelle. "Queen Bean. Wake up. Momma told me to get you up and ready." Annabella whispered loudly, "I get to practice all by myself today." Hearing a mighty grunt, the young girl tossed her covers off. The cold air hit, causing goosebumps on Clara's skin. She slid her legs off the bed to grab her robe.

"Good morning, Annabelle."

"Good morning," she commanded flatly. "Now, I have an outfit for you. Momma picked it. I wanted you to have the pink one, not green, because you would look prettier, but she didn't listen. Sawyer is taking you on a trip. He said your riding skills have improved enough to leave the castle. I wish I could go, but I'm not allowed." Annabelle fumbled to unfold the clothes, working swiftly on the twisted corset when Holly entered the room.

"Annabelle. My word, child. You took off with that frock faster than lightning. Are you sure you aren't part horse?" Annabelle giggled while giving up on the bodice and the idea of doing this herself. Holly stooped to retrieve the discarded item, encouraging the little girl to stand still to watch.

A full skirt split in the middle with a green corset. The attire was considered a proper ladies' outfit for travel, although pants were commonly worn. Having completed the task, Clara wondered how a woman around here managed to dress herself. "Holly, have you ever ridden a horse before?"

"I used to enjoy a relaxing ride now and then. No need for horses now, for which I'm glad. I can't see myself bobbling about on horseback. Anything I need is right here at the castle, it 'tis."

"Oh, okay. I don't think it's that bad. So far, I've only ridden in the fenced-in area or the outskirts of the stable. Sawyer didn't say how long we'd be gone. Wish me luck, in case I need it."

"Prayers to the stars for your safety. But I'm sure you'll be just fine. I'll make a special snack once you return." Holly squeezed Clara tightly, and Clara left the room, anxiety close behind her.

Leaving the castle was a little scary. *Who knows what lives outside the castle walls?* Sitting to eat, Clara's anxiety brewed as she whispered to herself. "What happens if I fall off? What if I break a bone? It's not like they have ambulances around here." Her overthinking kicked in...

She mounted the brown mare. The horse skittered about. The powerful energy under her was anxious. Trotting down the lane, a monster came out of nowhere. The mare bolted, sending her flying through the air to eat a solid meal of dirt. Sawyer and Jade galloped ahead, unaware she wasn't behind them.

Spitting out gravel, her head raised to see the beast barreling toward her. The monster, aware of easy prey, advanced quickly. Trying to get up, she fell back into the dirt. Her leg was broken and a hideous bone protruded from her shin. So gross. The beast drooled; she was an easy catch. Hobbling, she tried to scream, but it was too late. The monster had gotten her...

"Clara, your daydream doesn't seem to bring you joy," Sawyer said, breaking her trance.

"Huh? Oh, Sorry."

"Perhaps you should use some of that imagination to project that secret magic you have locked up inside," added Jade.

"Sorry guys, I'm just really nervous about the whole riding without the protection of a fence thing."

Onyx sat next to her. "Clara, you like either land or water." The man was already shoveling his food down at an alarming rate. Clara waited for him to continue and just as she picked up her fork, he said, "You hate the mud. The messy, messy middle, don't you? The mud is slippery and dirty, for sure, but it's also the most fun. Learn to love the mud. You'll smile more."

After the crew finished their meal, Clara eyed the horse whose reins were handed to her by Rory. Rory smiled and said, "I'm giving you Stormy. He's a gentle gelding who's accommodating to a new rider. Also, he'll grow with you. As you improve, he tends to grasp your expertise and act accordingly. I think you'll find him a pleasure to ride. He has an extraordinary gait."

"Hey, Stormy." She stroked his nose. He was black, save for some white on the bottom of his lip and two white socks above his front hooves.

Jade was already seated on her steed, but Sawyer waited until she mounted before doing the same. With all three in the saddle, they met Onyx at the gate. Looking past her white-knuckle hold of the reins, she noticed Onyx didn't have a horse. Instead, he was astride a large metal bike that resembled a magical beast.

"Wait, how come he gets a motorcycle, and I have to ride a living, breathing animal?" Clara asked.

"I can't relate to the motorcycle, although I wish I thought of calling it that. This is my Dragonmare." The Dragonmare, he explained, was an invention he created from random parts and a bit of infused magic. A dragon head made from metal parts protruded from the handlebars and a simulated tail from the bumper. Wings were created from tiny gears and iron rods in the side panels for show. "I originally thought of creating an iron stallion, but since most my friends ride mares, I decided to join them."

"It's pretty cool looking, too." Onyx smiled as he revved the engine. Pulse in her throat, Clara followed the others out the gate and into the open field. The safety of the castle faded as they progressed further away. Everything was explorable, exposed. Long grass rustled beneath stomping hoofs, and a vast blue sky spanned endlessly above the pure wilderness. It's true that she loved a controlled hike on a paved path, but roughing it out in the woods? Not her idea of fun. What if her companions left her? What if someone got hurt? There was no way she could fend for herself, especially if monsters attacked.

Sawyer rode beside Clara, matching Stormy's gait, "There's nothing better than looking straight into a wide-open world. I find that I've learned more about myself during an adventure than all the time spent within the castle gates."

"It is beautiful, for sure," Clara replied between breaks, it was hard to talk and ride at the same time. But after a few hours of travel, she felt like a pro. "Good boy, Stormy," she praised. Loping on, Stormy sprang forward, unannounced, with a kick of his heels. Bolting, Clara tried to turn him in a circle, but was unsuccessful. Screeching, she jostled around. Unable to keep her balance, she slid off, hitting the grass with a thud. Luckily, she seemed unscathed. As she wiped the dirt from her pants, she froze.

The creature had three long, snake-like limbs. Its head, beak-like, snapped and lunged. Arms solid and squirmy, the towering beast squalled.

"Clara," Sawyer's expression was wildly excited. "It's the perfect opportunity to learn." He positioned her in front of him, which was right in front of the squirming monster. "We can never assume any beast, big or small, familiar or unfamiliar, has ill intent. We must negotiate first."

The beast slithered, swift with intention. The legs, moving with agility but never twisting, advanced with a snap. Clara gasped. The knight pulled her away with merely a second to spare.

"Creature, do you understand my tongue?" asked the knight. The beastly monster squalled and lurched again. The other battle mates stood guard. They would join in if the need arose. "Clara, unsheathe your sword." Trembling hands pulled the rapier from its sheath. Holding it to parry, it trembled in her hands.

The creature lunged again. This time, Sawyer's sword made a connection with its leg. Spewing red, the other snakish limbs squirmed to regain balance. Pushing Clara aside, Sawyer charged the beast to strike another limb. Jade rushed to pull Clara out of harm's way.

"What were you thinking? You didn't move. You'll die if you don't do something. We aren't asking for you to fell the entire beast, but at least try to scrape it," Jade hissed before joining in the battle.

Clara wrung her hands together. Sawyer and Jade seemed to enjoy the skirmish. Watching the fight unfold, she spotted Onyx creep towards the woods where a beautiful woman stood at the edge of the treeline.

Onyx seemed entranced by the beauty with the alluring sway, calling him towards the woods. Her long, floating hair glistened from the setting sun. She smiled coyly. "Come hither, kind alchemist. Let me take you to a place where your wildest inventions can come alive."

Clara felt uneasy. "Onyx, I don't think that's a good idea." She rushed to pull him, but he was too strong. Yanking his arm harder, her scream for help went unanswered. "Onyx, this doesn't feel right. Even if it were, who follows a stranger… ugh… stop… into the woods. Gah, don't do that." Onyx shoved Clara aside. With a final push, the alchemist dislodged from Clara and rushed into the forest without looking back. Clara ran towards the fighters, arms waving.

"Whew, that was invigorating," Sawyer said as he searched the beast for anything of use.

"Been some time since we teamed up," laughed Jade, collecting a purple liquid into a vial. "Onyx would be upset if I didn't collect this for him. Where is he?"

"Guys," Clara panted, "Onyx… he went into the forest."

Jade put a cork stopper onto the jar holding the purple liquid. "He's probably collecting a herb or root."

Clara shook her head. "No, a woman was standing by the edge

of the woods. She was talking to him, and his face… it looked different, like he was in a trance or something."

"Sounds like a witch," Sawyer announced.

The team searched the woods. Jade stopped at a modest clearing. "Here's her shanty."

Clara only saw an empty clearing. "Where?"

Jade explained, "She was trying to hide it from us, but her spell is basic. That's a witch for you. They only do the bare minimum to get by." Jade cast a spell that revealed a disheveled shed.

Slowly peering into a greasy window, Clara gasped when she saw Onyx soaking in a steamy cauldron. Her anxiety kicked in at high gear. "She's going to eat him. What in the world! First the hag wanted to eat me, now this. Do all the beasts here feed on humans?" Clara whispered harshly.

"The fire looks new. We have time." Sawyer shrugged and knocked on the window.

Clara, mouth open, glared at the knight. "What are you doing? She's going to see us."

"Trust me." Sawyer rapped again and waved cheerfully once the witch saw him. Opening her door, she craned her neck around to glare at them. The once gorgeous woman was now crusty and thick-skinned.

"Ah, company has come. I see you found my house. Very precocious."

"And what a place you have," Sawyer said, stepping over a pile of rundown planks that scattered a few bugs. "My name is Sawyer. Tell me why you're simmering my friend in basil. He's thin as a rail, I'm not sure he'd make the perfect stock."

"Are you saying you'd make better?"

"You can try, but I'm probably pretty tough. You know, all this muscle," he shrugged confidently. "She'd probably taste pretty good," he motioned to Jade, who gave him a glaring side-eye. "The problem, I'm thinking, has nothing to do with my friend being skinny, or my muscles being too… well, impressive. The real issue is why are you resorting to cooking humans instead of your normal cuisine?"

"Oh, I'm not going to eat him. No, no, no."

"Other plans in mind?"

"I'm not telling you, human. Begone." She tried to shut her door, but Sawyer held it open.

"Fair enough, although, I'm letting you know we aren't leaving without our friend. You decide. You can either release him or watch us take him."

"Come, brave knight." The witch transformed into a beautiful woman who sashayed seductively. At the first swing of her hips, an electric beam from Jade smacked the witch off her feet. She thumped to the ground. The trance broken by her fall freed Sawyer from joining his friend in the hot tub of death. Heading inside, they ducked to avoid the cluster of cobwebs. Reaching into the cauldron, the three pulled Onyx from the pot. Having felt the water, none of them mentioned how the temperature was much hotter than they had expected.

"Wake up, Onyx. Come on, buddy." Sawyer slapped his friend's face until he stirred.

"Hmmm."

"That witch almost boiled you alive!" Clara exclaimed. "We need to get out of here before she wakes up." Clara wiped sweat from her brow caused by the thick cauldron steam and the realization of the tough competition to survive in this world.

Jade put a hand on Clara's shoulder. "Clara, it's fine. Witches have no power over mages. As long as I'm here, there is nothing to be worried about. Onyx is fine. We found him in time."

With shoulders to lean on, Onyx made it back to his Dragonmare. Once seated, he grimaced as he pulled a lock of hag hair from his belt.

CHAPTER 17
Brave Together

CLARA

HORSEBACK RIDING across the open world evolved from anxious restraint to an enjoyable union. She was finally comfortable in the saddle, but her brain was not at all settled with what had happened. How could everyone so easily forget that mere moments ago their friend was stewing with spices? She could only imagine the smell or sight waiting had they arrived later. *What have you gotten yourself into? You were so uninspired by the coffee shop, so unhappy. Now look where you are. It's riddled with danger here. You had to have adventure, didn't you? You couldn't be happy where you were.* Clara's eyebrows furrowed, and she frowned at the laughter directed at Onyx when he pulled a damp sprig of thyme from under his arm. *This is ridiculous. What next? Zombies? Maybe. No reason to rule that one out. It seems nothing is out of the picture here. Making coffee doesn't seem that bad after all, now does it? And that beast with the snake legs… horrible! All this… It's what nightmares are made of.*

Onyx smiled as he recalled the story from his point of view. "I saw something very different than what you witnessed. Herbs were hanging from the ceiling, fluffy cats sitting on puffed stools, and sunlit windowsills. She laid me in a cozy bed and covered me up. It's no wonder that I started to feel hot and sweaty. Here I thought it was the thick blankets."

The rest of the crew laughed at his recollection and chatted contentedly, amused at the idea of Onyx soup. They all had a turn, even Onyx, with guessing what spices would pair best with the alchemist besides the rosemary.

Jade laughed, "Witches are tactful in the dark arts but unlikely to comply with rules. They're notorious for causing trouble, and I think they like it. Nothing but pests if you ask me. But, she got what she deserved. Now, she'll have to hide her house again. Witches hate that. Not only does it expend magical energy, but it's a lot of work for them. In some ways, we won for that reason alone."

Clara's distaste lessened upon seeing lazy smoke puffing in the distance.

"Welcome to Rafferty Hills, Clara," Sawyer announced, turning in his saddle. "You just made your first journey."

Clara grinned, leaving the soup horrors behind. She survived her first adventure. They all survived. After crossing a stone bridge, the townspeople spotted the crew and crowded around the visitors. Many seemed to recognize Sawyer. "What pleasantry to see 'ya, Commanda'," exclaimed a weary-looking woman.

"Glad to see 'ya, Sir, Commanda. 'Erfect timing, I might say," another chimed in.

Watching the dirty, threadbare townspeople, Clara's thoughts stirred. *Feels like a movie. Like the part when the heroes ride into the poor town. Usually right before something big happens.* Clara's thoughts were interrupted when a wrinkled man with an infectious smile spoke. "'Elcome, travelers. Sawyer, good ta see ya again."

"Boyce, it's a pleasure, as always." Sawyer dismounted and tossed Willow's reins over the worn hitching post. Onyx, unwilling to pass up some herbs, sped off to gather them from the hills, after politely excusing himself.

Jade tied her steed to the pole. A smirk formed on her lips as she watched Clara struggle to dismount. "Saddle sore? I promise that'll go away. Before long, riding will be just a means of travel."

"Good to know. I feel as though I can't properly shut my legs."

Clara returned the laugh and followed the crew, bow-legged, into the inn. "I've never ridden that long before."

Boyce ushered the companions to sit with him. Once drinks were served, he filled them in, "We appreciate your comin'. I 'pose you mustn't got word from our messenga'."

"We haven't heard from anyone. Is something the matter?" Sawyer asked.

Boyce nodded. Pain painted his expression as he retold the eerie chain of events. "A few days pass, er… Kit, one of our youngins', stumbled into town, crying n' pale. She didn't say 'er word. Refused to move. Her eyes, they were empty… only a shell of 'erself. We 'ave so few youngins', ya know. The little gal, she hasn't been the same since. Did you 'appen to bring an 'ealer with ya? Please say that you 'ave." Boyce looked at Clara.

A sick feeling hung in Clara's gut. She diverted her eyes away.

"Are you sure it's only the one child? No one else was affected?" Jade asked.

"Yes, Sorceress. But I cannot say fer what tomorra brings, but the rest of us seem to be unscathed fer the moment." Boyce's thin lips quivered, and he nervously rubbed his arms.

Jade pursed her lips and grabbed Sawyer's shoulder to excuse them both. She motioned for Clara to join them. Standing outside the inn, they spoke quietly. "Typically, I wouldn't jump to conclusions, but I already feel it. There is a power here that I haven't felt before. Let's send Onyx to get Eleanor once he returns," Jade said.

Sawyer brushed his hand across the shadow of his incoming beard. He quickly rubbed his eyes, catching his breath.

"Are you feeling alright?" Jade asked.

"I am, but… after rescuing Clara from the swamp… I can't believe I haven't mentioned it before. I'd forgotten about her, till now."

Jade grabbed Sawyer's shoulders firmly. "Who? Sawyer, who are you talking about?"

"While bringing Clara home. I noticed a hazy phantom. She didn't speak a word, yet had the power to… remember. Thoughts I hadn't entertained in years came alive. I managed to escape her spell. Although, I don't know if that was my doing or hers. After she disappeared, I thought I had imagined it. She didn't seem real."

Jade planted her feet firmly. "How do you know it wasn't a dream?"

"I don't know. What I saw could have been her, the memory of her, or a nightmare."

"That's vague data to make any harsh opinions about. Perhaps it's an omen." Jade shifted from one leg to another before pacing. "Zerpith's chant mentioned how Clara was cursed with a power. Could this be what we're against? Clara, have you seen anything? Could it be possible the phantom came from your world with you?"

Clara shrugged. "I haven't seen anything. I only remember waking up in the cart. Besides that, my world doesn't have phantoms. Nothing magical. No phantoms, no curses, no Lectus. Why do you think the shadow has something to do with the sick child? Kids get sick often in my world, I'm guessing it's the same in yours."

"We can't be certain what caused the child's sickness. I never became sick from the shadow. She was simply showing herself to me."

Jade shook her head. "As soon as we get home, I'm speaking with Zerpith. He needs to be informed. As does the king. Sawyer, I'll leave that to you."

Clara followed the two inside. The old man's wrinkled hands rubbed his balding head. Beads of sweat rolled down his face. His eyes pleaded for hope as they reentered the room.

Jade asked, "Boyce, have you noticed anything odd? Suspicious shadows or dark feelings?"

"Can't say I 'ave... thankful fer that. 'Ave you seen 'em fer yerself? Should we be——"

Sawyer interjected. "No cause for alarm. We're just speculating."

Clara surveyed the inn. Something felt familiar. It was as if deja vu or some forgotten memory pierced her mind, altering her emotions. She felt angry before sadness cloaked her. She wanted to cry and scream, but she did neither. *Sawyer saw the phantom only after he found me. Is this what I've done? Could the phantoms be my fault? No, can't be. I can't project the tiniest magic. Nothing. I'm nothing in this world, and I am nothing back in mine. The hero they're looking for doesn't exist. I have no information about the phantom, but if they want me to fight it, I don't know how.*

Boyce grabbed Clara's arm, snapping her from her internal dialogue. "I feel there's a reason you are here."

She gasped and pulled her arm back. "I'm sorry… so sorry. I'm not the hero. We should probably get Eleanor. I know she can help." Ignoring her, Boyce reclaimed her arm. His eyes brimmed with tears. Clara gave in as he pulled her from the table, leading her to a rundown hut, only a few homes from the inn.

"I'm nothing here," came a small voice from another room as soon as they entered. The hair on Clara's arms stood. A cold wave washed from her chest, spilling into her gut. The room was dimly lit with the smell of dirt, moisture, and old blankets. A small bed, lifted by a crudely made pallet, held a child. Clara greeted the mother. Thin and exhausted, the mother held the hand of her daughter.

"Always wanted a baby girl, I did. Met Huckle later in life, not as a young spring chickin' like me friends. Never thought I'd have one, though. She be my world." The mother's eyes brimmed with tears.

"What's her name?" Clara cautiously kneeled next to the mother. A few bugs scattered around her knees. She rested her weight on her legs to keep them at bay.

"We call 'er Kit. 'Er given name is Nora, but we 'ave been naming her Kit since the day she came to us. Kit for Kitten. Yes, that's what we say."

"Kit. I like that. I heard her cry. She said she was… nothing. Do you know why she'd say that?"

"She always been a tiny one. Came 'arly, too," the mother wiped tears from her eyes. "She be always the one to catch ill, 'fore anyone else. She 'as troubles, you know. She 'as trouble keeping up with the rest of the chil'ren 'round 'ere. I keep tellin' 'er she be jest as good, but they pick on 'er, they do."

Clara bent to hold the child's other hand. A deep sense of

knowing and compassion flooded her in a way she could not comprehend. Unbeknownst to her, she closed her eyes. The atmosphere altered. Darkness came, washing over the room like thick black paint that sucked Clara into a gloomy forest. She stood from her knees, arms hanging and heavy. Anger welled into bitterness. The woods were dense and colorless, with only enough light to cast shadows. In the distance stood a hazy figure. It pointed a finger at her. The hair on the back of Clara's neck stood until her surroundings changed once again…

Clara bit into the noodles. Across from her, Angel looked tense. "Clara, I know things have been hard lately. I understand you're struggling, but you need to snap out of it. You can't stay like this forever."

"Why would you say that? I'm fine, really I am." Clara smiled dryly.

"You're different. I can't tell you exactly why but I sense it. Clara, please—"

"Seriously, I'm okay," Clara got up to walk out the door but stopped at the threshold at Angel's plea.

"Then tell me why your eyes are dead. The spark you once had, it's gone. You're still my Clara, but only a withered portion of her."

A searing pain pulsed on her forehead. In an instant, the woods were gone, replaced by the dusty planks and musty smell of the room. Tears streamed. Her breath shallowed. For a moment, Clara forgot about herself and her pain. All her attention was directed at the still, small child lying sick on the bed. She dropped to her knees and rubbed the child's brow. "Kit, please hear me. You are more. Believe me. If I know anything, little one, I know this." Placing her head against the child's, she whispered, "Once upon a time, I lived in a place called America. I always thought America was hard to live in. I believed that… that I wasn't good enough to make something of myself. I never felt like I belonged. I felt like a nobody."

The girl stirred, her eyes slowly opened. She reached to touch Clara's brow. "Pretty…" Her voice was small and weak.

"Hear me… I somehow came here, and I still don't feel like I belong. The worst part of all of this is how everyone is telling me I'm someone who I don't feel I can be. They say I'm capable of doing great things, like defeating Lectus, but I don't believe them. I don't know how to feel good enough to believe them. But in America, I was so sad that… that I lost who I was. I'm still trying to get her back. We are the same in this. But please, Kit. Don't lose yourself. We can be brave together, can't we? Would you… be brave with me?"

Swallowing hard, Kit wrapped her arms around Clara. "I will."

Crying together, Clara whispered, "What scares you more than anything?"

"I'm afraid of the kids who make fun of me."

"Next time they bully you, stand up for yourself. You are worth being loved, even if you are the one who has to do it."

"I will."

"Just don't be mean back, okay? Instead, maybe ask them why they want to hurt you and what they're seeking to accomplish."

"I won't be mean, I promise I won't be like them."

"Go kick their butts with kindness. I hope one day I get to hear about how you made yourself proud," Clara said, laughing at Kit's surprised reaction.

"You kick Lectus's butt," Kit replied with a giggle.

"Good. You'll stand up for yourself, and I'll… I'll defeat Lectus."

"Kit, my Kit," cried her mother. The girl sat up in time to feel her mother's firm embrace. Her pale complexion steadily showed signs of life.

Sawyer and Jade waited until Clara left the child's bedside. Jade ran to Clara first. "Whatever you did, it was amazing. Well done."

"I didn't do anything… I mean, I don't think I did."

"The signet upon your brow glowed fiercely. More than that, there was something incredibly powerful present. Seeing it—seeing you—brings me hope. I second-guessed it many times, but now I'm sure," Jade said.

"Really? Thank you. Maybe there's something more after all." Clara reached for her forehead, but the burning sensation was gone.

Sawyer squatted to meet the child, now sitting upright in the bed. "If you ever need someone to stick up for you, let me know. I will send a knight to defend your honor." He winked, and the child laughed.

"Yes, sir," she said in awe. "I'll let you know."

"Hey, Jade," Clara said softly, "I'm really tired. Do you think we can stay the night here and leave in the morning? I don't think I have it in me to ride back today."

"Are you okay?"

"I think so."

"Of course. I'll get you a room."

Sawyer beamed admirably at Clara. "Great job. We're proud of you... I'm proud of you."

Clara smiled through the weariness. She wasn't sure what happened, but maybe, just maybe, it was enough to hold onto.

CHAPTER 18
Times are Changing

SAWYER

THE TABLE where Jade and Sawyer sat was splintered but clean. They had only been seated a short time before Onyx appeared, wearing his usual accessory—mud. "Guys," he said, having proudly picked up on Clara's verbiage, "I found some great resources I think I'll make a tonic with. Wheatworm Stem is scarce, although this town seems to have no shortage of it growing on their hills." He began to write in his journal. "With it, I think I can make a base oil for your sword that will extend the life of an infused oil. So… the spirit tonic, that usually lasts… would you say… five minutes before it wears off? With this Wheatworm Stem, I think we can extend the effects to at least seven." Onyx looked at his friends, "Fill me in."

Jade retold the story. "Hmmm," Onyx uttered while stroking his chin.

Jade took a swig from her cup. "My thoughts exactly. Clara didn't seem to know what happened. It's obvious she has no control over her power… no sense of awareness of it, at all. It's perplexing."

Sawyer shook his head. "It's a crazy notion. The mark on her forehead was gleaming; I knew she had power. We must do all we can to support her in understanding it."

Onyx sat back in his chair. "That's some powerful elaboration. I'm sorry I missed it. It would be hard to think someone of great power wouldn't know it, but then again, she tends to overthink."

"If she felt anything, she didn't say, although she was extremely weary. I saw her reach for her forehead, but she never said how it felt. I don't want to wake her, so come morning, we'll discuss it. I'm anxious to speak to Zerpith as soon as we return. I wonder if he's seen anything like it before, or if any of his prophetic dreams revealed it." Jade dropped her fork, no longer hungry. It was going to be a long night waiting to get back to the castle.

Boyce sat at the table with them. "I can't thank 'ya enough. Things be tough around 'ere and 'aving the youngin' sick jest adds to our struggles."

"Tell me," Sawyer began, "how is the living situation? Do you have enough to eat? I noticed many thin villagers."

"No Commanda', harvest has been slow this season. We're doing our best, 'tis true… but 'ere jest ain't enough to go around. Then, 'ere be the taxin'."

"Taxing?" Jade and Sawyer said in unison.

"A group comes 'er ever so often. They be asking fer taxes fer the king. Vittles 'ere, cow 'ere."

"The castle isn't taxing anyone at the moment," Sawyer said firmly.

The man sat silently. A frown slowly pulled down his face. Loose wrinkles molded into his chin. "You don't say…"

Sawyer addressed Boyce, "Once I arrive home, I'll inform the king. For now, only surrender your resources if you're threatened. I'll send a knight or two once I get back to Ancora Castle to check in. Until then, hide your goods, if you must." Boyce's eyes filled with tears, and Sawyer continued, "If you need anything before then, please send word."

Leaving the discussion behind, Boyce and the companions chatted casually. Even Jade picked her fork back up to join in on the conversation while finishing her food.

As the sun rose, the friends promptly left town. Seeing the disoriented look on Clara's face, Sawyer asked Jade to wait before speaking with Clara until she properly recovered. After an uneventful journey back, they trotted through the gates.

While the companions were adventuring, the rest of the group continued their preparation for the journey. Rory packed and stored supplies in the designated shed. Once ready, they would be used to stock the wagon. They didn't know how long they'd be, so each inch of space was considered strategically. Salted meats and dried fruit were stored in tight bags, as preserved food would be the most efficient. Flavorful spices were also stored, waiting till the time they were needed to season fresh game.

When the group entered the stables. Rory dropped the leather straps he was holding. He waved joyously with both hands before meeting them. "Welcome back," he said, taking Willow's reins. Two other squires came to tend to the other horses. No one took the Dragonmare, as many were afraid of it.

"Thanks, Rory, we had a fine trip. Guess what? Clara is a great horsewoman now," Sawyer informed.

"That's great news!" Rory replied before asking Clara, "Did you like Stormy's gait? He's smooth, isn't he?"

Clara nodded. "I did. He's the perfect horse for me. You did great picking him. And I only fell off once."

Rory laughed. "Eleven more falls and you can call yourself an expert." He winked, something he saw his mentor do often. After dismounting, each went their own way, but Sawyer grabbed Jade's arm.

"Do you mind if I accompany you when you speak with Zerpith?"

"I don't mind at all. He may want to get your account about the phantom. Give me an hour to freshen up first. Meet me outside the mage's wing."

"While you freshen up, I'm going to speak with the king. I'll update you once we meet." Anxious for advice, Sawyer headed straight for the King's Audience. He'd need to give an account of what had happened and discuss the state of Rafferty Hills, as well as the ever-prevalent Gohmer.

The King's Audience presented the typical scene. The court chatted at tables adorned with food and drink. Always spying, always gossiping. But unlike normal, the king wasn't seated on his throne. Cutting through the room, Sawyer exited out the back door and headed to the king's personal chamber. A knight was standing outside the king's door. It wasn't opened for him.

"Commander, state your business."

"Garret, Good to see you. I'm here to speak with the king. We've returned from Rafferty Hills. I need to provide a debrief to King Henric."

Garret shook his head. "I'm sorry, but the king will see no one."

"Are you certain? Can you tell him it's me requesting a visit? I have news about Clara and an update about the town. I'm sure he'll make the exception."

"I don't think it's a good idea. He didn't want to see the court this morning, and he definitely hasn't been entertaining visitors today. He specifically told me that no one has permission to enter."

"I hope he's feeling well, but I need to see him if at all possible. Please, step aside."

"I can't let you do that. Please understand—"

"Then I'll need to force my way in."

Garret sighed. "Wait here." The guard entered the room and reappeared shortly after. "He said you may go in, but only briefly."

The king sat at a small round table when Sawyer entered the room. Scattered papers littered the table and spilled across the floor of the dimly lit chamber. Old text, many from children's fables, lay strewn across the room, some open with bent corners and others with pages ripped from their binding. After bowing, Sawyer stood at the edge of the table. "Your Majesty, thank you for allowing me to enter. I have returned from Rafferty Hills, Clara's maiden trip. I have an important update to share."

"Do you feel this would be better served with an official round table?" The king didn't release the book he was holding in one hand. Binding bent, it flopped over his hands.

"I agree, a round table will be in order. However, there's a few issues you may need to hear before the word is shared."

"Then, I suppose you order a round table, boy." The king waved his arm, dismissing the knight abruptly. "Now go. What you have to say should be for all to hear."

"Your Highness—"

"Leave my presence. Now, knight!" The king slammed his fist onto the table. The book fell from his grip, crashing to the floor and cracking the binding. Mumbling, he swiped it from the floor as he gathered the dislodged pages. "I won't repeat myself. Go away. Lectus. The castle without windows… a forest…"

Heart in his throat, Sawyer left the room and turned to Garret. "How long has he been this way?"

"I cannot say, as I have only recently been assigned to his watch this morning."

"I see. He seemed to be more of himself just days ago but I've noticed how his demeanor is…. well, altering. Have you noticed the same?"

"I can't say, even if I did."

"Perhaps he's unwell. My apologies for bothering him. Thank you, Garret, and keep an eye on our king."

"Until next time, Commander."

Merrick's quarters were only a short walk away. Seeing the knight guarding the door, he stopped. "I need to meet with Merrick. It's important. I must see him promptly."

"I'm sorry, Commander. He left for Cauldira a few days ago."

"Cauldira? Did he reference his agenda?"

"No, sir, he did not."

Sawyer excused himself; it appeared that requesting any additional information was futile. Running his hands through his hair, he sent a page to give word of the upcoming round table and waited for Jade. The sky was cloudy, although lacking rain. Yet, the moisture in the air was a sign rainfall was coming. Sawyer didn't wait long before Jade arrived. Upon entering the mage's wing, they made a direct path to the main room, where the mage assumed they'd find Zerpith. The kooky-eyed ancient sat on a simple wooden chair. Hands on each armrest, he grinned madly as he watched a young mage conjure up fire in a stone fire pit.

"Ooo, there you are! Concentrate on growing the flame. Fire comes with a price, young man. Feeeeel the price of power! You're going to remember that burn after, but you'll learn to overcome it, even welcome it. Yes, welcome it. Always save enough strength to cool the burn. You know this from your studies." He rubbed his hands together. "If you don't, the fire will consume you from the inside," he shouted madly. "The stronger your fire, the more energy you save for the cooling. Balance. Errr. Balance your energy. You'll learn to reserve it. Especially after a good burn or two. If you don't, you'll burn alive." The ancient one threw his arms up and cackled.

The horrified young mage whimpered. Smoke escaped from his ears. The fire in the practice pit roared untamed. Sawyer stepped back as Jade rushed to help. "Nash, listen to me, summon water. Only feel the water. Forget you ever had fire."

The boy cried as smoke billowed from his eyes, he desperately rubbed at them. Jade's voice raised. "The water! It's cold within you. Feel how cold. Mix ice with it, if you need to. You can do this. Look at me, Nash!"

Fire flickered across the boy's eyes. Closing them so tight his eyelashes disappeared, he relaxed after a minute. "Good job." Jade smiled reassuringly. He did not smile back. Instead, he shook his head.

"I don't want to do this anymore."

"But Nash, you were born into the Hethro family. All Hethros are born mages. Few bloodlines are so consistent. Your body was made to harness magic. That's an honor. So many would give anything to do what you can, despite the pain."

"I don't… I don't like this," the boy cried. Zerpith, unamused, rose from the chair, eyes rolling. Ignoring the boy, he waited for Jade and nodded his approval to Sawyer.

"I sense you have something to tell me," Zerpith said.

"Yes, Master Zerpith." Jade walked a few paces behind the ancient one. Sawyer kept his distance.

"Come, young sorceress. Come, knight."

Following Zerpith into his chamber, they each sat on one of the large pillows placed in front of a twisted wood chair where Zerpith was seated. The ornate chair was decorated with a thick cushion embroidered with stars and the four elements. The magic-infused stitches glowed, trapped within the fibers. Tassels hung from the cushion, swinging as Zerpith shifted. Twisted tree trunks formed the chair's armrests, winding their way up, over Zerpith's head until they connected to the ceiling. The same twisted branches made up the tall back of the wooden throne. At the very top, galaxies were carved into the wood while spilling across the ceiling.

"Tell me, Jade, what did you see at Rafferty Hills, ehhh?"

"I saw Clara's powers. It seems to stem from the signet on her brow. She doesn't appear to have any control over it, but it's there. I doubted your prophecy. I ask for your forgiveness, as I was sorely wrong."

Zerpith nodded his acceptance, and Jade continued her retelling. "We have a new adversary. Sawyer mentioned a hazy, foggy-like being. Sawyer, tell Zerpith what you saw."

"When I rescued Clara from the swamp, on the way back to Ancora Castle, I encountered a shadow..." Zerpith's eyes shone intensely. *I feel as if I should keep these details private.*

Zerpith folded his gnarled hands into his lap, but immediately placed them back onto the arms of the chair. His long fingernails clicked onto the wood. "Your account is vague. A shadow, you say? We must be aware. He is here. What else did you see, knight?"

Sawyer fought the urge to break eye contact with the ancient mage. Zerpith's wayward eyes rolled about his sockets, which provided a valued release from their grasp. "It was only but a flash. Possibly a nightmare due to lack of sleep on the road." Sawyer looked at Jade, her expression questioning.

"Dream or reality, the shadow appeared. Hmmm," Zerpith's eyes were popping from their sockets. He leaned forward in his chair.

Sawyer didn't lean away from the ancient mage's advance. "Ancient one, shadows appear everywhere."

"Ah, and so they do. But, a shadow or phantom did you see?" Zerpith dropped his head and seemed to doze off instantly.

Jade spoke up, "Thank you, Master, for your time. I'll return." Zerpith said no more, so they rose from the pillow and walked back to the mage's quarters. Nash was now gone. Jade glared at Sawyer. He shook his head to silence her. When seeing Jade's perplexed look, he spoke under his breath, "Let's discuss this outside."

Rain fell hard. The two kept under the roof leading from building to building, but not protected enough to stay completely dry. The occasional spray of water misted them as they watched it pour. Sawyer noticed Jade's far-off gaze. "What's on your mind?"

"It concerns me how Nash didn't desire his powers. No mage ever said such a thing, but I guess times are changing." Jade's jewel-toned eyes darkened. "Speaking of unwanted powers, do you suppose that Clara has something to do with the shadows?"

"The phantom wasn't present at the swamp, like I said. Assuming the worst is a terrible idea. Many creatures roam the plains we know nothing about. We shouldn't be hasty to say Clara has anything to do with it."

"I think it's worth investigating."

Sawyer changed the subject, dismissing his agitation. "I saw King Henric in his quarters. Literature all over the place. They were largely about Lectus and old fables. He refused to even look at me. I sought the advice of Merrick, but he wasn't here. He left for Cauldira, so I was told. I think he knows something isn't right."

"If that's the case, I wonder why he went to Cauldira instead of Eros. The mages and healers would prove to be a better resource than warriors."

"Merrick is tactful to a fault. We must trust his judgment if the message is true."

They walked towards the dining hall until Jade broke the silence. "We're running out of time to train Clara with magic. She tries… over and over again, but she isn't progressing. It's frustrating for both of us. Yes, there's more hope now than before, but I'm not sure what to do from here. If only we could tap into that again. Perhaps when we speak with the Preceptor when we get to Eros, he can provide insight."

Sawyer nodded. "He'd be a good resource. If anyone can enlighten us, he'd be in my top five. Has Clara said anything more to you about what happened at Rafferty Hills? She was fairly quiet on the way home."

"Nothing. She doesn't know what happened. That's it. She only had an encouraging conversation with the child."

"I'll talk with her later tonight, if she's up to it."

"Would it matter? I asked her, and her answer was simple. She didn't know. For now, I'd let it go. If there's something more, she'd tell us."

"I'm sure she would."

"Sawyer, listen. We still don't know much about Clara. I know you've spent a lot of time with her. My stars, every spare minute you have, you're together. It's not a bad thing, but…" Jade sighed. "All I'm trying to tell you is to take it slow. I've never seen you this… interested before. If she doesn't make it, you're going to get your heart broken."

"Duly noted," Sawyer said coldly.

CHAPTER 19

One More Day

MONTHS LATER

CLARA

CLARA DEEPLY BREATHED in the smell of honeysuckle mixed with fresh grass from her open window. Leaning over the edge, the wind tugged playfully at her hair. Still in her lace-trimmed nightgown, she closed the window, shutting off the outside breeze. Today, she was to only do one thing—rest. With festival plans in full swing for tomorrow and the journey to find Lectus the day after, everyone was tied up with other tasks. Having no agenda of her own, she had the day to herself.

Her scepter lay on the small carved table near the door. Clara paused. *Should I try to train myself today?* She shrugged it off. *Nah, but I bet that's where I'll find Sawyer.* Leaving the tool behind, she chose a simple dress made from cotton. The small daisies embroidered the entirety of the blue frock. She neatly tied it in the back. After french braiding her hair, she retrieved a ribbon from the vanity and secured the braid's end. Her stomach growled.

The click from the door opening and shutting echoed through the empty corridor. Walking the halls, voices could be heard from various meetings. Everyone seemed to be discussing one thing: the festival. Once at the dining hall, Clara grabbed a tin plate from the table and filled it. *It feels strange being on my own. I wonder if this is what it's like living here. Actually living here. Being independent outside of expectations and routine training.* Sitting at an empty table, she ate alone. Across from her was a table of young knights laughing loudly. Over in the corner was a group of white-haired healers. Each wore a simple white robe with Ancora's crest beneath a cross. *Those must be infirmary healers.* She looked for anyone she knew, but none of her friends were there. She smiled. She had friends.

Dropping her plate into the sudsy bucket purposely placed on the rolling cart, she strolled to the training ground. In the distance, she saw Sawyer, Jade, and Onyx. They were talking. Sawyer tossed his sword in the air and caught it by the hilt. On the last catch, they split. Onyx stood a distance behind Sawyer with Jade many feet in front of them both. Sawyer took a stance that Clara was now familiar with. They were going to spar.

Arms circling her head, Jade conjured sparks. Once she connected her palms, fire crackled and spat. The flames grew, licking at her cheeks and swirling around her waist and down her legs. It singed and smoked until it disappeared. Clara moved a little closer. They weren't in the mage arena. *Is this what a mage attack looks like without the barrier?*

As quickly as the fire disappeared, it shot fiercely at Sawyer and Onyx. Clara gasped. Sawyer held his shield against the fire. The fiery attack hit the metal and cascaded around the knight. Onyx dodged the leftovers, then tossed Sawyer a shiny stone and vial. The knight deftly caught both, downing the vial in record speed. Sawyer swiftly scraped the stone across his blade, the movement seamless, after drinking the vial. His sword glowed shades of red. Jade attacked again, this time with a tornado of wind. The tornado spun, growing as it traveled. Now the size of four Sawyers, the twister engulfed the knight into its core. Onyx nonchalantly hurled a bomb. The explosive struck the side of the tornado, which was now the size of an elephant. A sizzle turned into a crackle as it spun, swirling lopsided.

Crackling louder and louder, the tornado burst into a whirl of flames that parted aggressively. Inside, Sawyer was visibly ready to attack, sword flaming. Swinging his weapon in impossibly fast circles, the flames were enhanced. He charged at Jade. A trail of flames followed as he pretended to slash her. She fell to the ground dramatically. Onyx laughed at her performance. All signs of fire or wind vanished. A few nearby knights looked awestruck, and some younger ones applauded the spectacular performance. Clara relaxed. This was only practice after all.

The battle mates waved when they noticed Clara. Sawyer lifted his sword high above his head and flexed his free arm's bicep. She laughed, jogging towards them. "That was incredible! Do all the warriors fight like that?"

Onyx shook his head. "Not all knights can take a hit like Sawyer, or partake in drinking anti-spells."

Jade wiped the soot from her palms. "Sawyer has an unnatural ability. There are other Ancorian knights with extraordinary abilities, as well."

Sawyer winked at Clara. "All in a day's work. But without Onyx, I would have been burned to a crisp. Jade's magical attacks are strong. I felt the heat, even with the anti-spell."

Jade addressed Clara, "Shouldn't you be resting? There won't be much of it after we leave."

Clara stumbled over her words, "I was just walking around, seeing what everyone was doing."

"Is that so?" Sawyer arched his brow. "Well, since you're here, you could practice your running skills, since that'll predominantly be your avenue of battle." Sawyer feigned drawing his sword. Clara bolted. Rushing past the laughing, spectating knights, she could hear his footsteps. Lifted from her feet, her breath huffed out as Sawyer flung her over his shoulder.

Sawyer announced victory. "I've got the Bean Queen!" He ran. Clara laughed, watching Onyx and Jade running behind through bumping vision. Watching the ground pass by, a film formed around them. It was the color of liquid soap—translucent with the slightest shine. Sawyer's breath labored as he struggled to run against the friction of the film. The substance became thicker as walls enclosed them in a glistening bubble. Sawyer set Clara down as they lifted from the ground, his face beaded with sweat. Between labored breaths he spoke, "Eleanor's here."

They were quickly separated from the ground. Almost at the treetops. Sawyer smirked, rocking the sphere. Clara calmed the panic gripping her each time the enclosure swung. Eleanor's lavender eyes sparkled brightly below. Arms outstretched, her enchanting smile enhanced her already ethereal countenance. Sawyer rolled next to Clara, pressing his face deep into the barrier. Eleanor's smile burst into laughter.

"It takes incredible concentration and strength to create a magical shield, yet she makes it look effortless. She's our only combative healer. A substantial trade was made to acquire her. One of the best decisions Ancora has made," Sawyer informed her.

"She's so beautiful too," Clara said, looking through the bubble. Sawyer's hand brushed a stray hair from her forehead and traced the presumed circle on her brow. Her heartbeat increased. *Don't freak out. Be cool. Stay calm. Clara, pull yourself together, and don't say anything weird!*

Sawyer's voice lowered. "Healers are visibly beautiful, but it's only something you see. The beauty you feel is so much deeper..." He pulled his hand back abruptly. "I didn't mean to touch your brow, your hair, it was—"

Heat rising to her face, her skin flushed pink. "Thank you. For brushing it off... It's okay. I—I'm not mad about it."

Sawyer laughed. "I didn't mean to fluster you. Especially when you're stuck in here with me. Please excuse my rudeness." The knight's voice faded from a deep emotional tone to one of cordial entertainment. "Clara Rivers, since I have your undivided attention. It would be an honor to have your company tomorrow for the festival. Would you care to join me as my lady? We could explore the wild amusements that the festival bestows upon us."

"I'd love to go with you!" Clara didn't hold back the excitement in her voice. She wanted to tell him she thought he was cute, but was that appropriate? Did she need to play coy, or was their dating system similar to America? *I never can tell what's traditional or modern here. Maybe I'm thinking this way since I compare everything to what I know.*

Sawyer's hair pasted to his forehead, and his eyes shone boyishly, "Brace yourself. Eleanor's going to dissolve the barrier shield."

"What? We'll fall!" Clara exclaimed. The shield erupted with an alarmingly loud bang. Falling towards the dirt, a soft, stretchy, cloud-like tarp caught them both. They were safely on the ground.

"Eleanor, that was amazing! I'm blown away by your gift!" Clara said.

"Thank you. I had a bit of fun. Only two days away before the carefree life dissolves."

"I already feel safer. I have the greatest people surrounding me. What more could I ask for?" The faces around her smiled; she felt safe with them. Jade interrupted the conversation to excuse the group. Clara waved them off and left the training grounds.

Skipping like a child, Clara entered the castle. *I should visit the library!* Walking the hall, she opened the door to an extensive library spanning floor to ceiling with books. "I never know where to begin," she voiced aloud.

"Are you looking for something in particular, Clara?"

"Hello Rory, it's nice to see you! Are you reading anything in particular?"

"Sawyer requires me to read *The Swordsman Companion of Theorems and Logic, Junior's Edition.* It's boring."

Clara snickered under her breath. "I hear ya. I wasn't a fan of schoolbooks either. Hmm. I don't know what I'm looking for. Any books about Lectus?"

"Unfortunately, no. Sawyer already searched, but the king must have taken them all, and he isn't sharing. All I remember is what my parents told me. They'd say, 'Rory, Lectus is going to hear you and swallow you up if you don't obey.'"

Clara paused. "That sounds like a terrible story."

Rory shrugged. "It's only a story. What if there's more than one Lectus? Or what if he's just another person, like us?"

"Hmm, I hadn't thought of that, but Zerpith's chant spoke of fairytales."

"Maybe the 'fairytale' isn't talking about a fairytale but a figurative warning? Mages, especially ancients, like to talk in puzzles."

"Maybe. I definitely wouldn't complain if that was the case." *I could only hope.* "Any book recommendations for me?"

"There's so many. I love reading. Well, at least when it's not school books. You could start at *Mister Magic's Miserable School of Mages*. It's one of my favorites. It's about a mage who keeps making mistakes." The boy snickered. "He turns his teacher into a chicken. She lays an egg." Clara followed Rory towards the section where the book should have been. The boy smiled the entire time while searching the shelves. "Ah, someone already borrowed it. You'll have to wait till it's returned."

"It's okay, I'll just look around to see what catches my eye." Overwhelmed at the options, she settled on a short book about courtship. Skimming the pages, she quickly lost focus. *It's not like I'd have time to read it anyway.* Putting the book back into place, her foot kicked something. An old, thin binding peeked from under the dark wooden shelf. She dusted the cover off. No title. Flipping through the pages, they were blank. Huh? What was that? *There's only one picture?* Clara paused. The drawing spanned across both pages in the center of the book. The image painted in muted shades gave her chills, goosebumps tingled her arms. *The forest looks dead.* The depth drew her eye to a broken path etched into the thick paper. The path traced across the break between pages.

Instantly, blank pages began to fall from the binding. Clara shut the book, trapping loose pages inside. Placing it on the shelf, she noticed her hands trembling. *It's just a book. Relax. And a very old one. No wonder the pages fell out.* She promptly left the library. The sun was setting, revealing hues of pink brushing across the sky, blending effortlessly into shades of orange and yellow. The sun, not ready to retire, highlighted a section of clouds. *How did time pass that quickly? I swear it was only lunchtime when I entered the library...*

The maids were prepping her room for the night when she opened the door. The bed was turned back and a carafe of fresh water was placed on the nightstand. "Good evening, Lady Clara," the servant said with a smile.

"Good evening. Thanks for the snacks you left last night, Opal. Every night I stay here, I look forward to the goodies."

"Ah, you are welcome! Got more fer tonight, as well."

Clara peeked into the basket left on the small table by the chaise. A few tea bags infused with lavender, three canvas bags containing a trail mix-like concoction, paper-wrapped jerky, two wax-covered cheese balls, a loaf of fresh sourdough bread, and a small, curious crystal vial plugged with an exquisite matching stopper. Clara paused on the bottle before plucking it from the basket. She searched for a label, but was unable to locate one. "Looks yummy again today, but I haven't seen this liquid before. What is it?"

Rolling a cart of leftover sundries towards the door, the maid stopped to survey the room. "Oh my. I apologize, Lady Clara, for not explaining. It's a beverage infused with magic. It's supposed to help you sleep and increase your focus. The Preceptor gifted it to you, sent all the way from Eros to wish you well on your journey. He said it will give you a mental and physical boost the next morning. You need to drink it tomorrow night. What a thoughtful idea!"

"Oh nice! That's really kind of him. I don't think I know who he is. Is he friends with Sawyer?"

"The Preceptor is an important official reigning over Eros. The Enchanted City, in case you didn't know. He's both healer and mage! Eros united with Ancora a long time ago. We be talking over a hundred years ago! I can't say if he befriended Sawyer, but he's friends with the king, he is."

"I heard about Eros. Thank you. Is there a way for me to send him a thank you?"

"I'll ensure one gets sent. Would you like to provide official words?"

"Um, maybe. How about, 'Thank you for the kind gift. Your support means a lot.'" The maid smiled as she quickly retrieved parchment and quill from the cart to scribble the message.

"I'll make sure the scribe gets your thanks. He'll write it up nice with Ancora's seal, unless you'd like to write it yourself."

"That's okay. I'm sure the scribe will make it look much better than I could."

The maid nodded in acknowledgement and left Clara alone. Still holding the bottle, one last ray from the setting sun casts light into the room, reflecting onto the bottle. Swirls of glittery clouds twisted and crashed inside the bottle. *Mage and healer? I guess they have hybrids. I'll ask about it once on the road. It should make for an interesting conversation while traveling.*

Placing the bottle by her bedside, she still had the rest of the evening to enjoy. Clara took a visit to the gardens. At night, the flowers were illuminated by the many lanterns strung across the stone arches and fixed to decorative pillars. Locating the Lily Weed, disappointment replaced her excitement. All the flower heads were closed. *I guess even some flowers need to rest.* A jumble of laughter across the garden wall led Clara's steps into one of the courtyards. Sitting at a small table, she watched the usual jester toss eggs. Children laughed as the jester feigned slipping on the snotty mess left on the ground. These antics, as simple as they were, filled her with more joy than anything she watched on TV. Soon after, the jester proudly bowed, causing his hat to pop off his head in a bang of confetti. The hat fell to the ground in a puff of smoke. The crowd laughed, followed by cheerful applause. The jester then announced a group of bards who began to play a melodic tune encouraging melancholy daydreaming. Listening to the music, she thought about Angel.

"Going out for a bit will do you some good, I promise. I know you aren't a fan of big groups, but I found the cutest spot for us. It's a new place, just opened up, and it's only a walk from our apartment." Angel locked the door with an indifferent Clara standing behind her on the steps.

"Thanks for thinking of me, and moving in… especially since you and your parents are footing most of the bill."

"Don't think about that now. Let's think about fun things. You can make it up to me later." Walking the sidewalk, the girls entered a hip coffee shop. Clara, laughing at the name, turned to Angel.

"The Bean Queen?"

"Isn't it fun? They're having an author visit today. I thought you might like that. It's one of your favorites."

"Sharlene Hastings?"

"The very one. We're early, so we can get some food before she does all her author stuff. I'm craving some pita and hummus."

"She only writes fantasy. I thought you didn't like that."

"Yeah, but I like you, and that's enough."

Clara snapped from her thoughts when Jade appeared. "Oh, this group is one of the best. They come around every month or so. I hear they may be hired full-time," the mage informed her as she sat on the seat next to Clara. Eleanor joined them.

"This song fills me with love and reverie." Eleanor sighed, brushing her shining hair off her shoulder and looking ethereal, as usual.

"Eleanor, it's good to see you. I'm afraid we haven't had much time to get to know each other," Clara said.

"Time, isn't it relative? Don't take me as rude, but I tend to keep to myself. We shall have much time together on the road, I'm certain."

Jade slid her chair from the table. Everyone clapped when the song ended. "Clara, Eleanor and I were discussing your powers."

Clara's hands turned clammy. *I bet they're going to tell me I'm worthless and that it's time for me to leave. That's why they both came. Then they'll escort me away. I'll have nowhere to live…*

"Sweet Clara," Eleanor softly addressed. "Jade mentioned how you healed a tormented child. What an excellent and entrancing tale that is."

"Thank you, but I feel that I don't deserve the recognition. I don't know what I did, or how it happened." Her breath lightened in relief. Maybe she wasn't getting discarded after all.

"What did you tell the child? You might have said something that caused the reaction to take place. Whatever it was, it must have been powerful." Jade leaned on the table, interest piqued.

"We only talked about what issues she was having in her personal life. She was getting bullied."

"That's all? Getting bullied doesn't account for being physically ill. The child's skin looked almost gray. Anything else you can remember? Anything at all? There must be something more than that," questioned Jade.

"I'm sorry, it wasn't anything spectacular, really. I asked her to be brave with me… does that mean anything?"

Jade's sarcastic expression wasn't suppressed. Eleanor's soft velvety voice covered for Jade's facial transparency. "I presume," Eleanor smoothed her hair out across her shoulder, "although I'm not getting the sense, perhaps you're a healer instead of a mage. It's worth exploring, even if I doubt it. Healers typically possess a soothing grace. We can easily recognize each other, even from a distance. I don't feel that with you." The healer did everything with dignity, even if rudely.

Jade, getting up from her seat, put her hands on her hips. "And that is an interesting concept. I can't speak for you both, but I'm starving. With everyone tied up for the festival, they're serving a variety of soups. Care to join me?"

Dinner came and went. Clara, back in her room, looked out her large bedroom window. Fireflies floated like tiny lanterns over the grassy field. Two maids pushed carts of dirty dishes below, the cobblestone walkway softly clacking with their footsteps. Leaving the window, she studied her reflection. There was nothing on her brow.

One more day till they leave.

One more day till she leaves the comforts of the castle.

One more day till her life was going to change.

CHAPTER 20
The Festival

CLARA

A SWEET-LOOKING pink cotton dress hung on the wrought-iron hanger against the wall. Empire waist and belted with a ribbon, white lace danced along the hem. Cute leather flats completed the look. Clara was obsessed. Sighing, she realized how much she would miss the castle and the nights at the Puckett hut. The late-night chats with Sawyer by the fire, she hoped, would continue as she presumed there would be campfires while traveling. It was possible that once everything was said and done, she might never see Ancora Castle again. Her mind clung to the thought…

Clara stood, covered in the blood of Lectus. She had won, but barely. Her friends stood around her, cheering. Confetti fell like shimmering rain. Of course, she realized that confetti wasn't realistic, but this was her daydream, and she wanted confetti. *She jumped into the air, magic lifting her off the ground. Floating gracefully, she found herself in Sawyer's arms…*

The dream halted. "Of course, we can't be together," she interjected, "Even if I like him, enjoy his company, and find him really cute, I don't know what'll happen after the whole Lectus ordeal is over…" Her words slowly faded. Well, maybe she'd entertain the idea…

Sawyer spun her in fun circles and leaned in for a kiss, but the atmosphere faded. Gone were the confetti and joyful friends. In their place was a gaudy pink bathroom. She was home. She cried complex, happy tears when she saw Angel. Of course, her Ancorian friends would be confused, as they didn't know what happened. Her happiness would then fizzle. She would never see her beloved friends at Ancora again… She would never see Sawyer again.

"Will there be no happy ending?" Clara said aloud while violently shaking the dress from the hook. Just then, a maid came in.

"'Tis time to dress, no time to waste. I'm already running behind." The maid helped Clara into the frock and tied Clara's hair back with a pink ribbon, half up and half down. It was simple, comfortable, and lovely. Remembering to straighten her back, she lifted her chin. When a knock was heard, Clara opened the door. Jade appeared on the other side.

Wearing what looked to be heels, the mage's already tall stature towered over her. *Heels? Nothing should surprise me, but then heels come into the picture. I guess fashion is important wherever you go. I wonder if they hurt her feet or if she uses magic.* "Jade, your shoes are so cute! Do they hurt your feet?"

"I'm a mage, or have you forgotten?" Jade's eyebrows rose. "If my feet hurt, I wouldn't know. I always put a trivial spell on my heels before I slide them on. I rarely get the opportunity to dress fancy, as I'm usually in battle or training. But today, I finally get to wear them."

"You look incredible. I could never pull that off."

"Thanks, it feels great for tonight. Come tomorrow, I'll be ready for my usual gear."

"The Festival seems like a big deal. It happens every year?"

"The Festival of Reformation began about a hundred years ago," explained Jade. "It was created as a day to remember our blessings and the hard work that made Ancora what it is today." Jade continued to walk deftly in the high stilettos. "Hundreds of years ago, there was a great battle. The stronghold of Melburn had captured Ancora. Melburn turned Ancora from a respectable kingdom into a place of hatred and poverty.

"During that time, there were many wars, but I see no need to mention them right now. After all, today is a day to celebrate the overall victory." They turned down the hallway and out the door. "To sum it up, both peasants and nobles alike will be mingling to celebrate the win. It's fascinating, actually. Many young, love-seeking people will be hoping to catch the eye of an eligible partner. Some are aiming to gain popularity and status." Walking into the crowd, Clara visibly spanned the connecting courtyards, each with an assortment of activities. "Watching the desperate romantics is probably my favorite part," Jade laughed. "Games, dancing, eating, entertainment, you name it, it's here for enjoyment. Speaking of entertainment, there is a rather amusing man right there."

Onyx stood behind Sawyer, both dressed in matching armor, but a nobly decorated version of it. Onyx haggled over a piece of junk with an irritated vendor. Sawyer smiled with delight when he saw Clara. "If it isn't my Bean Queen. You look lovely." He bowed gallantly.

"Thank you. You look rather dashing yourself."

"Did you expect any less?" He gave her a cheeky wink, which made her laugh. "Since you find me incredibly hard to resist, please allow me to escort you around. You are my date, after all."

"I mean, since I already agreed, why not? And, since you find me such a lovely enchantress, I hope you buy me something to eat." Clara took his arm.

"Say no to food? I think not," Sawyer agreed lightheartedly. Lights strung between rafters and hung from trellises, contributing to the already festive atmosphere with their warm glow. The cheerful aura was proof of the much-needed reprieve from daily life. Stopping at a booth, Clara searched the surface of the table. Wooden boxes lined with waxy cloth were displayed tactfully, all with the hope of catching the attention of a hungry buyer. Clara stared blankly at a particular bin containing rows of eyeballs stabbed on a skewer.

"What is that?" she choked. Red pupils glared at her from sticks.

Unblinking, they looked like highly-glossed candy, save for the stiff dangling veins still attached.

"Glommer eyes. Appetizing, aren't they? Many find them a special treat since they're rarely found outside the festival. Would you care to try one? They don't taste as horrid as they look, but I wouldn't say I'd go out of my way to find them. It's mostly the pop, once bitten, that ruins the experience."

"No, no thank you. I'll pass this time." Still looking at the box with peering eyes, she could almost feel the pop they'd make.

"I know something you'd like," Sawyer said playfully. "That sweet tooth of yours might find some sugar fluff satisfying." Looking for a particular stand, hand-in-hand, Sawyer led Clara to a vendor spinning sugar. The vendor waved them over.

"Sugar fluff for your lady, Commander?" promoted the vendor, newly crafted treat in hand.

"Of course, a pink one, please. To match her dress," Sawyer requested. The shopkeeper sprinkled caramel over the rosy fluff and rolled the sugar into a pan of slivered, thin shards of hard candy. The man handed over the puffy snack to Clara while Sawyer paid. Taking a bite, it melted in her mouth. The slight crunch from the candy shards paired nicely with the fluff that fizzled on her tongue as it melted.

"This is incredible. We call this cotton candy where I'm from. But if you tried to put caramel on it, it would probably dissolve."

"So, it seems our worlds are not that different after all. Sugar fluff, cotton candy. Magic is dust." Clara punched his arm, marveling at the strength she now had. The knight just grinned, unharmed by the jab.

"America or not, I'll always love sugar fluff," Clara informed while tearing off another piece. Leaving the stand, another attendee waved them over.

"Take your chance at Dunk the Monk? All proceeds go to benefit the orphanage. You win either way!"

Clara looked at the one with the money. Sawyer nodded and purchased two tickets. Going first, he chucked the ball at the target.

It hit the center but didn't budge. "Hey now, shouldn't the monk be dunked by now?"

"Depends. I don't think you hit the target."

"Sir, I believe you are in error."

"No, I'm not, Commander," the attendee gaslighted. "But, you get another try."

Tossing the ball again, the target moved. "Your game is rigged."

"It's a moving target. As Commander of our noble army, surely you are prepared for moving targets. Too bad, Commander. You can always purchase two more tries. The children will benefit." The vendor called for Clara. "Ma'am, it's your turn."

Clara threw the ball, but between the shifty rules and her bad aim, there would be no hope of her winning. She gasped when something grabbed her around the waist.

"Bean Queen! Sawyer!" It was Annabelle, and Dave and Holly were close behind her. Her pigtails, tied with purple ribbons, matched her dress. "Momma, can I try?" she pleaded.

"Good luck," Sawyer huffed. "You might have better luck, since you're a cheater."

Annabelle hastily took the ball after Dave paid. She hurled it, but missed. She tried again, but the ball barely reached the target. The monk, seated on the chair, clapped for the effort. "Momma, you go," Annabelle said, handing over her other ticket.

Holly, already red with embarrassment, sheepishly held the ball. Closing her eyes, she threw the ball, hoping to miss. A heavy splash flung her eyes open as the monk splashed into the water. Both Annabelle and Sawyer gasped in surprise.

"You did it!" they cheered in unison.

"Oh dear, you poor man." Holly ran up to the tank with a large number of apologies. The group laughed as the wet monk climbed from the tank. "Are you okay, dear?" Holly took the towels from a nearby stand to hand them to the soaking monk. Her cheeks were increasingly flushing many shades of red. She stopped to push her hands against her cheeks.

With continued celebration, the sun started to set. The warm hues added to a perfect wind-down for the festival. Feeling hungry for a good meal not involving sweets, the couple searched for dinner. Finding an aromatic booth, they ordered two delectable plates filled with lamb chops, potatoes, and green beans. Casually chatting, they sat on an empty picnic bench. Jade joined their conversation, her plate holding a serving of turkey.

The mage was having a hard time holding back hysteria while explaining how watching Dave participate in an arm-wrestling match was the best part of the night—even better than watching hopeless romantics get rejected. "My word, he tried so hard I thought his eyes would pop out."

Sawyer laughed. "I'm surprised he participated at all."

"He might have decided it was a bad idea afterwards. I saw him rubbing his arm. He held the other guy off for some time before losing, so I'm sure his muscles cramped," Jade said.

Darkness fell far too soon. The golden lights now burned brightly. Strewn across trellises, they showcased their sparkle, creating a relaxing ambiance. The dim light beckoned for slow dances and secret kisses, both of which would happen. Clara and Sawyer stood at the edge of the dance floor, waiting for the next song. Heart light, Clara's smile grew when Sawyer took her hand and squeezed it. They joined the other dancers when the next tune began. Thankful for the many dance lessons at the hut, she followed each number with ease. Song after song, they danced freely. The music slowly wound down with a waltz. Sawyer dipped her gently when the dance ended. Meeting eyes, Clara blushed. A slight breeze added to the perfect night, cooling the sweat from their foreheads. The lead bard announced a close-out song dedicated to all the lovers. While dancers left and others joined, the two stayed in place.

"Does this mean we're lovers now?" Sawyer said with an amused grin.

"Ah, you're dashing and cheeky!" Clara replied, laying her head on his chest. He squeezed her closer, his heart beating into her ear.

Sawyer's voice deepened. "I'm excited for our adventure. I'll always keep you safe, even at the cost of my life. I know the unknown frightens you, but I'll be with you."

Clara answered softly, "I'm thankful...I don't know what I'd do if… but I don't want to think about tomorrow. I only… Can we just focus on dancing, and… um… this moment?"

Sawyer's chin rested gently on the top of her head. "I like how you're thinking." Clara moved her head to meet his eyes; he placed his forehead against hers. "Your brand pulses."

"It does?" They released the position. Clara laid her head back on his chest.

"But," Sawyer lowered his voice, "not as hard as your heart is right now."

Clara's breath caught in her throat. "I don't know what will happen when everything is… over."

"Clara." He lifted her chin. "And here I thought your heart beat was for me." He smiled gently as his voice softened, "What happened to focusing on this moment?"

"It's… it's tomorrow. Tomorrow, all this… it changes. What if I get hurt to the point I can't be healed, or worse, what if someone dies? What if—"

"Clara."

"But so much could happen, and I don't feel prepar—"

"Clara."

"Sorry, but… What if I get captured and hidden in some treacherous tower high in the sky? Like Rapunzel?" Sawyer slowly spun her, dress billowing. Returning to his chest, Sawyer answered.

"Then I'll climb the tower to find you."

"What if there's a gate protecting the tower and lots of guards?"

Sawyer spun her again, this time faster. She slammed into his chest with a giggle. "Then, I'll storm the gate to save you."

"I'd wait for you."

Sawyer let out a deep laugh, "No doubt you would. And—"

Clara paused as Sawyer leaned closer. Her heart raced. The music stopped, but neither noticed. He halted when his lips were an inch from hers. "I'd stop at nothing to find you. Regardless of the reason."

Clara slowly leaned towards his lips, but a gust of wind blew her hair around, breaking the moment.

"Whew, the breeze feels great," Sawyer said while running his hand through his hair.

"It really does." Clara wiped her own brow to pull a stray, blown hair from her mouth. "It got cold fast, don't you think?" She rubbed her arms to get the chill off.

Sawyer searched the sky. "There's been no mention of storms tonight. I wonder if a mage is messing around."

The wind grew stronger. Everyone ceased celebrating. Women held their dresses in place to keep their petticoats hidden. Mothers rushed to find their children. A few men looked in amazement, pointing, as the lights swung from the trellises, flickering and sparking. The amazement turned to panic as the wind increased.

"Think we should go home?" yelled Clara to Sawyer, wind overpowering her voice.

"This wind is unnatural." Sawyer hollered back as he pulled Clara close. "Hang on as tightly as you can."

Clara hugged the knight around the waist and buried her face in his chest. He wrapped his arms around her and tucked his head on top of hers. The wind, now uncomfortable, slid them around the dance floor. The crowd scattered. Running and screaming, they held their belongings tightly while searching for safety. Vendor stands, decorations, food, and all sorts of merriment were turned over and tossed through the air.

"Watch out," shouted Jade as a jagged, broken piece of metal from a nearby stand targeted the couple. With a shout, she shot an electric bolt that knocked the danger away. Stumbling under the pressure, the wind gushed harsher the closer she moved towards the couple. No longer able to keep upright, she fell, shoes blowing off. The red heels flew through the air like pretentious, stylish daggers.

Sawyer's legs buckled. Clara, arms squeezed tight, pressed harder into his chest. The wind pulled her hair, ripping out the pink ribbon. Her locks blew wildly, in Sawyer's eyes and sticking in his mouth. They both tumbled to the dance floor. Screaming, Clara slipped from his embrace. The knight stretched to grab her forearms. He grasped them so tightly Clara felt bruises forming. She gripped his back. Checking tears, Clara kept her face towards the dance floor so the wind didn't steal her breath. The dance floor was now empty, save for Clara and the knight.

Sawyer raised his voice so Clara could hear him above the loud bursts of wind. "This wind… It's strategic."

Clara kept her face tucked. "What?"

"The wind is… it's pushing everyone… everything away from… you… including… me." He coughed when the wind slapped his face.

"No. That isn't possible. Please… no!" Clara cried. Her body shook, loosening her grip. She scrambled to regain her composure. "I'm scared. I can't die now. Lec…tus.." A renewed push of energy filled her when a haunting screech ripped through the breeze. "What was that?"

"Clara, listen," Sawyer pleaded to the waxed floor. He pulled her closer, arms shaking. "This isn't going as planned, but don't… don't worry. I promise you'll be okay."

"What do you mean? Just have a mage stop… ugh… the wind."

"If we… separate… I'll… I'll find you. Like—" he coughed, catching his breath between squalls of wind. "Like we said."

"No," Clara gagged back the great sobs threatening to escape. A large shadow cut through the starlight and loomed above the festival. Screams muffled the air. Her arms burned and were bruised from the pressure of holding on. She now understood. The wind, the haunting cry—the beast was after her. Energy fading, they slipped from arms to hands. Their clasp broke when the wind swept strongly under Sawyer, twisting him to his back. Clara screamed as a large, dark beast swooped down, breaking the dance floor between her and the knight. The impact tossed her to her feet. Wind trapped her in the midst of swirling debris until the dark beast snatched her legs. She dangled upside down while hurtling into the sky. Sawyer was blown off the dance floor into a pile of rubble.

Clara's heart pounded in her ears. The voices below were faint. She shut her eyes, holding her breath so she didn't have to slowly see the festival disappear. A cry spewed from her gut as she pulled in panic, trying to free herself. Eyes open, she stopped fighting the pull. A tight cord from below rubbed her shin and constricted her circulation. Wrapping her leg, a tight yank pulled her towards the earth. It was then that she got a good look at the beast pursuing her. Her face paled.

It was ginormous. Dark wings pushed against the sky in smoke-like flaps. The creature bit the cord with force. It snapped from her leg, separating her from the ground below. Frozen in air, she became light-headed. Thick claws wrapped around her in a scaly cage. Trapped within the sharp grasp, she shivered and gasped to stay coherent.

The strength of the creature mocked her each time the wings pumped. Every swoosh took her higher, wrenching her stomach like a ruthless rollercoaster. There was nothing she could do to stop it. Her tears ceased when all sight of the festival was gone. No one would hear her now. Her stomach dropped like lead weights. Time slowed. She closed her eyes, and her life flashed before her as if she were a bystander.

The room was silent as the author read a section of her book. It was Clara's favorite chapter. Angel munched on avocado toast and leaned over to Clara. Angel whispered, "Nothing against your author, but I think you could write something better. I mean, really. You have so many stories just waiting to come out."

"Shhh, I love this part," Clara hushed.

The author read on, "It was then that she found her sweet, sweet, freedom. It was always with her, but only found in doing the things that scared her the most."

Clara flashed her eyes open. *This bird… it's taking me to Lectus.* Her senses stabilized. She forced herself to move. The treetops were far below. Falling would certainly kill her. *If I have any powers at all, I have to trust myself enough to fall.*

She wiggled. She thrashed. She pried at the scaly claws. Her face scratched against the rough feet as she pushed her head through the space between its toes. Scales tore at her dress and skin. Pushing her head back through, she rubbed the blood dripping down her temples. Pressing her feet against the beast's palm, she pushed and kicked. Her spine stiffened when the creature cawed hauntingly. Survival kicked in. She had to fight.

Grabbing a tough scale from the spiked foot, she pulled.

Yanking and bending, it ripped off, leaving exposed soft skin. Slick, jagged, and sharp, it would be her weapon. She stabbed it in the fresh wound. Blood squirted into her face. Spitting it out, it left behind a metallic taste. She yanked another scale, which was easier to loosen than the last. She pulled another, then another. Each time, digging and stabbing into the sores. Pull, yank, stab. Pull, yank, stab.

More and more of the creature's tender skin was torn apart. More and more, the damage from her stabs oozed and sprayed red. The creature's grip was failing. She forced herself through the wounded toes. Her decision became too real as her dress caught on a jagged scale.

Flailing, she swung without control. Bile burned her throat. The bird shrieked into the night air, but the sound that scared her most was the ripping of her dress.

CHAPTER 21
Banshee

CLARA

IT WOULDN'T HAVE BEEN the first time Clara had seen some progression in life only to find herself back where she started. Spitting out a greasy lump, her senses were harassed by a familiar putrid smell. A rush of thankfulness overcame her. She had somehow landed safely. A sour clump of mud slid down her throat. She dry heaved and gagged dramatically. "You've got to be kidding me. Nothing surprises me anymore. Nothing!" Her frustration increased the more the pungent waft of the swamp gurgled. "I'm… I'm back at Giant's Pass." She thrashed her arms in an attempt to expel the rising anger. Thick bubbles popped while she smacked the mud in rage. The motion didn't help release her ire, but it did cause a stir.

Offended by the beating, the mud grew thin beneath her. She slid off a messy lump with a huff of her own and a moan from another. The deep groan grew louder as the swamp suctioned to release something previously hidden. Something slapped her on the back with surprising force, but it wouldn't be the crusted clump of mud she called her hair. Looking up, mouth agape, she forgot about the sour taste in her mouth. In this moment, nothing else mattered but escaping. The large form lumbered to its feet. Thick globs of mud plopped around him. Wiping off his face, he smiled with thick green teeth.

"It's a giant!" Clara screamed shrilly as she scrambled around, sliding but going nowhere. She scraped and clawed for stability until a hard substance under her hand provided the momentum needed to pry herself forward.

"Ahh, you wake giant," came a booming voice. He frowned. The giant shook tremendously, releasing the remaining blanket of mud. Swamp flung through the air, covering unsuspecting trees and splattering the ground. With his shake, he made sounds that Clara couldn't decipher.

Battle cries. There are probably more. More hags, too. More giants and witches and hags. I wonder what it's going to feel like if I die? Maybe it only means I'd wake from this terrible nightmare. Clara, despite her frozen body, had enough imagination to keep her overthinking fueled.

The giant finished his ruthless dance. He'd accomplished what he needed. His prey was petrified. Good for him. An easy chase. He salivated with victory. The snack would give him the energy to ransack the local town. Roaring again, he would pluck her from the swamp, just like a wilted flower, and bite her head off, spitting only enough to discard her hair from his tongue.

She tried to cry, but only mumbled noises were heard—if they were even hers. The giant stared, but did nothing. If she didn't run, her life would end where it started. Her friends would carry on with life, destroy Lectus without her, and she'd be nothing more than a useless pawn in this story.

"Why you wake me? It's rude. Now I hungry," pouted the giant.

"I'm sorry. I didn't mean to. I mean, I…" The giant put his hands on his hips before bending towards her, but she didn't wait around to know what exactly he thought of eating. She did, however, have the sudden urge to move from her paralyzed state. Rushing to the bank, she frantically climbed the ridge at the swamp's edge. She scrambled a quarter way up when something entangled her leg.

"Let me go," she pleaded, but further investigation showed that it wasn't the giant holding her back.

It was herself.

Looking at her leg, her overly friendly face peered back. "My badge…" Nostalgia took her, but only for a second. Untangling the badge, she tossed it away, distracting the giant. "Here, look. This… this is a… um… gift. Take it. It's all yours."

Heated and greasy, Clara rushed from the swamp, leaving the confused giant with her image. Running against the drying mud, she checked to see if she were pursued. Instead of a chase, he was looking coyly at her badge, smiling oddly. She sighed, thankful for the success. Perhaps she wouldn't be eaten today. At least, not right now.

"I didn't say hi," the giant frowned, badge held close to his eyes. "Cla, Clar, Clara. Clara left me a smile. I like smiles. I have smiles too." The giant grinned back at the badge. "My friend, Clara, she ran away."

"*Riding along, the ladies will lead. An assortment of goods, count me to bring.* Ha, good little ditty there, ladies," the man said to his horses. Ears turned back, the mares listened to their master's song. "*Another day out, roaming the land, selling fabrics, soaps, pots and some pans. A monster part, for an inquiring witch. A needle, a thread for a lady who's rich. My spices are valued by cooks all around, and my voice will be the envy of bards.*"

The off-key song pierced the air, disrupting wildlife as the peculiar man beat two pots together in rhythm. Standing on the wagon seat. Both arms waving, he banged the pans harder.

Clara purposely ignored his call.

"Hello there. Hello, my friend," the man shouted. Leaving the pans on the seat, he removed his floppy hat and waved it excessively.

Clara stopped, and the wagon clopped closer. She was barefoot, dirty, and covered in scratches.

The man whistled low when he saw her. "Barefoot banshee, you're looking snappy today. Much like a visualization of a grand adventure!" Clara purposely diverted his invitation to chat. The man didn't give up. "Come. Come now, take a look through my wares. No doubt you'll find anything you might need. Herbs, tonics, hmmm." He loosened the sheet from the wagon's hood fastened behind him. "I believe I might even have a useful giant foot or bat tongue." He whipped out a dried, shrunken foot in victory.

The foot was disgusting. Thick, split toenails protruded from spread, dry, hairy toes. Head swimming, she wanted to puke. Last night had been a nightmare. After finding a stream to wash some of the grime away, she was unable to locate food or clean water. Her stomach growled, and she was dying of thirst. Feet slapping the ground, her matted hair crusted on her shoulders, causing an annoying crunching sound as she walked. A small stab of hope sparked, but she wouldn't be so lucky. He probably wasn't going to help her. Chances are, he was going to rob her, or dismember her, just like that hideous foot.

I'm sure, by now, the word's out I'm gone. Although I have no idea how they transmit news here. If he knows, he's going to see me as a way to gain reward. Maybe torture me to ensure I don't run away. Don't look at him so he'll leave you alone. Just keep looking down. Watching the dirt, she moved forward. Feeling the sting of tears, she exhaled a larger-than-expected sob. She walked. She wailed. She wiped copious amounts of snot from her tears. Tired, hungry, and barefoot, she wanted nothing more than to rid herself of the man selling body parts. More so, she wished to rid herself of ever jumping into a ray of light.

The man leaned across the edge of his wagon, bending around to watch her walk past. "Banshee, if you knew what I had for sale, surely you would stop." Clara walked by his wagon without acknowledgement. The man slapped his hat back on. "Oh!" he exclaimed as he hopped off the wagon once his body could not bend further. The horses pulled the wagon to the edge of the path for a quick snack of grass. "Banshee, friend," the man called. "If it isn't a foot you need, I have an endless supply of daggers and machetes. Sharp too. One swipe will sever a head quickly and with little effort."

Great, he has a wondrous supply of sharp, deadly weapons. She picked up her pace, lifting the hem of her dress. His steps pounded behind her, and she mustered all her strength to run. The man did the same.

"Help. Help!" Clara yelled. The man rushed in front of her. Once a little way ahead, he twirled around in the most spectacular spin to face her. Skipping backwards, he sang. *"The banshee ran away in fear. She cried, she yelled, her voice I hear. Her tears, albeit, she did not blot the ever-flowing loads of snot."*

Clara stopped. "What?"

"Nice to meet you. Snot and all. My name is Charlie, I'm a peddler, the best around! Charlie Bales. You can call me Char. Isn't that fun to say? Like a fire smoldering. I enjoy it myself. Now tell me, Banshee, what's your name? It doesn't have to be your given name; whatever you want me to call you is fine. You can even make it up."

"I'm not a banshee." Clara started walking, with Char continuing to walk backwards.

"What are you then?"

"Nothing. That's what I am. Nothing… but lost. That's what."

"Woowee, nothing is the best. A day of nothing, a week of nothing. But a person of nothing, I've not heard of. You'd be the first. If it's anything like the other nothings, you must be extraordinary."

Clara stopped. The man's eyes were large without a hint of ill intent. "Char, I give up. I'm in trouble, actually, like, really really lost and in trouble… and my name is Clara."

"Isn't it wonderful!"

"What is?"

"Being lost, Clara. It's my favorite. I'm lost right now."

"Wonderful."

"I know! Let's be lost together. The only thing better than being lost alone is being lost with someone else. Ladies!" Char whistled. The two horses hitched to his wagon ceased their munching. Lazily, they strolled toward the peddler. "The ladies here, they travel with me. Thimble and Beet." Char motioned to his horses before he swooped into his seat. "Come, Banshee Clara, sit next to me." Clara gingerly followed his request.

Searching the wagon, he began to rummage through his stash, careful to hide any body parts, seeming to realize she was sensitive about them. He returned with two bent tin cups and a clean linen hankie. Pouring liquid into each cup, he offered one to Clara. He then handed over the hankie.

"Sorry, I didn't have anything to wipe my nose on. I wasn't expecting to be lost. I don't have any money though."

"Good thing, too, because there's no charge. Now, let's celebrate! *Cheer, cheer. Banshee and peddler! To being lost. To nothings. To Thimble and Beet. We'll travel the road, the ladies will lead! We'll sing. We'll laugh. Have fun, indeed!*" Char's smile went crooked. "Banshee, that wasn't my best song, but… the sentiment. It's exciting, entrancing, and I love them. Now, you go."

"Me?"

Char motioned towards his horses. "Thimble and Beet keep their songs to themselves. Unfortunately, we'll need to skip them this time around."

"Oh. Um…" Clara thought but no unique songs came to mind. Remembering a popular tune from America, she sang it. After finishing the song, she turned to Char. Both hands were smashing his hat against his face."

Woowee! You're good at this."

"I guess I am," she said, taking credit. Since no one here would ever know, there were many songs she could own. Too bad she couldn't sing.

"Again," Char propped his feet onto the bar that separated the seat from the hitch. Clara sang another, this time just a chorus. It was widely out of tune, but that didn't dampen the peddler's amusement.

"Woowee. Today has turned out to be an exemplary day for songs!" The peddler threw his hat up in the air and caught it. Smiling broadly, he let the reins drop before slapping his hat back on. "All this excitement tired me out. The ladies will decide where we go. Lean back, put your feet up and let's relax."

Clara laughed. "You're crazy. I guess the stars were looking out for me by placing you in my path. I'm glad I found you."

"Me too, Banshee. Me too." He leaned back into his seat, shifting the braided cushion under him and placing it behind his head. "Finding me was one of the best times. Finding you, a close second."

She watched a warm grin lift on the peddler's lips. The wrinkles around his mouth showcased how much he smiled. "Char, what did you do before becoming a peddler?"

"Those days have faded. It's all mere recollections of another time. I tend to enjoy the way I am now. No point in reliving anything else."

Clara folded her hands, unsure where else to go with the conversation. Char seemed to be devoid of additional words, though his grin never faded. Springing into life, Clara jumped from Char's sudden movement. "Clara, life is incredible! What's your favorite part?"

"Well, I'd say… I mean, I guess it's the ones I love… the people I care about."

"Tell me who."

"Back… um, home, I have a best friend. Her name is Angel. We did all sorts of fun things."

"Like what?"

"Well…" Clara drifted back in time while telling her story.

Child Clara, full of life, raced the group of friends to the top of the rock. "I bet you won't jump!"

Angel, huffing from trying to keep up, was second in line. "Clara, I didn't bring a suit to jump in."

"And?"

"I don't want to get wet. I just got this shirt, and I don't want to ruin it."

"It gets wet every time you wash it," Clara replied, waving her hand dismissively with a dramatic eye roll.

"Clara," came the voice from another child, "my mom will be mad if I come home all dirty and yucky."

"Then don't do it. I'm just saying that I'm not missing out and neither should you."

She looked at the edge of the rock. Lifting her arms over her head, she bent slightly forward. On her tiptoes, she rocked, flirting with the edge. She imagined becoming a mermaid once she hit the water. Then, all her friends would be amazed and wonder how she had kept the secret for so long. It would be amazing.

The rock was a common swimming spot many would jump from, but none of her friends, herself included, had succeeded with the plunge. "I heard there's sharks in the lake," cried Penny. Her pigtails swung as she shook her head.

Hands on hips, Angel groaned. "Penny, it's a lake. There aren't any sharks."

Penny sneered back, "You never know. I'm just saying. I heard on the news…"

Ignoring the voices behind her, Clara looked over the edge, teetering on the balls of her feet. Her heart leaped into her throat. She felt the fear, but liked it…

"And did you jump?" Char leaned in close, his smile gone but the fine lines remained.

"No, I didn't."

"But why not?" He swished his hat on his head and tugged at the brim.

"I listened to my friends."

"But what about your voice?"

"Huh? What about it?"

"Why didn't you listen to that? What a fun adventure that would've been! Right now, you could've told a different story."

"I don't know, but there isn't anything I can do about it now."

"Well spoken, Banshee! Next time, you jump. It's really that simple."

"We'll see." *Nothing is ever that simple.*

Char stood on the wagon seat and threw his arms up, stretching into the sky. "There's nothing to tell if you don't jump. It will just be the same story. So, next time you jump." His smile returned to its creases. He offered a hand to Clara, "Banshee, join me!"

Clara laughed as he jostled around, his thin legs keeping balance as the road bumped him around. If he could stand, why couldn't she? Gathering her wits, she carefully stood. The wagon felt unsteady beneath her. *I'm going to fall and break my leg. If that happens, how in the world will I get help? It's not like I can take out my phone and call 911. I'd have to travel, who knows how far, until we found help. Even then, what can they do without a healer?*

Char stretched his arms up higher, waiting. "Next time you jump!" he said again, this time louder.

Finding her balance, she shot her hands up. The wagon bumped, and she caught the side of the tent but steadied herself. Reaching to the sky, she lifted her head and shouted. "Next time I jump!"

"Together," Char cheered. He grabbed her hand. After they scrambled to stabilize each other, they shouted, "Next time, jump!"

The laughter continued as they returned to sitting. The excitement refreshed Clara. They peacefully chatted about stories and songs. As the sun set, Char pointed to the horizon. "Look, do you see that?"

"See what?"

"A group of healers. Right there! Camped." Char guided the horses to the edge of the path, exposing a small clearing in the woods beside the dusty road. The cluster of healers were only a mere ten feet away. He swung himself around the side of the seat and balanced on the wagon's iron step used to climb aboard.

"Healers? Do they typically travel? How can you tell they're healers?" Clara asked.

"You can tell by their hair. All white." The peddler waved with gusto. Clara shyly did the same.

"Healers, friends. Your luck is of the best kind. I just so happen to have an assortment of goods. It's just what you need."

"Thank you for the offer. We could use some replenishment. We'll look through your wares," said a healer who looked to be their leader.

Clara's mouth went dry. All the healers, just like Eleanor, were beautiful and seemed full of confidence and gentle self-respect. She felt small in their presence, but the smallness felt safe. Char already disappeared to pull out bits and bobs from his tent. He didn't seem to have any insecurity around the healers.

"Hi, I'm Clara." The healers, some seated, some standing, stared without introduction.

The lead healer who spoke walked toward her. "Clara, welcome to our camp. They call me Silas. Do you typically travel with the peddler, or did he find you on the road?"

"Not till today. I mean, I was on the road by myself, but I've been traveling with him since he picked me up."

"I see. What can you tell me about the circlet on your forehead?"

"I have yet to see it myself. I don't know anything about it." Instinctively, she reached for her brow.

The atmosphere darkened. Clara was in the woods, alone. The smell of cedar and moss was thick. The wetness intensified the smell. She searched recklessly, but for what? "How did I get here?" Her heartbeat quickened as panic squeezed her chest. Her breathing shallowed.

A figure watched her, pointing.

"Your name." The hazy phantom breathed in shallow spurts. Her hair, shielding her eyes, tossed back and forth. Clara sucked in a breath. "No, I'm not telling you my name." Her brow burned into her forehead, but it did nothing to protect her. She would always be a nobody. She could help no one, not even herself. Her legs grew tired. Her mind wearied. Her hair covered her entire face, and she felt as if she were shrinking. Tears streamed down as she gasped for life. The phantom's eyes lit up when she saw Clara masked in sorrow.

"I need your name. Tell me... your name!"

Clara jumped from her blankets.

"Woowee, where've you been?" Char asked as he crouched inches from her face.

Struggling to stand, she felt a strong hand support her back. It was Silas. "You had a vision." His clear gray eyes displayed uncertainty.

"I don't know. I don't know what I saw." Char's arms circled her, hugging her tightly. Her throat ached from holding back the tears.

Another healer, a woman, approached, taking Clara's hand. "Dear one, take comfort. You're now safe."

Silas helped Clara to her feet after Char reluctantly released his embrace. Clara placed a hand on her brow, "I felt something. A presence. I can't see the spot on my brow that everyone talks about, but I sensed it. I felt it deeply."

A different healer, who had not introduced themselves, nodded supportively. Silas guided Clara to the campfire with a hand on her shoulder. "Sit, tarry here tonight. You're in no danger here. Your friend is welcome as well." A holy silence stilled the air, giving her peace.

Char broke it with a whistle. "Now, let me show you what I've got. It's the best around!"

That night she dreamed a castle towered above her. Thorns and thick vines riddled the hill on which it sat. The castle, without windows, towered menacingly before a dense wood. Her friends were not here. She stood alone.

The woods, thick with brush, smelled damp and moldy. She'd smelled it before somewhere, but couldn't remember where. She walked, each tree looking like the last. Three colors existed in this place. Green, brown, gray. There were no flowers, as nothing of color would bloom, and no clouds wandered the sky. Dense woods obstructed her view, making it difficult to find direction. She would walk, but go nowhere. Tripping over a root, she fell into the rotting earth. Mud smeared her knees and elbows. She tried to rise. Nothing held her down, yet she couldn't move. A dark, cloaked figure towered over her, his body casting a multitude of shadows. The shadows joined in, "Tell us your name." Panicked, she pulled at brown twigs, trying to stand. "Tell us your name," the shadows repeated, but she couldn't remember.

Clara screamed as she grasped the dead twigs, now loose from their plant. "What's my name?"

Clara woke with a gasp, "Clara! My name is Clara!" Her heart pounded, but settled after seeing Char, squinty-eyed and grinning from a bowl of porridge. He carried his half-eaten bowl and a freshly made one to her bed.

"Nice to meet you, Clara." He stuck out a hand that Clara slapped away.

"Did I say that aloud?"

"And what a memory that is! The very best. Now, grab yourself some food. Our new friends left you a bowl. Isn't that grand?" Sitting up, she accepted the nourishment.

Silas approached with the other healers behind him. They all rode white stallions. "Take care, my friend. Travel safely, to wherever you're headed. Most importantly, remember who you are."

Huh? Why would he say that? Clara dismissed the thought. "Thank you. Thank all of you."

CHAPTER 22
Caffè Americano

Clara

THE HORSES WALKED AWAY from the camp, hooves clopping. The days passed. Spurts of conversation, all full of curiosity and adventure, were had sitting on the bench seat of Char's wagon. Char loved dwelling on life and all it had to offer. He also enjoyed reliving their newly shared experiences and pondering all the ones ahead. Amidst his ramble, he pointed a finger, as if part of their normal exchange. "Look, bandits."

"Bandits? For real? What do we do? We need to hide. How do we…?"

"Welcome, friends," Char said, waving openly with no attempt to hide or ignore the riffraff. A scraggly rider rode to greet them. Four others were behind him, all equally as scruffy. "What do you 'ave 'ere, peddler?"

"Only the best around," Char proudly announced. Clara slapped a palm over her mouth. Surely they were after "the best around."

"Stop yer horses, peddler," sneered a bandit. The ladies halted from the gentle pressure on their reins. Clara discreetly reached for the machete Char had given her days ago. He reasoned it'd come in handy since everything seemed to frighten her. She kept it hidden in the wagon bed behind her seat, within easy reach. She grabbed the handle.

"I'll take a gander at yer trash, peddler," the bandit said.

Char was unaffected by the pressure. Retrieving his displays, he showed some potions as if at a local country fair. "This one here, I tell you, it's the best. Mark my words, your beard will feel as smooth as a dove." He smiled as he picked up another bottle. "Oh, yes, yes, yes, this one… I know you'll love it. This salve can heal some of those scabs you have there, on your arms. Smooth as baby skin. A healer bless—"

"Enough. I'll look meself." The bandit dismounted, as did his posse. Strutting toward Char, he grabbed him by the collar, slamming him to the earth. He ransacked the wagon.

Char casually rose from the dusty gravel and dusted himself off. "It's all good, and worth the money spent," his voice held less enthusiasm.

"I ain't be spending any money on yer junk."

The wagon shifted as the bandit entered the covered bed to search deeper. Keeping the machete behind her back, she flinched when another bandit climbed onto the seat beside her.

"You ain't going anywheres."

"No, of course. I… I…"

"What's ya got behind yer back?" The bandit leaned closer. So close Clara could smell his foul breath. "Whatcha hidin' from me?"

Sweat formed on her forehead. *What do I do? Do I use the knife or run? What if I use the knife and hurt him unnecessarily?* A face popped into her mind. Sawyer's. *Negotiate.*

"We are mere, poor travelers, s-sir. Nothing but the basic stuff, you know. Were you looking for something in particular? I'm sure we can help you f-find it."

"Garber will do the lookin'." His eyes rested on her brow, confused.

My brow… Confidence strengthened her courage; she could embody her higher self. "I'd tell Garber to find somewhere else to loot. Behind my back is a machete, but it's the last thing I'd worry about, if I were you." Her heart pounded. She prayed he didn't notice the quiver in her voice. "Now, I'm sure we can strike a deal for you to leave us alone. Before things get crazy."

The bandit paused before calling his leader, eyes never leaving her brow. "Garber! Git over 'ere!"

"What ya yammering about, Henry?"

"This 'ere woman wants to bargain. Us leaving and such."

"I'm no mere woman, Garber," Clara announced, "Do you see this mark on my brow? I'm a banshee! One wrong move, and I'll pulverize all of you." All five bandits gathered. Char took advantage of the distraction to quietly and quickly return items to the wagon. He purposely left one vial in his hand, hidden in his clenched fist.

Clara stood on her seat, legs wide and machete lifted. "My name is Clara Rivers. I'm from America. Leave now or forever hold your peace. I will smite you into ash and sprinkle your remains into coffee using my dark brewing power of Caffè Americano with an extra shot of espresso!"

"Whaddahs she mean, Garber?" asked one of the bandits.

"She's tricking us. See how 'er legs be shaking? No banshee would tremble at the sight of bandits," Garber replied, weapon raised. "I'll take me chances," Garber stated before grabbing Clara's leg to pull her off the wagon. Falling onto the seat, Clara grasped the iron hand railing while holding the machete away from her head. Before her leg could be tugged further, a cloud of smoke filled the air, causing immense coughing and gagging.

"Banshee, let's go." Char regained his seat. The ladies needed no command to gallop. Bumping along the path, the bandits weren't far behind.

Char beamed at Clara, eyes bright. "Woowee! You are brave."

"I'm not brave, I did what I had to so we'd survive. And don't thank me yet. I didn't even use the machete. I… I don't know if I can bring myself to hurt anyone with it, and the bandits are close behind us. All I did was buy us time."

"The most precious resource there is."

"They're closing in. Maybe less talk and more going faster,"

Clara said, panic in her voice as her arms moved to show the increase of speed she referred to.

"We don't worry. If they catch us, we decide what to do then."

The highly agitated bandits circled the wagon till it slowed. Garber held his thin, rusty sword above his head and charged. His ragged blade sliced Charlie's arm once the wagon stopped.

"Stop," Clara cried as she grabbed her friend. Blood trickled down his arm. She hastily jumped from the wagon with unexpected rage. Her heels hit the earth first, causing pain to shoot up her legs. The pain contorted her face and increased her anger. The brand on her forehead shone.

"She's gonna sprinkle us into coffee with her dark Americano power! Garber, you was wrong. She be a right-real banshee!" cried a bandit when he saw her brow beaming brightly.

"Imma gettin' outta here. Ain't werth the trouble." Garber galloped wildly away from the wagon. His posse followed, leaving a cloud of dust.

"Woowee, what an adventure that was. You saved us, Banshee." Char tossed his hat into the air and caught it.

"Your arm." She wiped his wound against her sleeve. "Oh good. Whew, it's not too bad, thankfully."

"Clara, you saved the ladies, me, and my wagon. You should have seen you!"

"Char, what exactly did you see? I mean, when the bandits ran away."

"The most beautiful confidence. Nothing more beautiful than that, you know."

I can't believe this. We almost died. They cut Char. How much longer is this charade going to continue before someone really gets hurt? But then she remembered she scared the bandits, and this wasn't a game. This was real life, and she was brave.

Char slid back in his seat. A clean linen strip of fabric covered the cut that bled moderately. "All that adventure deserves a proper nap." Char pulled his hat over his eyes and quickly drifted off. Clara leaned into the tightly secured curtain behind her. Feeling tired and happy to have done something useful, she fell asleep. Things might be looking up after all, but it was hard to believe otherwise with the peddler around.

The ladies clopped on, never really knowing where they're going, but always happy to make the decision. Walking without direction, they reached a town called Gohmer. There, they parked themselves at a nearby post, waiting for their master and the barefooted banshee to wake.

CLARA JUMPED at the sound of clashing. The peddler was out of his seat and making a ruckus loud enough to wake the dead. He tactfully showcased some pans to a townswoman. "Glenda, these are the best quality. Made with top-quality iron. You'll find no better elsewhere. They'll last for years. Trust me, your great-granddaughter will use these with her great-great-grandchildren."

The innkeeper owner, head tilted, wiped away a wispy hair greased to the side of her face. "How much?"

"Ten coin, that's it. No better deal you'll find, near or far."

"Five."

"Oh, Glenda. Five is just not right. It simply can't be five. But seven. Seven is the best number out there. It must be seven."

"Seven, then you shut yer mouth. It 'etter be good or the next time ya come, I'll hit ya with it."

Char smiled wryly, his right eye twitching. "Glenda, no need to be a bore. You'll love the pan. Everyone loves my stuff."

Clara stretched and climbed out of the wagon. Judging by the line of threadbare peasants and tireless negotiation skills, they'd be here for a bit. Walking into the inn, she met the very woman who bought the pan.

"Hi, I was wondering if you had a bath and maybe some clean clothes."

"It'll be two coin fer the bath. As fer clothes, ask the peddler. Ain't no one 'round 'ere got anything extry."

"Thank you. Um… I don't have any money. Do you happen to have a small job or chore I could do?"

"Check that 'ere board." The woman pointed to the side of the room where a crude board was nailed.

Wood stacker, pay in kindling and wood for yer herth

Vermit hunter. Ratz and snake. Can pay with milk rations

Henry Forman is a fraud! Don't trusts him with yer stuff! He stole my cattle and me best gal!

Yikes! I guess no matter where you go, relationships are messy. She continued to search. *Are there any paying actual money?* Lifting a few notes to search behind them, one caught her eye.

In search of server. Must have all teeth and keep good appearance. Uniform provided and employmentship will be for one night only. Very prestigious company coming! – Mayor Hans Gribble

She pulled the note from the board. One evening with a mayor couldn't be all that bad. It was worth a shot. Turning to the lady at the counter, she asked, "Where can I find Mayor Gribble?"

CHAPTER 23

A Healer's Warning

SAWYER

SAWYER PRIED off a cracked board pinning his leg against the tree. Brushing off, he appeared unharmed, at least physically. Jade rushed to his side, panting her words from being out of breath, "Clara…"

Sawyer shook his head. "The bird… the wind. I couldn't stop it. I couldn't…"

"No time for regret. We need to find the others." She grabbed Sawyer's arm, pulling him from the rubble and into the crazy mass of confused and crying people.

"Rory, hold his head," Eleanor cautioned as she bent over an elderly man. His leg snapped; the bone protruded sharply from his shin. Closing her eyes, she chanted. Rory soothed the man by stroking his head, as there were no pain-reducing tinctures to ease his discomfort while relocating. It was the price paid. The injured must trade pain for healing.

"Rory, Eleanor!" Jade shouted.

Noticing the healing, they were careful not to disturb Eleanor. Once the old man's skin was tightly sealed, they approached. "Eleanor, let the other healers finish up. We need to regroup,"

Sawyer commanded. The healer caressed the old man's cheek. He smiled weakly as she rose gently from the ground.

"Sawyer, is Clara going to be okay? I saw the monster bird fly off with her," Rory said, eyes wild and open-wide.

"We'll do our best to save her," Sawyer reassured.

The four looked for the others. Jasper spotted them first. He was wearing most of the food he had for sale from his stand. "What a surprise that was." His voice prompted the others to turn around.

Rory furrowed his brow. "Jasper. Did you see the bird? It was so big! How are we going to fight it? How do we know where it went?"

The cook squeezed the boy's shoulder. "Leave that to the fighters. We'll do all we can to support the effort."

Jasper yanked Onyx from a mound of junk. During his retrieval, however, Onyx managed to grab a curious piece of metal from the pile of wreckage. He met the others after seeing them. Sawyer, taking the lead, faced his friends. "I'll find the king. We'll need to have an emergency round table, if he's open to it. Meet me in the debriefing room in ten."

Moments later, he found the king on the balcony overlooking the festival remains. The royal's blank stare overlooked both wreckage and untouched festivities. The lights, once bright and cheerful, hung limp, twisted and broken among each other. Tables blown and broken lay in piles. Festival decorations were tangled and strewn across the courtyard. The farther from the dance floor, the less damage was taken. Some parts seemed unharmed, while others were demolished, and many were somewhere in between.

"King Henric," Sawyer bowed hastily, "We should—"

"Silence, knight. Why didn't you save her?" He pounded his fist on the balcony rail.

"Your Highness, I did everything within my power. I'm sure you saw the beast. That was no ordina—"

"Your duty is to protect and save. Do not mock me with empty excuses. Heed my words, Commander. If you don't find her…" A dash of black haze flashed across the king's eyes. "Unharmed, mind you! You'll no longer be welcome. Do whatever you need to, but do not speak to me until you find the girl. Leave my presence. Never have you disgraced Ancora more."

Heat filled Sawyer's heart, ears, and eyes. Breathing deeply from his chest, he departed from the estranged king, confused and heartbroken. Walking the shock off, he opened the door to the open table room to see his friends in a circle. Standing tall, he addressed the room. "King Henric won't be joining us. He is a bit out of sorts. I don't think we should wait till morning. The winged beast will be far gone by then, if not already. If we leave now, our chances of finding her increase."

Jasper put his hands on his hips. "The wagon can be ready in no time. Rory and I had it properly stocked this morning. We just need to grab the perishable items. Say the word, Sawyer, and I'll tack the donkeys."

Jade stood. "I'm ready, too. Just give me thirty minutes to gather my things."

"No better time than now," said Onyx, standing.

Eleanor crossed her legs. "Well, I'd need to gather my silks and toiletries, of course, but I suppose I can do that swiftly."

"No time to waste. Meet at the stables, ready to depart. We'll leave in an hour. If everyone can make it quicker, even better." Sawyer left, not looking back. Rushing from the castle, he surveyed the festival till he spotted Holly. Seeing each other simultaneously, she ran to hug him.

"Oh, our sweet Clara," Holly cried.

Annabelle, tightly hugging Dave's leg, wailed. Eyes red, she detached to grab Sawyer's arm. "The bird took Clara. It's so big. Sawyer," she pleaded, pulling at his pant leg. "You'll save her, right... right?"

"Of course, don't worry. If anyone can, it's me." He bent to hug her. "I'll be leaving in an hour, hopefully less. There's a few things I need to pack, but for the most part I'm ready. I wanted to say goodbye—at least for now."

"My dear boy," Holly cried, taking his face in her hands. "When you come back, I'll make a feast. We'll celebrate the victory and gather round the fire to hear the story." Holly hugged him tightly.

Planting a kiss on his cheek, she moved away long enough for Annabelle to hug him fiercely. Dave, not one to give out hugs all willy-nilly, embraced the knight before finishing off with a wordless, yet firm, handshake.

"I'll see you soon," Dave's voice cracked. "Love you, boy." With an emotional nod, Sawyer left.

Forty-five minutes later, the wagon set the pace. The donkeys, annoyed at being roused before morning, needed a snap or two of the reins to move their stubborn legs. Jade projected light at the front of the line from a crystal around her neck. Magic-infused crystals hung from the wagon and the brow strap of bridles to project light. Despite being together, loneliness weighed heavily on everyone. Nobody spoke.

Sitting next to Jasper, Rory turned to Sawyer, who was riding close to the wagon's side. His youthful voice broke the silence. "Where do you think the bird took Clara?"

"It's hard to say. It's possible she was carried directly to Lectus at the windowless castle."

"Maybe she got away. Maybe she's looking for us."

"Perhaps." Willow snorted, chewing on her bit. Sawyer patted her neck. "I think we should head to Eros. Perhaps they'll have the insight we need to find the windowless castle."

Tired from a lost night of sleep, the traveling group witnessed the sunrise. The colors were vibrant and reassuring. In the distance, a group of travelers gathered around a newly expired camp. A strong man, gray and weathered, approached them. Spotting the badges, he looked relieved.

"Commander. My name's Barney. We're from the city of Yorne."

Sawyer halted, followed by the rest of the party. "Barney, a pleasure. Sawyer Lydon. What brings you to the outskirts of Ancora? I don't think we've heard from any Yornites for some time."

"A sickness, Commander. Unlike anything we've witnessed. Our town is shrouded in thick fog. Many are unable to leave their beds. We've yet to find a tincture or healer able to help. We've been on the road for weeks, and Ancora is our closest ally, so we are headed there."

Eleanor deftly dismounted her white stallion. "I feel the hurt. You've brought them with you."

"Rightly so, wise healer. When we left, Jen and Marco were as healthy as me. Now, they are bedridden and ghastly gray. It seems you've come in time. Will you please help us? There's no one else."

"Yes, I'll go." Eleanor needed no direction to where the sick lay. Upon reaching them, the healer kneeled. Grabbing the hand of the limp woman, her thick lashes brushed against her cheeks when her eyes closed. She started her chant.

Barney looked instantly relieved. "Maven Healers are so hard to find these days. You should be thankful to have her. Yorne only has infirmary healers, to which we are thankful for."

"We have a small handful of healers at Ancora, but Eleanor is the only Maven. We feel lucky to have her a part of the kingdom."

Eleanor's chant abruptly stopped. The healer remained on her knees, unmoving, eyes closed. Her grasp on the woman's hand tightened till her knuckles became white. "What's wrong?" Barney asked, his hopeful expression fading.

The healer opened her eyes, her pupils missing. Her teeth clenched. Jade rushed to her side, jerking her from the trance. "Eleanor, are you okay? What did you see?"

"This sickness… it's stronger than my resolve to stop it. Thank you, Jade, for pulling me from the blackness that surely would have devoured me."

"But healer, what did you see? What do you mean by 'the blackness'?" Barney pleaded.

"I saw… I saw—it doesn't matter what I saw. I'm sorry, I won't be helping after all. I'm sure you understand." Eleanor gracefully rose to her feet.

Barney's plea escalated, "Miss Healer. Please, try. It's spreading fast. I believe it's only a matter of time before we're all consumed. Please, I beg you."

Eleanor turned her back to the man. Looking over her shoulder, a tear slid down her cheek. "Be strong for your friends." Mounting her bareback stallion, she cantered a distance away. There, she waited.

Sawyer stepped back. *Healers are intuitive beings. Eleanor is sending a warning.* "I apologize. To all of you. Barney, I'm afraid we cannot help you. At least not yet. Ancora is healthy, from what I know. If the sickness appears to be contagious, I ask you not to bring it there."

"Commander, is there any other way? What else can we do? Wait for our family and friends to die without hope?"

Sawyer's heart was burdened, but he couldn't take the risk. "I'm sorry we can't help."

"Ho!" Jasper interjected. "Before we part ways, take some rations." He was already out of the wagon, packing up a bag of supplies for the small group. "It's the least we can do."

Sawyer nodded his agreement, "I wish we could do more."

Barney took the resources. "Thank you. I understand. I just ask… pray to the stars for the lives of my friends and the future of yours."

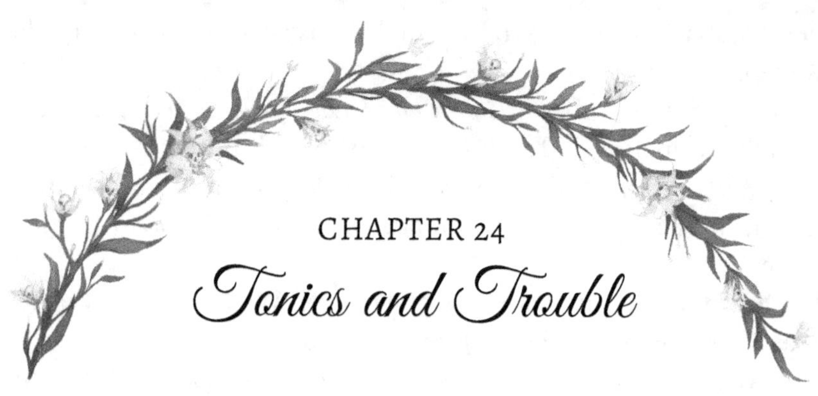

CHAPTER 24
Tonics and Trouble

ELEANOR

THE TEAM MOVED ON. There was no more talk of the curse, nor of the group left without help. Onyx, coasting on the Dragonmare, yawned and wiped his eyes. Night was closing in. "Hey guys, do you suppose we should retire for the night? I can't live off energy tonics anymore."

"I'd agree to that," an exhausted Jade seconded. "If I have to drink one more, I'm going to scream. An early night's rest would allow an early start come morning, and we'll be fully rested instead of the fabricated energy from the tonic. I'm grateful for them, but I wouldn't say they're refreshing."

"I think we should keep going," Sawyer urged. "We have plenty of tonic syrup."

Eleanor trotted her stallion to the front. The knight's aching heart was a painful motivator for him, this she was sure, but the idea of shaking up another mixed vial sickened her stomach. "I can't make another mile, and I refused to drink another oily tonic."

Sawyer softened his tone. "What if Clara's close by, and we miss her by that very mile?"

"I highly doubt that's a probability," Jasper said. "I need to eat a real meal, not convenience snacks."

"I see I'm outnumbered. I comply. Let's stop."

The team made camp, complete with a dinner that satisfied their hunger. The fire, mature and roaring, provided a welcoming heat and a cozy place to linger. Full bellies and tired heads lay on pillows. Many didn't wait for sunset to close their eyes. Eleanor refused to sleep on the ground around the fire like everyone else. In exchange for the makeshift beds crafted from camp blankets, she spread a fur rug across the wagon seats. There, she fluffed her pillow for a comfy night away from the suffocating fire and dusty ground.

Her pillow still smelled of rose water, but she knew after days of travel, it would reek of campfire and dust. Closing her eyes, she recalled the phantom in the woods during her chant. Somehow, it knew. Somehow it made her remember when...

Aesian turned the framed picture of Eleanor and himself face down. "I got word that Ancora needs you. They recently lost a healer. The counsel mentioned you. You'd be the perfect match."

"What do you mean? Ancora? Of course you don't agree to this."

"I think you should go."

"Surely you're joking. I... I live here, in Eros. Why would you want anything else?"

"You, me. Love, family. All nonsense. That's not in the stars for us. I think you should leave for Ancora as soon as possible. Start a family there, I know how much that would mean to you." His voice cracked slightly.

"No. I want to stay. Here, with you. Don't you see? How can you not feel this? Feel us? I know you love me. Aesian, all those memories. The lake... even these very candles in this room light up for us."

"Our plans... they mean nothing. Just a distraction from everyday stressors. I ne-never loved you, and I don't now."

"You don't mean that."

"I do."

Pain shadowed Aesian's eyes as he slowly set the picture upright. Wooden candlesticks held white candles, dimly glowing, around their framed image. The room was quiet. Nothing moved except the flames. Eleanor's eyes searched Aesian's. He must be teasing. "So you're saying..."

"Us." The fire in the hearth roared. It crackled with a romance that would not be fulfilled. "We'll never be, nor… will we ever be… together." In a flash of light, he was gone.

Even after all this time, the art of dematerializatin amazed her. Aesian was one of the few known to possess the capacity to vanish. Being a healer instead of a mage added even more excitement to the mix of bridged magic. A healer's heart was vulnerable to outside magics. Few healers in history have accomplished such a dangerous endeavor. It was more likely for mages to bridge the gap in the healing arts than the other way around. He was indeed gifted.

Mixing magic was a dangerous experiment. Some would try, only to find themself mangled—or worse. Magic didn't naturally mix well within a body, but Aesian was an exception to this rule. Due to this, he was revered by all who knew him. The sound of a nearby creek trickled, but the calming ambiance did nothing to ease the painful memory. The night Aesian left, she dismissed any hope that the life she desired would blossom. Instead, each day she felt more wilted.

SAWYER

Morning dawned in shades of red and pink. A giant thump followed by a loud wake up cry from Jasper woke the camp. Sawyer sprang from his bed, flinging his camp blankets behind him. The others stirred with weary faces that turned to astonishment as they saw a large giant smiling at the edge of their camp.

"Hi, friends," said the giant with an awkward wave.

"Hello, friend… What brings you to our camp?" Sawyer placed his hand on his sword. He knew little about giants, surprisingly enough, and had never seen one, till now. Usually they kept to themselves and, despite their large size, walked among men unnoticed. Some called it magic while others called it scarcity. Standing close to fourteen feet high, this giant was of average height, and no giant ever grew to more than seventeen and one-quarter feet.

"I smelled good bites."

Sawyer wasn't sure what giants ate, but he hoped it wouldn't be them. "Are you hungry?"

"I smelled meat."

Jasper cautiously offered the rest of the cauldron of deer stew to the giant. He could easily make something else in exchange for peace. Scooping up its contents with dirty fingers, the giant gobbled it down, not paying one notion to its heat. Ending with a glorious belch that could raise the hair of any witch, he put the cauldron down. Happy with his meal, he took a card-like paper attached to a ribbon from his pocket to swing it in full circles.

Jade prepared herself. "Giant, we're not looking for trouble. How can we help you?"

"Trouble? Trouble is bad. I no like trouble. Other giants not like me. But, I like Clara's smile. She ranned away. She's my friend."

A fresh energy rushed through Sawyer. "Who? Who did you say?"

"Clara," the giant replied, this time louder since he was not heard before.

"When did you meet Clara?"

"She came to my home to visit me."

Sawyer's eyes widened. "Where do you live?"

"The swamp. It's my home there. I left to find Clara, she gave me a smile. I like smiles. I want to give her one. I'm lost now," The giant's words dropped with heavy regret.

Of course she was there. "I've met her there myself," Sawyer said, recalling the lifeless, crusty lump. "I see you have a trinket. May I see it?" The giant looked hurt by the question. He held it to his heart.

"I promise I'll return it."

"I need to go home, but I'm afraid of… of hags and witches," his large bottom lip quivered.

"If you allow me, just once, to see what you have, we'll take you home and fight off any trouble along the way." The giant paused. With a shake of his head, he handed over the item.

Sawyer took the lanyard. Wiping the badge, he found it surprisingly durable and resistant to the traces of swamp. Behind the mud a familiar face looked back at him. It was Clara. Wearing a strange hat, she smiled wide, despite the sparkle lacking in her eyes. There was a crest of some sort beneath her name, but he wasn't familiar with it. "The Bean Queen" was inscribed at the top. A flood of emotions spilled into his heart. Hesitating to pry his eyes from her image, he addressed the giant. "We're looking for Clara, just as you. A beast took her and she needs our help."

"Clara needs help." The giant's eyes watered.

Jade, impatient with the conversation, said, "Giant, we need to find Clara, and fast. Let's just call it a plan since we're all looking for her. We'll take you back to the swamp, then we call it even."

"Even," the Giant said, happy with the arrangement. "Friends take me home." He patted his belly.

The camp packed up quickly. When the party was ready, the giant followed.

Giant's Pass. The reeking, bubbling, greasy mud pit. Oddly enough, Sawyer felt sudden nostalgia when the wafting smell of swamp greeted them. The giant was thrilled to have company and a safe trip home. As a reward, he allowed Sawyer to keep the badge, his gift of gratitude. Accepting the gift, Sawyer shook the large hand.

"Find Clara. Bring her home." The giant said seriously. His big eyes conveyed concern.

"That we will, good friend," Sawyer reassured.

Now safe from hags, witches, and all sorts of calamity that could surprise him, the giant covered himself with an ample layer of mud. The rest of the team opted out of seeing the giant off in the swamp and waited outside the banks. After watching the giant blanket himself, Sawyer took the opportunity to search the area. Willow didn't share the same nostalgia as her master. She halted. "Come on, girl." He nudged her forward. Ears back, she bobbed her head. Sawyer dismounted. Taking the reins, he didn't notice the swamp bubbling behind him.

The mud produced two double-lidded eyes. They blinked. A hungry swamp hopper watched the knight with interest. Her tongue, thick and long, spewed from her mouth, snatching the knight by the shoulder and pulling him into the mud.

Cursing from surprise and disgust, Sawyer splatted onto his back. Stinky swamp washed over his face as the massive tongue wrapped around his leg, dragging him through the mire. Switching from astounded disgust into battle mode, he composed himself. A clear head with quick thinking was needed. Negotiations were out of the picture. A swamp hopper would neither care what he had to say nor would it understand. She was hungry, and he was her target. For some beasts, it really was that simple.

She dragged him closer, pushing mounds of mud along the way. He shuffled to grab his sword against the push of the heavy mud. After many unsuccessful attempts, he failed to grasp his weapon from his side.

Swamp hoppers were as basic as a beast could get. But basic wasn't always easy, and easy wasn't always simple. That being said, they weren't that harmful if you encountered one in the field or on land. It was when they were at home, in a swamp or body of water, that tact was a top priority. This one, sporting bumpy light green and red spots, knew her advantage. She was in control. Her whip-like tongue could wrap, and that it did, to pull and trap anything—or anyone—small enough to fit. This was her turf, and he, according to her, was her dinner.

Sliding under the mud, she dragged him closer to her gaping, expectant mouth. Her eyes rolled around in expectation. Fighting would be a waste of energy. He had to let her win. The initial gulp wasn't as bad as he imagined, but once inside, it was a bit more cramped than expected. Warm and wet, it wasn't the most comfortable place to be. He had only just arrived, but the lack of fresh air told him he didn't have much time to visit.

His breathing was labored against the putrid, hot bile gagging him. Feeling his sword by his side, he wiggled to squish himself against her stomach wall. He hoped to create just enough space to grab his weapon. He wiggled and pushed. The swamp hopper jumped, sloshing him around. *What a fine mess this is,* he thought. He wiggled again, as did the swamp hopper jump. Each time she leapt, the knight rolled tightly around her stomach. Each time she moved, he squished against her stomach wall and splatted.

Closing his eyes against the bile that would surely burn, he fought for air, but the supply was running out. Praying to hold back his own bile from spewing, he bent his knees to his chest. With all the force he could muster in such a cramped space, he pushed his feet against her stomach wall, stretching from all limbs. Unfortunately, his effort didn't produce enough room to pull his sword from the sheath. Even if he had been successful, there wouldn't have been room to wield the sword safely.

It was then he remembered the magical rock Jade had infused. Squirming enough to reach into a pocket, the stone glimmered in the dark of the belly. Seeing the white light, he groaned at the decomposing animals left behind. Thanking the stars, and Jade, he sighed, close lipped, with relief and focused on the wind stone.

Eyes bulging, the creature had more than indigestion. Her belly filled with pressure. Her eyes strained and popped as she bloated. Shaking with tremors, the beast grew. Belching, she instantly felt better. Slapping her tongue at her newest victims, she only had a moment of relief before the bloating resumed. She bloated then belched. Eyes popped, her skin stretched. She expanded and contracted. Then, when she expanded again, she began to float.

Body enlarged, her legs were now nonexistent as her belly grew. She expelled air, but she couldn't belch enough to keep up with the bloat. Her skin could only grow so far, and, sadly, the bloat would exceed the belch. She combusted in an explosive blast. Bits and parts splattered the air. Amidst those in flight was a disgusting knight. Sawyer flopped into the mud close to the bank. Standing up, he shuffled through the knee-deep mud to meet the astonished spectators.

Onyx and Jade stood with expressions of astonishment and awe.

"Looks like you're having adventures without us," Onyx said.

Extra-thick strands of slime slid off Sawyer's hair. "Quite," Sawyer answered, followed by a forceful spew.

After much scrubbing and cursing from the nearby stream, Sawyer dried by the fire. "This slime is persistent and difficult to manage," he told Jade. "Especially from my hair. I couldn't get it out no matter how hard I scrubbed."

"You could always shave it off," Jade joked.

"Horrible idea. Remind me not to seek your advice for serious issues. Can't you use some magic to rid me from it?"

"Where's your respect? I'm not a barber. But okay. Good thing I like you. Let's try this." Jade sent a forceful wind, drying his hair. It stood on end, pleasing her immensely, but it worked to fling off any stubborn goop. "I think being wet was making it stick. Now that it's dry, I don't see any more slime." She raked her hands through his hair to check. "Yep, got it all. Just look at you, classy." She slapped her hands together. "Just another day on the job."

They both laughed until Jasper's voice bellowed. "Come and get it!"

Rory jumped from the log where he sat. Sawyer's armor, taken apart, was lying in two piles—one clean, one muddy. "Goodness, all this scrubbing has me starved!" the boy announced.

The group gathered in line to fill their plates. Smashed potatoes with herbs and field greens. The meat of choice: swamp hopper. Sawyer frowned at the sliced meat, then gagged. Amused, Onyx took a large bite. "Tastes like victory to me."

"Nothing better. But if you smelled it from the inside, you may think victory tastes like bile and rotted flesh." Sawyer reluctantly took a bite to find it delicately tender and full-bodied with flavor.

"Ah, see there? Not bad after all, is it?" Onyx teased.

"I'm surprised. I find it's typically not the taste but the memory that changes the outlook of the taste," Sawyer replied as he finished his plate.

While Jasper washed the dishes, an angelic song echoed from the woods. Eleanor jumped from the wagon. A group of healers were in the distance carrying golden lanterns. As the song drew closer, the lights got brighter.

"Healers, come. Tarry with us. Our cook has enough for all." Eleanor held out her arms. With grace, the healers dismounted their white steeds and joined the group. Each greeted her first before addressing the others. One of the healers, who looked to be the leader, said, "They call me Silas. With me, my friends and fellow healers, Fiona, Tranden, Caspian, and young Vada." As he pointed to each one, they bowed slightly with their hands pressed together.

Sawyer extended a handshake to Silas, which was reciprocated. "What brings you out of your homeland? It's not typical to find healers traveling without a strategic group."

"With our circumstances dire, we saw no other choice, yet I'm not able to discuss the nature of said circumstances. We've been on the road for some time and are quite weary."

Jasper banged on the pot that still contained steamy nourishment. "Ho, fine healers. Not another word. Come. Sit and eat. I'm sure you'll find my cooking more than satisfying. The meat is fresh from our knight, Sawyer's, efforts."

They graciously accepted the heavy plates and sat around the fire. The company waited for the healers to eat. Once finished, Sawyer retrieved the badge with Clara's picture. "Silas, during your travels, have you seen this woman?" He handed the lanyard over.

"Clara. I met her mere days ago. She was with a traveling peddler."

"A peddler?" Sawyer felt a spark of hope, but he calmed it quickly. She was alive.

"A peddler. They visited our camp about a day's ride from here. They had an assortment of goods, some of which we purchased. Why do you ask?" Silas kept his eyes on the picture, a confused look on his face. He slowly returned it.

"Was she okay? Can you describe the man she was with? We are searching for her and are worried."

"She seemed unharmed. The peddler had brown unkempt hair and I'd say middle-aged. In human years, of course. Nothing out of the ordinary, although he liked to talk and sing silly songs. We merely saw them a few hours before we retired for the night. They left promptly the next morning."

"I see. And Clara? Anything you can tell us would be useful."

"She was shy, but fell asleep rather quickly. Unfortunately, there wasn't much time to converse."

Sitting on the ground, crossed-legged and listening, was Vada.

She chirped in, "Char, I meant the peddler, mentioned they might end up at Gohmer. His ladies like to take him there when they're close by." She giggled, "He said there's a woman there who likes to give them treats. I think that was where they probably went. The ladies are his horses," the child recalled.

Silas addressed the young healer, "Vada, the peddler tends to ramble. I wouldn't count on his stories. Now, child, it's time we leave." Standing up, he nodded to Sawyer and briefly to the others. He made a respectful bow to Eleanor before mounting his stallion. "Thank you. Your kindness was water to our dry souls."

"Leaving so soon? You're welcome to camp with us for the night, if you choose," Jade offered.

"We can't reside for long. The world has been in disarray of late. Even now, I cannot be certain of the company I keep."

Sawyer nodded. "You can rest assured no harm will come to you from my companions or myself. You're safe with us. In any case, the best to you and your companions. Be vigilant on your journey. There seems to be a sickness overtaking many communities. We encountered a group the other day that was afflicted. Even Eleanor was not able to rid the disease."

Silas and Eleanor shared a knowing glance. "I'll take heed. Goodnight to you all." With that, the healers nudged their stallions onward and disappeared into the woods.

The next morning, the companions packed early. They traveled till late afternoon when they heard a roar from the sky. The monstrous bird circled in the sky, peering at the ground and swooping down periodically, unconcerned by the team. Flapping her wings unalarmed, she headed in the direction of Gohmer.

CHAPTER 25

A Familiar Voice

CLARA

CLARA CLIMBED the outrageous hill to the mayor's house. Glutes burning, she reached the weathered porch, panting. Stepping on a crunchy beetle, she wiped it from her bare foot into one of the many rotten floorboard cracks. The door opened promptly when she knocked.

"Jest one minute." A woman shuffled to the door. "What a mess ya are! I can't be 'aven you bringing that in."

"Um, sorry. My name is Clara. I'm here for the job posting. The one about the server. I promise I clean up well. I only need a bath, some clean clothes and shoes."

"Errrr, we 'ave one but you'll need to show yer teeth."

"Huh, ahhkay." Clara opened her mouth to display a full set.

"Oh good. Ain't missin' a one. It's important to the mayor for 'is servant to 'ave all teeth." She smiled, as if to prove a point. "The 'ath is right 'round the corner. Jest pump the spout, I'm sure ya know 'ow." The maid folded her hands as Clara turned in that direction. "Now, jest wait 'ere a minute. I 'ave yer uniform." She shut the door to open it a minute later, handing Clara a basket containing a neatly folded stack of clothing, a bar of soap, and towel. Taking it, she thanked the maid, who introduced herself as Henny.

Looking for the tub, she found a lonely feeding trough with a metal spigot upgrade. Pumping the handle, cold water filled the metal bin. Lowering into the icy water woke her mind. *I wonder what will happen to me if my friends don't find me. It's a big world with no viral way to spread information. The best-case scenario is getting cleaned up and a night's rest. Then what? Travel around with Char... or wait here in hopes of being found? Or. Or do I find a random job that pays less than The Bean Queen and live a new but even more miserable life?*

Another voice spoke in her mind. One she'd heard before, but pushed away unconsciously. *But what if the stories you tell yourself aren't true? What if everything works out? Remember the woman you dream about? What if you lived as her?*

She grumbled as she washed, twice. Once to rid herself from the grime, and another to rid herself of any ideas of what might happen. Whether it be America or here, she was still the same 'ole Clara. Dry and clean, the cold water sparked a fresh energy that livened her steps. She once again knocked on the door.

Henny nodded in approval but wrinkled her nose at her brow. "Oh, that won't do. No, no... but I jest don't 'ave any other options this 'ere time. Come inside." The house showcased a clean but unfashionably rugged interior. A dried monster head was proudly displayed on a stand. Seeing the cross-eyed beauty rotting on the peg made her gag. To the left was an odd-looking bowl filled with candy, and to the right, fresh flowers. A coarse hair lay suspiciously in the candy bowl, matching the centerpiece.

"Oh, that's nasty."

"Eh? Ya, 'ere's candy. Would ya care fer some?"

Clara politely shook her head. "No, I'm good. Thank you, though."

"Now Clara, that scar on yer 'ead jest ain't proper-like," Henny tsk tsked, shaking her head. Rooting around in a drawer of the stand, she pulled out a roll of lace. "I've 'ept this around. Good thing, too." She took the lace and wrapped it around Clara's head. "Hm, 'ill do."

Henny nodded approval while whispering, perhaps to herself, or perhaps so Clara would hear. "Henny, clever as a fox ya are. Mayor Gribble will be 'oud. He 'etter be glad he hired you over Nonny. Nonny ain't 'alf as smart..."

While Clara listened to Henny discuss her own positive attributes, she glanced into an aged mirror hanging over the stand. *Everyone keeps talking about the scar... I still don't see it. Either they're crazy, or I am.* Lifting the lace, she leaned closer to her reflection. *Nothing's there. Not a mark.*

"Ahhh, put that back!" Henny grabbed her arm to pull it down. "No teching it, ya hear? Right now it be stayin'. Jest as I planned." The maid nodded to support her warning.

"Yes, sorry, Henny. I do have a question. The statue—it looks real. What exactly is it?"

"Awr, that be a hag."

Her eyes that never wanted to see a hag widened. "Did the mayor kill it or something?"

"That what he tell me to say, anyways. Yep, yep. That what he tell me to say." Henny placed her hands on her hips while shaking her head. "That's what I say now. Now, fer yer job. Tonight is a 'inner party. Our Mayor Gribble is hosting, after all. Best of 'anners." Clara straightened her back. "Great leaders 'ill be visitating. Tonight! Yep. Hup we go. Only few 'ours away. Follow me, this way."

Henny led Clara into the kitchen to instruct on how to properly serve a meal. At this point, Clara had taken enough meals at the castle to know basic formalities. Henny, though, was confident in her ignorance. Realizing one night wasn't worth bickering over, Clara smiled and nodded like a newbie as the maid covered the basics.

With the lesson complete and the last of the food cooked, Clara was commanded, rather forcefully, to wait in the kitchen while Henny properly greeted the guests and offered seats. Mumbled voices spoke while the maid gushed over the visitors. *Why am I nervous?* Clara began to overthink, answering her own question. *What if I spill something, especially the soup. It would stain, too. I've never seen such a dark soup before. I guess I'm afraid to fail, but I've never spilled a coffee on someone, so there's that. But the floors are so uneven, one misstep and I'd ruin the important dinner.*

I mean, it probably won't happen but even aside from this dinner, what will happen to me if I don't have a job? If Char moves on, I can't stay here. I could be back wandering the streets alone and… the hag. I wish I'd never seen her hideous cross-eyed head. Then, there's the witch. Might as well be both out to kill me at this point…

"Clara, such an ugly 'ace you 'ave."

"What?" Clara wondered what happened to the rule about manners.

"Don't be making 'aces now. You got all yer teeth to 'mile with. First course to 'erv. Remember, no yammerin' to the company. Any 'erds need sayin' I'd be sayin' 'em." Henny picked one of the two plates of appetizers, leaving the heavier one for Clara.

Both men had silver hair with unnaturally beautiful features. The man at the head of the table had slicked back hair. A mustache matched his beard, each was pristinely maintained. To the left was another well-groomed man. His silver hair was shaved on the sides with the rest tied behind him. Clean-shaven, each tendril of hair shimmered once the light hit it. Striking cold-blue eyes bore into her.

To the right of the table was an awkward man who looked just as much out of place with the silver-haired men as they did in this room. He, too, had a fair amount of hair, although his looked unnatural and a little skewed. Large drops of sweat rolled down his nose. *That must be the mayor.*

The sweaty major was nervously inching his small glasses from the tip of his nose while trying to push himself closer to the table. Fighting against the chair leg wedged against the floorboard, he gave up. "Supreme Dignitaries, we've prepared a fine meal for us all today," the mayor said with a roll of his tongue. Clara followed orders as she approached the table and offered food. "I'm sure you're finding your timage here enjoyable. Gohmer will be an exemplarity… exemplaritority… exemplarly town under my tutalarage." His face reddened.

"We've noticed your… exemplary work," the man with the blue eyes said with slightly feigned compassion. His eyes lingered on Clara. "Gribble—"

The mayor cleared his throat. "Mayor—"

"Formalities are unimportant, Gribble. The important thing is whether or not you received the potion from the witch. It's the only reason why we are here," scoffed the man with the beard.

"Oh yes, yes, yes." Mayor Gribble tapped his fingers together. He felt very important now. His tone spoke confidently to the man with the beard. "Odin, I'll have my maid fetch it fer ya."

"I don't believe we're on first-name speaking terms at this time, Gribble," the man with the beard cautioned.

"Of course, of course… accept my apologies. It—it shan't happen again. Lord Odin."

"The potion," Lord Odin repeated, taking a bite of the appetizer. He unashamedly spat it into the napkin and took a drink. He didn't touch the rest.

Henny left to retrieve the bottle, and Clara followed, eavesdropping from the kitchen. "Your servant. Tell me about her." This time, it was a refined voice from the blue-eyed man. The voice sounded vaguely familiar. *His voice is very distinct. It can't be… is it the voice I heard from Ancora. The one who tried to trade me? The nerve!*

"Henny is the best of maids 'ere and around. Yes, it's true. I'm sure you've noticed her ex-exemplifary cooking skills and servicings." The mayor puffed his chest, causing a button to pop. Hiding it, he pulled the vest down to cover the gap.

"Not that one. The other. The one wearing the misplaced lace."

"Oh, her? She jest a temporary. Nothing of impertinence." Gribble waved his hand. Before the conversation progressed, Henny entered the room carrying a murky liquid in a clear glass bottle. A small doily was placed beneath it.

"'Ere 'tis it." She handed it to Mayor Gribble, who snatched it. The doily fell from the tray. "Henny, yer excused!"

Mayor Gribble handed over the bottle. "You'll find it high

quality. I'm sure you can tell, I only collect qualitative things. I sourced a woodland witch, yes I did. She used the best of ingredients. I paid 'er nicely with resources. As I mentioned earlier, my leadershipness has spanned into nearby towns and they are happy to pay for my knowledges." He puffed his chest out again, hair poking through the busted hole. "As you know, ahem, finding a woodland witch 'tis hard to do. I 'ad to find me a mage to locate one and such."

The blue-eyed man inspected the potion, holding it up to the light. "It looks more concentrated than before. That's good. The last stock didn't work as swiftly as we'd like. As we mentioned, we needed a stronger brew. This looks acceptable."

The men exchanged glances. Lord Odin began, "Good work Gribble, we'll be on our way now."

"But the meal. It's only jest begun. We 'aven't even gotten to the good part."

"Good day to you, and thank you for your hospitality," said the blue-eyed man empathically.

Clara moved from the doorway as the two men vanished from the table in a swish of light. The poor mayor sat alone. He stared at the tableful of uneaten food. *They disappeared… how in the world? It's obviously magic. Zerpith disappeared like that, too. The power here is incredible, but it's a shame how they treated that poor man. I kinda feel bad for him.* With the thought of the Mayor, Clara realized that she still had a job to do if she wanted paid."

"Henny, was there anything el—" Clara turned and bumped into the blue-eyed man's chest, who materialized before her.

"Hello, I hope I haven't been rude. My deepest regret if I frightened you. You look a little out of place. Are you from Gohmer?"

"Oh. Yes'm. Fer as lang as I'r can remembery," Clara said, wincing at her own attempted accent.

"Your name?" His eyes bore into her. The iciness made her freeze.

Shaking her head, she stammered. No names would come, not even her own. Eyes darting to see Henny being chewed out by the mayor, she spouted, "Jenny. Name's Jenny. Yep, born and bred right here in this ole towny."

"Jenny…" His voice was deep and mysteriously enticing.

"Yessiree," she creaked.

"Tell me, Jenny. What's the purpose of your headband?"

Clara wrung her hands together, backing away. "Jest, you know… a fash-fashion statement. Every… all the… gals are wearing them, ha. Yeah. You know how that is. I thought it'd be a good idea… er… don't ye like it?" Back against the wall, she felt the sill of an open window. The curtain stuck to the back of her uniform from the incoming breeze.

"I'm fully aware of the latest fashion, but have yet to see that one. If you don't mind, please remove it."

"Remove it? Isn't that a bit uncouth?" Just then, a cry ripped from the sky, shaking the house. Screaming from outside filtered through the open window. Something grabbed the back of her dress, jerking her out the window. She slammed to the grass. Looking down at her was Charlie Bales.

"Banshee. Time to go. Adventure awaits! There's an incredibly massive bird outside to boot. The ladies are anxiously waiting for us. No worries about your job, they can do without you, and I made enough money for us both. I even got you some snappy clothes."

Running from the house, Clara and Char tumbled down the hill to reach the wagon. The horses shifted around, waiting for their cue. The bird circled in menacing fashion high in the clouds, searching, crying. Cawing, more roar-like, she shook the dirt by pounding her claws onto the ground and scraping the earth with her sharp claws. Pedestrians scattered frantically.

With a slap of the reins, they left town without drawing attention from the monstrous bird. The ladies galloped, bumping the wagon up and down in haste. Clara wiped sweat from her face and gripped the bar in front of her seat. Looking at Charlie, he had a strange smile on his face.

"What in the world is wrong with you? We're running for our lives, and you're laughing!"

"Clara, the creature doesn't know who we are. Why it would be after us? But I was thinking. Just one plop from that beast would surely cause great damage."

"Why is that funny right now?"

"You need to cover all areas when fleeing a situation, Banshee. If it were to drop, let's say, a dapper pile, the wagon could slip and slide all around." Char grinned, expecting to share in the laugh, but Clara glared. "Don't be afraid. Relax, be free." He slowed the horses down.

"Char, don't slow down… Ugh. You're going to hate me after this. I'm so sorry to bust your bubble, but the bird… it's after me."

Amazed, Char slapped his hands over his hat. "You don't say? Why didn't you mention it before? I guess you'd better hide. Quick, under the wagon's hood. The creature won't find you there." Untying the curtain, she flopped into the back, hiding among the piles of items. Char sat nonchalantly in his seat, whistling low and calm. The horses clopped lazily.

Clara peered out from the back of the wagon's hood when she heard an explosive sound. The bird flapped uneasily as sparks crashed around it. Sawyer, Onyx, and Jade were attacking the bird! Her mouth gaped open as the battle unfolded before her. The fighters were quick, deft, and entrancing to observe. *It's almost intimidating to watch them…* The winged monster roared, causing an angry wind. The horses bolted, throwing Char back into his seat. Clara rolled among the mass of goods. The nasty foot slapped her face, and she forcefully hurled it away.

A nearby tree blew from its roots in the increasing wind. In a crash, it blocked the wagon's path, scaring the horses. Rearing up, the steeds turned sharply, toppling the wagon over. Valuable cargo spilled and scraped across the dusty road—Clara and Char included. Jade focused on the enemy. A shock of lightning shook the beast. The monster hit the ground with a shocking tremor.

The group worked as a team, each one playing a part. Onyx tossed a vial, which the knight caught with keen peripheral vision. The dance was well-rehearsed and masterfully executed. Pouring the vial across the sword's edge, he deftly swapped the vial for a fire stone. The blade burst into a scalding inferno. Swinging the weapon over his head to stoke the fire, the fire caught, sending raging flames off the glistening blade. Rushing the bird, he slashed into her side. The creature flapped and screeched. Hobbling in a jolted motion across the ground, one wing dragging, she left behind a trail of fire. Finally gaining leverage, she roared like thunder, sending a shiver through the earth, shaking the team.

Clara rolled, scraping her knees across the gravel along the way. Still in her uniform, dirty and awestruck, she watched as the team battled. Sitting up, she surveyed a mass of chaos. The bird was now in the air, although not as confident as before. Fire scorched across her side, reaching for her head. A thick cloud of smoke followed her. The monstrous bird's eyes darted, her head buckled in when she saw Clara.

Scrambling, Clara searched for something to hold. Without bothering to brush off debris from her tumble, she darted for safety. Char followed her, all while holding his hat firmly to his head. Clara and Char watched the battle unfold as her friends prevented the winged creature from reaching her. Clara held onto the tree; Char held onto her. The peddler's hat finally blew off, exposing shaggy brown hair.

Eleanor, struggling to maintain posture in the increasing gusts, cast a protective shield around the fighters. Sawyer deftly wielded the fiery blade. Onyx, not to be outdone, used various objects and potions to attack, protect, and deflect oncoming advances. Eleanor, not breaking a sweat, lifted her arms of protection to counter the wind and deflect. Jade projected fire and lightning. Angry, the bird swooped into the barrier, breaking the seal.

Jade concentrated magic in the form of water and shot it from her palms with a cutting force. Now steamy and wet, the bird snapped at the barrier with a deep cut severing her wing. Jade summoned electricity, the perfect counter to her previous water. The lightning struck, causing the beast to fly wildly in a dazed stupor. Eleanor, slowly getting weak from the new barrier, fell to her knees to save energy.

Back in the sky, the bird plummeted onto the shield once again, breaking the protective barrier a second time and sending Eleanor to the ground. Not wasting time, she rose to her feet to cast protection again, but failed. The fowl retreated into the air, now unsteady. The water had smoked out the fire. The wind dried her feathers, nursing a new flame not doused.

Once again, the beast found Clara. She swooped to grab her. Caught in her grasp, Char was carried with her, dangling from Clara's legs. Both screamed as the bird gained flight. Jade shot another bolt that clipped the creature in the tail. The bird swayed and dipped, up and down, back and forth, unable to keep balance without its tail intact.

Onyx rushed to Eleanor's side with a small tube. She drank the contents, placing her hand on his cheek gently. Revived, she stood tall. The beast once again plummeted. Injured, she dropped her captives. The bird, the banshee, and the peddler fell in a disorganized manner. Eleanor chanted a protection that caught the humans, then swiftly moved them to safety. The bird landed with a mighty crash. Sawyer, flaming blade in full swing, chopped into the creature's neck, hack after hack. Feathers and scales came loose and caught fire. The creature's remaining flesh erupted into a raging bonfire. With the fire spreading rapidly, the bird charbroiled until motionless. They had won.

Jasper and Rory caught up. They missed the action, but not the aftermath. A circle branded the ground from the protective shield, an upturned wagon with two frantic horses, and spilled contents spanned before them. A large, smoking bonfire raged, smelling much like chicken.

Jasper waved as he saw his team, Clara included. "Ho, looks like a job well done."

"Banshee. Woowee." Charlie exclaimed as he rushed to get his hat. "Of all the stories we shared, the monster crow and your friends weren't one of them." He swung his hat into the air, catching it on his head as it came back down.

"I guess it never came up…"

"And now we shall sing of it."

"Clara," Sawyer embraced her freely. She hugged him back, fighting sobs of relief.

"Thank you. For coming for me," she whispered. She held him close as long as possible before the rest arrived to greet her.

"Clara, they killed the bird! You're safe now, right?" Rory pulled at the cook's sleeve. "Jasper, are we going to——?"

"No lad, hard to say what curse has tainted the meat of that fowl. We'll not be eating this one."

CHAPTER 26

Lectus

SAWYER

REUNITED, the party continued on their way to find Lectus. The sun retired, surrendering its duty to the shining full moon. The night sky blanketed the heavens with her usual companion of stars poking out from her midnight cloak. Char, who was more than a little thankful to meet new friends, was seated around the fire with the companions. The horses, unhitched, roamed free for a midnight feed. During the great wagon spillage, a wheel was broken. Not having a spare, Jasper had given the peddler their extra, which was a perfect fit.

The fire was hot, offering the seduction of food. It was a good night; they were together. Sawyer forked the dinner, juices exploded into complex flavors on his tongue. A saltiness with notes of rosemary... and wait... a sweetness too. Field greens were wrapped around the girth of each carrot; he bit a chunk off.

The peddler had respectfully removed his hat when offered a steaming plate of food. Sawyer intently listened as Clara told him about her adventure. Her arms moved expressively. *She has no idea how captivating she is*. The mark on her forehead told a story that he didn't completely understand. Although she was an anxious spirit, the carefree moments, like this one, made her vibrant with freedom.

"I've missed you," he laughed as Clara stopped, blinking with wide eyes, after telling him how she survived the flying beast.

"I've missed you too… I didn't know what to do. When the bird dropped me, I thought I was finished, but somehow, I didn't get hurt."

"Somehow, you always think you're done for," he said. "Maybe it's time you see how capable you are." *If you only could see yourself the way I see you.*

"Really? I guess I never noticed before. I don't know why I think in worst-case scenarios. I'll try harder. I promise! But… do you think I can take down Lectus?"

"Lectus, you say?" Char abandoned his seat to grab his mandolin. "Lectus. A fable. A tale to be told, mhmm." The peddler shook his head, hat flopping to the rhythm. He strummed a few chords before continuing. "They say Lectus was a man who desired more from life. Perhaps more from the people around him, but even more for himself. Persistent! Stubborn! He craved adoration and power. So the tale goes."

Char increased the tempo of his strumming. "A lot of things are said about Lectus. But the truth is always in the middle. You see, in my travels, I have learned how he had come to be. They tell of the day he lost himself. It was the day he met the water nymph…"

Lectus limped. Apprenticing at the apothecary became a bitter afterthought, prying at his nerves. His cane pounded the ground, a reminder he'd always need it. How dare they! For all the good he'd done, nobody saw any of it. Another day of misery. Kindness was a mere manipulation to get what you want. It wasn't real. No matter how many times he tried to please, no one returned it. Not at the apothecary, not anywhere. He could barely walk the street without hateful words from the townspeople. And all because his family practiced malefic magic. He, himself, has never dabbled in the art, but they didn't care about that. The bruise ran from his brow bone to his eye socket. Angry blues and purples blended into the redness of a swollen eye. "Just as the other," he sneered.

Fight after fight these days, but someday, they would pay. They didn't know he'd come into magic of his own. They believed such power wasn't in him, but they were wrong. They wouldn't know how he practiced spells in his shack at night. He'd show them how they overlooked him. He just needed to keep practicing until he was ready. It'd be an unfortunate discovery for them.

"One day, their hateful words will transform into fear and adoration," he said loudly. He swallowed blood from a broken tooth. "And then they'll regret how they treated me." Lectus limped ahead, as did his ruminating. He had a great deal of memories of how he'd been treated. All his life, rejection targeted him. Now, he was the only one left in his family. The replay was a torment he now welcomed. He would use it as fuel.

He continued for some time, limping, sneering, cursing the sky, pounding his cane. They would pay. They would learn. They're at fault. But soon, they'd love and adore him. They would have to. Once their eyes opened to who he had become, he would scoff and laugh as they pleaded for forgiveness while shaking in awe at his power. Head down, his foot swished into soft dirt.

"A pond... when did this appear? I don't take wrong turns." The lake glistened with sparks of light. "It's captivating."

A pale greenish-blue head popped from the water, circled by a ringlet of seaweed and water lilies. Thick braids were tied and twisted around her head. She splashed from the water with a shell in her hand. Dancing upon the surface, she sang. The shell, which she blew into, created an eerie yet beautiful accompaniment.

Char strummed while humming, lost in the story, then picked up the momentum. "My friends, as you can imagine, at the first sight of the nymph, he instantly fell in love. His emotions overtook him as he desired to have her. But Lectus harbored too much hate to see true love, and he pondered the stories he learned about the mysterious, beautiful creatures.

"Their songs, as beautiful as they are, can lure a man into their ponds for certain death. Of course, that's what he chose to believe. You see, nymphs can grant wishes, if you can overcome the call of their song. But first, you must take her shell. Inside her shell lived a light. This light contained her life, but also a wish. To set the wish free, you must first break the shell. This releases her life. He didn't understand it then, that the wish was not separate from her life. In fact, the wish was her life. Woowee, what a sight she was, and woowee, his dream could come true."

The nymph blew into her shell, singing a song of enchantment. Lectus plugged his ears with moss before entering the water. He carried his cane with him, but the buoyancy of the water removed the need for support. Lifting the cane over his head, he waded waist-deep. "Nymph, you have invited me to your home. I'm but a crippled man. You don't need to fear."

The nymph swam to him. As she came closer, he spun the cane over his head and splashed it across the water. His plan paid off as it broke her concentration long enough for him to swipe her shell.

"Sir, please return my shell. It contains my life." She lurched forward to take it, but he cracked it in two. The nymph's hands trembled. The wish released from the shell with a sparkle of light. Flashing, it hovered above the broken pieces.

"I wish to be all-powerful! The most powerful of any mage or healer." Lectus's lip twitched.

"Sir, you know not what you've done, as I'll die without my life. Please, spare me this day. I'll be gone soon, if you don't return the wish." She struggled to stay afloat, her legs already beginning to melt into algae. "If you return my life now, I shall still live."

He treaded water. "You lured me to this very water to die. You're no different from everyone else. Compassion is a joke, and life, the jester." He pushed the nymph away with rage. "I'll not retract my wish but enhance it. I desire to be more powerful than any mage or healer, as I just told you. I crave a power all my own. One that will stand the test of time. Everlasting life and—everyone will know me. I'll rule and be adored across kingdoms. They'll pay for how they treated me. They'll all pay. I'll live off their sorrow and feed on their remorse. I'll devour their regret to grow from their sorrow. Forever they will remember me and fear."

The nymph weakly sang as she slowly melted into the water, "To him that wishes... his heart will open. His mind of mayhem, his body broken. God of the Lake, grant him his wish! I'll surrender my song, and the life I could live," she cried at the end. "Your wish has been granted. I'm almost gone... I'll ask one more time, spare me this day."

"I do as I wish. I can already feel the power coursing through me. I will not take it back now!"

"Then I'll die," she cried into her arms that were foaming into the water. "You think you've won, Lectus, but your thoughts elude you. Power without control is more dangerous than death." Her body was dissolving fast, and she

lifted her face, now the only part of her left. She met his eyes. "By conquering me, you have conquered yourself." And with those words, she was gone. Lectus left the lake, his cane floating in the algae.

Char did a fancy ditty on his instrument. "Lectus's pain would be his doom. The siren granted him powers, that's true, but not in the way he had hoped. You see, she gave him the power of necromancy. Lectus failed to understand the truth. In his haste for love, he only saw revenge. Wishes are not always granted in the way that we imagine, and nymphs, not as malicious as one would think."

Sawyer saw the look of confusion on Clara's face. He whispered to her, "Necromancy means talking to the dead."

Char progressed. "Not realizing what he was bestowed, Lectus happily left the nymph, who was reduced to a pile of algae and foam. The lake dried up into a muddy hole. As you can imagine, he was a bit more than a little excited to show off his newfound powers. But, as he would soon realize, he got exactly what he wanted. A power all his own."

Rory interrupted the tale. "My mom told me that Lectus would haunt me if I didn't stop picking on my sister. She said he'd terrorize me in my dreams to teach me a lesson. I was afraid to fall asleep."

Char nodded, his shaggy hair swaying under his hat. "It's true, you know. What grows from hate, flowers as sorrow. But, perhaps it's all rooted from fear. Lectus is a testament to that. Walking, limp free, Lectus approached the town that produced his once black eyes. But before entering, he passed through an old graveyard. The graveyard of shadows. As he wandered by, his powers increased. Elation soon turned to horror. Instead of feeling powerfully happy, he felt fear, regret, and doom."

Char, lost in the story, increased the intensity of his rhythm even more. "The cries from the dead overtook him. He was a part of them now, and they him. For the rest of his existence, he'd carry their memories, and if you remember that would be, well, forever."

Sawyer brushed hair from Clara's brow. The firelight reflected onto her shiny scar. Her cheeks flushed pink. Casting her gaze to the ground, she whispered, "How am I supposed to fight someone who's immortal?" Sawyer put an arm around her, pulling her close.

Char continued. "The story goes on. Wherever Lectus went, he sucked up the shame and inadequacies of those who passed on. Before long, he was no longer a man, but a projection of the voices of the dead." The story ended, and Char set his instrument down to pick up his plate. "If you don't mind, I'll have some more. Must have gotten a bit hungry after all that."

Jasper motioned to the pot, still steaming. "Help yourself."

Scarfing his second plate, the peddler finished with a poorly controlled burp. "Goodnight, good friends. Rest well and dream of adventures. I'd say that I'd come along, you know, but the ladies will decide."

Sawyer escorted him to the wagon. "I can't thank you enough for taking care of Clara."

"She takes care of herself and does a good job doing so. She even saved my life."

"I'm happy to hear that. With all the dangers roaming the land, it's always nice to have a friend. Thank you for being that to her and us."

Salty moisture brimmed in the peddler's eyes, threatening to overflow. "Woowee, what a day it's been, and the night is still new. Just think of the songs I'll write! They'll be the very best yet. No bard around will be able to match the tales of this peddler." With that, he swung himself onto his seat. Reaching behind the passenger seat, he pulled out a carved-handled machete. "Give this to Clara. She was fond of it and good at using it, even if in her own way."

"I'll make sure she gets it."

Clara rushed over. "Char, wait. Will I see you in the morning?"

"This I never know, Banshee. This I never know."

"Okay, then… I—I can't thank you enough. I… you…" Clara's eyes watered.

"Banshee, our paths will meet again. I can feel this. I know this. Journey on and be brave. It's the best way to be. Laugh, cry. Feel and be free."

"Goodbye—"

"There are no goodbyes for people you care about. Even when

they pass, they never truly leave." With that, he disappeared into his tent with an energetic swing.

Clara plopped onto the makeshift seat next to Sawyer. "The story about Lectus…" She stared into the fire. "I wish I never heard it."

"All we have are stories. Most of which are very old. We don't know where the truth lies. Besides that," he said, lightly punching her arm, "as long as I'm here, you'll be fine. You'll have all of us to protect you."

"How am I going to help? Am I supposed to fight him in my dreams? And… what happens if we get separated again?"

"Well, then you'll use your machete." Sawyer laughed heartily as he handed over the weapon.

"My machete!" She laughed while lovingly placing it onto her lap. "I'm pretty good at using it to negotiate. Can't say much about how it works any other way."

"You negotiated with a machete?" He scooted a bit closer, intrigued.

"I didn't know what to do, so I just swung it around like a wild woman. I'm not sure I could hurt anyone with it. I'm just glad I didn't cut myself in the process."

He firmly put his hand on top of hers. "I'll show you."

The pause was heavy. Their eyes connected. She diverted her gaze. "Oh, um… that sounds perfect." Heat flushed into her cheeks, but he knew it wasn't from the fire.

CHAPTER 27
Eros

CLARA

DISAPPOINTMENT CLOUDED Clara's emotions when she woke to find the peddler gone that morning. Now, she put pressure on Stormy's side to urge him into a canter. *We're almost to Eros. Then, we'll know how to find Lectus and his hideously stuffy castle. But what then? Will I somehow magically return home? What if I get home and so many years have passed? Then everyone I know will be dead—or old. What if I get back home and I'm the old one? What if I die and nothing happens at all?*

Rory rode double with Sawyer on Willow. Both were discussing something they found hilarious. Eleanor cantered off into the distance alone. Jade, alert as always, kept close to the wagon while Onyx stopped far ahead, picking up some plants from the roadside. Jasper flicked the reins to encourage the donkeys to speed up. Agitated, they eventually complied, albeit stubbornly. They traveled uneventfully till they reached the towering city.

"Hello there! Do you have clearance to enter the city?" asked the watchman peering over the wall, hand shielding his eyes from the afternoon sun.

"We're traveling from the Kingdom of Ancora," Sawyer replied.

"Commander Knight, Sawyer Lydon." He turned his shoulder to show his badge.

"State your business, Commander."

Eleanor interrupted. "Eleanor, of the Enchanted City of Eros. I worked under the tutelage of Aesian. Our business is our own, but it's imperative we meet with the Preceptor."

"Eleanor? What a pleasure to see you again, young healer. It's Pete, Pete from the Knighthood. I've met you before, back when I worked at the citadel." He smiled. "You're just as lovely as I remember."

"I recall, and thank you. My party and I need passage into the city. I'm exhausted from traveling and would adore the comfort of home."

"Yes, m'lady! I'm sure Aesian will be glad to see you." Pete smiled broadly. "The infirmary is to the left, if you need it. Lodging to the right. You'll find many things to entertain you in the city, no matter which way you go—although, Eleanor, I don't need to tell you that. I know that your friends will have a pleasant time while they're here. Many new shops have recently opened, as well. I know you'll enjoy your stay."

"Thank you, Pete."

Jade led the way into the inn after they passed through the gates. "Slumbers Inn and Spa, looks like a good enough place to me."

An attendant standing by a podium sparkling with blinking lights greeted them cheerfully. "Need a restful night's sleep, weary travelers? No better place than Slumbers. We have expanded our menu and our spa services. Hot baths in each room, and waterfalls for a relaxing wash. Our waterfalls are exclusive to Slumbers, by the way."

"That would be delightful. Let's see, we'll need three rooms, if you have them. Also, we need a stable for our steeds and a space to keep our wagon," Jade said. Clara gazed over the room. Lush rugs and chairs sat around a roaring fireplace made from golden stone. A bottle or two of wine chilled in a golden tub here and there, with glasses stylishly waiting. The high ceiling was painted with mosaic-like charm and a few curious-looking guests with enchanting eyes chatted quietly in random seats.

Jade, keys in hand, handed one over. "You'll room with me tonight. Here is the secondary key in case you need it. While I'm here, I'm going to do some shopping tomorrow evening. The lights are really nice at night. Do you still have the money Sawyer gave you? Feel free to pick up some things for yourself. You're safe here, in case you were concerned. There are knights on every corner. It's also the birthplace of Eleanor and myself—although I don't remember it as well as Eleanor. Tomorrow we'll find the Preceptor to schedule a meeting. He may be able to tell us more about Lectus and the windowless castle. At least, we hope. I know he does a lot for the city so we may be here a few days while we wait. I'm not complaining though, Eros never gets boring. They also have an incredible training arena for mages. It's far better than what we have at Ancora."

"Maybe we'll have a breakthrough while we're here then. Are you planning on shopping?"

"Not right now. Sawyer and I are planning on doing some strategic planning. But you should go."

Clara followed Jade up the marbled stairs until they located their room. Jade left her belongings on the table, then excused herself. Clara peeked out the deep-set window. A beautiful big city, full of activity, was waiting below. Tall, castle-like buildings held a magical intrigue, like a modern storybook.

I have to check out the waterfall! Akin to a shower, the waterfall had a large golden showerhead built in, covering the majority of the shower's ceiling. Marble walls enclosed the space. A few steps led down into the shower, producing plenty of steam. Smiling, she turned the flow on and then off by pressing a crystal knob on the shower wall. It'd have to wait until after her exploration. *This is like a real-life city. There are things to do, food to eat, and things to buy! Maybe it'll take awhile for The Preceptor to open his schedule.* She grabbed her satchel from the table and made sure she had everything. Money, the key…

"That's all I need. No car key, no ID, no credit cards or phone.

What a strange sense of freedom." Smiling, she stuffed the light satchel in her pocket and headed out the door.

"Can I come along?" Rory pulled on her bag as she walked towards the double doors of the inn.

"Of course."

"Thanks. Sawyer and Jade only want to drink and talk by the fire. They said they're going to visit the pub for dinner, but I don't want to wait around. That's boring. Jasper wanted to nap. I don't want to do any of those things."

Merchants lined the shining white cobblestone streets. "Would you care to try my famous dough nuggets? I have samples. Strawberry, cinnamon, coconut."

"Strawberry for me, thanks." Clara took a sample on a small stick.

Rory anxiously waited. "Cinnamon, please." Each skewer had one nugget. They resembled tater tots sprinkled with shaved crystal. Once bitten, they crunched from the crystallized flakes, and a sweet, thick filling oozed out.

"Oh, yum." Clara wiped the syrup from her chin. She paid for a full-sized skewer.

"These are the best. I had them last year at the festival. Although I didn't see them this year," Rory also purchased a full helping.

"Have you been to Eros before?" Clara asked as they wandered the streets while eating the nuggets from the skewer.

"No, this is my first time away from the castle. Someday I'm going to be a knight, just like Sawyer, and then I'll travel all around. I'll fight beasts and rescue townspeople. I can't wait."

"Some of my best memories were being a kid. Don't rush it. Sometimes, I wish I could go back to those times."

"Did you work in a castle when you were a kid?"

"No, the castles in America are for tourists. They don't hold an official purpose. But, if there was that chance, I probably would have loved it. Instead, I hated my job, serving drinks and snacks."

"Why didn't you like it?"

"I don't know. I guess as you grow up, responsibility takes over.

You go to work because you always have bills to pay. If I tried taking a chance, I'd have nowhere to live if it didn't work out. You play things safe, I guess. These responsibilities weigh you down and one day you wake up and realize you stopped doing all the things you did when you were little."

"Sawyer doesn't play safe. Neither does Jade."

"I'm not like them. Here, people seem to like danger, for some strange reason. But for me, I'm not hoping to risk my life battling things." Clara pretended to swing a sword at Rory, who laughed and feigned evading.

"But you are now, right?"

"I promise it isn't what I'd choose to do."

"Maybe you need to do things like a kid again. Not worry about what happens as much. If it matters, I think you're going to defeat Lectus. It will be so cool. I'll get to be a part of it, too, won't I?"

"Of course you will. Especially since I'll need to borrow some of your trust in me." Clara looked to her feet. *I guess I'm afraid the more they believe in me, the harder I'll disappoint them if this doesn't work out.*

"Clara, look," Rory said, tugging on her bag. "Crystal Balls and Magical Notions. Maybe they'll have something you can use to fight Lectus." They bee-lined into the shop. To the left was a counter that looked very old. Carved wood and etched jewels trimmed the edges. A young man stood behind the aged cabinet. His pointy ears and yellow eyes paled in comparison to his green hair.

"Welcome to The Magic Notion! If you need help, please let me know. We have both modern and ancient wares. For ancient notions, come see me. I'll need permission from the keeper, of course, and also your credentials for any viewings."

"Thank you," Clara said while scanning the shelves with wands, staffs, crystal stones, robes, jewelry, and all sorts of trinkets. Some things looked old and knotted, others slick and polished to perfection, but all full of the wonder of a world not her own. Picking up a jar, something floated inside. Seeing an eye blink, she swiftly put it down. Each jar was unique with crafted glass and stoppers. Beautifully detailed, though many descriptions were not legible, at least not to her.

Light pierced Clara's eyes. A crystal ball reflected a ray from the bay window in the corner. Standing on a pedestal, it gleamed dangerously. Examining the tag, it read, "Dreamcrystal Ball, see attendant for price." The prism-like intensity was mesmerizing. *Must be expensive.* Looking into the glass, it showed her nothing. Moving closer, she peered into the depths. Her concentration faded. Her head thudded, pounding against her brow. Her eyes shut as she pressed her temples. The thumping intensified, beating like a drum to the rhythm of her heart. The pulse banged against her eyes until they opened to see an old, haggard face. "Zerpith!" Her body jolted back, knocking over trinkets and bottles from a table behind her. The attendant rushed her way from behind his podium.

"Are you okay, miss?" he inquired, more anxious over the fading gleam from the ball than her.

"She's okay, sir," interjected Rory, "I was playing a parlor trick on her. You know, scared her a bit. It would have been much funnier had she not made such a mess."

The attendant wasn't impressed, but Rory took Clara's arm and left the shop quickly. "What happened? Are you okay?"

"I saw Zerpith in the crystal ball." Clara covered her mouth with her hands until her breathing calmed. "I'd know that face in a second."

"Are you sure?"

"No doubt. None at all. It was that janky old man's face. He was looking at me with his creepy, veiny eyes. I think he saw me for real, too. I promise." She sniffed. "Rory, he's watching us. I think he wants me to fail."

"Clara, it's okay. We're with you. Zerpith is entrusted to Ancora. He's probably watching over us to make sure we made it safely, if it was actually him. I don't understand why he'd work against us."

"I don't know. All I know is that I didn't feel safe. He gave me a headache. My head is throbbing now."

Rory looked confused. "I don't understand. Zerpith wouldn't harm any of us. Many times, it was his protection that saved Ancora. I don't think he'd change now. Do you need a healer for your headache? I can get Eleanor."

"No, it's almost gone. I'm sorry. I suppose I'm overreacting. Let's… let's forget about it and enjoy our time here. I'm getting hungry. The nuggets didn't do much to fill me up, so let's find some food and forget about it."

A river split the city in the center. A few translucent bridges closed the gaps of the extensive waterway, allowing pedestrians to cross. Sparkling and clean, many vendors shouted to potential customers in the city center on the walkways. Crossing one of the bridges, Clara paused to see straight through the bridge and into the clear water. Many colorful fish swam below. A particular cluster darted back and forth in frantic motion, showcasing their flowing fins and lively colors. The translucent bridge turned into stone once they stepped onto the street. Hopeful merchants called, each wanting a sale. One guy in particular looked directly at them.

"Beautiful lady! You've lucked out. It just so happens that I'm gifting a free bracelet. I have a new shop and need someone to spread the word about my quality products."

Clara shook her head. "I'm sorry, but I don't live around here. I can't help you with that."

"No matter, traveler, if you report back to me in a few days, simply on quality, it's yours. Of course, I'll need you to show it off to your friends and spread the news." The merchant pushed the bracelet at Clara.

"Thanks anyway." Clara kindly pushed it back. She whispered to Rory as they left. "Did it seem to you that he was forcing that bracelet on me. Suspicious, if you ask me. Is that common here? Do vendors typically give things away?"

"You worry too much. Everyone wants to make a profit. I wouldn't think too much about it."

They rounded a corner that left the vendor stands behind and opened to a double street with buildings on each side. In the center was a line of trees blooming with glowing flowers. "My best buddy, Nash, told me they have a game room somewhere. He loved going before living at Ancora. He told me about all the games he loved playing. Maybe we can go there after we eat. Whatcha think?"

"I'm game for that! Get it? I'm game?" Clara snickered at her joke.

"Clara?" Rory spun around, almost bumping into her. "Clara?"

"I'm right here, silly."

"Clara, where are you?" Rory turned and retraced his steps, jogging slightly.

"Rory, wait up! Seriously, I'm right behind you. Stop running."

"Clara? Clara!"

"Rory, I'm right here behind you! Come on now, this isn't funny."

"He can't see you," boomed a voice behind her. Someone grabbed her arm, tying a blind fold over her eyes and pulling her off the street. "You could have just taken the bracelet and made this a lot easier on us, but I see you're going to make this difficult. I've been tasked with bringing you to the citadel, and I'm not leaving without you."

The body behind the voice picked her up and ran. She cried for help, unheard. She tried to kick, but her legs wouldn't move. She tried to pound on his back, but her arms didn't budge. Eventually, she heard multiple doors open and shut before feeling the plushness of a bed.

She couldn't see, but she felt in her gut there was another person in the room aside from her captor. He spoke in a voice that she remembered. "Great work. I see your venture was a success. The bracelet I crafted was also a success, I presume."

That's the blue-eyed man who approached me at Mayor Gribble's!

Someone yanked the bracelet from her wrist. "Thank you, Aesian. It's been a pleasure helping our esteemed Preceptor."

Clara's heart quickened, and she brushed the inside of her top lip to release the dryness. *The Preceptor is Aesian? The same Preceptor who was supposed to help us find Lectus?*

The man continued to speak to Aesian, as if she wasn't in the room to hear how much of an easy target she was. "At first, she wouldn't take it on her own accord. We had to snap it on her wrist ourselves, but she was an easy target. The coating made sure she felt nothing. Pretty much no trouble at all," her captor bellowed.

"Well done, I'll use that as a premonition for things to come."

CHAPTER 28

Angels

CLARA

THE ROOM WAS WHITE, accented with silver and gold. Thick curtains hung heavy above the windows. Furniture encrusted with diamonds and precious stones sat tastefully throughout the room. Ornate, silver-plated candles cast a sleepy glow. In any other situation, it would have been beautiful. Clara lay on the bed, sinking into the many pillows. She stood when a tall, lean woman entered the room.

"Clara," she said with an unfamiliar accent. "My name is Alora. I'll be your personal assistant."

Haven't I done this before? Just like when I first went to Ancora. Rory… he didn't hear or see me. They mentioned the bracelet. I knew that merchant was fishy. Ugh. What's next? Princess-like attire? Hot baths and hearty food? A death wish from an old cranky mage? At least this time there isn't any mud.

Alora opened the shimmery doors to the armoire. The candles reflected golden light across the walls from the door's mirrored surface. She pulled out a dress. "I think this will suit you well." She smiled and gestured to a small, partitioned room. "The shower's behind that wall."

Blinking back tears, Clara walked behind the stone wall,

236

entering a pearly stone shower with a diamond showerhead hanging from the ceiling by vines. Undressing, she piled her clothes upon the stool behind a frosted partition. Not finding a spigot, she stood under the shower to feel a steady stream of perfectly heated water.

From behind the wall, Alora raised her voice just enough to be heard over the shower. "The ladies and I will return shortly. Until then, we'll give you privacy. Enjoy your shower. There's a bath, as well, if you prefer that. I'm sure you have already located the spa items. If not, let me know."

Clara answered from under the shower's flow. "Yes. I see them. Thank you." Once the door shut, and Clara was alone, a rush of emotions engulfed her. Tears turned to sobs. Eyes red, she studied the decorative ceiling. A mosaic of an angel was crafted from stained glass. Golden hues accentuated her clothes. Intricate detail brought the image to life using shading and shadows. The angel held out her hands as if she had something to give. She wished she could go home to her own Angel. Back to when life consisted of walking to work and expected daily activities. Even a boring life was better than this. The emotional roller-coaster of the months prior whooshed upon her like a raging tsunami. She wanted to scream. She wanted to get dressed and run until she found another ray of light leading her home.

"Why do things keep happening to me? I don't understand! Why am I even here?" she yelled, voice wavering under the water's flow. "I went from cold claw-foot tubs to modern... freakin' showers. Will I... keep bouncing from realm to realm... failing no matter where I go? I just..." She fell to a whisper as she spoke to the mosaic angel above her. "I hate this. Zerpith mentioned how there's something I don't see. It's obvious it's this stupid mark on my forehead, but... that isn't the whole story. I can't see the purpose of my life here! The Preceptor. What was his name? Aesian! He was supposed to help us but the creep abducted me instead. This... it can't be a good sign. All that effort to get here only to fall straight into a trap and now... we... I—I don't know how to find the windowless castle."

Clara pushed her brow against the hard stone. It felt cool upon her skin, even with the warm water streaming from the showerhead. She cried without restraint. "I miss home… I miss Angel." She slid to a squat. Placing her head into her hands the water cascaded over her hair, she pressed her hands harder to shield her face from the water. "I think I love Sawyer, but I can't… I'll never have both worlds. I know he'll come for me but I don't know when. I need to tell him how I feel, but how can I? I don't know what my future looks like to surrender to love. I don't—" Broken sobs released, and she rose to her feet. Slamming a fist onto the shower wall she screamed. "No one promised me a happy ending! I can't fall in love. Not now. It's what I've always dreamed of and after all this time, when my life is uncertain… love finds me."

Clara stared at the Angel mosaic again. "I love him. But, I don't know what to do next." A steady stream of tears fell from down her cheeks, mixing into the shower's stream. Closing her eyes she faced the pouring water, allowing it to cover her face until she gasped for air. Letting the water wash her tears away, she left them in the shower. Taking the soft robe hanging on the outside shower's wall, she tied it around her waist. Stepping to the mirror, she met her reflection. There was still nothing on her brow. She sneered at herself and her puffy red eyes. Her voice sounded strained and small, "I'm tired of crying."

Opening a large curtain covering three connected windows, the candles dimmed in comparison to the light shining in. Outside was a large bustling city. People and creatures all walked the streets below, looking small and insignificant from her height. They didn't know she was trapped. Life moved forward without her. Yet. Yet, her friends were down there, somewhere, most likely looking for her. It was an endless, cruel cycle. Closing the curtains in anger, the candles once again had their moment to shine.

CHAPTER 29
Spinning in Circles

SAWYER

RORY BURST through the door of Slumbers, gasping for breath. Sawyer and Jade, goblets in hand, watched as the boy ran to them.

"Hey, Rory," Sawyer lifted the goblet to toast the boy's arrival. Jade lifted hers but upon seeing Rory's face, they both quickly lowered them. "What's wrong?"

"It's Clara. She was right next to me. I promise, she was…"

"She's gone?" Sawyer stood, his breathing shallowed.

Rory's lip quivered. "She was right next to me. I turned around, and she was gone. It happened so fast. I don't know where she is."

Sawyer slowly put his glass down and bent to meet the boy's eyes. "Thanks for telling us. Where was the last place you saw her?"

"The bazaar. We were going to find something to eat."

"Did she eat anything up till that point?" Jade set her glass down, her eyes sparking with angst.

"Only a sample of something, but there was this man with a bracelet… He wanted her to have it, and she kept saying she saw Zerpith."

"She saw Zerpith?" Jade swooped down towards Rory. Her

goblet fell from their table, spilling a tiny crimson river onto the floor. "Where did she see him?"

"In a crystal ball."

"At the bazaar?" Sawyer said.

"No, at a notion shop. I thought it was him ensuring we arrived. I..." Tears began to pool in the boy's eyes, and Sawyer gentled his tone.

"Go find the others. Let them know. We'll find her, just like last time. Great work filling us in, by the way. There was nothing else you could have done." He rustled the boy's hair with repeated assurance. "We'll find her."

Sawyer ran straight to the bazaar. Using Clara's badge, he showed it to the vendors, asking if they'd seen her. "Commander Knight, I did see this woman," a vendor informed as Sawyer put away the badge with Clara's face. "She was talking with the merchant next to me. He offered her a bracelet, which she didn't take."

"Did he look familiar? Do you know where we can find him?"

"No, Commander. I haven't seen him before, or his stand."

"Did you happen to speak with him? Did he sell anything other than bracelets?"

"No, sir. He kept to himself. He had a few pieces of jewelry. They looked to be high quality."

Sawyer spoke to Jade, his voice stern. "Tracking her won't do any good. I'll head to the citadel. They might have word about her whereabouts." Crossing one of the bridges to the massive building, a guard stopped them as they reached the steps.

"You're not to enter, Commander."

"Hurly, it's me... We played cards together a few months past. Surely you remember how I beat you. And, if I could add, by no small amount."

"How can I forget?" the guard said with a grin. "But I'm sorry, I can't let you in."

"We need to see Aesian. We need his help."

"Aesian has requested that you and your party leave at once."

"Then I'll go in, if you can't let him through," Jade tried to push through the guard, only to be stopped by another.

"Nor you, Jade. None of your party shall come a step closer. Now that you're here, I'll need to ask you to leave Eros entirely. It's not my choice, I'm sure you know, but it's my duty to tell you."

"Outrageous." Jade put a hand to her hip. "I was born here. I won't be leaving."

"Please, comply. I don't want to send for the forces." Stepping away, Sawyer backed from the guards and motioned an angry Jade to follow.

"Who in their right mind gave him the authority to tell me I can't enter the citadel? It's a mage's right to do so! The audacity. The crassness of that man." Jade paced.

Sawyer calmed his internal rage. It wasn't going to help them find Clara. "He's only doing what he was told..."

"This is bullcrap," Jade sneered, providing some much-needed comic relief to Sawyer.

Jade's lip tightened at Sawyer's weak laugh. "What?"

"I think this is the first time I've heard Clara in you."

Jade rolled her eyes. "Of all the crazy things she says, that'd be the one that won't leave. What is bullcrap anyway? You know, each time we turn around, she's gone. This journey is taking us in full circles."

"And I couldn't love it more." *Clara, I'm coming. Just as I promised. I'll always find you.*

"Well, what I'm not going to do is watch you spin like a top over it. It's obvious she's in the citadel. Their message is a little less than subtle. But why? That's the question." Jade dropped her arms to her side and grabbed Sawyer's sleeve in an attempt to quicken his pace. "Zerpith..."

"Are you suggesting he has something to do with this? I had my suspicions..."

"I'm reluctant to suggest anything, but Clara just disappeared. It could be a working of his, or maybe she was just taken without Rory noticing."

"Rory told us about the bracelet. He must have crafted it. You work with him closely. Have you noticed anything off?"

"Pause that thought for now." Jade let go of his sleeve, but it remained bunched from her grasp. "I need to move with caution. We don't know what he's planned. But, this I'm sure of. He can peer into a mage's thoughts if they're nearby. I'm no exception. We can't let him—"

"Then it's settled, Jade." Sawyer brushed his fingers through his hair anxiously. "I'm going into the citadel. One way or another. You'll… you'll need to sit this one out."

"I agree, to an extent, but it worries me. I understand you're capable, but are you going to survive without me? That's the real question. One thing you can't do, lover boy, is spin in circles trying to rescue your lady in distress. Keep focused, and stay collected."

Sawyer smiled coyly. "Tornadoes spin, and are pretty dangerous. I fret for the one that stands in my way."

Jade huffed. "I'll find Rory and Jasper. Take Onyx with you. This may not end up as anything in the end, for all we know. Oh, and Eleanor. It would be good to have her with you as well."

"Aye, aye, Captain Jade," Sawyer said with a wry wink.

"Your charm does nothing. Off you go. I'll be thinking of everything other than what I should be." Sawyer jogged off, but before he got too far, Jade called to him, "By the way, be careful, okay?"

Stopping and turning to face her, yards apart, he saluted. "Aye, aye." He resumed his jog down the walkway, ignoring the looks from the ladies who watched him pass. At one time, he would have indulged in the attention, but after meeting the mud-covered lady at Giant's Pass, all that had changed.

Onyx was buried shoulders-deep in a pile of small trinkets when Sawyer found him rummaging in a remnant shop. Escaping the junk with a new random treasure, he smiled upon seeing his friend. "What do you think about staying a few days after meeting with Aesian before we move on?" the alchemist asked while observing a small magic-infused gear.

"I think we don't have much choice since Clara's gone, but I'll warn you, we aren't exactly welcomed anymore."

"We lost her again? Well, we like excitement, don't we?" Onyx replied, holding a bag of rusty gears to go with his other item. Sawyer waited while the alchemist studied each one. "You mentioned we aren't welcome?"

"That seems to be the case. I'm positive Clara's trapped at the citadel. We need to find a way in. I have to find her."

"The citadel has many side doors and entrances. I don't see why we can't enter another way. We'll need to disguise ourselves or find an alternative entrance that isn't widely known. Yet, I've been in this shop for some time, and not one person has told me to leave. Are you sure we aren't welcome?"

"It's a recent command, but if word travels as fast as it does at Ancora, we're short on time. But you might have something there about disguises. I wonder where we can get uniforms. Jade can't help. If she uses her magic to cover us, every mage around would know. Besides that, Zerpith might read her thoughts and ruin the whole plan."

"Why would Zerpith care?" Onyx asked before he paid for his stuff.

"I'll tell you while we walk. We need to find Eleanor."

CHAPTER 30
Two Funerals

ANGEL - MEANWHILE IN AMERICA

ANGEL GRIMACED AT THE BULLETIN. She'd been dreading this day for weeks. A memorial of life that seemed more like a giving-up party. Candles danced alongside the funeral home walls. Smiling mosaic angels cast a colorful glow around the pews from stained glass windows. Seats were filling for a body never found. The police called it a mystery, ending the investigation without answers. The rented casket was empty. Beside it was a smiling picture of Clara, taken by her…

Clara spun in a circle. This was the first time she had worn the lilac dress she'd obsessed over for months. Clara didn't want to spend the money, but it was the perfect celebratory splurge. The ruffles, the eyelet detail, all gave her friend fairytale vibes, so she said. A bow around the waist snatched her in the middle nicely. The breeze was soft and the sun gentle.

"You're a mess," Angel laughed as her friend continued to watch the folds of her dress flutter during the circles. "But I wouldn't have you any other way."

"It just makes me so happy. This day, this dress. Do you feel that?"

"The only thing I'm feeling is a hot coffee and maybe pita and hummus. Nix the maybe. I want some now."

"No, but yes... to that. The pita and coffee, I mean. But that wasn't what I was talking about. I feel free... don't you? It's only been a week since graduation. We have our whole life ahead of us. We can be anything. Literally, anything with our one life." Clara stopped twirling to push her dress down from the velocity, laughing heartily.

Angel smiled, shaking her head with feigned irritation. *"How about you spin the crap out of life? Make a mess, get a little dizzy. Like you are now."*

Clara side-stepped to catch her balance. *"How can I not? Isn't life the most beautiful thing? We're done with monotonous school, and now we get to... we get to choose what we want to do. We are full-grown adults now. It's so exciting."*

Angel snuffled back a cackle. *"We always got to choose. Crazy lady."*

Clara wrinkled her nose and flopped onto the blanket. Her dress billowed around her. *"I'm glad we got into the same college. I know we didn't have to rent a dorm, but imagine all the fun we'll have together. Eeeeek! Maybe we'll find the love of our lives..."* She laid on the grass. The thick trees gently rustled in the breeze, making the moment even more peaceful.

"Clara, cheese." Amused, Angel used her phone to capture the look of pure joy on her friend's face. The smile was genuine, her eyes shining. Lilac looked good on her, but it was more than that. Life looked good on her.

Angel watched more people filter in, each quietly taking a seat. A few from the coffee shop and a couple of friends from college. Clara's estranged mom, who hadn't stopped crying from the time she entered the church, looked tired. Clara's mother hadn't seen or spoken to her daughter in over a decade. And now she must regret it, when it's too late. The sadness was overtaking her, consuming any viable signs of vitality. Clara's mother looked more like a zombie now.

Angel fiddled with the corner of her bulletin. The edge was bent and crinkled. She tried to smooth the paper, but it wouldn't go back. Angel whispered. *"You're not gone. Somehow, somewhere, you're alive. Most likely crying and making up stories that only make you more afraid... but you're not dead. I'm not going to mourn your death... I refuse to. Instead, I'll celebrate and remember. I should've done that more when you were here. You deserve to be celebrated."*

CLARA - THE CITADEL IN EROS

The Next Day

The coffin was empty. The hard pews held only a few bodies. Angel, seated at the front, was wiping tears, but still looked as beautiful as ever. Her mom didn't cry, but sat in cold silence.

Next to the casket was her picture. The one from her badge. She cringed. "Why would they choose that one? It's a terrible picture of me!" She wanted to push it over and smash into its center. She wished to jump into the casket to hide, bury herself away to sleep in the confined darkness.

Everyone was seated, sparsely apart and mostly choosing the back of the small room. Angel was the only one to stand. She walked to the casket. A small arrangement of flowers lay on her closed coffin. "Clara... you had so much potential, if only you could see it. If only you knew." Angel turned her head. She was staring at her in her dream. "You need to wake up."

The words echoed through the room. Angel's face grew red. Screaming at full volume, she tossed a small, balled-up piece of paper onto the floor. "You're not dead!" In rage, her friend clawed the flowers off the coffin. Ripped apart, they fell onto the aged carpet in pieces. Yanking on the lid of the casket, she pried and tugged, trying to open it.

Clara no longer watched. The scene turned dark, deathly silent. The blackness held a familiar clout that she didn't mind. "Is someone calling me? But... I don't know. I don't remember my name," she tossed around, but it was a tight fit. The sentiment was curious, but not frightening. "What's my name again?"

The lilac dress was made of silk, high-waisted with white rosebuds accentuating the bodice. Sheer sleeves, cut with a "V" for ease of movement and tied bows, hung shapeless from the sides. As beautiful as it was, it was only a dress. But the woman in the bed tossed and turned as the covers tightly wrapped around her.

"Lady Clara... Oh my, time to wake up." Alora tried haphazardly to unwind the woman from the tightly twisted sheets. "How did you ever manage?" She chuckled until the sheet-twisted Clara sat upright. As Clara's matted head of hair birthed from the top of the opening, the woman laughed. Clara spotted a glimpse of herself in the large standing mirror across from her bed.

"What the... Gosh, just call me spawn. Spawn of the bed!" Clara joked.

"Here, lie down... Yes, roll this way. A little more. Perfect." Both ladies giggled as Clara was freed from the twisted blankets. Stepping onto the cold floor, she brushed her hair out of her face.

"Thanks for the help."

"Of course, I'm here for that reason. So my next task, after unwrapping you, is to get you dressed and ready to meet the Preceptor."

Alora helped Clara into the intricate dress. "It's lilac..."

"And incredibly gorgeous, don't you think? Crafted by the finest, of course. It fits you like a dream. It never ceases to amaze me the skills of our in-house tailor."

"Yeah, it's beautiful." Clara drifted.

Angel put her phone away, happy with the capture. "That color looks amazing on you."

"Thanks," Clara said, beaming. "I really didn't want to spend the money, but I'm glad I did."

The day would soon end, as would the week. Boxes would be packed into an overflowing trunk. The truck would empty to fill the shared room of modern decor mixed with shabby chic details. Angel's modern fur and simple art mixed among Clara's vintage boho decor clashed and complemented each other in a marriage only the two would understand.

She'd wear the dress once more, but it would be for the last time.

Clara felt her sides. The soft fabric felt smooth. No pockets.

"The Preceptor requested I give this to you, on his behalf," Alora informed as she handed a small box to Clara.

Clara hesitated before accepting the gift. *Stars only know what's inside...* She tugged on the elegant bow. Bubbles of light sparked as the box fell open, unveiling a brilliant necklace. White in presence, but gold in reflection, it stole her breath away. A small crystal star hung from the center of a larger loop. Rays of light cast colorful, magical reflections. The room danced with the illumination. Her mouth dropped showing a surprised emotion contrary to the sadness filling her heart. "I can't take this. I mean… I'd like to keep it but… this looks too expensive."

Alora carefully took the necklace from the box and clasped it around Clara's neck. "The workmanship is impressive. Don't entertain any thoughts of objection; you might offend the Preceptor." She grabbed Clara's hands. "If I were to be forthright, you may find him handsome." Alora laughed when she released Clara's hands.

Clara nodded but her emotions were numb. *Handsome or not, he isn't Sawyer. I wonder if everyone knows what happened, that Aesian stole me against my will? I hope Sawyer doesn't think I've agreed to any of this. I've searched this entire room for a secret escape, but there's only one door. I can't jump out the window, either. It's too far.* Heat rose to Clara's cheeks. *It's only been a day. Maybe they think I just got lost, but I doubt it. I just don't know if they suspect Aesian. What if they meet with him and he acts like he has no idea where I am? What if he tells them I'm somewhere else and they leave?* Hopelessness shaded Clara's thinking. "I may never get out of here," she unconsciously whispered.

"I'm sorry, Lady Clara. I didn't hear what you said."

"Oh, it's nothing. I was just admiring the necklace. That's all"

Alora smiled, "It is the most lovely pendant, isn't it? Now, come with me. I'm taking you to him now. You'll dine together this evening."

Clara followed her lady's maid down the hall. Lights appeared and snuffed out as they passed by. Each seemed to know when to light and extinguish. "How does Eros have so many modern inventions?"

"Modern inventions?"

"Compared to other places I've been. Eros seems to have everything."

"We are well developed. The Preceptor has done a fantastic job at keeping us comfortable and guaranteeing we can provide the absolute best to everyone who enters the city. He's one of the superior ones. A healer turned mage. A mage of healing, many like to say. He manages both, which is a rare talent."

"So he is both healer and mage?"

"Precisely so. In that right alone, he warrants respect and reverence. Many have tried to bridge the gap, but few come out alive."

"So if he's so important, why am I the one to have dinner with him?"

"Clara." Alora stopped and grabbed her shoulders. "Please be respectful of the decision he's made. You're of rare power as well, and you both suit each other nicely."

"Everyone keeps saying that about my power, but…" Her words were taken away by the exquisite balcony spanning across the vestibule. Peering from the landing into the vast floor below, she saw Eleanor. She opened her mouth to call, but no words escaped. *Please, speak. This is your chance. Eleanor will get you out of this. Speak up. Speak up!*

Eleanor spotted Clara, but the healer focused on the necklace hanging from Clara's neck. Her eyes narrowed. Grabbing the hem of her dress, she locked eyes with Clara, flipped her hair, and walked promptly out of the citadel.

Eleanor. Please, tell them I'm here. I know you will. Grabbing the banister, she pulled away from Alora to run down the steps. Her feet stopped her before she could descend.

"I'll not repeat myself. For your safety, and mine, don't do that again. Aesian could kill us both in a glance," Alora said, her tone dark but then quickly lightened. "Now, let's go." Clara's feet were once again mobile. Understanding that many had power over her, she complied. All the anxiety over Lectus… replaced by a man she was meeting for dinner. The feeling of being the least powerful mixed as well as ice cream and ketchup.

Alora took her arm to guide her down the steps. At the bottom was a silver-haired man with a dashing smile, the same blue-eyed man in the dining room at Mayor Gribble's. Her eyes dried from lack of blinking, and she rubbed them.

"Beautiful Clara. What a picture you paint. That color is stunning on you." He grabbed both her hands. "I see you received the necklace." He nodded to Alora. "Alora, I'll take it from here."

"Thank you, Preceptor, for the beautiful necklace," Clara said, heat flushing her cheeks. The sentiment felt fake.

"Call me Aesian. No need for formalities," he said, offering an arm that she took. "Tonight, I'm going to take you to the most prestigious restaurant in Eros. All around, to be exact. The King's Table. They serve a limited but creative cuisine. I think you'll find the options to your liking. Due to the current state of the city, I'll transport you from here."

"Current state? Is something happening?"

"Not for you to worry about. Hold still. I'm transporting us now." Aeisan wrapped his arms around Clara, and they vanished.

The air was light. Fluorescent colors whirled and whipped. As soon as dizziness set in, her feet felt the pressure of solid ground. Set over a river, vines covered the roof of the establishment. Greenery cascaded toward the ground. Small white flowers popped against the greenness. Dark wood columns structured the entrance, standing proud at the restaurant's entrance.

"Preceptor," the hostess said with a curtsy, "I have your table ready. Follow me." A private table overlooked the river that expanded into a large lake, with boats drifting among the waves. The hostess pulled Clara's chair out, then placed napkins on their laps before leaving. Another man approached the table, bowing before speaking.

"Preceptor, Lady Clara. I'm the owner of The King's Table, Hethin Nohly. It's my utmost honor to have you dining here tonight. I've personally prepared your courses, paired with the finest wine." Motioning to the waiter beside him, he continued, "Mallory, alongside our best of staff, will be serving you both tonight. Of course, should you need me directly, just ask." Bowing once more, he left the table while Mallory provided sparkling water.

"The view is really pretty," Clara said, fiddling with the necklace before letting it drop back to her chest.

"As time passes, you'll expect no less from me." He reached out to grab her hands. She pulled them away to hold out the necklace.

"Tell me about this beautiful gift. It must have been expensive."

"It's an heirloom from my ancestors. A rare piece. It's said to possess unknown powers, much like yourself. It suits you."

"It's passed down? Are you sure you want to give it to me? Shouldn't you save it for someone special?" Oysters interrupted the conversation, along with a fancy cheese board clustered with grapes, crackers, and an assortment of meats. She resisted the urge to dig in like a starving monster. In all the rush of things happening, she didn't realize how hungry she was. Aesian motioned for her to go first. Clara carefully put far less food than she would have liked on her plate.

"Tell me about America. Would you like to visit your home one day?"

"I'm surprised you have heard of it. Well, I'd love to visit, but that's not possible."

"All things are possible with the right connections. America has been the talk of many. You aren't a secret around here. That knight happened to find you. That's simply how it came to be, but you were never destined for Ancora. I apologize for the rude way we've brought you here, but your friends wouldn't understand. It was a necessary transaction. However, this morning I invited them for breakfast, and they agreed. They're packing to head back to Ancora."

Clara's eyes burned. "I need to use the bathroom, if that's okay." Sniffing, she grabbed the napkin. "I'm sorry, my allergies have been acting up today."

"And I'm sorry, because you can't leave the table. However, I can help you with your allergies later..." Aesian's eyes softened. "Sawyer only postponed his marriage to Princess Adeline so he could help with your mission. Now that you're here, his task is complete. Going forward, he's planning on taking his role as future king with his new bride."

Clara didn't notice the emotion that flashed in Aesian's eyes. Staring at her hands, she held her breath. *It can't be. Sawyer wouldn't leave without me. There's no way I read him wrong but... marriage to Princess Adeline? How could I be so stupid. I should have known. No, I did know deep down, but I didn't want it to be true.* Clara's heart cracked. She wanted to cry all over again. When she looked up, Aesian's gaze stared blankly downwards, shielding her from his face. Was that? No, it couldn't be a tear.

He's lying. I don't know what happened between Sawyer and Princess Adeline, but it's not what he says. Clara stared at her wine glass. The deep red liquid sat motionless. Unblinking, she imagined her higher self. It had been some time since she thought of her...

Grasping the wine, she splashed it across his face. "I don't believe you!" she screamed. Turning over the table, she opened the window next to her, splashing into the river below. The water was cold, but it only pushed her to swim faster. Just as her power helped her escape the bird, it allowed her to breathe under water until she was beyond the city gates. She'd catch up with her friends, and they'd figure the rest out together.

Breaking her own daydream she lifted her chin and straightened her back. *Perhaps Lectus was nothing more than a tactful story to get her to Eros. Perhaps there was nothing to fear after all.*

Aesian stared behind her, intensity piercing his eyes. He lifted a brow when he noticed her watching. She quickly glanced behind her, nothing was there. She cleared her throat. "I guess it's for the best," she lied back. Clara stopped any additional words from spewing. *He could kill you in a glance. Play it safe. Keep yourself alive long enough for someone to find you. Or, when the time is right, make a break for it.* Her nerves hung in her throat and sloshed with the oyster as she swallowed. She coughed quietly and took a drink of water. Lifting her head, she looked the preceptor in the eyes. There were no traces of tears. "So what does a preceptor do?"

"Intrigued by me?" He took a sip of wine. "I advise, teach, and plan the future of Eros. Nothing you need to worry about. I've mastered both the ways of mage and healer, as you might know. This power gives me prestige and social standing."

Clara lost connection with his eyes. Lifting her eyebrows, she stabbed at a grape. It rolled around, avoiding her fork. *So he is what they say. Lovely.* The next dish, the main course, arrived. Seared aged meat with rosemary, potatoes, and an unfamiliar vegetable. The savory food lightened her urge to stab her own throat from making forced conversation.

After longer than she had hoped, the waiters came with the final dish. The small, delicately decorated cake was the perfect portion for two. Aesian smiled, showing his dimples. "Dearest Clara. I have enjoyed our meal together. This wouldn't be the way I would prefer to ask, but heed my question and answer wisely. As fortune would have it, we cannot stall for a proper courtship." He leaned in and grabbed her hands. "Some of the most important decisions we make are ones made quickly. Ancora was never the proper fit for you. I'm sure you know that. If you were, they would have unlocked your magic by now. As with any great power, we should pair it accordingly. It's sudden, but I feel it. We... we are meant to be together." Aesian spilled the last part out awkwardly.

Clara groaned. She pulled her hands away. Aesian didn't flinch. He kept talking, "Your powers are tremendous. Zerpith confirmed, and I agree. With my watchful eye and experience, we'll be an unstoppable pair. You'll live like a queen and want for nothing. Join me for a lifetime together." His proposal felt indifferent, despite his cheery tone.

Dropping to one knee, he presented an incredible ring. Clara stared. Her eyes fixated on its shimmer. She swallowed. Mages and healers alike were watching. They were smiling, happy to have a small part in the special day. A hard lump formed in her throat. Jumping out the window wasn't going to be an option and everyone watching possessed power she didn't. They all were on Aesian's side and not one would fight for her. *Just say yes and figure it out later. If you say no now, you'll have more trouble to deal with. If they don't kill me, I might have to live with something worse.* "I... I..." Aesian waited. *It amazes me, this entire thing. Am I really that powerful? So powerful that this man would give up his entire life to marry me. He doesn't love me. It's his eyes. They tell a different story.*

Her attention darted from his gaze to the ring. It was stunning, but she didn't want it. *I can be anything here, and no one would know any different. I can be the person who says yes, only for now. Please, forgive me, Sawyer. I have to do what I need to in this moment to survive. I'll figure it out later.* The excited faces held big smiles. Her heart raced, hands sweaty. *Just tell him yes! You have to!*

"No."

Gasps erupted around her. "Clara," his voice lowered. "This was a question without a choice. For both of us, you'll need to proceed with caution."

"I said no." Reality hit her. Actually, it slapped her across the face. She could already feel the emotion burn from the hit. She gasped and covered her mouth with her hand. *What did I do?*

"My dear Clara!" Aesian announced gleefully. Jumping, he pulled her from her seat to hug her. The tables of people clapped and cheered. He placed the ring on her finger and pushed her into her seat. The waiter, wasting no time, cut the cake. Tiny white rose buds sprinkled the air.

Leaning over the table, Aesian connected eyes with her. "I'm choosing to ignore your words, dear Clara. In case you didn't know it already. You will marry me."

Bravery filled her. She was powerful too. At least that's what she was told. "Aesian. Need I remind you? If you hurt me, or kill me, my powers will grow stronger. I will rise from the dead and hunt you down…" *Where am I going with this…* "Then… I'll bury you under an unmarked stone. But! I'll wait until winter, so a cold sheet of ice covers your grave." She deepened her voice. "Not even the angels will mourn your passing."

Aesian's eyes squinted as he concentrated on her brow. She felt it pulse. He backed into his seat, but only for a second. Then, he laughed.

"Dear Clara, I don't fear you. Now eat a piece of cake to celebrate our new beginnings together. It looks divine, does it not?"

Heart sinking, she took a bite of the celebratory dessert. There was nothing else she could do, at least not now. She might as well enjoy the cake, nevertheless. The ridiculous meal complete, Aesian paid the bill and transported them back to the citadel. He opened the door to her room.

"Rest tonight. Think about your future. I'm patient, almost to a fault, but not forever. I do not fear you, nor will I ever. Keep that in mind and repeat it. This can go two ways, but you make the choice. Let's make sure it works in our favor." With a hand on her back, he pushed her gently into the room and sealed the door.

CHAPTER 31
Eros' Secret

SAWYER

ONYX AND SAWYER passed the crowds of people gathered at the market. Yesterday they had no luck finding their healer. So far, as of this morning, no one demanded they leave, but the increasing rudeness from the residents demonstrated they were short on time. The day almost over, they finally found the healer sitting on a crystal bench by the lake, many yards away from the busy shoppers. Fists clenched, her jaw tight.

"Eleanor, are you alright?" Concern shaded the knight's eyes when he saw she'd been crying.

"I was exci— Never mind. I searched to find Aesian, but he wasn't in his room. Although I didn't find him, I did find out about something else."

Sawyer saw the pain in Eleanor's eyes. *She's in love with Aesian.* "What news did you uncover?" he asked gently.

"Our heroic Clara is getting married. She's deserted us… abandoned the journey for a life of luxury. We should probably leave. Let her live her life out in—in peace."

"Where did you hear this and from whom? Seems rather fast." *Certainly Clara isn't going to marry by her own will. It's possible Eros wants her for something, and this is their way of keeping her. That has to be the reason. It must. I doubt they'll hurt her, but if any man lays a hand on her, I'll disregard all thoughts of negotiation!*

"It happened this very evening. At The King's Table. He proposed. She said yes. She's even wearing his family's necklace. That's all I need to know."

"Who proposed?"

"Aesian."

I don't believe it," Sawyer cautioned. "She's probably said yes out of fear. We must find her before the marriage takes place." Sawyer calmed the heat of anger that brewed.

"Then don't. But it won't change a thing. Aesian will be the love of her life, and she'll forget about us… and the mission."

"Why would he want to marry Clara?" Eleanor shrugged, and Sawyer continued. "We need to get into the citadel."

"Best of luck," she said with a flip of her hair.

"You know the layout better than any of us. Unfortunately, none of the usual entrances will be an option. We'll need something more obscure… if that's even possible. What do you suggest? We need to rescue Clar—"

"Clara seems rather happy," Eleanor snapped.

The knight dropped his arms to his sides. "Trust me, she isn't. She probably doesn't know what else to do."

Eleanor paused. "The bottom chambers of the citadel connect to a tunnel line. It's big enough to travel through. Don't ask me how I know and don't bring it up while you're there. You can find it from the root cellar behind the Briggit's Barrel. Just… tread with caution, and don't be alarmed at what you find."

"Won't you be coming with us? We could really use your assistance."

"No. I—I can't. Not this time, but take care and be careful."

The local bar, Briggit's Barrel, was highly recommended for its historic significance as the first building built in Eros. Rumored to have hosted men and creatures of all kinds through the decades, it wasn't a place to skip when in town. Both Sawyer and Onyx had visited before and enjoyed a card game or two while eating the famous food. This visit would hold a different excitement, one that wouldn't involve foamy beers and a stack of cards, but instead a reluctant, moss-covered cellar door.

"This must be it." Onyx tugged on the door. "Locked." Taking out a thin metal tool, he picked the lock. Sawyer checked for anyone watching. Only the lights from the street kept them from complete darkness. Eros was a picture of activity come evening, and this night was no exception.

"Sounds like a party happening in the center square." Sawyer shifted legs as he waited. "Good thing, as it's probably the distraction we need."

"Eh…" Onyx picked away, consumed by the challenge and focused on winning against the metal puzzle.

"I love a good party, don't you? Sounds like they're having just that. Clara would love it. I'm thinking, once all this is over, I'll ask her to stay… at Ancora."

"Eh…" *Pick, pick, pick.*

"Holly would be delighted to have her as part of the family. Annabelle too. I've been impressed with how her riding skills have improved. I already miss her and the way she seems to disappear within herself. I wonder where she goes? I wonder what she's thinking?"

"*Grunt.*" *Pick, pick, pick.*

"I think I'm in love with Clara."

Onyx stopped. Without looking, he pulled the lock. It opened. "You finally noticed?"

"It's that obvious?" Sawyer said, sheepishly. "I haven't ironed out the details yet, but once this is over, I'm going to ask her to officially court." Sawyer climbed down the ladder fixed to the opening of the newly unlocked hatch. The alchemist followed. The blackness was thick. Sawyer lit a torch and handed another to Onyx.

"Princess Adeline's a smart woman. A simple conversation should clear things up." Onyx waved the torch across the wall to illuminate anything lurking and to search for anything he could collect.

"So you've heard? It's never that easy. They left so abruptly. I don't think King Boren was happy about the delay."

"Everyone knows. Well, maybe not Clara, but we didn't want to bring it up. Did you talk to Adeline directly?"

"I haven't," Sawyer mumbled under his breath. *What a fine mess this is. I'm open to the idea that a conversation would help, but it isn't just me involved. King Henric and King Boren have to agree. King Boren, maybe, but King Henric…?"*

"Night Honey!" Onyx exclaimed, holding a few empty vials. Taking one, he reached to pick a wilted flower from the musky, dingy wall. The stamen, chunky despite the frailty of the petals, released a sticky substance once pressed. Onyx beamed. "What a find that was. Rare, too. The tunnels aren't so bad."

"And here I thought you were calling me honey," Sawyer laughed.

Onyx joined the laughter while tucking the vials away into a soft pouch. "I'll leave that to Clara."

Each step taken was paired with an eerie thud. It wasn't wet or dry within the tunnels, but earthy and damp. Their torches highlighted areas where shelves had once stored goods. Long since unused, pale vines, dirt, and cobwebs now filled what hadn't already decomposed. A few ladders appeared, all with sealed exits. Night plants hung limp from the ceiling and crept along the walls. Onyx stopped now and then to collect whatever caught his eye. Sawyer never discouraged him. Around the half-mile mark, muffled, soft voices were heard.

"I can't do this anymore. It hurts," said a weak voice.

"I'm so tired… so tired," said another.

"Death would be a welcomed visitor. My powers are waning. If I don't get out of here, please tell my parents… I love them."

"If you don't get out, none of us will. Just stop talking. I don't have the energy for useless conversation. None of us do."

"Eros has slaves?" Onyx whispered in horror as they saw a line of chained mages and healers. Each one expelled magic into a small crystal in front of them that was connected to a thick, clear tube. Their life force of magic gleamed with prism colors and bright bursts of light while traveling through tubes into a larger glass pipe.

"Sawyer?" a small, weak voice squeaked out.

"Nash?" The small boy nodded his head, tears rolled down his cheeks. "How did you get here? What happened?"

"Zerpith was mad at me," he said, choking back a sob. "He… he sent me here for rehabilitation. He said—he said that once I came here, I wouldn't be afraid to use magic anymore. He said I was a disgrace. I promise that I can expel really well into the crystal. Can you tell him I'm better now? Can I please go home?"

"Onyx, take Nash out of here. I'll discuss it with Zerpith later. We can't leave him here." Sawyer scanned the other hopeful faces.

"Commander Knight, he can't go. The chains, you see, they do more than bind us," said a chained mage.

Another weak voice continued the story. "If we leave, not only will they find us, but they'll retaliate with punishment. I—I don't want to be punished."

Onyx picked the cuffs shackling the young mage. The disconnected metal clanged to the floor. "Mages have their ways, but never underestimate the brains of man." With pleading eyes, each held out their wrists. Onyx rubbed his brow. "I don't have enough supplies to free everyone right now, I'm sorry to say. I'll come back for each of you. Do you know if the crystals are transporting or absorbing magic?"

"They pull it from us. There's a reactor that stores our magic to power the city," an old and feeble healer spoke. "As you can see, I have aged physically. Even my hair is returning to its original color. I'm dying down here."

"I've never seen an aged healer before," Sawyer whispered sadly.

"I'm glad I cannot see my reflection. Not in this state. I shan't last much longer, for which I am grateful." The healer's head sank to his chest. Many others dropped theirs, as well. Bowed heads jerked when a crack of a whip cut the air. Sawyer nudged Onyx. "Take Nash to Jasper. I'll take over from here. A few guards shouldn't be a problem."

Onyx carried the boy and ran through the tunnel. Sawyer backed against the wall. Sliding on a set of opened chains, he draped them over his wrists. Facing the crystal, he bowed his head to his chest.

"I'm told that the lights are flickering at the party. Someone's not pulling their weight," the guard sneered and checked each line that fed into the glass pipe. Inching towards Sawyer, the guard muttered to himself. Each crystal was lit, except one. Sawyer noticed because it was his.

Discreetly, he pulled one of the infused stones from his coat pocket and covered it with both hands. Slowly, he released it into the line until it lit up. The guard, seeing it blend with the others, nodded his head. "I'll not have a one of you slacking on the job. A special event is happening as we speak. No excuses, hear me? We recently got word that Aesian will be marrying Lady Clara. Together, they'll improve the city. Who knows, we may not need your sorry magic much longer. As long as she holds the power they say, there shouldn't be a need for weaklings, like you." He randomly kicked a mage. She grunted from the force. A loud raunchy cackle escaped his chapped lips. The other guards chortled with him.

Without further inspection, the guards left. Once gone, Sawyer let his bangles drop. The stone was almost out of power, and he tucked it back into his pocket. "I'm appalled… and terribly sorry. Here I've been enjoying all the conveniences of Eros at the expense of each of you. This was unexpected."

The old healer squirmed. "There are many of us. All chained throughout the tunnels. Probably around fifty or so in total. The tunnels were once used for storage. It gave merchants an easy way to travel the city. But now… now they hold us… mere slaves. I was once proud of Eros, but no longer."

"I'll figure out a way to save everyone. Give me… give me some time. Until then, please hang in there." He squeezed the old healer's shoulder gently. "You'll see freedom again, friend."

Without hesitation, Sawyer continued up the steps leading into the citadel, careful to pay attention for guards. Without finding any, he turned the handle on the door."Locked." Turning to walk back down, a large object pounded him on the head.

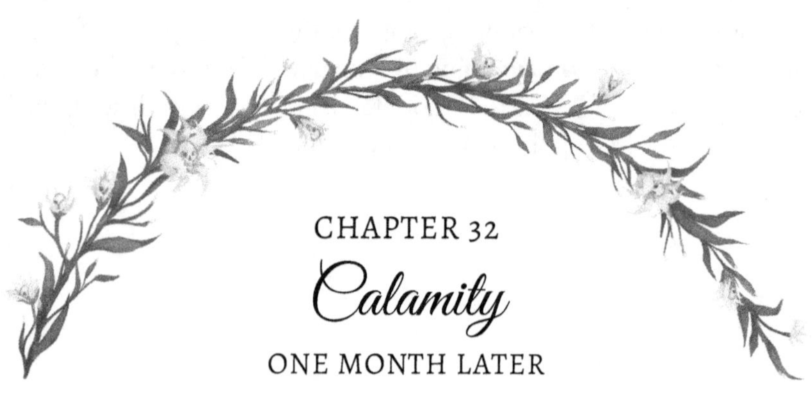

CHAPTER 32
Calamity
ONE MONTH LATER

CLARA

THE OUTDOOR MAT where Clara sat was woven with soft, thick rope. Cross-legged, she held a long baguette. The courtyard behind the citadel opened to a cloudless sky. It'd been weeks since she arrived in Eros. Unable to come up with a better escape plan, she played along with the engagement, at least for the time being. Tearing off a small piece of bread, she tossed it into the pond. Colorful fish rose to the surface to fight over the offering. "Don't worry. I have enough for everyone."

Aesian watched Clara coax the expectant koi. "Do I foresee a pond in our future home?"

"I think I'd like that. I always wanted a pond and a garden. Oh, maybe a secret garden that only I knew about. With a swing in it. I could disappear for hours, and no one could find me." Clara smiled at Aesian. For the last month they've been attending private events together and discussing magic theory. Although she felt bad for lying, the more she went along with the plan, the easier it was to mask her true feelings. Yet, she felt a trust in Aesian that was most unexpected considering how he lied about her friends, and Sawyer's marriage. *There's something that's making him act like this. I don't think it was his idea to marry me. Yet, he smiles when I see the regret in his eyes and when he doesn't think I'm looking, his face chances. It's as if he feels there isn't another choice.*

"A pond is most certainly an option. But do you truly wish to disappear? I know that our first dinner together made you... uncomfortable. I hoped, by now, that would be behind us."

"It's... fine. In America, you date before proposing marriage. You may even break up and date many people before finding the right one. You shocked me, that's all."

"It's much the same here, unless certain rules apply. Our arrangement was unconventional."

"Rules? That doesn't sound fun. I know everyone here thinks I have all these abilities, but ya'll are going to be sadly disappointed. I'm nothing special here. I was nothing all that great in America. Just call me Clara of Nothing."

"Clara of Nothing." His dimples showed as he smiled. "You say that now, but wait until we hit a breakthrough. I'll show you the way, no matter if it takes time. Sometimes, delayed power is the most intimidating. As soon as we marry, we can deepen your understanding of magic."

Clara picked at the grass by her leg. "Your dimples betray you. You appear to be this big bad guy, then you smile. Boom, baddy gone."

"Then they deceive you, as I can smite you with a glance."

"Well, then... then I'll bury you and cover you with ice so no one will find your unmarked grave." They both laughed, recalling Clara's threat from their first dinner.

Amusement lighted his eyes. "So that not even the angels will mourn my unfortunate passing?"

"Exactly. So don't forget it. That was the most important part. Being nothing is pretty dangerous, you know." She grabbed the remaining baguette and pointed it at him dangerously. He laughed and leaned back on his arms.

She scooted herself closer to Aesian on the mat. "I'm curious. I hear so many things about mages and healers, but what exactly are you? I know you bridged that gap, but I don't know how much I understand it. You were once an average healer, and then you somehow mixed your healing magic with mage magic? I noticed all the healers I met have white hair. Mages, their hair varies. But yours is silver."

"A fine observation. Healers are born with a variety of hair colors, just as a mage would be. We all come into this world the same. It's also worth knowing that not all children born to healers or mages can follow the legacy." He ripped off a piece of the baguette sword and ate it politely. "Some lineages can produce more children to the craft, but even then, there's no guarantee. No one understands what happens when powers enter a prospective wielder of magic, but there are theories."

"Like what kind of theories?"

"Some say that every child is born with the ability. They believe that magic leaves those children as they age or that they grieve it within themselves so strongly they're unaware they possess it. In other words, they mistake it for something else or kill it with their unbelief. Others think that only chosen ones can wield the power. It's all stories. Nothing's been proven."

"What do you believe?"

"It's not something I entertain. I felt the power at a very young age. I knew it was there. Whether it is there or not, only they would know. However," Aesian sighed, looking at Clara, "if they only believe they're nothing, so shall they remain."

"Well, it's hard to believe I have a special ability when I've been trying my best to find it."

"Wouldn't your own words figure into finding such power?"

"I'm sure it doesn't help to encourage the negative narrative, but I feel small in a very big world. Anyway, I have more questions."

"Go on, I'll answer what I can."

"The hair. What happens that changes it for a healer but not mages?"

"When a child of a healer heals for the first time, the very cavity of their internal nature changes. They're no longer bound to themselves, but to the well-being of others. The first healing is most painful as it paves the way for the future. This pain causes hair to grow white. Some say it's the pain of bearing the wound of another."

"How would they know if they're able to heal?"

"The voices. Pain calls to them. We can hear it, feel it. Many are even drawn to it as children. Some, it's later in life when the voices speak."

"So, when did you know, and why is your hair silver, instead of white?"

"Empathy's call was a strong one. I heard it as if it were standing beside me. It's a day no healer forgets. But the world of magic is complex." Aesian's face softened. "Rarely, a healer or mage can bridge the gap, I've mentioned that before. To explain, it all comes to one's tolerance of mixing magics. Healer and mage. When this happens, our hair becomes silver. The reason has never been studied. One other, Lord Odin, our Primus Leader, has done the same. A bridged mage."

"Do you still feel it? The pain of a healer?"

"It will always be there. The mage powers within me cloud the voices at times… I'm not as sensitive as I used to be."

"Why then? Why change at all? And what happens if you try and it doesn't work? What happens then?"

"Mixing magic is a catalyst for danger, no doubt to both the caster and receiver. For example," Aesian said, holding out his palms where a small, golden light formed. "This is the spell of Angel." He held the sphere in front of Clara. The spell intensified its brightness. "Angel can save a life from the very shadow of death. The first time I conjured it, I was weak for days. Now, I find it more effortless to summon. I've never used it, as the aftermath of pulling one from death's dark grip would be significant." The light grew brighter. Clara shielded her eyes. It grew brighter still, forcing her eyes to shut.

Angel… Clara opened her eyes to another place.

The woods were a burst of color and lush foliage, smelling of sun, flowers, and fresh running water. Wildlife scurried from bush to bush. The birds sang at the top of their lungs. A loud voice projected from the heavens. She called back.

"Hello! Aesian? We were just talking… about… Angel… that's my best friend's name. I miss her so much."

The voice echoed back as she walked. "Life's power. Is it not? Some flourish, while others wilt. Each has a time and place, but life, it's never fair. But how you use the one you have… that's what matters most."

Clara strolled down the cobblestone path. A single Lily Weed lay open and plucked on the walkway. She stooped to take it. The voice continued, "Now, on the other hand, there's the spell of Seize."

Clara carefully cupped the head of the Lily Weed, lifting it to her lips to speak into the hard bulb. "Why haven't you come for me?" She then whispered into the delicate petals, "Why did you leave me here?"

"Seize is used by advanced mages. It's hard to master, if not more than Angel. Even so, the risk may never be worth the summon. No magic is without risk. No magic will ever be without risk."

She yanked the center bulb from the Lily Weed and held it in both hands. It rolled around in her palms and across the dislodged petals. Her eyes ruptured into a river of hyperventilating emotion. "Where are you?" she screamed into the woods. A brown leaf fell from the tree above her. It landed upon the Lily Weed in her hands. She paused, watching as the dead leaf contaminated the fresh petals.

"The two are the same, yet different. One must have the other to survive. I think that's why those who bridge the gap are changed forever. There's no going back. Angel of the healer. Seize of the mage. One creates life; the other takes it. Some like to believe that death robs life, but I believe that death is a giver."

"My life. It's taken from me." Clara's breath became unstable. "I'm alone. I can't remember why." More dead leaves fell. The Lily Weed completely shriveled. She dropped it. The brown pieces fell to the dirt that was once the cobblestone path. The voice was strong now, pounding in her ears. She covered them fiercely, but it did not weaken the volume.

"Angel and Seize. Once combined, you have calamity. Calamity is an intimidating power. Once cast, it is impossible to deflect or recover from."

Clara echoed back, "It's impossible to recover from?"

The voice didn't acknowledge her. "The consumed one changes forever. And the one casting it will always carry it. Neither will ever be the same person afterwards."

"So what happens if someone is in calamity?" Clara screeched into the gray sky, her voice strained and high-pitched. All color was gone, the woods lacking *life. The once pristine cobblestone was broken, now covered in years of moss and dirt. She jerked her head up wildly, hair falling over her eyes. Feet away stood a lone shadow. "Where did you go?" Clara called to the voice. "Don't leave me with the shadows!"*

"Calamity. It muddles the insides. One's entire being can't understand it. The mind, the body, the soul. It complicates one's very internal being. This is what happens when life fights with death."

Clara wiped a tear from her cheek. The shadow ahead became two.

The voice boomed. "You need both to experience this world. Neither is good nor bad. Life can be an ugly reality, and death a beautiful release. The key is to be aware of how you use them. Death is beautiful when life is lived fully. And life is a gift when we accept death. Together, they abide alongside each other to create a beautiful story. Much is the same with magic."

The shadows rushed her on each side, blowing her hair back from her eyes, exposing her face. The voice from the heavens softened. "But when they can no longer see each other's beauty, they are muddled. When muddled, they create manic confusion. Chaos's mixture. Calamity."

The voice ceased. The shadows multiplied. Clara ran, stepping on the dropped Lily Weed. It crumbled under her foot. The shadows chased her. Down the ruined cobblestone she ran while they followed. "What's my name? Please, will someone tell me my name?"

The voice returned, laced with passion. "Calamity will tear you from life. You neither live nor die."

The shadows crowded her, merging and drowning her within their blackness. "No, it can't be." She lifted her arm, her hand reaching from the shadowy ocean.

"Clara, are you okay?" the voice asked with concern. The shadows raised their arms with her, hiding her reach from view. A cloud of darkness reaching towards the sky.

"I'm not strong. I can't do the things everyone wants me to. I have no control over this story." She hyperventilated when she sucked in murky air.

The voice became frantic. "Clara, can you hear me?"

Her arm still reached above the shadows, despite being outnumbered. "I hear you. I hear you." Her voice fell to a whisper. Trembling knees became weak. "I'm drowning here... in the... darkness... I think... I'm..." Her legs gave out. Before she became immersed in the darkness, a firm grip grabbed her wrist and yanked her from the blackness.

"Clara. You're safe." Clara opened her eyes. Aesian was inches from her, holding her wrist firmly. His eyes alert, his voice sympathetic.

"I—I he-hear you." She choked back lumps. He pulled her close to hold her tight, releasing her fear.

"What did you see?" he whispered into her ear. "You were in a trance-like state, calling for help."

"I—I don't want to talk about it right now. I just need to ask. What happens to those who might, you know, live in calamity?"

"If you must know, the first thing is never assume good or bad. Not all who wander between vitalities are unhappy. But you shouldn't fear this, as it's a very taxing spell. Only theories of it have been researched. Even now, with the tiniest of versions, I am spent. I cannot imagine anyone wanting to cast it. Tell me, is that what this is all about? Are you afraid you'll end up in a calamitous state?"

"I don't know, because I feel like I no longer know who I am. The victims, do they become ghosts?"

"I wouldn't agree or disagree with that theory."

"Well, that just makes me feel loads better. I don't feel like anyone should be allowed to have that sort of power. What happens if a bridge-the-gapper fails? What then? Can you mix different spells or just this one? What happens if you mix two spells, and they do nothing—or don't mix at all?" Her words spilled out fast and anxiously.

"So many questions. I promise in due time you'll hear all that concerns you. For now, you look pale. We should change subjects until you are ready. Would you like to see a play tonight? There must be some showing."

"Su-sure."

"Clara."

"Hmm?"

"From the second I saw you at the mayor's villa, I knew you'd be a worthy student."

"You knew all along? That I was the servant at the mayor's?" Color began to warm her face.

"Of course, Jenny," Aesian said with a smirk. "I knew who you were. The lace, although clever in its own right, did nothing to mislead me. Nor did that crazy dialect. It was an awkward, or should I say cringy, moment."

Clara's tone lightened, a laugh trickling from her. "I was really scared."

"I could tell. I apologize for being so brash."

"How did word spread so fast about me? I don't see any quick ways of communication around here."

Aesian's dimples appeared. "I can't say much about your world, but I can see that you have only just begun to understand mine. There are many ways to communicate, even if you don't know of them. Now, I have quite a few questions for you, but for now, why don't you enjoy this beautiful spread you've been feeding the fish?"

Clara breathed the fresh air in relief. She was safe. Aesian sat back on his arms while Clara made a sandwich of maple ham, she took extra care in stacking the ingredients between the bread. Aesian stared into the sky, beads of sweat formed on his forehead. "Clara, I think we should discuss the trance you were in."

Clara's attention was drawn to Aesian. For the first time his eyes clouded with fear, it frightened her. "Um, there's nothing to talk about."

"If there's nothing to discuss, then why am I haunted with the image of your hand reaching from the darkness?"

THE DAYS PASSED SLOWLY. Each day she hoped Sawyer would find her, but he never came. When she wasn't with Aesian, Clara spent most of her time with Alora. Confined to her bedroom, the two ladies laughed over a game of chess. Casually snacking, their second game was set between them. "They have this game in America too. I always liked it, but was never that great at it."

"You're better than me," Alora chuckled while watching her king be checked. "I noticed how you're warming up to Aesian. This is good." She motioned to the vase of flowers sitting on a small table by the window, accompanied by the fancy box of sweets.

"He's not so bad. The people seem to love him too, but…" *It's true. Aesian is fun, but he isn't Sawyer. Also, don't forget how I know he lied about my friends leaving. So shut up. Don't say any more to her. She feels like a friend, but you can't count on that. She won't be able to help you. She won't support an escape. Sawyer… he'll come for you. Just wait it out, play the game. Yet… it's been such a long time…* "But I think a little more time is needed before the wedding day."

"It'll be here sooner than you know it, ready or not. I can't wait to see the darling children you both will have. Aesian always loved children. I'll make sure to select the best nanny, but I doubt you'll need one."

"I always wanted children too. Even as a little girl, I loved taking care of my dolls. But, as for the nanny, I hope she knows how to play chess. I could use a little harder of a challenge." They laughed. Alora was turning out to be a pleasant distraction. An illusion of happiness. *Why hasn't anyone come for me yet? What if, perchance, Aesian didn't lie and my friend did leave? What if I read him wrong this entire time?* "Alora, I'm tired of chess. Did you want to go for a walk outside?"

"The gardens would be a delight today, don't you agree?"

"I was thinking of downtown. I'd love to do some shopping, see the city. Since I'll be a large part of everything, I'd love to meet the people and look around. All that life outside of the citadel, just waiting to be explored."

"I don't know… Let me see if we can get approval. I'd like to go downtown, myself, if I'm honest. Been quite some time since I've been there. I wonder if the Chicken Magic cart is still there. It's one of my favorites. They cook their chicken in seasoned oil. The crispy coating is an experience of its own. I'm hungry now. One moment. I'm going to check." Alora left the table and quickly left the room. In her haste, the door remained ajar, unsealed.

This is my chance! Walking to the door, Clara's heart thumped. *What happens if I get caught? What happens if they think… No. Do it. Don't go there. You got this. You got this… Be brave.* She pushed the door enough to squeeze through and slipped out. Looking left, then right, no one was in the hall. She looked a second time, to be sure. Walking quietly on her tiptoes, she turned the corner and down the steps, shielding her face with her arm.

SAWYER

Sawyer sweated profusely. Sitting up, he pushed himself to the back of the cell. A voice nearby spoke, "I'm glad you're awake. Are you able to hear me? Please, don't eat any more of the porridge they've been giving you. My name is Asher. I've been watching and trying to get your attention for some time. I think you're poisoned, but only enough to keep you sick. Otherwise, you'd be dead by now."

Sawyer lolled his head to his right to see a thin, cock-eyed old man in the cell next to him. The voice didn't match the face. The wrinkled chap smiled with his gums and muttered words Sawyer didn't understand.

"Over here. Across from you." Sawyer then saw the mage shackled in the cell in front of him. "Don't mind him. I'm not sure what his name is or why he's here. He's certainly mad, but not in a bad way. If you watch him long enough, he becomes the greatest of entertainment," Asher chuckled, referring to the wrinkled man.

The old man lurched closer to the bars that separated the knight's cell from his own. He reached to pull on Sawyer's leg. Sawyer yanked his leg away, resulting in a rush of dizziness. He placed his head in his hands to steady his mind and piece the story together. "I was in the tunnels. Something hit me."

"The guards dragged you here weeks ago."

"Weeks?" Sawyer rose to his feet with difficulty. The old man clapped and danced in circles, grunting incoherently. Sawyer watched in disgust as the old man sucked down porridge as if drinking from a glass. He squeezed it between his cheeks and stepped on what fell.

"I remember now." Sawyer looked away from the old man to study his bondages. "These shackles. They look the same as those in the tunnel." Reaching his hand for his hair, it crunched from dried blood and crusty dirt. The old man clapped and muttered. Licking his tongue around his gums, he smacked his lips. Sawyer feigned a smile at the haggard prison mate. *For the first time, I can't think of a plan.* A little energy filled him after drinking the warm, stale water left in the cup by the porridge. "What can you tell me about this place?"

"There's nothing to know. We're in prison. We're tracked. Guards are watching from the only door. I've been here far longer than you and haven't figured a thing out," replied Asher.

The old man laughed. It was a choppy, hard laugh. Both men stared.

"Is he dying?" Sawyer questioned.

"I wouldn't know. Poor soul."

"Why isn't he shackled?"

"I suppose they figure he isn't much harm. Those spindly arms wouldn't hurt a bug, and those knobby legs most likely wouldn't last long during a chase. Yet, he dances often on them."

The old man smiled broadly, showcasing a prominent snaggle tooth from his gums. He effortlessly pushed his cell door open. Sawyer gasped. With a spin, he hopped to Sawyer's cell. Reaching into his mouth, he took out a key, covered in porridge. With a rough cackle, he first opened Sawyer's cell, then Asher's. The doors creaked open.

"Thank you, kind man." Sawyer shook his head, looking at his hands. "I can't do anything about the shackles."

"Get back in the cell! I hear guards coming," Asher warned. The old man, with a wild grunt, shut both cells before skittering to his own. Sawyer leaned against the wall and bowed his head to his chest. The old man put the key back into his mouth and gagged only the tiniest bit.

"Dinner's here," one guard announced, sliding a plate for Asher and the old man. The old man, who had recently eaten his last meal, dug in with the same gusto as before. Asher bowed gracefully as he accepted the plate from the door slot.

"Porridge, porridge. It's one of my favorites. They spare no cost feeding prisoners," Sawyer's ears perked up. He knew that voice. "Hey, by the way, Hubert, I'll take it from here. I know you have

Algirtha waiting at the Smokin' Boar. Leave a bit early, maybe you'll get an extra kiss. Oh, and don't forget to buy her some flowers. If you want to show her how much you care, you need to surprise her."

Hubert flushed. "Ah, thanks, brother. Algy did say she loves petunias. I'll leave the rest to you. I got myself a new jacket for the occasion. It's our one-year courting anniversary, so I need to look sharp." A moment after the man left, the remaining guard opened the door to the old man's cell. "Hey there, buddy, I noticed you opened the cells. Great work." He high-fived the old man, who jumped ecstatically. Spitting out the key, he handed it over to the guard.

The guard shook it off with a sick smile before attaching it to his belt. He then opened his hand again, and the old man pulled out, from his baggy drawers, another key. This one glowed, although slightly less than what it should have. The guard frowned, but pinched the key gingerly. Entering Sawyer's cell, he held the glowing key to the shackles. An electric buzz sizzled, releasing the shackles from Sawyer's wrists. They fell to the ground. He did the same for Asher. He then reattached the shackles after fiddling with their mechanics. They returned to their shiny state. "Can't have anyone thinking the shackles stopped working, now can we?"

The guard pulled up his hat to show a familiar-ish face, he then spoke, "Whoa, you look terrible. I'm sorry it took so long to find you. Took more time than planned to gain the trust of the guards and acquire this uniform. I also befriended this fine fellow." He motioned to the old man jumping in circles.

Sawyer stared, his lips moving slowly, "Onyx?"

"The very one, although I'm sure you noticed I look a little different. Now, take this." Onyx took a vial from his pocket. "Drink it all. I know it's bitter, but I promise it tastes a heck of a lot better than that mush they've been feeding you. It won't restore you to full working order, but it will nourish and strengthen your body enough to escape without having to throw you over my shoulder."

Taking the vial, Sawyer drank it till empty. Onyx slipped a backpack from over his head and pulled out a uniform. "This should fit, although you are a bit skinnier than when I left you… and seriously more smelly." Helping his friend dress, he took out a pair of cuffs and turned toward Asher.

"Asher, good to see you again. Thanks for your patience while I got everything under control, and for looking after my friend. I'm going to cuff you, but not latch it. When we pass the hall, leave out the first door you see. No one uses that one. It's the safest bet. I've packed you a bag. It isn't much, but it should hold you for a few days."

"Thank you, I can't tell you how grateful I am."

"Not a problem, buddy." He turned to the old man who was having great fun opening and shutting his cell door with loud bangs. "Thanks for the help, sir. Well, you didn't quite get the whole plan, but your implementation worked. I'm proud, nevertheless." The old man nodded, flinging saliva, and squatted in the corner of his cell. Everyone looked away.

Onyx grimaced. "I think I'm just gonna let him do his thing."

"That's probably for the best," Sawyer winced.

"You doing okay?" Onyx asked when Sawyer wobbled while regaining composure. "I have a disguise for you. Well, more than the uniform." Onyx retrieved a box from his backpack.

"Yes, I believe so. I feel odd, but my legs have more strength than before. I don't think we should waste any more time." He put on the guard hat that was handed to him by Onyx. "We need to find Clara."

"We'll save her, soon enough. I know where they keep her. Now hold still." Onyx took two thin disks from a small glass box. "Clara once told me that in America, many people have trouble seeing, so they invented these things called contacts. Now, I don't know much about the seeing part, but I did manage to add some color."

Opening his friend's stubbornly blinking eyes, he proceeded to slip in the disks. "Don't blink. There, from green to brown. I also have some tonic to dye your hair. Black is the fastest, so that's what you're getting. Don't complain if you don't like it." Onyx led the knight to a rusty sink. He quickly took off Sawyer's guard hat. Having not been groomed, the knight's hair was shaggy. The color stained the knight's strands, but they didn't have time to wait for a full cure. It ended up patchy and uneven.

Onyx raised his eyebrows at his friend's new look after it was quickly towel-dried. Spots of brown flecked through the black. One area was left completely untouched beneath the nape of his neck. "Dashing, like usual. Let's move, friend." Wrapping an arm around the knight, Onyx helped him up the stairs.

CHAPTER 33
Requiem

ELEANOR

ELEANOR WAS A KNOT OF ANGER. She had seen enough, heard enough. The way Aesian held Clara in the courtyard was appalling. *What gall she has. Sawyer is incorrect with his assumption. Clara obviously loves Aesian. Who wouldn't? After coming so far, she's abandoned her purpose, endangering everyone. Tearing me away from my appointed home to travel—and for what? So she can live her life in happy bliss with the one I love? The team, our group, camped outside the city walls for weeks. They hide behind clothes and makeshift masks to disappear among the locals, but it's only a matter of time before they're discovered. I'll not have one part in any of this. Not one. They work for a worthless cause.*

She brushed her white locks. Living with her parents, she refused to hide. No one requested her to leave, and she would not do so if asked. At this point, she wished they'd sent her away long before she had to see Aesian with the traitor and all the sickening, joyous news. It was all everyone wanted to talk about, the wedding next month. No matter how many times she would change the course of the conversation, it led back to that.

Sawyer told her that it wasn't Clara who wanted to marry, yet the supposed heroine seemed pretty happy about it. Each time she peered around a corner or spied them from a distance, they looked excited enough. *All lies...* She seethed as she slammed the brush down upon the vanity. In the vanity mirror, another figure appeared next to her own. She jumped.

"Lord Odin."

"Sweet Eleanor. It's good to see you, as always. I hear the Ancora companionship is nearby. Some are even in this very city as we speak."

Eleanor rose from the padded stool. Another, older man, appeared in her room. "Zerpith?"

"Ehhh, Eleanor. A beauty, even among healers."

"Master Zerpith, Lord Odin." She curtsied gracefully, despite the way her heart pounded. "What pleasure brings you both here, to my childhood room, of all places? Your sudden visit is a bit improper."

Odin stepped closer, tapping his fingers together. "Proper or not, you bowed when we arrived, did you not? Remember your place, healer. We know the plans your companions have. Our request is simple. Help us dispose of them. They trust you, so it should be simple. We'll need to do it with as little disturbance as possible. Of course, we know you can handle this."

"Forgive my hesitation, my lord, but there is nothing to dispute. Clara willingly complies."

"False," hissed the old mage. "Her heart speaks otherwise. She does not plan on marrying the Preceptor, but she'll have no choice. Ehhh, you'll be rewarded greatly for your service to stop your pitiful friends."

Clara doesn't want to marry Aesian after all. Her heart leaped. *I should have known! Aesian does love me. Lord Odin and Zerpith must have threatened him. He had no other option! Jealousy has blinded my heart. How could I have...? I need to tell Jade.*

The smooth voice of Odin ironed out the creakiness from the ancient, "Get the group together in one place. Propose a meeting, dinner—whatever you decide to do, we don't care. We'll fund whatever. Tell us the location and time, we'll do the rest."

Zerpith locked his gnarled figures together. "The knight, the alchemist, they lurk. Ehhh, sneaking within the citadel walls. Find them, before they find her."

Eleanor folded her arms. "I'll do as you say."

"What a good girl, you are," Zerpith said, creeping closer. He rolled one of Eleanor's locks between his fingers. She moved away from his touch, and he released her hair. "You have two days." With that, both disappeared, leaving nothing behind but the echo of their magic.

CLARA

Clara crept down the hall, dress floating behind her. Even in the worst of times, she could appreciate a beautiful dress. Passing by one of the three dining rooms, Aesian appeared in the distance. *No, no, no, no. If I'm caught, the friendship we have will be ruined. What little trust he has in me will be gone. This isn't going to work.* Her mind kicked into gear, overthinking what could be. *If I'm caught, they might chain me up and serve me terrible food. What if I didn't have my own bathroom? Maybe they'd turn me into a ghost and then what? Roam around mindlessly? How boring! They could do whatever they wanted, and I can't really stop them. I'm one against thousands.*

She whispered to herself, "I don't want to die…" Then a small voice called to her from the depths of her mind. *"But what if you live? What if—"* Turning abruptly, she bumped into a guard. She held her breath. His brown eyes were weary but still full of character. "I'm just about to head to my room. Sorry… I'm going now." With a slight bow, she turned to leave when the guard grabbed her arm and gently pulled her into an embrace.

"Follow us," he whispered.

"I'm going to my room, I—I promise!"

"You could take me with you," came the cheeky reply.

"What! No chance," she pulled away to see a tired smile. Familiar freckles specked across his nose, but his eyes and hair were different. *What if it isn't him?* "Sawyer?" she whispered, unsure.

Seeing him nod, her eyes lit up. He winced when she wrapped her arms around him. Hugging him tightly, she held back tears.

"Hey there, you two." Onyx broke the embrace. "I don't think now is the time for pleasantries, especially with an audience."

The three frowned as Aesian, along with a group of mages, saw them. Onyx raced toward the steps to the lobby floor, pushing his friends ahead. Running, they came to the end of the stairs. Standing at the top of the right marble staircase of the vestibule, an army of mages, knights, and healers gathered below. Lord Odin was at the front, commanding the army to wait. The massive army pushed toward the steps, without climbing them. Coming from all sides, escape was increasingly impossible. Clara clenched her fists as her legs involuntarily shook.

"This is very bad timing, as I don't have a single weapon on me. What a fine mess this is," Sawyer said with surprising calm.

Lord Odin's voice rose above the masses, "Stand your ground! Don't advance until I command it!"

No one moved. Sawyer threw Clara in front of him and Onyx. "What are you doing?" she screeched.

"Trust that I'd never put you in danger."

Clara, standing unprotected in front of the two men, gasped out a horrible choke. The army looked even larger without her human barriers. Not having a plan, she waited. The army waited. Lord Odin smiled wickedly. "Taper your arms. We shall not hurt our Lady Clara." The army parried. "Do as you will with the rest, but do not touch her."

"Now what?" Clara asked with her arms spread protectively in front of her two friends.

Onyx shifted. He pulled out a bomb, lifting it high in the air, then paused. A small mage was crying in the midst of the army below. Clara watched him scan the crowd before throwing it far from the child's cries. It would only damage the wall and injure a few. Mostly, it caused a much-needed distraction. Light filtered through the gaping hole in the side of the citadel. The bomb did little to lessen the load or even distract the majority, but it did provide access to the city outside. Bodies lay injured, and the chaos ensued.

Lord Odin focused on Clara. A sinister smile turned his lips as he prepared a spell. Aesian materialized next to him. "Lord Odin, what are you thinking? We can't kill Clara. You just told—"

Pushing Aesian into the crowd, he addressed the army with lifted hands. "Forgo the ceasefire. If she escapes, she works against us. Each for themselves and spare none, but only I will deal with Clara."

Jade and Eleanor rushed through the jagged blown-out hole. Jade tossed unsuspecting militia away from their path with a gust of wind. She scoffed when she saw a shaky Clara protecting the confused alchemist and wobbly knight. This battle was going to be an interesting one. Battle erupted. Jade hurled bolts into the crowd while guarding the way out. As the battle commenced, Eleanor rushed into the crowd, chanting.

Eleanor

Eleanor cast a protective barrier around her friends at the top of the steps, a small one around Jade, and one for herself. She used all of her concentration to strengthen and guide the shields. It was a tricky feat to hold a strong barrier against attacks while allowing her companions the ability to attack through the shield, especially with multiples, but she would manage,.

Onyx took the arm of each friend and forced them down the stairs. Clara clung to an unstable Sawyer. The knight, despite his lack of strength, kept a protective arm around Clara. He would die if he weren't treated soon. Eleanor could see Death following him. Thankfully, Death was translucent, so there was still time. As for the shadowy figure following Clara, she wasn't sure what it meant or what to do about it. Her barriers were getting hit, but she didn't flinch at the pain it caused. She felt deeper pain than that. Here and there, enemy assaults bounced, trying to penetrate the hard shell. Yet, she would ensure no one could touch her friends.

Jade finally reached the others. It was time to merge the shields.

Sweating with exertion, she rushed into the center of the crowd to better manage the task. In order to complete the merge, she'd need to dissolve her own barrier and replace it with a mock replica. The mock barrier wouldn't protect her, but it may hinder others from thinking she wasn't protected. A warrior headed towards her. She saw him instantly, as her peripheral vision was sharp. She thrust her arm out, snatching his spear in motion, but she didn't stop it in time. The spear ripped into her side, lodging deeply into her gut. The pain cut into her body as her blood flowed into a crimson river trickling down her side. Holding her free arm firm, she kept the barrier going, but it would only weaken from here. *There's nothing I can do…* Blood soaked her dress, staining the delicate fabric. She felt her blood's heat as it touched her skin.

The deathly being, following the knight stopped. She met eyes with it. Opaque, she could see his beauty. He bowed his head before fading translucent. He silently continued following the knight.

Reaching her arms toward the ceiling, she displayed the spear she'd pulled from her side high above her head. Her wound, free from the weapon, poured freely. Adrenaline surged through her. She remembered the first time she healed, turning her hair white. She recalled the time she spent with her parents, crafting her art, her first battle and the day she met the man who changed her forever. *I… I'll never see this world again, nor… Aesian.* Her eyes smoldered black, clouding her vision. When her voice rose, beautiful and eerie, she couldn't see how the armies paused at the sound of her voice. Yet, she would make sure she was heard. The clarity of her soprano interlude would sear their ears and seep into their hearts. The battle stopped.

The citadel filled with her song, reaching into the street with a haunting warning. Aesian's voice rose with horror, and she heard him call to her. "Eleanor! Please don't do this! It was never what you thought it was. Lord Odin leveraged you! My sweet Eleanor, don't leave me! I'll join you on your quest, and we'd be un—" his voice cracked, "stoppable."

But it was too late. Her voice dropped into a deep velvety tone as she began to sing. *"A heart that beats from a life of pain. My final breath from the strength of the healed. Deep inside. The pain. It's free from my rein."* Her body quivered. *"The requiem of life sets me free. This... twisted manifest death. But I'll fly!"* She dropped the spear with a clang. Her voice lifted into a high octave. *"I'll fly towards my light."*

Agony screamed from her lips as white wings tore from her back, ripping her flesh open. Upon each feather was written a name of someone she had healed. Every cry of pain from them screamed into her ears, bursting her eardrums. She had healed them, but not without a price. Wingspan broad, the names shone with gold before each bleeding red. She levitated.

"Remembrance of those who lived from my pain. They are healed. They are free. My magic not vain. A healer's love is something unseen; the light shines upon them, but shadows my dreams. Her voice steadily, angrily, increased in volume. *When will they see?... I've searched for the light that's for me..."* Her empty eyes leaked dark rivers down her cheeks.

Her body shook and withered. She watched as her luscious hair fell in clumps from her scalp to be trampled under the frantic feet of the armies. Her skin grew thin, showing black veins beneath its translucent surface. The army, understanding, rushed to the doors, but she had sealed them. They pulled and pushed, but they would not budge. The enclosure of the gaping hole exploded into a black, fiery vortex, killing nearby warriors. Anyone close by would be sucked into death.

Aesian rushed to her, "Eleanor..." Her vision was cloudy, but she saw him through the haze. She smiled weakly. *There's no face more beautiful than his.* He levitated only enough to reach for her hand. His touch warmed her cold hand. He whispered, "Eleanor. I've always loved you. I won't leave you ever again, especially now."

Her dark eyes met his, he kissed her wrinkled hand. Her voice was quiet, shaky. "I'll love you until loving someone is no longer possible. Now, you must go." Tears fell down his cheeks. She released a sob that dripped with blood. Aesian released her hand. *"Love's in death... yet, I live... on. In... the... lives that are left."* Her limbs dropped to her sides. Her bald head dropped to her chest. Aesian's presence was no longer there, for which she was glad. Odin disappeared after cursing her choice. Eleanor's voice fell quiet. *"But it's worse. It's worse than my death. To heal in a world filled with pain."*

Jade cried to Eleanor, but she would not listen, she couldn't. Clara, eyes red and confused, rushed down the rest of the steps. The barrier had withered. Blinking, Eleanor struggled to hold her head up. The companions ran to the exposed wall. She winced to open a small opening in the vortex. They would be unshielded there, but safe from her requiem.

The energy of death pounded her weak heart in an unnatural rhythm. Taking control of her body, the power pulsed bigger until it spread throughout her entire body. She lifted her head and smiled as her body convulsed.

Her once loud voice became a tiny whisper as the light above her shone brightly upon her. *"I'm free."* A mighty blast shook the citadel and quaked through the city as the vortex broke. Streams of power came from all of Eleanor's limbs. Acid rain poured inside the vestibule. They were no longer trying to stop the companions from escaping the city. Each cowered for their own life. The city was in a panic as streets cracked and buildings crumbled. The rivers raged, spilling from their banks, and bridges fell with deathly vibrations. Black ash clouded the air, sticking to anything it fell upon.

Clara

They ran, pushing through the crowds and knocking people over as they barreled through the streets. Onyx let go of Sawyer, who was struggling to keep up. "Keep going. Take Clara. I have to free the slaves."

Sawyer halted, his legs shook from his lack of strength. "Onyx, buddy…"

"I can't leave them down there, and I can't be watching you."

Sawyer complied, "Be safe, and don't… stop to collect anything."

"I'll be back," the alchemist said as he ran from the others, jumping over bits of rubble and pushing people out of the way.

Clara's head pounded. *I don't know what to do. I feel you, I feel it. Whatever it is. I just don't understand how to use it. Eleanor, did she—?*

Sawyer gently pushed Clara's lower back to move her forward. "We need to keep moving."

Clara ran. She ran until she stumbled over a crack in the cobblestone. Scraping her knees, she pushed herself up. Looking behind her, Sawyer wasn't seen. "Sawyer!" she yelled into the panicked crowd. Retracing her steps, she jumped over bits of crumbled building and fallen pieces. Leaning against a broken pillar was her knight.

"Keep running! I'll be right behind you. You were going in the right direction; straight ahead is the gate. It's most likely crumbled to the ground by now," Sawyer said through gritted teeth.

Clara rushed to him. Putting an arm under him, she tried to help him forward, but he was too heavy. A pain unlike any other assaulted her brow as the shadow of Eleanor appeared in a flash and left as soon as she came. Sawyer stood strong. Grasping Clara's hand, he ran towards the gate, leading her with an unearthly force.

Jade stood outside the gates, reins in hand. Jasper, Rory, and Nash were already waiting with tacked horses and a fully restocked wagon. Once they arrived, the knight fell motionless. Jasper and Jade quickly cleared a space in the wagon before lifting Sawyer into the wagon's bed. Clara climbed next to him, brushing hair from the fallen knight's forehead.

Then, they waited.

The ash intensified. The earth quaked. The citadel was falling. *Please Onyx, hurry*, Clara prayed. From the dust emerged an old, senile-looking man wearing baggy, shabby drawers. He jumped and clapped when he saw them. Behind him was the alchemist.

Onyx waved, visibly out of breath. He called to his friends, "They are free… from the tunnel! I don't know how… but Eleanor was with me. She opened the sealed doors… so we could esca…" He stopped to catch his breath. "The tunnels collapsed. I wouldn't be here if… if she hadn't come."

The crazy old man followed the alchemist towards the entrance, where the gates swung wildly on the hinges. The ground, now a mass of ruins and bulging dirt, became a dangerous obstacle course. Amidst the chaos, not all who ran for safety forgot about their mission. As Onyx and the old man reached the towers, a rogue soldier shot an arrow into the alchemist's shoulder and another to his chest. He stumbled, quickly pulling down his spectacles over his eyes. He shook his head gravely and fell.

Jade ran to him. The soldier aimed, but the kooky old man had scurried up the ladder leading to the castle wall where the soldier honed his target. Jumping with unsuspected agility, he pulled the soldier by the back of the shirt and swung him around. The soldier tripped from the twirl and plummeted off the wall. The old man jumped and clapped his hands before hopping down the ladder to scamper off. Jade, mouth gaping, helped Onyx hobble to the wagon. They laid him alongside the feverish knight, who was quickly losing consciousness. Jade reluctantly drove the Dragonmare, and the riderless horses were tied to the wagon. The ash, now thick, darkened the sky, and all the lights went out. The friends didn't turn around when a deafening blow cut through the air, demolishing the city.

CHAPTER 34
Cauldira

CLARA

CLARA, red-eyed and exhausted, watched Jasper snuff out his pipe. The cook spoke aloud, but not to anyone in particular. "Some would say that warriors are the ones to triumph in battle, but the wise say…" he grunted as he rose from the stump, "it's the healer who wins the war." Dumping the ashes into the dying fire, he tapped the bowl against his hand to release the congested parts. He then returned to stir the leftovers for the fifth time. Clara bowed her head. *Eleanor's gone. Her life—snuffed out, just like his pipe.* Dinner had long since been eaten, leaving more leftovers than typical. Despite the calming chatter of nature, the atmosphere spoke at deafening levels.

The knight lay still under his camp blanket. Jasper turned from the pot. "If we don't heal him soon, he'll be the next to go," he whispered, cutting the silence sharply. Beside the knight, the feverish alchemist squirmed and sweated. He woke now and then in a stupor, only to look around and wipe sweat from his brow before succumbing to nightmares. "Not looking good. I don't like how his wound is turning black. Bad sign. I don't like it one bit. Not one bit." Jasper stuffed his pipe, once again. Puffs of smoke billowed towards the starlit sky.

"What happens now? Will Sawyer and Onyx die?" Rory asked Jasper with watery eyes.

"Ho, little lad. Life's a gamble. All we can do is play the cards we're dealt." The boy didn't break his gaze from the cook. Jasper blew a ring from his pipe and faked a grin, "But we play for aces, now, don't we?"

Rory perked up. "Sawyer's been teaching me about everything it takes to win battles. I'm going to be a knight soon. Then, I'll save all my friends. I'll play for aces."

"Calm, lad. You have plenty of time for that. Now, get to bed or help me with dishes." Jasper stacked a few random plates. The boy beelined to his blanket.

Clara gazed into the stars. Without streetlights, they shone unhindered. *I remember when I first saw them. The stars. I was in the wagon headed to some...* She swallowed. *Some adventure I never could have imagined. It's my fault Eleanor died. Sawyer and Onyx are hurt because of me. Stuff like this doesn't just happen. Had I been brave, I would've let that monster bird take me to Lectus. Then, Eleanor would still be here.* She cupped her hand over her mouth.

Rory grabbed her free hand. "Clara, don't cry. We're aces. We play to win. Jasper even said so."

"Then... I'm the joker."

A sweaty hand grasped Clara's with a weak squeeze. Sawyer. He sat up, hair plastered to his brow. "I love a good joke. I never," he coughed, "never once had an adventure I didn't like. And this one, it's... my favorite."

"But, Eleanor—"

"What an incredible friend she was. And... and what an honor to have been loved that much."

"I never thought she liked me. The way she'd look at me, even ignore me at times. I told myself all these things about her... but none of those stories were true. She had a big heart, bigger than any of us." The knight nodded, squinting his eyes from fatigue. "Here, lie down." Clara gently guided him back under the blanket. Tucking him in, she brushed his hair back and caressed his forehead till he fell asleep.

"Eww, gross."

"Rory, go to sleep."

Clara laid next to Sawyer and soon drifted to sleep…

Eleanor's vacant eyes bled red, her irises swirling with sadness, then anger. The healer's head turned, full circle, striking Clara with deep fear. Clara stumbled back, tripping over the newly protruding ground. Unable to move, her fallen body didn't agree with her mind. Run. Her head, free to move, snapped up to see a looming castle. A windowless castle.

The rain fell crimson with black ash. It stained her hands and face dark red. She pulled on her legs to move, but they remained still. The healer's jaw unhinged, dropping open to release a terrible screech. Transforming, her nose grew hard and long. Her arms sprouted feathers. What was once beautiful became a hideous, monstrous bird—the very one that once pursued her… and now did so again.

"I don't know what to do." She pulled each leg until they finally budged. "I don't know how to save myself." She limped towards the windowless castle appearing from the shadows. One heavy step after another. Thud. The hill was steep, full of thorns and covered with vines. Thud. Thud. Everything was gray and colorless. Now she ran in a cumbersome, jerky motion. Falling, she attempted to scream, but her cry transformed into a shadowy figure that sucked in a newly forming void. The process repeated itself. Thud. Thud. Thud. Screaming into a void and falling. Finally reaching the castle, she banged on the door. It refused to open but spouted sharp spikes. They stabbed at her fists.

Glancing at her injured hands, she held them out. The raining blood mingled with her own, collecting between both open palms until it seeped through her fingers. It gathered and poured into a pool by her feet. Overlooking the shaded woods from the hill, shadows gathered, looming below. In turn, they peered at her, pointed, and screeched. They were watching her, and perhaps always had. She covered her ears, but that did not stop them. One phantom approached her, holding its hands to its ears—a mirror of her. The shadow spoke in a voice raspy and deep, "Give me your name."

"No. I won't," Clara dropped to the ground and hugged herself tightly… but what is it? Panic ensnared her heart. She screamed back, "I don't know!"

"Clara! Wake up!" Rory pulled and pushed her from under her

blanket. "Bandits in the camp, and Jade left to bathe in the lake. I don't know what to do." Jumping awake, Clara retrieved the machete.

Jasper was pounding on a bandit with an iron pan. An especially hard blow sent the scraggly thief to the ground, accompanied by a few dislodged teeth. Pan in hand, hot from the roaring fire, Jasper swung it with brute force. During a swing, the cook blocked a dagger from another bandit. Hissing, the bandit growled at his bent weapon, then quickly forgot when the pan connected with his face.

Yelping, the bandit used his anger to rush Rory. Rory, junior sword ready, parried just as he was taught. Clara raised the machete and swung, eyes closed. Slicing through bone, the bandit's hand flopped to the ground. It took only a moment before blood spewed.

Two more bandits bolted, one swinging onto the companions' wagon seat. One slapped the reins. Jasper ran after him, scalding pot swinging. "No you don't!" Catching the rim on the back trailer, he dropped the pan and skipped one-legged while holding onto the wagon with all his might. The cook attempted to lift a stout leg, but it wasn't an easy thing to do. He hopped sporadically until his wide foot caught between the slats. Flopping to his back, he twisted and flailed as he was dragged. He pulled his body upright for a moment but failed to stay that way.

Running from the lake, Jade stopped the wagon with a burst of wind. Jasper gasped as his legs flew against his belly, and he spat out dirt. The bandit driving the wagon flew forward onto the donkeys before hitting the ground.

Clara's attention locked with the equally surprised eyes of the man she had partially dismembered. "I'm sorry. I—I chopped your… I can't believe…" Both peered at the lifeless hand before looking at each other. The bandit choked and gagged. Flinging her hands to her mouth, she dropped the machete and threw up. The bandit's stub bled profusely as he tried to stop the gushing flow. She puked again through her fingers. The bandit, newly covered in a fresh coat of spew, cursed while squeezing his wrist.

Rory dropped his weapon in shock, also gagging at the lifeless hand. Jade sighed and cast a trail of fire, sending the remaining bandits running, each trailed by a stream of smoke and flame. They yelped as the heat scorched their behinds.

"Jasper, get off the ground. Rory, gather supplies. Clara, clean up at the river. Seriously, can't I leave for just a few minutes? We need to travel to the closest town before everyone, save me, dies." She shook her head. "Next destination, Cauldira."

CLARA QUIETLY OPENED the door to Cauldira's infirmary. The room was peaceful, accented by the calming sounds from trickling fountains. Vines releasing blue flowers coated the walls. Many windows, some open, others shut, showered soft yellow light. A bed toward the back of the room held a familiar body. A nurse softly conversed with the man in a slightly inclined position. Upon seeing the visitor, the nurse left the chair to meet Clara.

"He's awake, but, as you may notice, a bit loopy." She placed a gentle hand on Clara's shoulder. "Just a reminder. Keep your voice low and refrain from sudden movements. It's a good thing he was so healthy before; otherwise, he may not be with us now."

"I promise," she replied, softly sitting in the chair beside Sawyer's bed. "I'm happy you're going to be okay. How are you feeling?"

"Clara, you look so… so lovely today. Your eyes… I see eons in them."

She held back a laugh. "You see eons in them?"

"And… I really love you. A lot. Ahhh, I think you know that." He winked, albeit delayed.

He loves me? I can't believe this. He loves me? "Sawyer, I lo—"

"That nurse… over there. You know. I love her too. She keeps giving me this…" he coughed, "…this medicine. I really feel really good right now." He chuckled in sporadic spurts. "Did I tell you how cool you are? Beautiful, too. Did I tell you yet?"

He doesn't mean it after all. He's only tripping. She laughed with him, urging him to soften his voice. "I'll be right back, okay? I want to check on Onyx."

"I'll wait for you. For eons! Just like your eyes." He flopped onto his pillow, but only for a second before lifting his head. He shouted, "Remember that. My words. Eons!" A nearby nurse rushed to calm and settle him.

To the far left of the infirmary was a private room. Frosted glass panels closed it off from the rest of the patients. Water flowed through the glass, shielding it from onlookers. A healer sat outside in a padded white chair trimmed with silver.

"I was told Onyx is here?"

"He's sleeping. We've induced a coma. The curse has spread, but we're hopeful for a favorable outcome. At this time, we can't allow any visitors as the healing spell is fragile, but it seems to be working."

"So, he's going to be okay?"

"We hope for the best possible outcome. Cursed wounds are tricky to heal, and contagious as well. If any of your companions, or yourself, notice a dark wound, please see us right away. We did check each of you over, but we cannot be certain."

"Of course. Thanks for taking such good care of him. Both of them." She left the partitioned area and sat next to the knight, now asleep from the spell cast upon him. Leaning back into the pillows of the chair, she dreamed of home. Of safety. Brewing coffee didn't seem like such a bad idea anymore. Maybe if she got home, she'd attempt karaoke. Maybe even a ballad about a love lost. *I think I'll ask about putting one of those fancy wood chessboards in the coffee shop. I enjoyed playing. Maybe I'll even get myself a fountain for my room. A small one. To help me sleep.* She brushed the hair away from the knight's forehead and ran her fingers through it. She whispered to him, "More than ever, I wish to go home, but it just wouldn't be the same without you."

SAWYER

Two weeks later, Sawyer picked at his breakfast while listening to Jade and Clara. "I think we should stay a week or two more while we wait for the poison to completely clear from Sawyer's system. While we tarry, it'd be a good time to practice your skills." Jade placed her fork down to dab her lips with a napkin.

"You're probably right. I saw a training area the other day during my stroll. Looked to be a pretty nice one."

"Cauldira has an excellent mage and healer program. Their training grounds are well-equipped and more than sufficient. Arlo, their Maven Trainer, is known to cultivate unique skills from mages and healers alike. He's a dynamic mage. Personally, I like him as a friend, but I'm not fond of working with him. Too unpredictable for me. I'll introduce you today."

"Dynamic mage? Those are the ones who don't always know the outcome of their spells?"

"They are. They seem, from what I can tell, to have a high resource of magic. Once highly trained, mind you, they are great assets in battle, but even then, you might get a random attack or spell at times."

"Then why use one? What happens if a bad spell is cast or—?"

Jade pursed her lips before speaking. "Because when they do work, they work well."

A tall man stepped to their table, cutting short their conversation. Sawyer stood in surprise. "Merrick." The two firmly shook hands before a quick embrace.

"Sawyer, Jade… Clara," he nodded to each, pausing on Clara for a moment. "I received word that you've come. I've been in extensive meetings with King Boren. It's good to see you. All of you."

Sawyer began to speak. "You left Ancora abruptly. King Henric—"

"No. Now isn't the time." He firmly squeezed the knight's shoulder. "The only thing you need to concentrate on is healing and getting Clara to her destination. When you return, there'll be plenty of time for future conversation. Once you finish your task, come back to Cauldira before heading home. Till then, let's make use of our time here. Tomorrow we'll dine together, which will be a needed distraction from your travels. I'm intrigued to hear about your journey thus far. I'd like to know what happened at Eros. I noticed Eleanor didn't arrive with you... and the city is in ruins. This is concerning." He stopped, but lightened his speech. "Till then, rest, eat, have fun. There's going to be some music tonight and a get-together. Nothing over the top, but a relaxing event. I trust each of you will be there." Merrick stopped. "Sawyer, Adeline is in the library. I suggest you speak with her."

As much as Ancora was adorned and flashy, Cauldira was practical and simple. Some areas were fully decorated, as all castles are, but for the most part, Cauldarians preferred things simple and functional. Where flowers grew in Ancora, greenery and herbaceous hedges flourished. It was beautiful in a simplistic way that led one to appreciate the minimalist style. Sawyer left the table with Merrick's words weighing heavily on him. Adeline was waiting. He felt weak and a little sick, but his mind was clear and sharp. He was, thankfully, weaned from the medicine, for which he was glad. He wasn't a fan of the lack of verbal control it gave. *I hope I didn't say anything stupid to Clara. I want to tell her how much I love her when the time is right. I don't want to ruin the moment due to a medicinal stupor.*

The library door creaked as he opened it. Adeline sat in an overstuffed chair, poring over a massive book. Another text, opened and marked, lay on the polished table next to a notebook full of sketches and notes. She turned the page without looking up. "Sawyer, a pleasure to have you here in Cauldira." She turned another page, indifferent to his presence.

"A pleasure, Princess Adeline." He stiffly bowed before sitting. "I'm glad you agreed to meet with me."

She closed the books, making sure to mark each opened page. She looked him in the eyes. "Dragons are curious creatures, don't you think? I have yet to see one. Have you come across any during your adventures?"

"A small one. I believe it to have been a hatchling." Adeline waited, so he continued. "He was more interested in the food within my bag than me."

"Bestiary intrigues me. Animals and monsters are largely misunderstood. I wish more people would learn about them before rushing to kill."

"I'd agree with that."

"Aren't we animals in many ways? I feel that of all the creations around us, we are the beastly ones."

Sawyer cautiously nodded agreement. He pulled on his collar to let a little heat escape. Adeline took the teapot and poured herself another cup of tea. "Care for a cup? I can have an assistant bring another glass, as I didn't prepare one for you in advance."

"No thank you, Princess." He shifted in his seat.

"I'm aware that you didn't come here to discuss dragons."

Brushing his hands through his hair, he breathed deeply. Her words hit like a mallet to his chest. "Princess. I... I..."

"Go on." She leaned in, resting her chin in her hands, as if understanding fully that she cut him off and the happiness gained from breaking a few golden rules was well worth it.

Sawyer shrank back, letting his intuition guide him. "I'm sorry. I —how do I say? How... I mean. Clara... She... I mean—you. You and me... and Clara. No, that isn't what I mean. Me and Clar—"

Adeline laughed, placing her cup down and tucking her legs under her. "How enjoyable that was. Better than I imagined, actually."

"I beg your pardon?"

"To see you squirm. To relish the awkwardness. Sawyer, your expressions. I think I shall remember this moment forever."

"You aren't angry?"

"Are you really that vain? Do you truly think that you're that important? So important that I would die of heartbreak if we didn't marry? Perhaps you imagined my wallowing in my tears over the handsome knight who broke my fragile heart. Oh, I'd never be the same after that. For my remaining days, I would never love another. Alas, my heart would grieve endlessly over the love we never had."

"Well… no. Maybe. Hey now. What are you saying?" His eyebrows furrowed.

"Handsome Knight, your smile is contagious and those freckles have won the hearts of many, but I'll have no part in such swooning. Looks are a minor attribute to life. And charm, just reckless manipulation. I chose another, much better for me. I have discussed it with my father, as well."

A flash flood of relief flowed through his body. He ignored the slight prick of resentment. "I'll take a cup of tea after all. Sugar, too, if you have it." He relaxed into his chair. "So, tell me about this other. Your one true love, I'm guessing?"

"Yes. The best of words could not explain the love I have for this person. Dangerously lovely and incredibly smart. Also wields a strong sword with quick wit, if I may add. What else could I ever want?"

"May I ask who has captured your heart?"

"And your brains explain themself, yet again. Are you genuinely that simple? It's me. Cauldira doesn't need a treaty. We never did. What it does need is a noble princess. Of course, partnerships are important for the survival of kingdoms, and to be clear, a very good tactic for prosperity. I'm not against them, but it wasn't in the stars for us, for which I am glad. My own father had such an arrangement, as did King Henric, but I don't see why it's needed for me, or Cauldira."

"Princess—"

"Call me Adeline going forward. It's the least I can offer you since you have saved me from the grimmest future."

"Adeline, it is." The assistant appeared and filled his cup with steamy liquid. Adding two lumps of sugar, he stirred, relieved to have a moment to collect his thoughts. "I'm happy for you. Both of you." Adeline laughed at Sawyer's joke. "I'm glad King Boren was understanding of that special union with yourself. I should have known that he would be. How did King Henric take the news?"

The conversation turned serious. "I haven't heard much about King Henric, but I'm sure Father has those details squared away. Unfortunately, he refuses to discuss it with me."

There's more to the story that she doesn't know, or she isn't willing to say, but Merrick will. I need to tell him about the strange mannerisms in King Henric. It may be the reason he came to Cauldira. "Since Jasper is here, we should ask him to teach your cook how to make those biscuits you like."

"What a splendid idea. Also, while you're here, I'd love to discuss the possibility of joining your companionship to Lectus. I understand that you're short two."

"But you're a princess."

"And you, a pompous knight." She picked up her cup. "And this a teacup, and this a book. Please don't tell me you are vain as well as shortsighted. If you want to exchange facts, I'm sorry, but you simply won't win."

Sawyer took a long drink of tea that emptied the cup. "I surrender, as long as King Boren agrees, of course."

CHAPTER 35
Rainbows

CLARA

"HELLO THERE, JADE!" Arlo waved. "Clara, a pleasure." He shook her hand with both of his. "Arlo Levisay." A small mage with red, puffy eyes clung to Arlo's leg, watching the newcomers as Arlo greeted them.

"Thanks, it's a pleasure to meet you too. Jade has said great things about you." Clara stooped to the young mage. "Hey there. My name is Clara. Are you okay?" The child nodded and pulled herself behind Arlo's legs.

"She had a scare, but she's doing fine. You were brave, weren't you? Did you want to tell Clara about it?" The young mage shook her head and clung tighter. Arlo smiled. "I understand that you're having some trouble with focus." The small mage peeked behind his legs with interest.

Jade interjected, "She is. I've witnessed her power but she has no awareness or control over it. I'm only guessing she's a mage. She may be a healer, or potentially something entirely different."

The child mage released Arlo's leg. She switched it for his hand.

Holding it tightly, she stared at Clara while Arlo spoke. "Clara, what are your thoughts? Do mage powers brew within you?"

Brew… "I don't know."

"Have you had any thoughts or feelings, deep inside, that felt like a sufficient strength you couldn't place? Or an undeniable intuition? Maybe pain, burning, a restlessness of any sort?"

"I don't know…"

"Have you noticed anything shifting that you wanted to move or instinctively read someone's thoughts or finish their sentences?" Clara shook her head. "Okay, how about a burden when people are sad, hurt? Can you sense when someone is sick or going to die?"

"I don't know…"

"Have you ever predicted the future or heard any voices?"

Voices. If I tell him about the shadows, they might expel me or think I'm the enemy. The voices I hear are not heroic, but they also aren't real. Just dreams or a trance… or something. "I don't know. To all these." Clara choked up. The little mage grabbed Clara around the shins to embrace her when Clara sniffled back tears. "I'm sorry. Why am I crying? I'm so sorry for breaking down. I'm just really frustrated." The small mage held her damp hankie for Clara to take. Clara took it, even though it was already wet.

Arlo spoke to the small mage. "Korlin, why don't you get yourself a snack? Tell Eunice I said you could have one." The child smiled and ran toward the castle, but not until she gave Clara's legs one last squeeze. "Jade, did you want a snack too?" Arlo asked with a sparkle in his eye. Taking the hint, Jade followed Korlin into the stone building.

Arlo addressed Clara, "Walk with me." The mage led the way until they reached a wooded area with a pond. "This is one of my favorite places to go, especially when I need to think. Life, it's so noisy sometimes. And although I adore this magnificent life, there's something to be said of only hearing one's own thoughts." Arlo patted the bench next to him. "Come, have a seat." Clara obeyed. She concentrated on the meditative white noise of falling water nearby.

"Tell me, what plays in your mind when you're alone with your thoughts?"

Clara sighed. "Nothing all that important. I mostly think of all the bad things that are going to happen."

"All the bad things? Why do you think about the bad things?"

"I guess… maybe because I can't make something from my life. I can't get ahead. It's like I expect to break all my own promises."

"Cauldira is the only home I know. Do you know much about dynamic mages?"

"Not really. I've heard they're unpredictable but worth it to some. That's pretty much all I've been told."

Arlo continued. "Early on, I had indicators of magic. Shortly after birth, strange things would come about. A toy was moved, or I'd be out of my cradle. One time, my mother produced extra milk at a rapid rate. Odd things like that. One time, as a toddler, I stoked the hearth fire so hot it burned our house down. I had no idea what I was doing. I was too young to understand." Arlo paused. "There are kingdoms destroying dynamic mages the moment they're discovered."

"What! But why? Why would they hurt a baby?"

"Because, as you've heard, we're unpredictable. Had I been born anywhere else, I might not be alive today. King Theo, King Boren's grandfather, would have none of it. Officials urged him to dispose of me, or at the very least, banish me. But the king stood his ground. He believed in life, and ever since, I held my allegiance to Cauldira."

"Why not Eros? Wouldn't they have taken you? Couldn't they train you?"

"Not even the magical population in Eros understands the ways of the dynamic ones." Arlo leaned his elbows onto his knees. "A decade ago, the Cauldarian militia was aiding the Gregrians." Arlo slowly shook his head. "I was in full focus to take down a large group of mages. Typically, an army may have 4-5 mages per kingdom, but our adversary had many more than that. Before the battle, I had practiced some new spells. Unfortunately, I failed miserably and found that it's possible for a single mage to stop a battle by wiping out both armies…"

"Arlo… I'm sorry…" Clara leaned onto her knees to match Arlo. "I know you didn't mean it."

"Tell that to the ones who died. There were twenty from Cauldira and many more from theirs. The Gregrians had tough mages, and both armies were weary. We were losing the battle. I didn't know how to regain control in Cauldira's favor, so I took a chance. I should have played it safe with a known spell. I should have played defense or kept out of it entirely. I should ha—"

"But you can't keep beating yourself over it. Your people trust you, so much so that you are still here, generations later. You were trying to protect your people. It was an accident that you learned from."

"But did that matter? The outcome remains."

Clara sat upright. "You can't change it, though. The only thing you can do is learn to live with it and from it."

Arlo smiled knowingly. "Is that so? You know what? It recently finished raining. Maybe." Arlo stood from the bench and grabbed Clara's hand to help her rise. "I'd bet there's a rainbow waiting."

They have rainbows here… They even have the same name. It's like a parallel universe. So many things in common, yet so different. She followed Arlo up the mountainside. Built-in steps made the climb simple. At the top, a prominent waterfall cascaded into a pool below it. It spilled off the side of the mountain and into a stony river. Arlo pointed to the vibrant rainbow.

Clara gasped. "It's beautiful!"

Arlo lay on his back in the grass, motioning for Clara to do the same. "I'd like to think of rainbows as a promise of a new beginning etched with the palette of dreams." He turned his head to look at Clara. "Come now. Lay on your back, Clara, and gaze into the sky. She's glorious, isn't she?"

Lying on her back, the rainbow beamed above. "Yeah, the colors are so vibrant. I don't think I've seen one so bright before. It's almost as if I could touch it."

"What about her?"

"Who?"

"The other rainbow. Do you see her?"

Clara scanned the sky. A faint bow of color mirrored the vibrant one. "Barely. I have to look pretty hard. I wouldn't have noticed if you hadn't pointed it out."

"As with each rainbow, so are you. Some rainbows… they show boldly for the world to see. Like the one you saw first. They are flashy and easy to spot. The other, she hides shyly behind a haze of vapors. She's a special one, but you will only find her beauty if you take the time to look."

Clara remained still. She reached her arms up towards the double rainbows. She concentrated on the faint one. *I hope I find you.*

Arlo stretched before sitting up. "Both are important; each one has its own array of colors, regardless of how bright. The rain was heavy earlier, but worth it, I'd say. The rainbows. Let them remind you that rain is only a season, and Clara… you're here for a reason."

CHAPTER 36
Shadows

CLARA

EVERYONE PICKED A SEAT. The small gathering space was modestly decorated with just enough to provide a minimalistic aesthetic. Jasper, who had been spending time with Cauldira's cook, helped prepare and disperse the food. Piled plates and animated conversation circled the table.

"I'm glad you joined me for tea earlier today," Adeline said to Clara, sitting next to her.

"Me too. I had a lot of fun getting to know you. It's been a while since I had girl time. Maybe once this is over, we can do it again."

"I agree. I foresee much conversation in our future. Perhaps you'll stay at Cauldira for a spell? Please know you are most welcome."

Arlo, plate overflowing, joined Clara and Adeline. "Clara, are you ready for training tomorrow? I'm thinking of starting with meditation. We'll take it easy."

"Absolutely. I'm excited to see what happens. I think… I hope I'll tap into something."

"And so you will, either way. Meditation is an undervalued tool," Arlo encouraged.

"Arlo, I've heard some things about bridging the gap. Do you think you have that power? I'm not sure why it's so interesting, but it fascinates me. I've been told that mages are a bit… moody, but you are the most laid-back person I know. Sorry if this isn't an appropriate dinner conversation," Clara said.

"Mages tend to be a bit temperamental, as you may have noticed. With so much surging power, restless and boiling within them, it's no wonder. As a dynamic mage, I cannot tell if the signs you see are a crossover into healer waiting to happen or simply the quirkiness of being a dynamic. But, I'm not prepared to explore it. At least not right now."

"What happens if you try to bridge the gap and you're wrong? Like, you find out it was only quirkiness and nothing more. What if you had no signs and tried? What then? And, the only two I've heard of are men, Aesian and Odin. Can women bridge too?"

Adeline joined the conversation. Arlo's eyes softened. He leaned closer as she spoke, "That's because women don't need to take such risks to be all-powerful." They laughed at her lighthearted joke. "Of course, I merely jest. I believe a woman was the first."

"Adeline is correct," Arlo began, "the very first was a woman. A healer. Her name was Aurelia." Clara, hands under chin, listened intently. "Some say she acquired a talisman from the stars. Others say she had a magical crystal star upon her brow suspended in a circle, much like your own brand, Clara. Aurelia's star could transport her to different worlds. It's said that through her travels she learned how to merge magics."

Clara grabbed the hidden necklace from Aesian. She never removed it after Alora placed it around her neck. Somehow, she hoped it would take her home or be of use when she needed help. She pulled the chain to show it off, but stopped as a tired knight entered the festive courtyard, yelling for help. "Help! Dougal is under attack! Please help us!"

"Call for Father. Quickly. We need to go to them," Adeline commanded as she jumped from her seat, but Merrick swiftly stopped her. "Princess Adeline, you serve your people better here and alive."

"Merrick, I plan to and will go."

"Adeline, you'll do no such thing," the firm voice from the king stopped her. "I'm sending an army right away. You will reside here, safe within the gates. No more questions. Check on your ladies. They have been asking for you. If you want to help, you can do so by preparing bags with provisions for the town."

"Father, please, I—"

King Boren's voice escalated, "I stand by my word. Adeline, find your ladies. Now." Adeline clenched her fists. Furrowing her brow, she left with her plate uneaten. Arlo followed but was halted by the king.

"We'll need you. Get your steed."

"Yes, your majesty," Arlo replied quietly.

Squires rushed to prepare the horses. Sawyer flung himself onto Willow's back. "Jasper, I think you and Rory should stay. Clara, perhaps you should stay, as well."

"Agreed. The lad will be safe with me," Jasper replied.

Clara quickly mounted Stormy. "I feel as if I should go. I can't explain it but I… please, I need to go. I don't know why, but what if this is the moment I find my power? Or maybe the windowless castle?"

Sawyer stared into her eyes, unblinking. "Then stay close to me, Clara."

"I promise."

They galloped off with King Boren leading the way. The sound of hooves clomping the earth and hollers from the soldiers became eerie music. Overcast, the mountain air cooled Clara's heated skin. *I feel like I'm in a movie. The part where things take a sudden turn from light-hearted and fun to dark and… and morbid. This feels like war, but from what I gather, it's a small town being attacked, not an entire kingdom. Are these bandits or something more? Something bigger?* She glanced at Sawyer as she swayed to Stormy's gait. Both man and horse were focused, despite breaking his concentration to ensure she was next to him.

The army entered the outskirts of the city. The small town gate opened, untouched by any attack. They trotted inside. Lifeless bodies lined the streets. Clara's eyes settled on a man covered in a dark cloak. He was standing over a motionless body. A thick, woolen hood covered his face as his head bowed. She dismounted and approached, leading Stormy by the reins. A sudden yank on her arm took her attention from the cloaked figure.

"Remember, stay close to me." Sawyer pulled her behind him. A townsman, streaks of black upon his face, rushed to the king.

King Boren dismounted to shake the man's hand. "What's happened to your town?"

"It came so suddenly. Unexpected. Phantoms. Shadows… Fi-figures?"

Shadow figures? Like the ones I dream about? Clara thought. *But, that can't be. Never have I seen one for real. They're only nightmares.* Her gaze rested back at the cloaked person. Arm stretched, the figure pointed to the lifeless body beside his feet. Clara approached, bending down, close to the still face. No breath.

"I wasn't ready."

Clara threw her hand over her mouth to contain the gasp. "Oh, I'm glad you're alive! I thought you were… Nevermind what I thought. I'll get you help." She screeched when she was lifted by the back of her uniform.

"Clara, it's best not to touch or go near the dead bodies," Sawyer said with concern. "I know this is your first time seeing such things, but please, stay close to my side. You promised."

"Dead? No. I was just—just talking to him. He must be injured, and that's why the cloaked person was trying to get our attention." She motioned toward the cloaked figure who wasn't there. *I'm positive I saw someone.*

"Clara, I've seen the deceased man, and no one has been near him, except for when a soldier checked his pulse. He's gone."

"But…"

Sawyer looked worried. "I'm sorry you had to see him. Are you okay?"

"Yes," Clara's throat tightened, spewing out her words in a high-pitched tone, "Why wouldn't I be?"

"I don't think it's a wise idea for you to survey the city with me. I know you wanted to come, but I think you should have stayed at Cauldira." Sawyer's eyes clouded with concern. He reached for her hand before pulling her to his side.

"No. I'm fine. Promise. I guess I got overly emotional." *I know what I experienced—at least I think I do. Gosh, I hope I'm not going crazy.*

Cauldira's commander addressed the group. "We're still surveying the town but we haven't located the source of the attack. Whatever it was, it seems to be long gone. We should camp the night here, to ensure there's no reoccurrence." Clara tried to concentrate on what else he had to say. Death had a smell, and she now knew its scent. It would be hard to purge it from her senses.

The commander continued, "We located a large group of unharmed civilians. They're gathered at the center of town. For now, secure your steeds and search all dwellings. Find those alive so we can question them." The army dispersed. Clara searched for Stormy to tie him, only to find she had dropped his reins at some point. She sighed in relief when she saw Sawyer tying both Willow and Stormy to the nearby hitch.

Sawyer approached her. "There's an inn two buildings down. It's a nice one, if I remember right from my past travels. A well-decorated sitting area, mulled cider, and comfortable beds. I'll take you there, and hopefully, they'll be open. We're only surveying the damage, so there isn't much for you to do anyway. I think a relaxing night would be good for you, and it's better than sleeping outside."

Sawyer held Clara's hand as they walked to the inn. Finding the establishment open, he paid for a room. Clara followed him up two flights of steps to a corner suite. "I'll come back soon. We're going to search the town, interview the townspeople, and take account of the lost or—or people who now live in the stars."

"Thanks for bringing me here. It's probably for the best." Sawyer opened the door. A huge fur rug, fluffy and clean, lay on a polished plank floor. A large bed was made with soft blankets, down pillows, and a smaller knit blanket, folded at the foot. Two chairs were set in the corner, overlooking a fireplace that was recently lit.

Sawyer turned down the gas lanterns so the room was dimly lit.

"Your tea should be arriving soon. If you're up to it, we can sit at the fire tonight, together. And… if you don't mind, I'd like to stay in your room, instead of sleeping outside. Of course, it would be to watch over you, and… I think having someone you're familiar with would be comforting. Let me know what you decide." Sawyer gently took her face in his hands and kissed her tenderly on the forehead, right in the center of her brow. "Clara, the timing is odd and a bit inconvenient, but I wanted you to know—" Guards were yelling downstairs in the inn, calling Sawyer's name. "Clara, I love you."

Clara stood speechless, heart thumping, as Sawyer backed away. He didn't wink, he didn't make a joke, or change the subject. Instead, he carefully laid her room key on the dresser and left the room, softly closing the door.

Clara's brand pulsed. She rushed to the vanity mirror. Nothing. She leaned closer, not even the slightest discoloration. Pushing the stool away from the dressing table, she held her hand over her still-pounding heart. *I can't wait to tell him that I love him too. I can't believe it! I'm in love!* A knock at the door stopped her celebration. Her tea was here. The maid rolled in a cart. She carefully took each item and neatly displayed them on the low table in front of the chairs overlooking the fireplace. The maid took the cart with her when she left.

The table had a full tray of tea sundries with a porcelain pot painted with flowers and a matching tea cup. A plate, accented with fresh sprigs of baby's breath, lay tactfully around the biscuits, fruit, nuts, and salted meat. In a wicker basket lined with white linen lay fresh flowers and a wrapped box. Clara sat on a chair, sinking into the cushion. Grabbing a piece of salted meat, she retrieved the flowers, placing them in the included pre-watered vase. Nine roses and two Lily Weeds were surrounded by lush green filler. Opening the box, there was an old, rusted key.

Clara lifted the skeleton key from its paper. Something was inscribed across the shank. She brushed it off to read it. *Senka Graveyard.* The fire spattered ash onto the protective shield.

The light highlighted shadows across the room. They danced across the walls and onto the floor. One Lily Weed in the vase wilted, petals falling from the bulb. The bulb fell next, plinking onto the table and rolling to her feet. She cautiously picked it up. It sat perfectly in her palm. Inside was an empty shell quickly filling with red smoke.

One shadow appeared.

Then another.

A swarm of shadows.

A shriek outside her window.

Clara pulled back the curtain. The cloaked person stood still, facing her, hood still blocking his face. Her mouth dried up, sticking her tongue to the roof of her mouth. The cloaked man lifted his arm, pointing directly at her. He slowly moved his outstretched arm towards a graveyard outside of town.

The glass vase broke, spilling the flowers onto the table. Opening the window, she yelled, "What do you want from me, huh? What?!" The figure remained, pointing. Clara let the curtain drop, legs shaking. She peered into the vanity.

Her reflection was missing.

The shadows peeled themselves from the walls, the floor. They flashed and swayed. The fire spat ash against the shield. The water from the vase dripped from the table onto the fur rug. Clara grabbed her sheath with her machete, securing it to her belt. With shaky hands, she grabbed the skeleton key. Rushing from her room, the door slammed behind her. The hall was unaltered. She ran, full speed, down the steps and out the door, heedless of the warning from the inn attendant to remain in her room.

Unbothered, Stormy ate from the trough placed at the hitch. She ripped his reins from the post. He shook his head anxiously when urged into a hard gallop. Clara dismounted when she reached the rusted gate connected to an old stone wall that the cloaked figure had pointed to.

Senka Graveyard.

Holding Stormy's reins, she walked towards the gate. Retrieving the key, she pushed it into the lock, creaking the door open. The path was worn, old, and surrendered to weeds. Stones and dead twigs crunched under her feet.

"I didn't mean it," said a gruff voice, muffled and shrouded with reverberation.

Clara paused, squeezing the reins in her hand.

"My life was taken," cried a sad voice. Its cries echoed across the graveyard.

Clara surveyed behind and around her. No one was there.

"It meant nutin'. I jest love me some beauty. 'Tis all. Time would let 'er 'eal, but she hadn't the time."

A cautious step forward. Stormy pawed and bobbed his head, chewing on his bit.

"I didn't do it. It didn't matter in the end. It didn't matter. Not in the end… It didn't matter. It didn't matter…" another voice lamented, mixing with the others.

"Where are you? Why are you doing this to me?" Clara yelled as she spun, searching, only to find herself in the center of the cemetery.

"Missed my kids growing up, I did. I rot without them…" this voice whimpered.

"Stop! I didn't do anything to deserve this!" Clara wailed into the darkness.

"Wasn't my fault, it 'twasint. 'Twasint," came another voice.

Dropping Stormy's reins, Clara pushed her hands onto her ears. "Stop!"

The voices continued, all joining each other in a mass of chaotic cacophony. Clara screamed at the top of her lungs. Her cry burned in her stomach, searing her vocal chords and cutting into her palate on the way out. All of the noise quieted. Clara moved her hands from her ears. They hurt from the released pressure.

Silence.

Not even a tree rustled.

Clara found herself chanting among the graves, breaking the silence. *"You're gone, departed in a shroud of mystery. Where did you go? I wonder… where did you go? You slumber in nightmares and live within death. What goes in your heart comes out with your breath. Your heart to be feared, you want to be heard as you plead for a freedom unknown, yet absurd. You live in regret for the life left un-lived. The cries which you sow are because... you just didn't know..."*

"You will never know her," a small voice whispered. The voice sounded like her own.

"Who? Who will I never know?" Clara asked the silence.

"You'll never know," a wicked laugh, soft and menacing, echoed in reply. The voices began again, this time louder, more angry. The shadows circled Clara. With outstretched arms, she reached towards them.

Then, in the faint distance she heard a familiar voice... "Clara, stop. Can you hear me, love? You don't know what you're doing!"

Clara's head swayed back and forth, hair falling into her eyes, peering from the tresses, her chant continued. *"They're dead, but I hear them!"* Her heart slowed with her breath. Time passed just as slowly. Before her was a human man, but she didn't recognize him. This man was deliciously afraid. She licked her lips.

"Clara, wake up!"

The man pulled her arm harshly, ripping her from the pull of voices, "Get off me!" Clara screeched, pulling against the force holding her back. It was Sawyer.

"Clara, what were you thinking? The inn attendant told me you left your room. Please tell me what's going on." Sawyer's voice was tactfully paced.

"I have to follow him, or he'll never leave me alone!"

Sawyer raised his voice, "Who do you need to follow?"

Behind the knight stood Jade, hand over her mouth. She shifted her feet while holding the reins of Willow and her steed in one hand. The cloak figure stood behind Jade, still pointing at the clearing of the woods.

Sawyer's eyes narrowed, as he spoke low and calculated, "Clara, talk to me."

Clara pushed past Sawyer, but he grabbed her waist, swinging her over his shoulder. "I'm sorry. I'm taking you back to Cauldira."

Clara struggled against his hold but couldn't lodge herself free. The cloaked figure remained. The voices from the grave surrounded her. They faded in and out in different frequencies. "Come find her, then you'll know."

"Who am I supposed to know?" Clara screamed into the night air. "Stop this terrible game. I'm not going to wait until you slowly drive me crazy!"

Sawyer carried her from the graveyard. Setting her back on feet, he held both of her shoulders. "What's happening, Clara? Please, tell me," he pleaded softly.

Clara shook her head. "I—I just need to rest for the night. Can we go back to the room?"

Sawyer sighed, "Of course. Come, ride with me on Willow."

Clara nodded. As Sawyer led the way towards Willow, he stretched out his hand for her to hold. But she swung herself into Stormy's saddle instead. Frantically, she urged Stormy into a wild gallop. The horse foamed at the mouth and grunted. "You keep hurting people. You keep tormenting me!" Big drops of salty emotion rolled off her cheeks. Her forehead seared hot. "I'm going to end this. Now!"

All of Clara's worry, fear, and anger that had been wrapped up in an anxious package untied as the gust from Stormy's gait wiped her tears. She was lost, but she kept moving forward. The figure disappeared and reappeared, guiding her. Tormenting her. The brand upon her brow burned as she felt the pulses. She roughly brushed her forearm across it.

The voices mocked her. *"You're looking for her... but you'll never find her."* Riding faster, she was deep in the woods. Thick and covered with haze, it smelled of moss and stale puddles.

Clara heard the clopping of hooves behind her. The calls from Sawyer and Jade were disregarded. Stormy shook her head and reared when they encountered a muddy pond. Clara tumbled onto the ground. Stormy took off, scaring Willow and Jade's steed as he galloped by. Clara pounded the ground with both fists before pushing herself from the earth. She abruptly fell again. Something pinned her. She ripped at the brush that kept her from standing, forcefully freeing herself from the roots. Breaking free, she sprinted towards the log covered in moss, the cloaked figure leading the way.

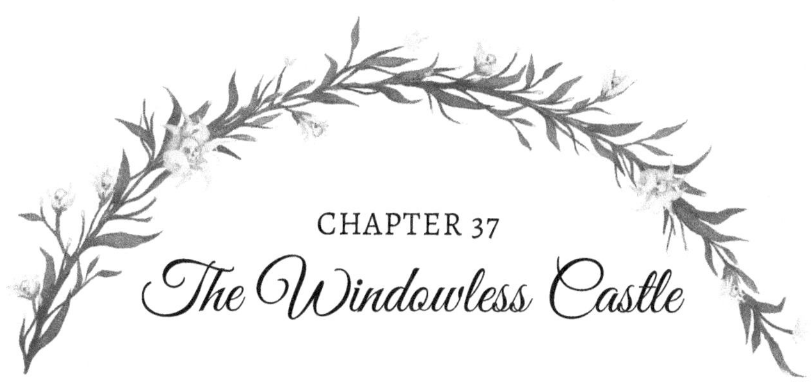

CHAPTER 37
The Windowless Castle

CLARA

THE CLOAKED FIGURE GUIDED HER. Always mere steps ahead. Always pointing. Always just out of reach.

Lumbering through the remains of a gravel path, she carefully stepped on a thin, slippery log that spanned over a green pond. Slowly, cautiously, she began to cross. The moss, thick and slippery, caused her to slide. Reaching for support, her hand grasped a large stick protruding from the pond. *A cane?* Using it to pull herself upright, she tossed it aside after reaching the other side of the pond. Both the knight and the mage endlessly called Clara's name.

Other voices called to her. Louder than her friends, these voices pushed her forward. *"Come to us. Come find her. We have her. You need her."* The air, once cool and crisp, filtered in hazy smog. Darkness shut out the sky, replacing the once blue sky with gray.

Clara stopped when the cloaked figure did. *"Your story begins,"* the figure breathed out in harsh shallow tones before disappearing. Dead leaves crunched under her feet. Atop the hill was a castle. A windowless castle. Ash speckled the air, sticking to her clothes. All signs of plant life sucked into the earth, leaving it barren. Replacing the greenery was a wasteland of dead skulls. Tripping on one, she stumbled until she fell. Face to face with the bony face, it appeared to be nothing but dead remains.

"Clara!" Sawyer cried loudly, catching up. He stepped on a random skull, breaking it into pieces. His voice cut through Clara's daze.

"Sawyer." She pushed herself from the ground to run into his arms.

"I'm not sure what kind of magic this is," Jade said, inspecting a skull but finding nothing strange about it.

Not letting go, Clara clung to the knight. "Get me out of here. I can't do this anymore. I thought I was ready to… to take Lectus down, but I'm not. Take me home… back to Ancora." Sawyer held her head to his chest, his beating heart pumped into her ear. The strength of his arms calmed her breathing. She stayed in his embrace until the ground rumbled. Skulls rolled and cracked under bulging dirt. They pushed at the unmoving skulls, encouraging them to waken.

One skull opened its mouth and screeched, shrill and threatening. A throaty scream joined in, along with many others; a melody of death, harmony of sorrow. Jade jumped over a large skull emerging from the ground beneath her. "These skulls… they're evil!"

A skull screamed. Something akin to blood spewed from its mouth, catching Jade's ankle. It pulled, stretching a sticky tendon of blood around her. She reached for anything to keep from being dragged towards the large skull, but there was nothing. Scraping the dirt, she rolled to her back. Jagged bolts crashed from her palms into her menacing attacker. Separating into multiple bolts, lightning rained back down, bouncing from an unknown source and breaking into pieces, recoiling and crashing. More skulls were born from the dirt. Each screamed their own deathly song. Sawyer, sword drawn, tried to smash the skulls but could not crush them or smash them into the ground. Clara kept close behind him. The knight fought, trying to reach the mage. He dodged misguided bolts and bloody tendons, but the skulls were populating, robbing space to walk.

The skulls cracked their jaws open, spewing blood in stretchy crimson ropes. Jade's arm, caught by another bloody grasp, pulled in the opposite direction from her leg. Sawyer drew his sword, swiping it horizontally in front of his eyes. He then wrapped an arm around Clara, sword in his other hand. He clobbered the skulls, but they only dislodged from the ground and bounced like misguided shots. They cracked and bled from bloodless bodies. "Jade, I'm coming!"

"No! I can't use my magic here. I—I won't be any good at helping anyone. Don't take another step. Common sense—" A skull wrapped a sticky cord of spew around her head, pulling her chin up. The skull mirrored Jade's words, "I won't be any good. I won't be any good."

Jade wept. "Can't you see what's happening? The lightning. It's multiplying. I won't get out of this one. Get Clara out of here!" A large crack of lightning crashed through a cluster of smaller skulls. Twice as many erupted from the earth's depths, replacing the broken ones. Electricity dispersed and rolled. Dodging a wayward bolt, the knight stumbled backwards. Jade's eyes widened. "I'm sorry, Sawyer…"

Clara felt a nudge from behind, but her feet wouldn't move. She was unable to divert her attention from Jade. The mage's vibrant eyes closed. She didn't fight as the skulls pulled at her limbs, severing them from her body. The knight carried Clara, and as he ran, she diverted her eyes to the dark, ashy sky.

Lighting crashed, multiplying with every strike. The battlefield was a mass of skulls ricocheting and crimson tongues. Sawyer leaped over obstacles while dodging bloody attacks, veiny ropes slapping the ground at his feet. He stopped once they reached the bottom of the hill, which was currently devoid of skulls. He placed Clara gently on her feet. She fell to her knees. Looming above, built on top of the thorny hill, was the windowless castle.

On her knees, she froze, her voice stoic. "I can't do this anymore. Just leave me here… and go home. Ancora needs you, Holly… you have family here. I have no one. For the first time… I'm okay with it. I no longer care where this story goes."

"Clara," Sawyer shook her shoulders hard. "Listen. No! Really listen! Get on your feet!" He grabbed her around the waist, out of the path of oncoming spew. The skulls were inching towards them. "I would carry you up the hill, but," his voice fell to a whisper, "I'm not going to. You must do it."

The heaviness of Clara's body pulled her down. So heavy that each step she took was intentional and labored. Sawyer dragged and pushed, encouraging her up the incline. Exhausted, they were safe from danger. Clara's legs shook, and not solely from the ground starting to quake.

She swallowed and glanced at Sawyer, who was leaning against the castle, breath labored. His eyes brimmed with tears. Sinking to his knees, he covered his face with both hands, his shoulders shaking. "Sawyer," she whispered, "are you afraid?" The chaos below continued. The skulls snapped their jaws open and closed. The gnashing of their teeth was an eerie companion to the deafening silence. Clara touched his shoulder.

"This is it," he said with feigned confidence as tears dripped down his cheeks. She brushed them off with her sleeve.

"You didn't answer me, Sawyer," Clara sat on his lap, facing him. She took his face into her hands, staring into his sad green eyes. "Please."

He inhaled a deep breath, body tense. "It's the ash that's…" he let his words drop as he attempted to stand, but she wouldn't get up. Sawyer spoke, pain coloring his tone, "The door has to be here. Let's rise. Follow me. I'm going to scan the exterior of the castle till we find the entrance. From there—"

Clara let her dead weight keep him from rising. "I'm sorry about Jade… I—I feel responsible. I loved her. She… she was amazing. Sawyer, I know you cared about her. I'm here for you, just like you've been for me. It's okay to cry, even if you're a courageous knight. Take this from someone who… who does it all the time."

Sawyer shook his head, his stubborn cowlick rising, untamed, from his hairline. "We need to continue the task."

Clara grabbed his collar, demanding eye contact. "Sawyer Lydon, Commander Knight of Ancora, I love you too."

Time stopped. They gazed into each other's eyes, searching, yearning. Sawyer's voice, emotional and soft, broke their connection. "When I told you, back at the inn, that I loved you, I meant… how I can see my life unfolding with you in it. Until we grow old and depart for the stars. I wanted nothing more than to see you happy, safe… loved."

Clara touched her forehead to his. Her brand cooled from the clamminess of his brow. She fell into his chest, and he hugged her tightly. The vibration from his voice soothed her nerves as he spoke, "When we first met, in the… back of the cart… you were curled into the corner, looking fragile, alone. Then, in the Ancora Gardens, you came alive, enjoying the world you were in, regardless of what had happened. That version of you was just as endearing as the last. Every time I think I know everything about you, you surprise me."

"I remember. I was scared and even wanted to hit you with a crowbar, if one had been available." They both laughed tightly. "But when I saw your eyes… I saw only kindness in them. I didn't want a relationship, yet, the more I got to know you, the more I pictured leaving everything I've known in America to stay here, even if Lectus was a part of it. You've encouraged me with a patience that deserves an award. But more than that… you have loved all the versions of me the same."

"There's nothing I'd change about you."

"Sawyer," Clara whispered.

"Yes, love?"

"Are you afraid?"

"I—I don't know what will happen once we enter the castle." He took a shaky breath. "But it's not me I'm worried about. It's the… the unseen wound I fear. Everything else isn't worth it. Fear, it's only an emotion telling a story of something deeper. But what wounds the heart, you can't bandage or spell away. Instead, you must feel it to find any kind of solace. That is what I fear. A wound that binds you to it. My love, you are wanted. Please never say that you give up on life. Clara Marie Rivers, the only thing about you that I want to see is… for you to be brave."

Clara lifted her head from his chest. Raising her chin, she kissed him gently on the lips.

SAWYER

Sawyer fervently kissed her back. He matched her kiss, frantic and tender. He pulled himself away to kiss her once more, just to ensure the first had, indeed, happened.

Standing, he helped Clara to her feet. Above where they once sat was a rusted doorknob. He drew his sword before turning the knob. It creaked when he turned it. Opening the door, Clara entered first, but he could not follow her. A harsh wind pushed the knight from the threshold. He struggled to stand, his sight clouded with blowing ash.

Clara, seemingly unaffected by the vicious wind, was beckoned into the windowless castle. Sawyer shuddered when a shallow, raspy voice whispered in the breeze. "Come find her." Her machete clashed to the ground before the castle swallowed her.

Tangled in Clara's weapon was her necklace. Sawyer unwrapped it from the blade, holding it to his breast. It was then that he knew. He stopped fighting the gust threatening to push him off the hill into the mass of chaos below. The wind died once the door slammed shut, sealing Clara inside. Dropping his sword, he ran his hands through his hair. This was not his battle.

IT NEVER WAS.

CHAPTER 38
Mayhem

CLARA

THE CASTLE DOOR SEALED. "We made it! Sawyer, I can't believe it! We—" Clara turned with a tear-streaked smile. "Sawyer?" She looked around. "Sawyer…?" Anger flashed through her before sadness cloaked her. She banged on the solid stone wall where the door once was. Legs weak, she fell to her knees and slammed her fists on the floor, disturbing dust that made her sneeze. Brushing back her hair from her face, the lingering wetness smeared the dirt on her hands. *Sawyer…*

Her scream echoed down the vacant corridor as it tore through her throat. "No! This wasn't supposed to happen! I don't know what my power is yet, and… we were supposed to do this together." Red-eyed and coughing, she stood. Each step felt heavy as she shuffled down a cold, endless hall. There were no lights, yet she could see. There were no doors, but one long, endless hallway. Her forehead seared and throbbed as she shook her head in vain to lessen the pain. She should have figured it out by now. Somehow, she'd jump into bravery, powers blazing, with a team of friends to back her up while she was victorious over Lectus… but it's a frustrating thing not having the answers. The cloak figure appeared at the end of the long hall, looking downcast at an opening. She paused.

This was it.

The cloaked figure disappeared, leaving behind the cold draft from a newly opened entrance. With shaking hands, she peeked into the room. Bones. A room full of bones. The air was stuffy and hot, smelling of decaying flesh. Skeletons hung upon hooks across the walls, dangling lifeless. She sighed. In the center of the room a single wooden chair was placed. She clenched her fists."I guess," she yelled at the sightless bodies, "that I'm supposed to… to sit in that chair while each of you magically spring alive to kill me." She lifted her chin, straightened her back, and sat.

She waited. Tapping her foot on the stone floor, she heard the clinking of chains. Just when she thought she was mistaken, a skeleton jiggled. Bones fell from a rusted hook. The head rolled to her feet. She jumped from her seat. Stooping to investigate, the jaw hinged open and hauntingly spoke. "Woe to me. Spent me last coin on a drink. Leave me alone, I'll not stop, I won't!"

Her heart skipped in her chest. The skeleton's jaws snapped. "Get away from me!" she cried, hurling it across the room. It smashed upon landing. Pressing a hand over her now racing heart, another skeleton fell from its hook. *I have no choice. I must be brave. If I can't be brave for myself, I'll do it for my friends… for Sawyer.* The bones rose, intact, scraping together as it stepped forward. Another fell from the wall beside it. Struggling to pull its bones in place, the second skeleton stepped towards it. The two embraced, bone against bone. Swinging around in a deathly waltz, their heads barely stayed connected to their necks as they danced to the scrap of clicking bones. Around and around they circled Clara and the single, plain wooden chair.

One skeleton turned its head backwards to look at Clara with empty sockets. "Dear, I won't allow you this dance with him. Not one turn." The skeleton's head remained facing Clara until it snapped off with a sickening pop. The dancing couple whirled out and closed in, the headless body unbothered. Again and again in pointless circles. Without its body, the head rolled around in its own insane dance on the dusty stone floor. After hitting a large gap in the stone, the bodiless head talked. "I cared for nothing else, save him. Oh, you should have seen us dance the night away. Now, dear. Remove yourself from him."

A fiery redness filled the empty sockets, gleaming deadly. Clara tried to escape from the dancing circle, but the dancing bones moved faster. Around and around they spun. The other skeleton pried its head from its spine and threw it towards the other skull. "Relax, dear. No one else will ever take me from you. I know the right way, the only way." His eye sockets glowed, mirroring hers. "And I… will solely," he said, his voice dropping, "fulfill your needs."

Clara moved behind the vacant chair. The headless dancers closed in. Fear overcame her as her trembling body shook the chair. Their skulls, still on the floor, bounced from opening jaws, propelling themselves towards her. "Leave us!" they warned. She kicked the rolling heads away. They snapped and screeched. Grasping the back of the chair, she crashed into the dancing bones till they scattered on the floor.

The other skeletons lined across the wall shook, some dropping their arms from their shoulders to inch forward. Others reached to pull themselves from their hooks. Each one chanted in hollow, deep voices. All desperate for a chance to speak. All yearning to be heard. One small pile of bones lay dusty in a corner, without a hook. It cried, "Nothing will change. Nothing will change." The words, laced in pain, repeated, unending. Crawling on its elbows, the bones dragged themselves across the floor, carrying cobwebs as it labored towards her.

There has to be a way out! Still holding the chair, she scanned the walls. The skeletons were slowly closing her in. Trapped, she swung the chair around, crashing it into the crowd of skeletons. They fell like dominoes. Bones scattered into the wall and across the floor. As soon as they fell, they assembled again using whatever pieces were nearby. Heart in her throat, she swallowed the bile threatening to spew. *I have to be brave!*

The skeletons, once again, closed in. With all her strength, she swung the chair, spilling the skeletons to the floor a second time. Bones hurled across the room. Parts of her chair went with it.

"I broke it!" she whispered painfully. Staring blankly at the dismembered chair, she breathed deeply as skeletons reassembled their bones. *I have no other choice than to fight!* Still grasping the back of the chair, she pushed into the group of skeletons, using what was left of the pieces. The skeletons bit and clawed at her. Pulling at her hair and clothes, she fell. Lying on the floor, she turned to see the small skeleton dragging cobwebs. Hopelessness settled in. *I don't know what it feels like to die, but… I wish I didn't have to do it alone.*

The small skeleton reached out to her, clawing her skin. "Nothing will change for me. Nothing will change for you!" it cried through sobs.

Frozen, Clara stared into the depths of the eye sockets. The small skeleton pulled itself closer. "No!" Clara yelled at it as it tried to touch her cheek. Adrenaline filled her. She leapt from the floor onto her feet to see a circle of skeletons holding hands. Scanning the walls in panic, she noticed one hook that looked different from the rest. Wide-eyed, her voice didn't sound like her own when she cried, "Get off me!" She yanked the head from the small skeleton, which had been biting at her leg. She ran as fast as she could muster. Pushing through the skeletons, she broke through and yanked the oddly formed hook.

Cold air rushed in, cooling her face as the opening appeared. She rushed through the doorway. The door slammed behind her, sealing the door without a notion it had ever been there.

Standing before her in the hallway, many feet away, was the cloaked figure. It pointed to a newly formed opening. She rushed after it. This room was full of reflections. A collection of mirrors, most of them cracked and broken, each had a different size and shape. Some in frames and others frameless, they hung from the ceiling facing all directions and were plastered against the walls. There were so many mirrors that no portion of the room was seen.

Seeing her reflection, many times over, a searing pain urged her to grab her shin. A small bony hand, grasping tightly, was digging into her skin. She ripped it off, leaving behind a bony handprint. Alone, she left it on the floor, reaching for something to hold.

Each way she turned, her reflection followed. Walking cautiously, the mirrors changed as she passed by. Her image was represented in each, but none showed her happy. One mirror played a story she knew well…

She shifted her apron. It was her first shift at the coffee shop. She had quit college. She quit hanging out with her friends. She even quit dreaming. "This is my life now, find a small comfortable place to live and die."

In this mirror, she served endless cups of coffee, each person demanding another. The line continued on and on until her hair turned white, and her face wrinkled. She eventually disintegrated into a pile of ash.

Her chin quivered. Tearing away from the story, another reflection caught her attention. Wrapping herself in her arms, she watched. In this mirror was a small Clara holding her mom's hand…

My sweet little girl, come here. Baby, hold my hand." Her mom's ponytail bounced as she walked, squeezing the little hand gently while they crossed the street. They had been walking a while. Her little short legs hurt. She remembered that moment and how she had imagined a cloud falling from the sky to scoop her off her feet and ease her weary legs.

"This time next year, we'll have a car. Won't that be fun? Then we won't have to walk everywhere."

"Momma, I want to tell Daddy about my interwhew."

"Daddy will be so proud of how well you did. Kindergarten is right around the corner, and you'll be in the next group."

A cloud would visit her that day, but not in the way expected. They reached the sidewalk and walked up the stairs to their small apartment. Opening the door, they gasped. Half the furniture was missing. On the empty table, a single letter. As her mother read it, tears welled up. Clara cried, not understanding why.

"Never mind your father," her mother said, blowing out a long breath. He wouldn't get to hear about kindergarten. He'd never get to see how she wrote her name, perfectly, on the paper.

Their world had stopped but life didn't. Each year that passed left her with less of the mother she knew.

The mirror froze on their faces. The story replayed. Not willing to watch the rerun, she turned from the mirror. She sniffed and rubbed her brow. *I wish I didn't have to see that.* At some point the pain had to stop. At some point she had to stop crying. Another mirror played, then another. Some stories were true, but most were spiraling stories of negativity created by overthinking. Her fears of falling off the horse. Her thoughts about being eaten. Story after story that didn't end well. Nightmares created by her. The utmost parts of her mind, shown in live motion. She watched them like a bystander.

Only one played something different. She laughed in this mirror and dreamed. She was happy and loved. She was calm and focused. But she didn't notice this mirror. Lifting a mirror here and there, she couldn't find a door. Even the opening leading into the room had been replaced with mirrors. *So, I'll be living with my own reflection? Here, in this room?* The unseen mirror of her happiness broke. Shards of glass scattered. On the other side stood the cloaked figure looming from a newly created doorway. She called to it, "Wait, I'm coming!"

Her feet ran for her. Her legs carried her body while her brain tried to keep pace. She didn't think, just moved. Entering the new room, a fresh breeze filled her lungs. Her legs felt light. A cloudless sky opened before her. Lush flowers lined a walkway, with white wooden chairs carefully lined in perfect order. Flowers tied to the chair backs swayed in the breeze. A trellis with cascading vines was beautifully displayed at the back of the room, situated on a platform, and perfectly centered between the rows of chairs. White rose buds hung delightfully from their branches. It was perfect. Exactly how she imagined the day would be.

To the left was Angel, holding a bouquet of Lily Weed mixed with roses. All of her friends were present, even those passed on and in America. Two worlds merged seamlessly together. Under the trellis waited Sawyer, dressed in his celebration armor, the same as he wore at the festival. Jade was at his side. He winked and bowed.

Her hand magically became full. A bouquet of Lily Weed, but she couldn't remember when they appeared. *How long have I been standing here?* Dainty lilac ribbon held the Lily Weed together. The loose ties tumbled gracefully to the ground. Adorned in white, delicate, pearl-sewn lace embellished her gown. She took a step forward, the luxurious material brushed against her legs.

Birds chirped, and the smell of honeysuckle perfumed the venue. The sun even smiled on them, lightly caressing each attendant. *The rays. They feel so warm.* She closed her eyes, feeling the heat on her face. She smiled. Not one thing was out of place or against what she pictured in her mind. As she walked, the seated familiar faces smiled widely. Charlie, hat in hand and tears in his eyes, smiled extra big as she walked by. No one broke their smile, not even for a moment. They looked alive and full of life, yet their eyes…

Angel took the flowers from Clara. Sawyer took her hands as soon as they were free. Between the couple was a white podium, behind which a man suddenly appeared, wearing a pinstripe suit and a red rose pin.

He smiled unnaturally wide. His smile upturned so tightly that his lips grew tight and his teeth seemed to grow. His nose, pointy and large, shrank his eyes into their sockets. Clara studied him. She wasn't afraid. He quickly addressed Sawyer.

"Do you take this woman to be your beautiful bride?"

Sawyer grinned. "I do." The loving words fell flat on her heart. Clara locked eyes with the knight. Something was seriously wrong.

"Do you take this man to be your wedded husband?"

Clara turned to the crowd. Dead blank eyes paired with beaming grins. Goosebumps prompted her to release Sawyer's hands. A sudden cold caused her to rub her arms. *What happened to the warmth of the sun?*

The man managed to smile wider and repeated, "Do you, take this man to be your wedded husband?"

Clara glanced at Sawyer. He smiled proudly. Dead eyes.

She glanced at her friends. They smiled so wide. Dead eyes.

"I, ugh…"

"Do you take this man to be your wedded husband?"

Fear crept into her. "I, um," Clara's voice shook. She tried to release Sawyer's hands but he held them tight.

The man increased his volume, "Do you take this man, the man you love with all your heart, to be your wedded husband?"

"No, I'm sorry. I can't get married."

The man looked irritated. Sawyer didn't release her hands. The man leaned over the podium. "You can stay here, live your life with the ones you love." He waved his arm over toward the guests. "Abide with us. You won't have to worry anymore. Isn't that what you desire? An easy life?" Sawyer squeezed her hands. She pulled them away. He reached again, snatching them into his. She tried to yank herself from his grasp, but he wouldn't let go.

The man behind the podium turned his head unnaturally sideways. His neck stretched to come inches from Clara's face. "Tell me what your name is?"

"My name... It's... it's..."

"Your name," he threatened.

"I'm not... I'm—"

"Now. Do you take this man?"

"No."

"No? No to your happy future? No to a life exactly how you want it? No to all your dreams coming true? Isn't this what you desired? Everything you wanted, given to you. Here. And. Now."

Petals floated around the venue. The man's neck shrank back to place. "Do you take this man to be your wedded husband?"

Anger replaced fear. She clenched her teeth. "I already told you! No!" Yanking her hands from Sawyer's grip, she grabbed the hem of her dress and jumped from the platform. The wedding scene faded into Holly's hut. Sawyer laughed as he bounced a little girl on his shoulders; she resembled her. They both smiled when they saw Clara watching. Angel laughed too, two children of her own clinging to her leg. Sawyer held out his hand.

The hut dissolved back into the wedding. She was back on the platform, the podium between her and Sawyer. "Just sign here," the man prompted, offering a quill with missing ink. "Just a simple signature, and your dreams come true."

The paper was old and creased. He stabbed her with the tip of the pen and Clara yelped. The empty quill filled red. His voice grew hauntingly dark, "Now sign."

Clara took the quill. She paused on the paper. "How odd… I… I don't remember my name?" She pressed her finger over the wound from the prick.

"Then sign anything!" he sneered, neck stretching until an inch from her face. "Put Frieda or Edith. I really don't care. Whatever you want to call yourself is fine. Just sign." His fake smile turned so uptight and wide that the corners of his lips split. Blood trickled down his chin.

"No, I won't…" Clara backed away from his face. "This… it isn't real. I won't live a fake life! I can't. I won't." She grabbed the edges of her dress and turned to the crowd. Down the aisle she ran as black eyes and hollow, deteriorating faces watched. "Sign the paper," they called together. "Sign your name. Any name will do."

In unison, they pointed at her. The sky darkened as the large dark bird swooped across the sky, scattering the flower petals. False smiles reversed into equally dramatic frowns. Getting up, the wedding attendees moved together, simultaneously walking toward her. There was no way out from where she came.

Retracing her steps behind the podium, she jumped off the back of the platform. "I will not do it!" The room went dark. Gone were the white chairs and pretty flowers. Floating petals were replaced with ash. All that remained were piles of rotten wood, bones, and dried brown flowers. The man lay dead, neck stretched long across the room. His face looking towards the wall, his eyes moved in the direction of the cloaked figure. A door creaked. She had nowhere else to go but through it.

CHAPTER 39
In Her Mind

CLARA

THE ROOM WAS CYLINDRICAL. A large stagnant well had been dug in the center. In one area of the room stood an old mirror. She shuddered. Wetness rolled from her eyes, spilling onto her cheeks. She walked to the mirror. Grimacing, she asked her reflection, "Who are you? I used to be… someone. Wasn't I? Or, have I lived my entire life in this castle?"

Brushing dirty hair from her brow, she didn't see any markings. "Why did I do that?" she asked with a faraway voice. *What am I looking for?* "That's right. My name is Clara. I'm from America. My friends. They talked about a circle on my forehead. I was supposed to do…" She leaned into her reflection, "I think I was supposed to do something with it."

Before she could contemplate what, a large floppy head emerged from the well behind her—a decaying beast with eight arms that thrashed and splashed. Old, still water spilled out of the well. Gooey eyes rolled and rotated. Locating her, they stared while each arm wiggled, a bony appendage clinking deadly.

She looked around. There were no weapons. She turned

towards the mirror to watch herself fade. She bowed her head with a shaky sigh. "I can't fight you." She let her arms drop. "This… it no longer matters."

The beast grabbed her with its dead appendage, crunchy and rotting. But death from another no longer mattered as it would be her heart that would kill her now. Wrapping around Clara's waist, it pulled her from her feet. But she did not fear or fight it. It shook her around, and she allowed her body to be thrashed willingly. She briefly imagined the ways she could die, but thinking was a mindless escape. Instead of becoming her undertaker, the appendage lifted her into a cage suspended high above the well. Opening the door, it threw her inside.

The door shut with a bang, causing the cage to swing rapidly, like the pendulum of her life. She waited on her hands and knees until the movement calmed. It was then that she began to rethink her life and everything about her existence. Parts of her missed the mundane atmosphere of The Bean Queen. The restitution of what she had known. *I miss the comfort of the fabric-filled futon at home. I even miss that ugly pink bathroom. I miss… I miss coffee. Will I ever taste it again?*

Actually, nothing about this world was familiar to her. She felt uncomfortable, scared, and cold—in every sense of the word. The cage was cold. The air was cold. Even her insides felt cold. The smell of metal permeated her nose, causing her taste buds to tingle from its metallic scent. "It smells like blood." Her words sounded small and insignificant in the big room. *How long have I been here? Days? Hours? It's always dark. I suppose the sun doesn't live here either. Nothing of life does. Even I am dead, at least, I think.*

Dread weighed her down. The poison from her mind seeped into the depths of her heart. Longing for the familiar, she licked her lips. Her throat was so dry. *Is this what it is like to die?*

Angered sprouted into a scream. "Whoever sent me here, you played a cruel joke. I—I didn't ask for all this!" she called out as if someone would care. Resting her head against the bars, she noticed how its coldness made her forehead feel wet. The vignette rust smeared across her forehead as the bars warmed from contact.

"Sawyer," she creaked. Her voice was giving out. "You

promised." Her plea wouldn't matter. No one would hear her anyway. Hope filled her heart each time she called his name, each time praying for a new outcome. If only he would rescue her... but her voice was failing, and her body was weak. *You're too late.*

Sawyer had failed her. Her friends had failed her. She had failed her. She tried to cry, but her tears were gone. The dryness burned her eyes. Never in her life had she felt so dead. Never in her life had she felt so alone. Even during her worst times, she never felt like this.

The mirror, only a few feet from the cage, glistened. A small crystalline ball rolled inside it. She felt a familiar presence. A voice inside her mind spoke to her. "Your knight. He isn't coming." Her head lifted as the voice continued. "How many times must he rescue you before you rescue yourself?"

"I'm not for this world. I don't have powers. How many times do I have to say that? For once, someone listen to me!" She shook the bars on the cage. It swung from the impact. "I am nothing. Nothing!"

"Your knight isn't coming."

"Shut up!"

"Open the door."

"It's locked. Someone. Anyone. Help... me."

The voice was calm. "You've been here before. This cage is only as strong as you. So... open the door." She slowly crawled towards the iron door. Carefully, she reached for the handle and paused. Her entire body trembled. The voice spoke to her once more. "Fear. It has always been your king, and you will bow to it forever, unless you open the door."

She pulled. It creaked open without resistance. *It can't be...* Hope filled her, and she repurposed her heart. She knew what she needed to do, even if she didn't want to do it. The fear grabbed at her like icy hands pulling her away from the opening. The mark on her forehead pulsed. She curled her knees to her chest and sobbed broken sobs. She felt that a great deal of responsibility was waiting for her outside the cage. More responsibility than she wanted to own.

In the deepest depths of her mind, she recalled all the times she let herself down. All the promises she made to herself left unkept. The many times her fear was more important than her future. This fear grew within her and rose to her heart. It was familiar. She acknowledged it.

Fear would always be a part of her, but she wouldn't let it control her any longer. The jump would be steep, but she could do it. "I'm scared," she pleaded to the voice that didn't answer. Despite this feeling, her heart was at peace.

In the waters below lived the monster. It would notice when she hit the water. What she'd do then, she didn't know. Standing, she approached the edge of the cage, toes balancing on the rim. She gripped the sides while teetering. The cage, angry to let her go, swung on its rope. She fell backwards, slamming against the bars, her forehead hitting the cold metal. The door banged wildly open and shut.

Without thinking, she didn't dwell upon what would happen once she hit the water. She didn't shame herself for not checking the door sooner. She didn't think at all. Instead, she spun on her heels and ran. Reaching the edge of the cage, she leapt. Her heart retreated to her throat as she fell. By the time she had a moment to second-guess herself, it was too late. She had made her choice. She chose to jump.

Hitting the pool, she held her breath until her head surfaced above the water. Swimming frantically, she climbed out of the murky well. The monster never stirred. Shaking, an odd happiness overwhelmed her. She screamed into the room, "I jumped!"

Looking around, she was alone. But, that didn't matter.

She was enough.

Standing, she squeezed water from her clothes. Walking to the mirror, she saw herself. The shining circlet upon her forehead glowed brightly. The white light pulsed. She still didn't understand it, but she didn't have to.

The mirror showed something else. Something behind her. A shadow. Unable to lift its head, the figure's head bobbed up and down. Each time it bobbed with a little more force until its head was upright. The room transformed. A colorless forest filled the space.

Clara walked through the woods to meet the figure. It held out a shaky hand. "Staaaaay…"

"Why should I? And, more importantly, who are you? I want to know your name."

"We are the same."

"No, we are not the same," Clara said strongly. The light from her brow shone upon the shadow, permeated through its face like dust.

"If we are not the same, tell me your name?"

Darkness fell, her brand shone brighter. Her light beamed across the shadow, exposing more dark phantoms. The woods dissolved, and now she sat, knees tucked, on the dirty wet floor. Water puddled around her, and she slipped while getting up. A large, tall door, previously overlooked, creaked open on rusted hinges. The ground beneath her shook. A jutting figure was coming through the rusted entrance. Dread pulled at her with a commanding force. All the things she was not invaded her mind. It was true. She would always be just Clara from The Bean Queen.

One giant leg stomped from the doorway with a labored step. He moved slowly and painfully, with jerking movements. Each step rumbling the floor. Clara felt immense emotional pain when she saw him. *I wish for death. Just like me, our hearts are missing hope.*

Her light began to die.

Then, she remembered. She was loved. She was also capable of loving others. It wouldn't be that she wasn't enough or that she was trapped. It would be that she was always enough. That even in her weakest moments, greatness was in her. It was then that she knew—there was a beautiful life waiting outside of the pain.

She jumped at her voice. It was as if she were two beings, one acting, one watching. "I won't be defeated!" Her fading light intensified. It was so bright, she could see into the mind of Lectus. There, she saw anger, hate, bitterness, and sorrow. They overpowered him, leaving no room for happiness. He wasn't her, but she understood him.

The lurching giant took a long, labored breath. Her brow shone upon him in sparkling rays. Her light reflected off various sets of eyes. She could see him fully now. Decayed bodies wrapped and clung to him, reluctant to loosen their grip. Entangled and rotten, they wept and cried. Piled upon each other, they all looked at Clara.

Lectus released a burned exhale and moaned. He had no other words, but none were needed. Built from lost dreams and lives halted by fear, the bodies spoke on his behalf. Each had a story to share, each desperate to tell it. Lectus only moaned. He had no voice of his own. A stabbing fear assaulted her. Lectus was hungry for it. His cry was stronger now. She felt drawn to him, yet she resisted.

Her voice shook. "You're hurting."

His head turned, moaning sadly. The pulse on her forehead shimmered. He moved closer and pointed down at her. One foot, then the next. Each one with great burden as the bodies weighed him down. Clara touched her brow. It caused her ray to cast shadows. She moved her hand, letting her light shine unhindered.

Her voice raised as she looked Lectus deep in the eyes. Behind the bodies, his eyes connected with hers—they were human. "I may never understand why or how I got here. But there's one thing I know for certain. Life can be dark, and sometimes, you feel alone…" Tears slid down Lectus' cheeks. Clara didn't break her eye contact with him. "But, even when nothing else shines, hope does! I will not become a part of… of you."

They stared, both unmoving. "I see you, Lectus. That's your name." He quivered. A body fell to the floor. She stood tall, lifting her chin. "Once upon a time, I struggled to live in my world. But you know what? I struggled to live in this one, too. The world didn't matter. I didn't like how my life was written, but I didn't know I was capable of more. That I could create a new story for myself." A cry escaped her but she did not break eye contact with Lectus. "No, they did tell me… but maybe I was the one who didn't listen."

The mass of intertwined bodies that built Lectus loosened. Another fell off. Then another. "We are similar, but not the same. I somehow lost who I could be. I thought so much about my own feelings… I only saw what I wanted to see. I think you did the same thing. But know this. I'm not going to join you. I won't."

More bodies fell. "I somehow created worlds, so much so that they became real. The stories I created about myself… they aren't always true."

A horrible cry echoed from Lectus, shaking the room. The bodies fell in mass quantities. The walls shrank and moved in. As the room became smaller, she felt bigger. "I don't care what happens. At least I was brave. I was brave!"

The shadows multiplied, circling around Lectus. "I'm not leaving until I see you. The real you. Lectus! My name is Clara Rivers. This is my story… and it all started with a childlike adventure and… a ray of light!"

Epilogue

CLARA

CLARA PUT DOWN HER PEN. She laid the signed book on top of the stack. *I can't believe I'm an author! Sometimes I still wonder. Did I create a world in my mind so lifelike that it became real?*

The white curtains casually blew from the slight breeze, tickling the leaves of the small plants placed on the windowsill of her country home. Well out of the way of busy streets, she had traded the sound of beeping for chirping birds and bright stars. Decorated to her liking, she had lovingly picked each item until she had created her small but dreamy cottage.

She smoothed the wrinkles from her lilac, rosebud-embroidered sweater. Angel had designed it and included it in the new line she named Eros. *The more time that passes, the fuzzier the memories become.*

A crash in her living room startled her. Arming herself with a fountain pen and scissors, she crept toward the main living area. The TV, left on, played a game show. The host laughed as the contestants tried running across a floating contraption, all of which was constructed for failure. But it wasn't the show that caught her attention, but a tall, broad figure.

The way he stood was familiar. Legs slightly apart, hand on the hilt of his sword. Yet, he seemed broader, more filled out than she remembered. He ran a hand through his hair. *It can't be.* Drawing his sword, the man turned. He smiled when they locked eyes.

"Hey," he said with a cheeky wink.

She smiled back. "Hey."

Acknowledgments

Another Voice was inspired by the magical memories of childhood and the conflicting reality of adulthood. Being a child through the 80s and 90s, I think of those days often and I owe my parents for encouraging my vivid imagination. Neither of you ever discouraged my daydreaming. Who knew I'd use it to write a book?

Patty and Janet, the worlds we created as kids, inspired *Another Voice*. May we never forget those days. If we never get the opportunity to travel to another realm, at least we had those adventures and Kermette.

A huge thanks to my best friend, Valerie. You've been there through the best and worst times. No matter where life leads, I know I can always count on you.

Katherine Nadene, your editing skills have elevated *Another Voice*! May the spicy carrot live on! I can't wait to work with you on book two.

Angela Matson, having another author friend, has been one of the best experiences. I think both of us are tired of reading *Another Voice* at this point! Cheers to your upcoming book and working together on book two of *Another Voice*.

To the Waynesboro, PA book club. Never would I have thought that being a guest author would result in some of the best friendships and a more polished version of *Another Voice*.

Much love to my dogs, Charlie and Angel, who are waiting on the other side of the rainbow bridge. This book wouldn't have been the same without you both by my side.

Special thanks to my beta readers, especially my niece Charity;

your support and feedback meant the world to me. Sometimes, it's what pushed me forward with my dream of becoming an author.

To Kellie, you always told me you thought I had a book in me. You were right.

Huge thanks to my artists, Jimmie Smith and Solafterashs. Your patience and talent brought *Another Voice* to life! I'll always be amazed each time I see your work.

Lastly, to all the dreamers. May we continue to find the adventures, because even in this mundane world, magic can be found within our imaginations.

About the Author

K. L. Busick grew up in upstate NY near the Canadian border. Being a chronic daydreamer since childhood, she rediscovered her love for fantasy while writing her first book, *Another Voice*. Now living in Waynesboro, Pennsylvania, where she has lived most of her life, K. L. Busick loves being an infatuated dog mom who enjoys a life of knitting, video games, and eating ramen.

In May of 2025, she graduated Summa Cum Laude with her English Literature degree and is a member of Sigma Tau Delta, an international English honor society.

instagram.com/klbusick

facebook.com/klbusick

tiktok.com/@klbusick